G000075178

Harry Buckle and Focks Schnauzer
THE KENNEDY ULTIMATUM

A funny thing happened to this book on its way to you. Back in the day, hoping for some early publicity, in Singapore we handed out advance storylines for our forthcoming thriller to Team Trump who were in town to meet N. Korea's President Kim. The book then being a simple *'easy going'* mix of fact and fiction back then due to be entitled *'Regime Change.'*

We got some amused if somewhat wry smiles, but days later we got phone calls seemingly from official US sources, suggesting we immediately *'Cease and Desist,' as encouragement of Regime Change 'By any means other than the due electoral processes of The United States' is highly illegal'*.

We were quite surprised and somewhat alarmed by the threats, but then various news stories and events suggested that *much of our original fictional plot was turning out to be fact.*

Had we stumbled on some ongoing secret CIA operation?

As not quite retired, but still interested, journalists we decided to see what we could find out...and what we found out, together with some info gems Harry had acquired over the years, changed the character and content-and indeed the title of the book considerably. Hence we present: *The Kennedy Ultimatum.*

To quote an early reviewer: 'As ever, Harry Buckle, who gained his first job as a journalist thanks to some family help from James Bond author Ian Fleming, wanders amiably through both life and this book, and remains constantly surprised when 'unusual and bizarre events' happen to him'.

Harry, always a music fan, moved on in the early seventies from journalism to start what became a successful music company, with which he brought the world many million selling records. En route, during his music business travels, he was accidently recruited by the secret services of both the British MI6 and Russia's fearsome KGB. So for Harry to be *'warned off'* publishing a tongue in cheek 'Plot to Puncture the President' seemed equally bizarre.

Four years later, with Team Biden Harris in command, and it is now confirmed our original plot is the subject of ongoing research by the US and others, and that's seemingly what still upsets the US State Department...*The Authors- Autumn 2021.*

We would suggest you do read the introductory pages, they set the scene for much of what follows: The Legends of Eagles...Events...JFK...Careless Talk...

To follow any on-going developments in this story...together with backstories, blogs, books & more... check out ... www.harrybuckle.com

The Legends of Eagles.

The imperial majesty of an eagle on the wing or perched fearlessly and steady eyed, cruel beak and massive talons at the ready, has been recorded in legend, myth, art, fantasy and fact since the birth of mankind.

With the mighty birds traversing between continents long before the earliest voyages of man and woman, there are many similarities in everything aquiline on the Aztec and Inca walls of South America and with the legends and smoky cave paintings of Mongolia, Persia, Western China, Northern Africa and Europe.

In North America and Canada 'The Eagle' held and holds sacred significance right down to a single lost or discarded feather.

For a thousand years, the most skilled of brilliant craftsmen and artists have put their best into the art and artefacts that record our awe at the hunting skills of various breeds of eagle.

Its flying ability-with eyesight that can focus on a mouse from a mile or so- to diving down, razor sharp talons and beak poised, at around 150 MPH, inch perfect control, wings and tail feathers streamlined back back in 'the stoop', with the last sound its quarry likely hears, being the almost banshee wail of the wind across the eagle's mighty wings.

It's no wonder those, often oh so similar, stories, fables, myths and legends, like the birds high on the wing, have traversed the entire globe, crossing those continents, timelines, languages and written forms. Golden Eagles, Sea Eagles, The Steppe Eagle, The Eastern Imperial, The Black, The Spanish, The Mexican and of course 'The North American Bald Eagle'- there are more than sixty, not always related, on the list. Some common, some endangered ...but all revered and many worshipped.

The eagle has four razor sharp and strong talons, three at the front and one at the back of each foot...but you'd need several humans with all their fingers and toes to count the number of tribes, creeds, clubs and countries that proudly display an Eagle on their flags, uniforms, crests, seals and badges.

Despite so many having appropriated the Eagle as a badge of strength and honour, apart from most Native North American tribes, humankind generally has not always been respectful of the eagle. This partly due to many of those legends also suggesting the Eagle is guilty of killing valuable lambs, goats, game, even deer and other larger quarry.

Then there's the almost identical Inca, Ancient Greek, Persian, Mongolian, Siberian, Tibetan and Chinese stories telling of eagles, despite their obviously limited lifting ability, carrying away a young shepherd boy, or in Mongolia, a girl collecting water...
...only for the victim to return years later, with their powerful eagles at their command, ready to remove an oppressive or tyrannical leader.

These days - as their wilderness domains become more restricted - the eagles foes are still mainly human. Mindless hunters, weedkillers, hormones and plastics coming down through the food chain , electric cable systems and an ever increasing number of windfarms. So much so that, with killing or harming of any eagle being a more than serious crime across all America, legislation to absolve windfarm operators from guilt is underway.

But there is hope, thanks to enlightened teaching, displays and demonstrations by falcon, hawk and other raptor friendly organisations, many dedicated to breeding and releasing much needed birds back into the wild.

Then there's the emotive, some if more than a little contrived, mainstream movies and documentaries, charting the ambitions and attempts to preserve the old ways undertaken by a few very modern Miss's in Mongolia.

No need for a 'Me Too' nudge or sentiment there- swathed in fur against the biting cold winds, with a massive Eagle on her gloved arm, she rides out to hunt game in the rugged mountains and plains of that still timeless wilderness ...and then uses her mobile phone to share the photos.

Meanwhile, to restore the good name of The United States of America it seems The Eagle, may be about to Strike Back...or is it just one of those myths?

'Events, dear boy...events.'

The quote attributed to 1950s and 60s UK Prime Minister Harold Macmillan, in answer to the question, 'What he feared most?' Books have a remarkably long shelf life. In the bookshop, in the readers hands, and quite often back on the shelves of a second hand bookshop or charity store. This means that certain of the fictions portrayed in this book, may well have become fact, or even have never happened - by the time you dip into these pages.

So a novel- with a realistic touch leaves both the authors and then the reader open to considering and comparing the content with 'Events' real, imaginary, past, present or future.

So, risky territory, even as we type this, but as ever we hope you enjoy it as much as we enjoyed the reality of creating it.
Harry Buckle & Focks Schnauzer. Dublin. Autumn 21.

JFK...and an event that shocked the world.
It's all over bar the shouting...

American President John F Kennedy was shot dead by a gunman-or some say-gunmen in Dallas Texas on 22 November 1963. *Despite the title of this book now being 'The Kennedy Ultimatum' it is neither all about the assassination of JFK, nor yet another exploration of the multiple conspiracy theories, some wild-others more measured, which the killing sparked off and which still proliferate to this day. Here for our younger readers- is a little of the background to that day which shocked the world...*

The killing of the personable, handsome and generally popular President set off a chain reaction of global grief. This swiftly followed in the USA -as the world watched ,wondered and worried-by an avalanche of accusations of national or even international intrigue, revengeful big business, political convenience and suggestions of organised crime...well...organising things.

All this with a scent of Hollywood scandal to add some glamour to the horror of the pictures on the front pages and most of the inside pages also. And for the first time, as news moved from the cinemas to TV, the endless re-runs of the shocking images.

It was when the accused assassin -Lee Harvey Oswald, who turned out to have extensive links with both Russia and the CIA, was himself killed just a few hours later-that the rumours started. When Oswald's - *convenient-too convenient-* killing was confirmed to be by Jack Ruby, a local nightclub owner with links to organised crime the rumour mill spun out of control.

Of course, in addition to the global media frenzy it sparked off a multitude of official tribunals, investigations, commissions and that lifetime of conspiracy theories.

Then, if the events of November 22 1963 were not enough, on 5 June 1968 JFK's brother Robert F Kennedy -'Bobby' was shot dead in Los Angeles. RFK was in the running to be President-and had previously, when Attorney General, also pushed hard to bring US organised crime under control. He was also a powerful campaigner against racial discrimination and for social justice. The killer, named Sirhan Sirhan had a rather well documented obsession with assassination because of RFK's support for the state of Israel, but it was all still fuel for the fires of rumour and the conspiracy factory not surprisingly went into hyper drive.

President JFK - whilst seen as a new broom, clean sweep, internationally minded modernist- had also been elected under somewhat dubious conditions. His well known father, who had been US Ambassador to London was, to say the least, very aware of the useful power of US Organised crime.

It was suggested he-The President and his wife Jackie-were the first political celebrities of 'The Television Age.' Any revelations of his various 'dalliances' or 'romantic assignations' as the media of the day described them played to that 'celebrity status.'

The President's many ambitious policies, including on racial equality, and his 'let's talk about it', ideas on international relations, especially with the Cold War hotting up globally and closer to home in Cuba, whilst popular with many, had also managed to alienate many well established and powerful figures in Washington and around the nation. This included those representing big business, sections of the military, law enforcement and the security services who had been used to operating to their own relatively unsupervised agenda's for years.

Over the years, confirmatory facts and evidence backing up some of the more exotic conspiracy claims have emerged , particularly those suggesting the Warren Commission and other investigations were seriously manipulated by the powerful elite of the day, and the results buried.

Equally over the years other facts have emerged that prove many others of the 'who did it and why' theories to be plain wrong.

So for the Kennedy story...for America... it is still not yet all over***...despite the shooting***...although you might want to check out what, as a young journalist, Harry learned on the day/night when JFK was assassinated.

...and today, 20 January 21, the day when President Biden proclaimed at his inauguration- 'Democracy has Prevailed,' the story of the past four years is all over *despite the shouting*...or is it?

'Careless Talk Costs Lives' and 'Loose Lips Sink Ships.' *Bars where expats gather, even inland, tend to attract some rum coves, many escaping from something - even in some cases, running from themselves.*

The famously sensible World War Two slogans referred to above, were particularly aimed at idle chat in the crowded pubs of beleaguered England and the bars of mighty America which was- a tad unwillingly -but oh so vitally-coming to Europe's aid. The stark posters warning of *'lives carelessly put at risk'* were emotively powerful and given the losses being incurred on all fronts, were much needed.

Although I have mainly lived in England, I worked as a journalist and then with my music company in many countries of the world. In recent decades, following the world of work took me more and more to Asia, where I loved the lands and their lifestyles.

Fortunately for me, my long time Irish friend, TV reporter Focks Schnauzer, usually resident and working in New York and Dublin, has a house in the north of Thailand.

So it's thanks' to Focksy that I have ended up spending so much time in the delightful old trading city of Chiang Mai with its still water filled moat, twisty turny little soi's -alley's- and a thousand streetfood stalls and little cafes shaded by old trees.

And it was in early summer 2018 in a not very girly local pub style bar in Chiang Mai, that over a few evenings we heard a rather amazing story. It was the beer and a youngish American doing the talking...'Careless'...Possibly. 'Loose Lips'...Definitely.

Those who know the region well are used to retired American gents- usually a way older than our chatty friend, quite often Harley Davison riders, or at least Harley Davison T shirt owners, often claiming to have been, or still to be: *Connected.*

Now, as an ex journalist turned music publisher and now author, I'm more than a 'Jersey Boys' fan, and years back when music mattered- I had various business associations with their wonderful music. So *'connected'* had certain connotations there. I later found myself sailing a tad too close to some interesting New York Italians also in the business of promoting music, but that's another story.

In Thailand *'A Connected'* American usually means Vietnam Vet- of which there are indeed many of about my age still hanging on here. For some others *'Connected'* means less convincing claims to have been a *CIA connection*. And others with even less convincing claims to have been a 'Raven' or 'Air America' pilot of which, in truth, there were very few. That's despite the deep 'in the black, off the books' nature of the action at the time, these days most of the names are all listed. There were certainly way fewer of them than there are claimants in modern bars around Asia.

Experienced expats and regular visitors to Asia also know better than to enquire of visiting Americans as to their political allegiances, as in most cases it only degenerates into a blame game.

The poor innocent Yank gets unfairly and boringly blamed for long and endless immigration queues for visitors to the US of A. Also for the proliferation of KFC, MacDonald's and Starbucks in the region, for the cost of Harley Davison spares, and in recent times for everything Bushist, Obamian and particularly Trumpian.

Even riskier, with memories really not so far back, those expats lucky enough to be married to charming Vietnamese, Lao or Cambodian ladies still try to figure out the age of the visiting Yank, and thus decide if they were likely to have been personally to blame for killing their wife's grandmother, grand-dad, aunt, uncle, brother, sister or indeed wiping out their entire village.

Of course, the usually good fun and mostly likable Yanks get their own back on those expats of various other nations with good natured accusations of them: 'Originating from a land of permanent fog and rain', Or being 'garlic breathing cheese eating surrender monkeys', or 'Having God Fatherly family connections only good for pizza making'.

Those stuck firmly in the Secret Service track, tend to allow the Brits to bask in the reflected exploits of James Bond... although there are always dubious late night claims of persons attempting 'The Roger Moore' re-entry maneuver.

But back to the story that we heard - as I mentioned, it came from an apparent chance encounter with a young American chap. Or younger at least than Focksy or I. Polite - of course, as as most Americans are. Name of Jerry, quiet, modest, and no codes or dodgy hints about his employers - although eventually it turned out - still modestly and discretely -but loose lipped all the same- that he *was* employed by one of the USA's many Governmental security departments.

Detailed conversations over a number of days suggested that he was less then impressed by POTUS the Careless Tweeter.'

Now this book does not set out in any way to denigrate the USA, in fact it was written because of our deep concern for the devaluation of it's once good name around the world.

I have loved the USA with a passion since I first went there in the Beatles days of the early sixties-as I said...*I was* a music business man. Over many years, I have been proud to share with my now grown children much that is wonderful from many of the 52 States, starting their own voyages of discovery of course, with their 'still in stroller days' in the various magical lands of Disney.

Oh yes. My Dad was a teacher, and remarkably good story teller...As a young lad, when I first discovered that various legendary Pirates and some earlier Dragons, did NOT live in the Cornish caves near my aunt's house on the beach, as he had always told me they did - I was seriously pissed off.

But Dad didn't apologise. He simply said: "Did you need to know the fairly boring reality that those caves were formed by a million years of tides and waves--or did you enjoy some good stories?" And so it is with what follows, file under true stories...probably.

Harry Buckle. Dublin & Cornwall. Updated Autumn 21.

Chapter 1. *Early Summer. 2018.*

The Temptations of a lost memory stick.

Harry writes: I'm sharing the writing and reporting duties with my great mate, TV journalist Focks Schnauzer...Focksy. To his chums...so you'll see some chapters with my by-line and others with his. It had been a long hot late June afternoon without even any of the usual thundery drama of the refreshing 'four o'clock' cloudburst. Well past time for a beer.

On our arrival at our local pub in Chiang Mai, Northern Thailand, Bim the bar lady, greeted Focksy and I with her usual smile and said, as she poured our beers, "Sawadee Ka, I got some stuff here for you two." Despite her 'I've got some stuff for you' sounding a bit dodge, it was, at first glance nothing of the kind. NB. *At first glance.*

Bim explained, "Mister Jerry he phone me from Bangkok Airport, tell me he have to go away on business very quick...but him forget him bag of clean laundry. He leave it in the bar last night, so he call and ask me to give it to you so you can send to him."

As Focksy and I settled into those first cold beers of the evening and tuned our phones into the bar's free Wi-fi, several queued Whats App messages arrived for each of us. Mine from Jerry, indeed asking if I could post his laundry on to him as he quite liked some of the jeans and shirts. Of course he would repay costs. Focksy's message, also from Jerry, seemed to have been sent earlier and simply said: Can't meet tonight had to depart urgently.

Given what Focksy and I knew about Jerry and his job, all that seemed quite reasonable, and so I asked Bim if she happened to have any tape and stuff behind the bar so we could bundle up the laundry for mailing. Her response was," I do it more good than you. All Thai lady now buy sell everything on line, we all big business every day so I got tape, box, stickers everything right here. Mooey, my friend here, she have account with DHL and FedEx and Kerry if you want. More quick than big line wait in post office."

As Bim started expertly taping up the package, Focksy's phone made another of its annoying 'cuckoo' sounds advising of an incoming message...the reading of which prompted a surprised 'Ah ha' from Focksy and he handed the phone over to me to see:

Mssg: Just boarded flight in Bangkok. Address for Laundry.
Jerry Smith. C.I.A. Exec Offices.1000 Colonial Farm Road.
McClean. Fairfax. Virginia. 22101.USA.

That it was the CIA was not much of a surprise, we had known Jerry worked with the State Department on 'Advance Security Planning' for the US President. But both Focksy and I thought it was a bit odd him requesting his old shirts and jeans-even if clean- be sent to his office and not to some home address. Or if to his office, with The CIA having thousands of employees, surely he would usually name a department or room number.

Then the picture became even more complicated as with a clattery sound something fell to the floor behind the bar, which prompted Bim to call out, "Oh look Jerry leave memory stick in him jeans pocket in him laundry," and she then continued, "Last night, after you go, some guys come in and have some drinks with Jerry. The guys and Mr. Jerry leave here very late, and him quite mau (drunk), maybe that's why he forget him clean laundry I think."

" I give the stick to you or we can put back in him laundry and post. But might have secret stuff on it and him boss go mad if Jerry stupid and lose the stick."

Given that this bar was, with many other little coffee shops, food stalls, cafes', condos' and a hotel, right next to the surprisingly large US Consulate here in Chiang Mai, all foreigners working in, or just visiting the consulate, were always called *'Hello James,'* as in James Bond, by the locals, so Bim's 'may be secret stuff' comment wasn't quite so surprising. Had she been aware of Jerry's 'CIA office address', it would have been even less so.

Now. Had Focksy and I acted instantly we might have been able to quickly get Jerry on the phone and ask him about the stick but then Bim followed up her comment with, *"Here in Thailand when we lose a memory stick then we call it 'a forgetory stick'."*

Which, given that English is her second or possibly third language after Thai, was really rather clever, and required Focksy and I to order another two beers and discuss same. I told him that when my Thai wife and I were recently waiting at an airport baggage carrousel I heard her on the phone telling that we were 'waiting for our luggage to be downloaded' which is brilliant.

She also, rather delightfully calls fireworks -'fire flowers.' I should stress, that like Bim, she has brilliant English, way better than my feeble attempts to speak Thai, even after ten years of marriage. When it comes to reading Thai script, to me it just looks like someone wrote mississippi in teardrops and then turned the letters upside down.

Consequently by the time we eventually tried to call Jerry there was no response as he was presumably by then settling into the first of his beers and peanuts at thirty thousand feet or so. In fact if he was en route Ex BKK to IAD for CIA HQ USA it was a long old flight, several flights in fact...nearly 24 hours...and that's a lot of peanuts. Whilst we pondered the situation further a couple of the evening bar staff arrived and after a somewhat rapid exchange of Thai with much arm waving, Bim had news to report.

"Jaap and Mooey they say very early this morning they going to Temple and see Jerry outside him hotel get into a car with some men. They said he seem upset and was pushed by one man who seem angry him, they not like to say anything then as not in their business. Jaap say she try call you this afternoon to tell you but your phone is off. She worry as Jerry nice man to she and everyone this bar."

Despite the popularity of insanely aggressive Thai boxing, generally I know well how 'unconfrontational' Thais are- even using the car or motorbike hooter is considered quite strong - and so I quickly told Bim to thank Jaap and Mooey very very much, and we understood very well why they could not get involved.

Bim then said, " You no good Mr Harry, always not have phone on in afternoon then may be Mr Jerry call you for help him."

My explanation that, in the Thai heat I always have an afternoon ' *siesta*' prompted a confused discussion with her, " Why you go afternoon party not ask Bim. I have Spanish boyfriend one time long before and he say me I would like *'fiesta'* very much."

The sound of very aggressive sticky tape ripping and sticking suggested that no amount of 'siesta- fiesta' explanation was going to win the day with Bim despite her language skills, so I let it rest.

Which returns us to the question of the Memory Stick... and what to do with it, that being another two beers discussion on the general morality of looking into a randomly found memory stick.

We agreed this was not really a random-completely unknown owner stick- and as the beers and the situation sunk in, we concluded that 'investigating the contents of a stick belonging to a friend' was worse than sniffing around one of unknown ownership.

But in the real world, could you resist looking into a memory stick that had fallen from a CIA man's pocket...

In the end Focksy... or to give him his full name Focks Schnauzer, which is rather more German sounding than the mainly Irish journalist - now TV news man- that he is. Think CNN's Wolf Blitzer but not so many jokes. So *'News Hund Focksy'* was all but demanding to check what was on it straight away.

Although then, as he seemed to be in espionage overdrive mode, he raised the potential problem of ' what if it was infected with some killer software virus...after all the CIA had been known to use such things in Iran and other places.'

In the end it was Bim who 'accidently' provided us with the answer. "Mr Harry, not you forget we still got your old lap top here behind the bar. The one you break the screen when you sit on it in the taxi...now you got the new one maybe you can give the old one to someone like one of us. It still work and screen not look too bad."

Almost as one Focksy and I jumped at that saying, "Good idea. Lets have it, we'll check Jerry's memory stick on it, and if there's anything evil on there it won't matter too much as that computer was dead-ish anyway. "

After some sorting of plugs and leads it powered up and indeed the screen worked fine...with just a jagged line across it, and so ...we plugged in the stick...and looking back I rather wish we hadn't...***Now it had all begun just a week or so earlier...***

'Could one order 'neaps on the side' when ordering Haggis in a Scots restaurant?

Harry writes: That question and the follow up, "As he had an allergy to shrimp would it be OK to order a 'Deep Fried Mars bar' as a starter?" had gained our attention somewhat. The questioner's final comment "I guess that *Mars* is like a fried cheese tempura of some kind." With us both knowing that with haggis being a traditional savoury delicacy and a 'Mars' a sweet chocolate covered bar of soft malted toffee, this left Focksy and I speechless.

Neither query being generally what one would expect to find as the main topic of evening conversation in a not very girly-ish bar in Chiang Mai. The earnest enquiries came around about ten days ago from the youngish American, or 'Jerry' as we had learned to call him after a few evenings of observing him in our local.

As is the way with such things, we had moved on from a few *shrugs, nods and smiles* at various sporting events on the big screen tv mounted on the wall behind the bar, to then exchanging a few words. The trigger to that first conversation and then an exchange of drinks, had been when a group of Aussie tourists had persuaded Bim the barmaid to change TV channels to the cricket.

Observing Jerry's distinctly puzzled expression as the Brits and Aussies in the bar exchanged knowledgeable insults over the almost motionless playing field, with white clad figures scattered around it in apparently random positions, I had, as the friendly chap that I am, attempted the usual explanations:

"*Cricket.* There's two sides of eleven, each has a go at being '*in*' until ten of the eleven of them are '*out*' and then they are all out. The two players from the team that are '*in*' are facing a series of overs- that's six balls...bowled from alternate ends. Whenever possible after a batsman hits the ball they run to exchange places once or more times. So that's good but it's also the most likely opportunity for the team that's currently '*out*' fielding to get out the man that's '*in*' batting or the one that wasn't batting but is running. '*Out*'."

Focksy raised a hand, "As a mongrel of , in this case American Irish German descent, I am not a cricket fan. So before the Brit. here gets on to fielding positions such as slips, long leg or silly mid on, and into the Duckworth Lewis formula. Or worse, starts telling jokes about googlies and *'the bowlers Holding, the batsman's Willy'*, or some other equally incomprehensible Wisden,* I suggest I buy us three a drink by way of apology for our Aussie visitors interrupting your evening baseball."

Jerry then insisted he would 'buy them' as he seemed to be a guest in our town...and this tropic heat did *'sure did make one thirsty'*, even if this bar full of cricket watchers hadn't been much in the lively US *'holler and swoller'* sports bar traditions.'

With politely controlled alacrity we accepted his kind offer, although the proceedings became a little delayed when Focksy insisted that, whilst in *matters sporting* he was an 'American Irish German', and indeed enjoyed baseball very much, in matters of lubrication and libation he was 'Irish German American' and 'thank you very much he'd have a Guinness.'

Jerry told us he'd been working in Asia for a few weeks, mainly shuttling between Korea and Singapore and had made Chiang Mai his regular half way stopping point of choice for some r&r as his dad had visited here in the mid sixties. Not only that but Bangkok was all full of self righteous American NGOs and modern day missionaries, looking to enjoy some girly bars...and remember dear reader that's an American view!

As it happens, despite me visiting Focksy at his winter quarters in Thailand annually for many years, neither he nor I frequent, 'girly bars' as our normal evening habitat. This not being a case of *'they would say that wouldn't they,'* but simply a matter of practical choice. When choosing a 'bar' to become your 'local' you need somewhere you can at least hear enough to have a chat with your chum about the days events or the plans for the morrow.

Given that both Focksy and I had been, or to some extent still are, itinerant journalists-me in print- him now on TV- there was usually plenty to discuss.

Of course, as the tabloids report there are many wild and unruly bars in the seamier streets of Pattaya and Patong, just as there are in the entertainment areas of most Asian cities and ports worldwide. Those tabloids should also report that most such girly bars are very noisy, as it is *vital their music is considerably louder* than the other bars that are usually less than an arms length away.

Many of those, girly bars that is, with scantily clad dancers on the actual bar, and other girls holding up signs advertising *'Twenty Sexy Girls Here - and One Dodgy Fat One,'* deserve both their seamy press and the shock and horror of passing PC tourists.

As it happens it is very well documented here in Asia that *'the dodgy fat one'* gets brought more drinks, and gets way more tips, than any of the other exotic creatures of the night. The reality being that confessional or TLC conversation more than carnality is the choice for most customers...but that's another story, and don't shoot the authors, we're only reporting on this.

Even in the wilder resorts, step back a street, take a longer look at what first glance appears to be a somewhat similar but perhaps a little quieter bar, and you'll find it much like any local bar or pub anywhere in the world. Pool table, dart board, 'lunch specials' and regular customers, often with their *'usual please'* delivered to their *'regularly occupied seats.'*

If the bar TV - in Asia at least- is showing US Football, NBA or Baseball, then the clientele are likely American. If it's Cricket, Rugby or F1 Car racing, then it will be Brits or Aussies...if it's *'Soccer,'* of the World Cup, Brit, Dutch, German, Spanish and Italian Euro leagues variety -it tends to be displayed somewhat universally in all bars, and is thus not a reliable sign regarding the nationality of the drinkers therein.

Should for some reason the bar TV be off- a monsoon rainstorm for instance reduces the satellite dish signals to blots of fuzzy illogic in seconds- an experienced passing visitor can tell in an instant from the style of beer pouring as to the likely primary language spoken therein.

The arrival of an icy glass with a good two inches or more of foaming *'head'* on the beer will strongly suggest that one of the northern mainland European lingos *'vill be zpoke here.'* To be fair the miserable and unsmiling faces in *'zutch a bar'* at that moment, are more likely to be due to the loss of *'ze TV zignal at a cruzial moment in ze important game'*, than than any lack of *'zense of humour.'* *'Ve can azzure you that many things are funny in*

Tchermany but not if the TV has gone off in the *vinal minuten of the Bayer Leverkusen playoff against Borrussia Dortmund.'*

That's enough to give one a headache and in need of one of Herr Bayer's best known confiscated trade marks: ie.ein Aspirin.

Another clue to the likely warmth of the welcome and potential for hospitality not hostility *used to be given* by a serious display of Harps, Shamrocks and dodgy plastic Leprechauns. Usually with lots of green faux Gaelic writing. This all suggesting an experienced clientele fully aware of the professional patience required by Guinness drinkers to allow their glass to settle and be topped up-before applying their first Dublin moustache of the evening.

Nowadays however, regardless how many green leprechauns and plastic shamrocks are on display they rarely provide much of a clue to the inhabitants nationality, as like soccer, a pint of the black stuff has conquered the world.

(Ed's note. As written this paragraph referred only to Guinness. But given that Focksy is, as he was partly raised in Cork, where there's a choice, a Murphy's man and Harry primarily a Guinness man - I thought it best to point out that 'other stouts are available.' The Ed.)

But back to window shopping for a suitable bar. If the foaming pints *are way less foamy, and carefully filled to the very top of the glass indicates two things:*

Firstly that the recipient of the ale, even if very chilled as is needed this near to the equator, that's the beer not the drinker being chilled, the quaffers - quaffists- are most likely to be Brits.

Secondly it suggests that that the smiley barmaid has been well trained in the all important art of instantly identifying the customers nationality and thus their beer serving preference from just a finger pointed at a beer pump. The customers polite words such as 'danke' or 'thanks' or even the Thai *'kop woon kap'* look very much the same to lip reading nubiles serving in a busy bar.

By day seven of this particular first week, Jerry tended to be waiting for us when we dropped in to 'our' local. He seemed to relax somewhat and told us a little more about his job, once he had learned that I really did hold both an Irish and a Brit Passport and Focksy had a US one a German one and an Irish one. I was surprised he mentioned the German one as his dad was born in what was East Germany, which has been known to make some US folks nervous.

Jerry it seemed 'worked' - or as he said- 'was overworked' - for the US State Department in a particular office that had had its staff numbers cut by fifty percent or more since the days of President Obama. So it seemed implied that the workload meant he was not therefor a major fan of his new boss President Trump. Actually as we got to know him better he seemed beside himself with anger about Trump abandoning the Paris climate change agreement.

Jerry explained he was a 'State Department *PARA*.'

When, moments later, he -Jerry - rushed out into the street as he did every time his phone rang- Focksy said. "Nice guy, but not too fit looking, I reckon that's bullshit about being a parachutist."

To be fair, on his return we learned that *'PARA' in* this case was the acronym for *'Presidential Advance Resources Agent.'*

'"I obviously can't say much, but as I've already explained I've been shuttling between Korea, Singapore and Washington- so from press and other media stories you can pretty much figure out what I've been doing."

Focksy said," From the many news reports over the years about US Presidential security, special armoured limo's, Air Force One planes, armed agents with cables in their ears shooting themselves in the foot, and such. I think we get it. "

Jerry nodded happily, but then frowned slightly as Focksy continued, "I hope you're not the guy who screwed up big time on May 23 in 2011 when the Presidential limo got stuck in the gateway leaving the US Embassy in Dublin."

Jerry replied, " Actually that is one of the things we have to be alert for, but why the hell you recall the exact date I don't know. It wasn't that big a deal?"

I replied, "Well actually it was quite a big press story at the time, because of course to most Europeans the huge car looks ridiculous, and as it happens May 23 rd. is my birthday. Focksy and I were in Ireland then en route to visiting our mutual friend 'Mick the Brief, and his family at Lahinch on the west coast. Given that your current boss has a golf course and hotel at Doonbeg just a few miles from Lahinch I guess you'll know exactly where it is."

Jerry nodded in agreement. I continued," Focksy's the golfer, and surfing, is or was, more my thing, hence me knowing the quite good surf at Lahinch, and Focksy all about the golf courses. I'd also guess from your *'Haggis and fried Mars bar'* enquiry that 'The Donald' may also be planning another trip to one of his golf courses in Scotland in the near future. That's despite the less than friendly welcome he received last time."

This time Jerry grinned broadly and said, "Well we are supposed to be discrete -but there's not much in what you say that hasn't already been reported by CNN, Fox and the BBC. In the main our concerns are keeping POTUS free of egg or paint throwing publicity hungry demonstrators and suchlike. In reality, whilst there's always a lot of threats, there's not so many Lee Harvey Oswald's out there- but of course we never know when one will turn up so that's our priority."

At those words Focksy opened his mouth to speak...but thankfully closed it when he engaged brain.

Jerry continued, "As Presidential Advance Resources Agents, we're tasked to discretely gain as much detailed local knowledge as we can so that we are well prepared. The problem I have right now, is that with all the cutbacks in staff I'm trying from here in Asia to prepare the local action and resources guide for a possible- I stress, as the White House says, *possible*, Scotchland and Eireland visit."

"To be honest all the help I've got is my assistant Wayne. He's on the ground now out there but he's having a hard time, he's only recently been promoted from his intern status and this is his first trip outside the USA. "

"Those calls I have to keep taking every few minutes are mostly from him asking about food and drink, and also because he can't understand a word the locals say to him. I just asked him to send on to me an sms he's just received from a local policeman in Turnberry Scotchland right now."

" To be fair it's got me baffled as well." He held out his apple thingy so Focksy and I could both read the message:

'This ane is too smale, widnae hold a puddock.'

Jerry looked at us expectantly, and to Focksy's amazement I said, 'May I tap in a response for you to send him?

Jerry handed over his tablet thingy and I sent: 'Wayne, tell the policeman that *'You'll get a bigger one , then Potus will be laughing like something's tickling his bahoochie.'* In seconds the response came back, he says *'Jings, that's fine then.'*

Following some intensive interrogation techniques involving fluids - Guinness in fact- poured in my face, I admitted that back in the sixties I had started my journalistic career with a Scots based newspaper group where I learned to appreciate -and understand the local vernacular of Scotland's legendary comic strip characters, the still brilliant 'Broons' and 'Oor Wullie'.

The following evening in the bar it seemed Focksy and I were now honorary consultants to PARA...Jerry saying ,"Look guys, I really need some help, I got more than a bit diverted having a good time out here in Asia, and I'm way behind in reporting back to my boss. You seem to know more about Ireland and Scotchland than anyone I ever met."

He insisted on buying us all the drinks we could handle- *"That's the least I can do, you guys are truly helping to make the world a safer place."* Which seemed a bit OTT, but then again a free drink is a free drink. Not only that, but the bar was empty of sports fans, as a passing truck had knocked the TV satellite dish off the bar wall, we had plenty of time, and peace and quiet to help.

The list of questions on his iPad seemed extensive and included: A need to know about prevailing winds in the Firth of Clyde. How many US pints are there in a dram? Should he be liaising with the Irish or British secret service about Doonbeg ? That one raised an eyebrow with Focksy and I to say the least.

Did we knew of a 'non alcoholic whisky?

And if not, would it be appropriate to toast the health of 'Her Majesty Your Royal Queen' in what he had been told was Scotland's second most famous and *non alcoholic* beverage: Irn Bru.

As apparently The Donald doesn't drink alcohol, they'd been recommended 'Irn Bru' and needed confirmation this would be suitable, oh yes, and 'was it usual for Her Majesty to take it on the rocks or straight up'?

Having set him straight about the sweet, rusty orange coloured Irn Bru indeed deservedly being Scotland's second most famous beverage- albeit a non alcoholic one, but not really suitable for Her Majesty...on a formal occasion at least...although we couldn't vouch for her private consumption.

Focksy also noted that there had just been a major press furor when it was suggested the Trump branded hotels in Scotland had banned the drink as 'it stained the carpets.' This slur on both their second national beverage and drink holding stability has incensed the Scots tabloids.

I did have to remind Focksy that, this was no lighthearted matter- and we were both *'making the world a safer place'* when he started to try and persuade Jerry that 'Buckie' or 'Buckfast Abbey Tonic Wine' was the regular preferred tipple of the entire Royal Family and Daily Mail directors when on their Scots estates.

(The Ed. For once Harry is being correctly responsible. 'Buckie' for all its excellence has become a somewhat notorious choice amongst Scots binge drinkers, vagrants and teenage troublemakers.
It has even been immortalised in a more than profane song by Billy Connelly. All a bit sad really as it is produced by well meaning monks at Buckfast Abbey in Devon way away at the other end of the UK.)

Meanwhile Focksy and I were pleased to note that Jerry seemed to be a quick learner as more and more Scotchland was becoming Scotland. We planned to give it another day and then start explaining the raw deep and complex historical political and religious differences between Irish Eire and the grudgingly Brit Northern Ireland...just touching on the 'The Troubles' as we went.'

When we told Jerry of that plan he seemed a bit insulted and claimed to be 'very big on global knowledge including Ireland.

"Just ask me anything- I mean- is the Pope a Catholic? Come on, I'm pretty up to speed guys." Focksy and I decided it best to give it a couple more days before we got into 'The Irish Question'.

Then there was some Asian not Scots or Irish confusion to be sorted out when the usually *'Coca Cola straight up please'* drinking Jerry, decided he'd earned a beer. "I'll have a Thai beer please," he said to the smiley and always attentive Bim the barmaid and she duly produced a bottle of 'Tiger.'

Now, Murphy's more than Guinness aficionado Focksy, is a bit of a stickler for ale accuracy and told Bim to replace the Tiger with a bottle of *'Singha beer.'* Explaining as he did so to Jerry, that " *'Tiger'* despite sounding like *'Thaiger'* was in fact originally a Singapore brew, and *'Singha'* which of course sounded as if it originated in Singapore was proudly made in Thailand."

Jerry looked concerned saying, "I really wonder if I am going to get the hang of life out here, the translator in my phone insists that the Thai word for rice is 'cow' (*kaoh*) and that the Thai for 'pork' is *'moo'*!"

We reassured him that his translator system was, in those two cases at least, correct...but the next crisis was not long in coming along when Jerry, having gulped down his Singha beer, quickly ordered another one causing Bim the Barmaid to say, " Now you take care Mr. Jerry, you girlfriend tonight get angry me if you *'Singha song'* all night." His auto translate phone started to suggest popular melodies to sing in karaoke bars, but Focksy and I explained that *'Singha-song'* was the usual Thai phrase for snoring.

With Jerry having given Focksy and I a bunch of homework, researching the areas surrounding the several Trump golfing establishments in Scotland and Ireland, we agreed it would be good to meet early in the morning to try get on and finish the job.

Jerry was embarrassed at suggesting the early start, but Focksy and I reassured him saying it was way more interesting than reading the news online alternately in the hot sun and the shade.

As we all left the bar, Focksy and I to find a Tuk Tuk back to our place, we observed and heard Jerry, en route to his nearby hotel, running the gauntlet of beer selling ladies at various nearby bars as they called out to him, *'Hello Darling,'* or *'Hello Dhaarkling.'*

When we met the next day at breakfast time to continue our now full time task of *'making the world a safer place,'* he mentioned it, saying, 'How smiley and friendly everyone was, all calling him darling' as he walked by.'

Neither Focksy nor I had the heart to tell that with the Thai word for monkey being 'ling' that in most cases the 'darlings' subtly changed if he didn't stop to *'Dhaarkling'*...which kind of means *'Monkeys bum.'*

(Ed's note. Sorry about all these interruptions but before we all get deluged in 'google translate' corrections and complaints, I would point out that whilst standard English has just 26 letters of which 5 are vowels- that the main Thai alphabet has around 44 consonants and 15 vowels which mix and mingle to create multiple tones and sounds. So, as global menus show, there's more than one way write Rice: Kaow, Kaoh, Kow and so on. OK...or if you really insist...OKAY.

To confuse matters even more the Irish Alphabet only has 18 letters. Lacking J,K,Q,W,X,Y, and Z, although they have those squiggly accents over the vowels producing unlikely pronunciations of Sile, Naimh, Seamus, Siobhan and many others.

Mind you when Harry was a lad, in an English Village, the local vicar was named and spelled Guinness... except he pronounced it as 'Guince,' or 'Gwince.'

Cricket. Dodgy old schoolboy smirks, smirked by those who should have known better, were the order of the day when top cricketing team-The West Indies-with their wonderful bowler Michael Holding, were playing against the Brits with their ace batsman Peter Willey.

This giving the commentators-probably radio then, more than tv-their chance to make their much anticipated and overly repeated: The bowler's Holding, the batsman's Willey.

And before you mention it, back a good few pages, still on Cricket, Focksy's words about 'incomprehensible Wisden' is for once on these pages-not a typo- Wisden not Wisdom, is the centuries old-still published official cricketers book of record.)

Chapter 3. *Early Summer 2018.*
Helping to Make the World a Safer Place.

Harry writes: Or as Focksy had now started to say in a slightly OTT style-as taught by Jerry: 'Proudly. Making the World a Safer Place.'

Focksy and I had happily abandoned our pressured daily schedule of relaxing by the pool, swimming ,chatting, snacking, sunning or shading and when 'conscience became conscientious' moving into the welcome shade and tapping away at our computers on our latest novels and other outstanding projects. All that effort closely followed by 'siesta' time. Today's earlyish morning now found us setting out to walk across over the Ping River Bridge to breakfast in the very bar we had only left quite late the night before.

As I mentioned earlier, the bar is one of several nestled in the side streets around the well defended walls of the considerably sized and very busy US Consulate here in Chiang Mai. So the choice of breakfasts available in the vicinity for consular employees, tourists, locals and visa hopefuls are many and varied.

Where fine ales, or at least the best available in the tropics, are served by the pint in *correctly unfoaming* style it also usually means that the bar staff have been trained with the necessary skills to provide a proper 'Full English or Full Irish' breakfast.

Several Eggs, well fried but runny looking at you. Real bacon, never ham. Porky sausages, baked beans, tomatoes, mushrooms, saute'd potatoes -never the insult to breakfast that is the chemically embalmed hash brown, fried bread *and* toast. Decent black pudding (blood sausage) optional. And a good mug of English Breakfast tea, not that wish wash often made from Lipton Yellow tea bags.

Finally, twin sauces in red and brown...and never anything GREEN. Green garnish or bloody sprinkled herbs, whilst fine for later, can spoil the start to a good day.

As a general rule, with sausages it is better not to consider what is in them...just enjoy. But with blood / black pudding sausage in the tropics, certain local customs involving hot tin roofs and fermenting uncooked pork seem hard to shift, hence black pudding being an option, only when its production heritage is well known.

Also regarding sausages, despite them being a little suspect in their manner of serving beer, the Germans generally can be trusted in matters sausageous. In fact Focksy and I have a plan to team up with a German butcher chum here in town and launch a brand of 'German made-English recipe' world cup schnorkers to be called *'Best Wurst.'*

(Breakfasts. Ed here again. 'Me Too' convention now makes it necessary to explain that ' Other breakfasts are available.' It's the shortage of oatcakes, tattie scones, and the general unsuitability of porridge in the tropics that makes the' Full Scottish' breakfast less common near the equator. I have also warned Jerry that if he keeps ordering waffles or pouring syrup on his bacon he could find himself suddenly short of two members of his 'making the world a safer place team.')

But first Focksy and I had to survive our walk across the Ping River Bridge, the narrow footway also being a popular and speedy motor bike shortcut for the thousands rushing to work.

With an average of three or four riders plus a small child or two per motor bike being the norm out here, the bikes can be counted in hundreds whilst the passengers transported can be in their thousands. But with a degree of smiling and dodging, the crossing rarely requires any pedestrian plunges to safety in the river below.

On our arrival at the bar, Bim the barmaid told us, as she quickly concealed the remains of a plate full of waffles, that Jerry had been in early , but had just departed as he had forgotten something...and in an encouraging portent of a good breakfast to come, she rustled up and served a couple of mugs of good looking breakfast tea-it steaming a little - even in the tropical morning.

Having logged on to the free wi-fi -using the day's special password written up on the blackboard behind the bar, we started to check the news on line. Focksy saying, 'It's crazy fast this Wi-Fi."

Bim, who was delivering an advance army of toast, sauces and stuff- to the table said, 'Well it's the US Consulate Wi-Fi, that's why we have to get the new password every morning. We get it from the Thai security guys on the gates as them and the consular staff have to check in with passwords before they can get into work."

So the Focks and I were just settling into the serious business of breakfast consumption when Jerry rushed in looking hot and bothered. "Sorry I'm late I had forgotten to pick up the wi-fi password of the day and we'll need it."

As Jerry then scrabbled to get the plastic wrap off the top of his now much needed new bottle of cold water Focksy pointed at his laptop and said, "*Bfmrm got it onn frmw hrt b rboard usl.*"

I translated- "What my mate is trying to articulate through a gob full of toast, egg and sausage is that we have both already logged on using today's password. It's pinned up on the wall there behind the bar as usual."

Jerry looked stricken, "But that's confidential information for US consular staff only. Christ...I'll have to report this. Can you image if those bastards in the goddam media get to hear about it. It'll be like Snowdon or Wiki leaks all over again."

Breakfast continued in a somewhat jolly manner with Focksy recounting tales of his '*Good Morning Vietnam*' days as a young but full on war reporter back in the day, where any and all top secret and confidential US military information was always revealed first in the girly bars of Hanoi or Ho Chi Minh city.

As Jerry went to stand up- Focksy put out a restraining hand, "Jerry, before you rush off to report about the Wi-fi, hear me out, as ,I hope, a friend. For sure a new friend, but friend never the less - and not one of those goddam media bastards."

Focksy smiled as Jerrys hand went to his face, "Consider the reality Jerry. Whatever we are looking at on our brilliant internet connection here is coming through a little black box somewhere in your US Consulate the other side of that wall. Now consider also, that any messages *we send as well as receiving* are also going through that little black box."

"As an experienced goddam media bastard I would be certain of two things. Firstly, if you think about it Jerry, you well know that anything seriously confidential in or out of the offices inside those large consulate grounds are for sure not going in and out through the same little black wi-fi box we are using."

" Secondly, again as you well know, there's a whole gang of NSA-GCHQ -CIA spook someones in Hawaii, Oman, Cyprus,

Cheltenham in the UK, or at some other establishments in the US observing everything we and everyone else using the free Wi-Fi are doing. Every key stroke, every bit in and bite out. They know who we are , where we 're going, where we live --and in the case of Harry here they know about his inexplicable preference for Guinness over Murphy's. And why. And the same goes for you. "

"What is probably more concerning to the NSA and others, is the fact that in the highish buildings round here- that hotel, those condo's, that building over the river, we can assume there are Russkies and Chinese in almost permanent residence, and they are really desperate to find out out about the truly secret US stuff that's being shared around that building."

" Unfortunately for the Russkies and Chinese they also have to deal with the data snow storm created by us lot. It's all flash flowing together down the fibre optics to Songhkla and Satun in Southern Thailand where the Thai fibers turn east or west to join the world wide net of subsea cables. So our data blizzard makes it just a tiny bit more difficult for the Russkies and Chinese to sort out the bits they really want, and a lot easier for the USA to check it all."

Focksy took a sip of tea and continued," My conclusion is, that a division of US security, possibly not directly connected to your own, is very aware that we are enjoying the free use of their better than most Wi-Fi. In fact they probably set it up that way, knowing that all those applying for visa's, or expats with any kind of problem, all use their phones to connect to the world and report home just prior to going into the consulate or immediately on leaving it."

" Unlike the old days when the world was connected by copper wires , it's actually more difficult to tap into, or listen to messages travelling at the speed of light through those fibre optic cables, so it really suits whoever wants to snoop, to simply tune in, right here, in all the cafes, bars and other places that think they've got a sneaky free wi fi deal."

Jerry sat back and said, "Wow. Now I'm embarrassed. Firstly about insulting you guys and secondly for getting it so wrong. Seems there's always stuff to learn about the real world of intel beyond my little bit of the Stars and Stripes. Thanks Focksy, you saved me looking more than usually dumb."

Focksy grinned and said, " I will add three more things. One. Your comments about the media generally are correct. In Harry's and my case we like to think we can be trusted because we like you, we can also afford to play a very long game. One day maybe, and you have a good story that needs to be 'out there,' you'll hopefully remember us."

"Secondly Harry and I will put your 'moment of madness' down to the insane sugar rush created by those bloody waffles and syrup...and we hope that tomorrow we will see you eating a proper nourishing breakfast. Blood sausage optional."

Focksy sat back and blew cool on the top of his still scalding tea. The Tea and Coffee cooling rate out here in the tropics is way slower than most countries. It should be noted though, that air-con can affect this cooling rate considerably and thus completely cockup the consumption of a good cuppa.

Jerry said, "Hang on you said three things, that's only two."

Focksy said: "Oh yes. Always remember. If at anytime on your late night walk back to your hotel you've been tempted, as many are, to accept the offer of some company for the late late evening , that the NSA now know all about it. "

" They won't disapprove - but they won't approve either-but above all they'll be so pleased they know. Sadly ,with them being based in a black box somewhere in middle America they won't quite ever trust you again. *Particularly if they observed your companion of choice being a lady boy. Out here it would be unremarkable and generally acceptable.* But in Windy Sky Ridge Montana or Soggy Springs Ohio it will be filed and may count against you one day."

I called Bim over and said, " Three coffees please the way we each like them, and three very small shots of Gammeldansk, I mean small...they are for medical purposes. Jerry's recovery from shock."

Jerry spluttered over his 'bitter tasting and very alcoholic medicine' and said, "Thanks' guys. Truly thanks. As it happens no lady boys or other companions last night, although I must say I am increasingly thinking that Bim is really very very nice."

My turn to speak, "Focksy and I have known Bim for more than ten years now, and she's indeed really nice. Hard working and straight. And like 99.9999% of Thai ladies absolutely NOT a bar girl, or easily available. But chat to her. You'll be insulting her and most probably won't get far, trying to drag her back to some hotel room for 'a quickie'...as many have tried and been rejected. As I said she's not that kind of bar girl, then again she might see a handsome chap like you as sex on legs, or a ticket to the future, so see how you get on. But right now it's us that better '*get on.*'"

" Half the bloody morning's gone already, oh yes...just one thing. If you treat Bim badly, Focksy and I will one day find you and cut off your internet or worse..."

" Now to work. Reference your bosses' two golf courses in Scotland. Before our breakfast even , Focksy and I noticed that one of them has a working rifle range not a mile away from it and there's a pub nearby called 'The Cock and Bull Arms.' Can't think why those two items came straight to mind."

Jerry looked fraught and serious and said, "Right now I'm getting confused and not sure what I should believe."

Focksy's response surprised him, " Actually, what Harry says about the rifle range and the pub are true. Not only that but the Turnberry Golf Hotel used to be a Royal Navy Air Force Hospital, where very sadly over the years many died, and so there's zillions of ghost stories about so many of the rooms. "

"Of course the internet produced multiple Turnberry ghostie results-most of which could be discounted. One seemed to be a promotional story in a golf publication in which a hotel manager gave considerable detail about 'ghostly activities' he claimed to have personally witnessed. Although as the pay off paragraph suggested that 'all hotels should have a ghost story or two', as it was good for business, it raised doubts about the validity of the whole piece."

Jerry already had already shared with us a remarkable listing setting out details of minor annoyances used to gain anti Trump publicity, and also details of fairly dramatic attacks or sabotage they regularly needed to head off, as they could inflict serious mischief or even injury upon persons and property associated with the President.

It's not everyday that over one's breakfast that the breeding rate of insects and rodents is discussed. The threat being that 'the anti brigade 'were planning on infiltrating infestations of everything from rats to cockroaches-even fire ants and very nasty brown recluse spiders, in Trump establishments to cause maximum disruption.

Focksy's comment that 'using the secret service as rodent inspectors seemed a bit demeaning' causing a more than little 'I bloody agree with you,' reaction from Jerry.

With him then remarking, "It's like a lot of this stuff, it all sounds quite amusing kids stuff until you consider the possible consequences. Take, 'stink bombs', 'fart smells', or 'maloderants' as they are more militarily called, they all sound like harmless jokes or schoolroom pranks, but evil smells are sometimes used to mask dangerous, even lethal chemicals. Just as if someone smears a harmless sticky gel over a door handle or elevator- it can take huge efforts and much time to establish if it's Novichok - Skripal style nerve agent or not."

"Those gels are more commonly available than you think. Taking into account that it's only a while back that someone set up a serious Novichok nerve agent poisoning in Salisbury England, and someone also killed the brother of North Korea's President Kim in a very public area of Kuala Lumpur Airport. It would seem unlikely the two events were related but they both involved nerve agents."

He continued, "Then did you notice that just before Kim Jong Un signed the peace accord in Singapore that the Koreans cleaned the pen he was to use." He was a bit put out when Focksy remarked ," Then their concern about the potential for such attacks, suggests they feel the dangers are in a two way street, the US may have coated the pen in a noxious substance."

Despite the maloderants of the conversation the wonderful smell of cooking from the little kitchen next to the bar, suggested it was lunchtime. Time flies when you're busy. Mind you Thai ladies, fairly diminutive in the main, seem to eat and snack constantly.

My wife says, "Most Thais 'eat for fun' when they have money, because for most of their lives they haven't had that opportunity." For us hard workers, busy making the world a safer place, spicy lime and herb minced *'laarb moo'* eaten with Romaine lettuce leaf scoops, hit the spot, so the lunch time discussion, was interrupted with lots of *'mmms- nice-wows'* and *'always great to have Thai food.'*

The parts of the discussion that were understandable through the munching mumbles were all about likely 'golf club events' and I don't mean Rory McIlroy or Tiger Woods comebacks.

(The Ed. I know, I know Tiger Woods is part Thai, and Rory a modern Irish hero-but we've already diverted into lunch details ...so please, 'lets get on!)

Potential risks, embarrassments annoyances on the golf course seemed to be a great concern to Jerry. Which, I guess is sensible considering the amount of time the Pres. likes to spend on the the links, and taking into account what happened on his previous visit to one of his courses in Scotland.

(The Ed reports: On 24 June 2016 whilst then a Presidential Candidate, Donald Trump was making a televised speech on the 9th Tee of his Turnberry Golf Course, Simon Brodkin-best known in the UK for his stage / TV comedy character-'Lee Nelson'- having been screened and searched, slipped through several layers of Police, Golf Course and Trump's own security, called out to the President that, 'He was delivering the golf balls as requested' and rolled sixty bright red swastika decorated golf balls all over the green. With Trump yelling 'Take him away,' Simon was handcuffed and taken away, and later released by some uber polite Scots Police. https://www.youtube.com/watch?v=Y8Ju8wZukYQ.)

One of Jerrys concerns included, Golf Cart sabotage. I have to be honest, Focksy's enthusiastic description of how his employers at the 24/7 TV news channel 'TNoTN' (The Newsiest of Television News) could cover the President perused by a whole line of golf carts in a *'wacky races'* style pursuit, caused a considerable pause in the serious proceedings, even 'Mr Serious 'Jerry laughed at that one.

Also on the golf courses, Jerry seemed very relaxed about the rapidly developing threat from widely available home and hobby drones now able to carry payloads of noxious sprays or explosives.

Given that we were just about to publish our latest thriller, which partly features just such attacks, we had some interest in the matter...and some up to date information to share. *(The Ed. Harry Buckle. 'Just In Case'. I have to say, it's a good read, but then again I would say that wouldn't I!)*

The drones referred to as home and hobby types, most used harmlessly, as a fun way to carry the few ounces of a Go Pro style camera...but given they can now carry a serious load of explosives or smoke making kit and 'self navigate ' to target they are a worry.

When Focksy and I mentioned these drones to Jerry he was quite dismissive," We've got that well under control, since Obama's day, we've had specialists with net firing guns. We can now block all the GPS Sat Nav type control signals- without also blacking out local first responder and our own communications. So for sure it's a worry, but I think we're on the case. I think we need to move on."

All of which left left Focksy and I shrugging slightly.

So, for him whilst all that's under control, the bigger problems are when someone wants to play golf! Again. Pretty much since 100 plus years back when William McKinley made the first Presidential putt in 1897, almost all Presidents have played. They mostly played the game in a way that reflects their personality, with the honour of being the worst cheat going to Clinton. Others learned to play as it 'was the done thing to do, to 'get on politically.'

Golfing Presidents have poleaxed spectators (Ford), built a putting green on the White House lawn, (Eisenhower), removed same (Nixon). In more modern times, both Obama and Trump have been much criticised for the amount of time they spend or spent on the golf course, but their numbers of good walks, spoilt by golf, pale into insignificance compared to President Woodrow Wilson, who played almost daily, and sometime twice daily.

When Ronald Reagan was enjoying a quiet round at a course in Augusta , an armed man crashed the gates, took hostages and demanded he talk to the President. The scary situation was defused without injury to anyone, but does set out the problem when any President wishes to play.

All buildings and equipment to be searched and screened for IEDs and other devices, the full Presidential protection service deployed, backed up by local police and other forces. Roads are closed, hills patrolled to avoid offering refuge or vantage to snipers. All of this of course after POTUS and his entourage including the 'just in case he's assassinated, body watch shared press pool' have been delivered safely to, and later from ,the course.

If his Trumpiness then decided he wanted a burger, after the strain of hitting his way to a round of 100 or more (sorry-officially, between 70 and 80) then once the food tasters, kitchen security, approved suppliers and chefs *not forgetting the ketchup sniffers have approved the Presidential squeeze (sorry Stormy)* he'll get his snack. So despite all this professionalism, especially amongst the ketchup purity operatives, the Golf Course is to some extent outside the concrete , steel, armour plated bubble from which he usually tweets.

One thing Jerry was very fixated on, were the rumours that protestors were planning on using courses over previous weeks, planting weeds, flowers & poison ivy. Or intending to mark out anti Trump messages on the greens and fairways with grass killer or fertilizer pellets- *the messages and symbols* to later grow up as 'extra green' or in patches of dead grass.

Again, the descriptions of 'grass killer sprays concealed in golf bags', or even 'golfing trousers adapted to allow pellets or sprays to be released down trouser legs,' caused more mirth...So much so that Jerry slightly lost his cool, and reminding us yet again, " Come on guys, you're supposed to be helping to make the world a safer place, writing out anti POTUS messages in extra green or dead grass is one thing, and quite amusing, but be aware that bad guys employing similar systems could also deliver deadly poisons."

Focksy and I avoided enquiring how the deliverer could release these deadly sprays down their trouser legs at no risk to themselves. The sniggers and then uncontrollable laughs started again as Jerry earnestly continued, "Every day POTUS wants to play, we're even having to check the groundsmen, greenkeepers and all employees with access to the sprinkler watering systems. I mean can you imagine if the water systems suddenly came full on when POTUS was putting."

Despite his efforts to keep on the serious track, Jerry's fairly obvious grin at that relatively harmless but 'oh so annoying' assault to his boss faded somewhat when Focksy said, "It may well spoil the hair do and make the orange leak a little , but it would be unlikely to change his scorecard, which other golfers suggest he fills in even before he's played."

Considering this was fairly early in our ten days of knowing Jerry he was still rather guarded and so said, slightly huffily "I don't know about all that, my greater concern is the real potential for exploding golf balls, or others loaded with smoke, weed killer, or even nerve agents finding their way onto the course. "

Focksy then sailed very near the mark in annoying our source of both free beer and a potential great news story when he launched off on a long speech about the likelihood that the CIA has also likely continued to develop such deadly items, hence Jerry's prior knowledge and fear of them.

Jerry frowned and started to say something but Focksy continued, " Protecting the President is not *directly* part of counter intelligence nor in the original CIA brief which was and still is in general terms, collecting, analyzing and disseminating international intelligence to Government officials.' "

" Having said that, somewhere along the line, both before and after The Kennedy years The CIA became more than a little embroiled in direct action often as a result of the extreme views of long time boss man Allen Dulles and some of his close connections with big business. Despite him eventually being fired by Kennedy, Dulles continued on his merry way making mayhem with his gang of 'dirty tricks hit men, all nameless of course and 'unconnected' with the CIA."

Focksy sat back, and continued, "Jerry, I can assure you *none of this is Anti American,* it's just a fact of life, shared in the backstory of many nations, how often the military, regardless of politicians, regulation, law, and national policy, decide their own causes to support and which battles to fight."

Even Jerry smiled at Focksy's," Mind you the outrageous indignation currently being expressed in the US over what may or may not be Russian meddling in US affairs is a bit rich considering the well documented and detailed history of around a hundred years of the USA doing just that in half the world."

Focksy and Jerry having concluded a political truce, the next few days were a continuous and convivial blur of creative thinking, although we were sidetracked into a discussion, about how it was seemingly impossible to embarrass this particular president.

In this case Jerry just nodded sadly at wild accusations - of Trump's extra marital dalliances with mainly buxom ladies, his own recorded words boasting of fame enabling much 'pussy grabbing.' So many allegations of apparent dodgy business dealings with big spending persons of apparently with Russian related origin.

The list went on and on...as did the president...even Jerry remarking, "It's the dissing and denigration of my beloved America that hurts me, I really see the high level smirks, ridicule and lack of respect for the President when we travel."

We sat back and considered Jerry's depressing words and eventually agreed we all needed an evening off...and as it was Focksy's birthday we had just the reason to take one.

Chapter 4... *Early Summer 2018.*
Hej hej der secret politico ist verboten ce-soir.

Harry writes: With an agreement that all Presidents, Security, Golf and Politics were all off the evening discussion menu, to celebrate Focksy's birthday we went to 'Nordern' a Swedish restaurant. One of Chiang Mai's best, and being Swedish it also seemed appropriately neutral.

Once there, Focksy's toast of *'Hej,hej, der secret politico ist verboten ce-soir'* seemed to be surprisingly clear despite being wrong and of appallingly mixed origin to say the least. We were joined by an old mate-Duncan, who, as a Cathay /Dragonair Pilot based in Hong Kong, came by Chiang Mai most weeks. He and Focksy played a lot of golf together, without any need for any close protection secret service agents as far as I know and hopefully no cheating.

The good news at Nordern, is that along with their Swedish specialties, they happen also to sell Chiang Mai's best rack of pork ribs. More international than Nordic but along with any of the Swedish dishes they are wonderful. So as it was a celebration we decided to share a rack of ribs between the four of us as a starter...along with a selection of herring, graved lax and several glasses of Aquavit.

(Ed Here, look I know this is an evening off and I know Nordern is really good, but these restaurant and other foodie details are slowing down the storyline...you guys ramble enough...let's get on with it, before something happens to the President).

Funnily enough it was Jerry's expert carving of the ribs to share that then got us back into that dangerous discussion ground of US politics. Several times over the preceding days he had made quite disparaging remarks about his boss, mainly based on his own deep rooted concerns about global warming and that evening when we complemented him on his carving skills he gave us a little more detail.

Turned out that he'd lived a very self sufficient rural life as a kid where he'd learned to handle carving and boning carcasses as a matter of course. It seemed his *'beef with the boss'* *(Ed Continuity please, the ribs were pork not beef)* harked back to those days. He went on to say that his right now his main grievance was about the current President's dismissive attitude of the Paris climate accord and the more immediate dangers of global warming generally.

Looking increasingly agitated, Jerry set off on what looked like a fairly regular rant," Even in Obama's day, whilst he made the right greeny noises like they all do, in the real world big business doesn't give a f*ck, and that means Congress does nothing. But the current president is the worst."

" Mind you there's way too much focus on 'rising tides and flooding cities' in the media, which can be very graphic and emotive with photo shopped images of flooded cities and famous landmarks ... but the real problem is out in the wilderness and down on the farms. One example is the pressure of big business to deliver more crops, which means use of more weed killers and artificial fertilizers. What is crazy is that *it's now proven that some modern farming chemicals are fast wiping out many species of bee. "*

"You can argue that global warming may take thousands of years, but the President's refusal, unlike Europe, to support banning certain chemicals is killing bees by the million. Every day. Now. As it's those bees and some other insects that pollinate and thus recreate almost all plant life as well as key food crops, that's a fast reacting disaster for the planet and for us."

He sat back, and apologised for breaking the evening rule of *'no business, no politics'*, but then couldn't restrain himself from adding, "*Quite frankly, I think that this goddam ignorant bloody President, imagines honey comes from a jar in a supermarket, not from bees."*

Focksy leaned forward and said, quietly, "Jerry we are with you on the creeping danger that is global warming, and your words about bees are a serious immediate global concern. But given your current employment and presumed security clearance it's probably best that Harry and I forget we ever heard your last few comments - but don't worry, as I said before we're both with you 100%. "

"As to the President, he probably does think 'Honey' comes from supermarkets, or *else it's just the name of 'a pussy to be grabbed',* but we'll drink to your well intentioned thoughts."

Which prompted a round of glass clinking 'cheers ' from the three of us and a muted 'thanks' from Jerry who then continued, somewhat quietly. "I thought about this a day or so back when you mentioned those security data storage facilities in rural or middle America and their small town morals. Not about what the NSA know, but more about rural life, in fact seriously rural. I was born in '73 way out in the deepest wilderness of Nevada, high up near the Idaho border."

"My dad's family, had a few hundred acres of scrubby farmland- only good for sheep and goats really, but they also had grazing rights on the nearby uplands and mountains. Our farming and sheep rearing family had come to America in the 1800s from North Eastern Spain, near the Pyrenees. They came to work as miners, so I guess they made some dollars with what I could imagine was back breaking work. "

" But they succeeded enough to encourage other family members to come over and they bought that cheap farmland. Cheap because it wasn't very fertile - but they, like others from the more inhospitable mountainous parts of Spain, Greece, Italy- across the Balkans and such, had a thousand years of skill- in overwintering their animals in sheltered valleys, and as the snows receded from the mountains in early summer, they'd herd the flocks up to the high pastures, where the meltwater and clear sunlight had created lush grazing lands."

He paused and took a sip of his wine, as Focksy added, " The Transhumance' is the name for, what someone once called 'focused nomadic farming'. The 'system' worked- mostly for sheep and goats, right across the mountains of Europe, although in Switzerland and other lusher uplands they did it with herds of milk cows. "

Jerry continued, "Of course in some parts of Spain and elsewhere the moving of the flocks was a big affair- with thousands of sheep and goats, walking through the villages and towns aiming for the high pastures in the spring, or returning in the autumn with their kids and lambs. Up on the heights, for the shepherds, on call and vigilant day and night-depending on their location there were wolves, cougars and other predators around then. It was a lonely, and self sufficient existence."

" Way back, in the fifties I think, my dad's brother had gone off abroad to do his military service, and somewhere along the line he invited my Dad- to visit him for Christmas. Whilst he was away he met my mom, seems her family didn't approve and although she was very young she eloped with dad."

"With with his older brother away on military duties, as Dad was the only able bodied male around to work the farm back in Nevada he took over, and lived there with mum."

"So as Mom, always said to me, 'Your dad and I were both outcasts. Which is why my sister and were were brought up very much living off the land and at one with nature, particularly when we moved the sheep and some goats up into the highlands we lived miles, often tens of miles from roads and even the smallest of townships. It was a lonely and exposed life -just as it had been for hundreds of years in the mountains of Europe and Asia."

" Just to tell you how remote our lives were- in many places there was so little light pollution that the stars in the milky way cast shadows on the ground on clear nights. So the wilds were home for us until we reached our teens. Even then in the early seventies we lived almost entirely off the land, hunting, fishing, trapping and foraging. If we stayed in one place long enough, we'd grow some vegetables, we usually had some goats that gave us milk, as well as a a good few hundred sheep. Back then there were millions of sheep all across the US, of course there's far fewer today."

" We hunted a lot, Dad was a crack shot but from an early age I was also good with a rifle-and bringing in plenty for the table. Mum and my older brother used to say that apart from our uncle who was a legend with a hunting rifle, that I was the best shot in the family. All of us, mum included, also trained our own hawks, falcons and even eagles to hunt down and catch rabbits or some bigger critters for the pot."

Jerry then launched into a rather graphic description of the lethal hunting and killing abilities of various breeds of trained hawks, falcons and eagles...so much so that I had to raise a hand and suggest "*I am more than a bit squeamish about such things and please can we move on before I have to give up- on this delicious food.*"

Jerry grinned and said, " Sorry, without going into more gruesome stuff, Mom explained to us that in various countries of the world, Mongolia, Persia, China and other places for thousands of years they had trained eagles as war birds to recognise and attack individuals. So we decided to check out the legends, and over several seasons, trained some fledgling eagles and falcons to recognise certain patterns on scraps of paper and learn that there would be food under just one of them."

" With us missing a lot of schooling when we were high in the mountains for months at a time, Dad said we were learning more, 'bringing history to life.' We did have some problems once when a rancher claimed our hunting birds had killed several of his sheep or young calves, but we showed him the trained birds and he backed down. "

"Mom always said ammo was expensive and so we were also pretty good with longbows and cross bows. We only cooked over fires, and we always took care to bury plenty of hot rocks left from the evening fire to make a good early breakfast and a hot morning drink. Although we lived in the farm valley cabin in winter, in the spring and fall up in the high pastures we really needed those warming fires."

As Jerry sat back, and we nodded our interest, Focksy asked, "So how the hell did you end up with the secret service- you need plenty of college or other qualifications for that."

Jerry nodded again and said, "Well both mom and dad made sure we had daily lessons of all kinds from them. Then in 88 Dad had gone away to do something with the military and never came back. Mom, had kind of had enough of being a nomadic shepherd and managed to get a job with a college in Idaho and both Terri and I got places at that college. "

" I think there was some kind of special deal for teachers kids, also we were both pretty handy at most sports which the college liked. In fact, I pretty much worked my way through college teaching rock climbing and guiding tours around mountains. When I grew a bit of a teenage beard they called me the 'The Goat.' "

" A year or so later I was seriously considering joining the military as there were quite a few survival skills centers around the region, but through various contacts at the college and something to do with Dad's brother I ended up joining the US Diplomatic Security service when I was about twenty two."

"Some few years later 9/11 happened and with all the new security services and stuff, I ended up transferring to where I am now. Looking back it was a very different up bringing, almost back in the style of the farmers and shepherds in the old country for hundreds if not thousands of years. Of course for us kids, it was all we knew back then, I don't think I watched TV regularly till I was a teenager.' "

He sat back, and we all contemplated his rather unusual story, until Focksy, as usual it was Focksy, proposed a toast.

"Good stuff Jerry, and great to hear all about it, and a story to take our minds off our current tasks. Also in many ways, it shows how much modern society has now lost from some of the old ways and values. Here in Thailand you don't have to venture too far from the cities, especially into the mountains to find farmers scraping a living on a just a few rice paddies...even still using buffalo to plow, and drying the rice on the side of country roads. "

"But for most of them, they are happy their kids have gone to the city life...the first thing they send home is a tv, and these days the next is a mobile phone. Does occur to me though, that next time it's my birthday, we'll forget the restaurant, and nip out to the hills near Lampang and let you catch and barbecue one of the many wild boar in the mountain forests out there."

Unbeknown to Focksy, Philip and the restaurant staff had been creeping up behind him with birthday cake, candles and chorus, so as the festivities continued he had to explain to Nordern Chef Phil his comment about, 'forgetting the restaurant and cooking wild game.'

Duncan, as a Hong Kong resident, had looked enthusiastic at suggestions of barbecued pork, as he had become a keen follower of the ever ongoing Hong Kong competition to find the 'best of the best' barbecue pork restaurants- Chinese style. Whenever we visit him there he seems to plunge us ever deeper into the back streets of Mon Gok or the suburbs where in noisy cafes sitting on tiny plastic chairs we'd be served - indeed brilliant pork.

Duncan, a long time Hong Kong renter was now buying a new build apartment there- as much as an investment as a home. He made us smile telling of his last trip to the tower block to choose kitchen tiles and such like, when the 'very Chinese' real estate guy asked him: "Mr Duncan, you want $100,000 HK parking place for your car or $200,000?"

"The inscrutable Chinese answer to Duncan's inevitable question, of "What's the difference?" was, "$200,000 parking have sea view!" The reality of course was that it was in a more convenient location, nearer the elevators.

Jerry was effusively congratulating Philip on his cooking, saying, "That's the best dinner I've ever had' since I was in Mont St Marsan in France last year."

Travels in France started another thread of conversation requiring yet more wine...during which 'birthday boy' Focksy suggested that, "Given all these stories of exploding golf balls and Eagles maybe Harry and I should go to Scotland when Trump's there. Plenty of both-Eagles and Golf there. It could be a good feature story, obviously not giving away any secrets or connections to you Jerry, but a general story along the lines of, 'It's easy for Europeans to smile at what appears to be the OTT precautions protecting the President of America...the big limo and crowds of secret agents. We're all aware of the many terrorist threats but in the real world there's a lot more to it."

This sparked off a predictable kneejerk reaction from Jerry concerned that we'd be revealing too much, but eventually he agreed that if-repeat if- we careful explain the realities of the dangers that the Secret Service faced each and every day, could be a good thing.

"Really in most places outside the US, people are quite uncooperative when we need them to move back or be prepared to have their bags searched. So maybe if they understood more it could help."

But by then it was time to wander back to the bar- have a final beer...*just in time for The Cricket on TV.*

Chapter 5. *Early summer 2018..*

Which brings us back to now departed Jerry's
found memory stick: *Harry Writes: Of course the first question
was, would it work? Given we were 'testing it' in my already
beaten up old lap top- now with a cracked screen after I sat on it in
a taxi, the portents were not too hot - unlike the evening.*

With no four o'clock thunderclap and cooling downpour yet
again - we were wondering if the rains had departed early this year.
But intrepid chaps that we are, we fired up the old lap top- inserted
the stick and bingo!

Instantly we had a cracked screen with the immortal and I
suppose not unexpected words still readable...

---- **Password please** **************

Despite both Focksy and I being seasoned and more than
slightly silver surfy, we are very up to date - on the ball-and
generally computer literate. Until something goes wrong that is.

But we do know that when paying attention to the screen the
correct stance is *'lean in'*...so we also know when to *'lean back.'*

Fortunately our leaned back attitude was the ideal stance for
supping ones beer and pondering the password demand.

"Ah." I said.

"Feck. " Said Focksy, betraying his Irish roots.

"49**JSinCMTH " Said Bim.

Having clarified that she was talking password not Thai, "I
see him put in 100 times every day." we asked her to confirm it as
Focksy entered it.

Bim correcting him..."No no last four are 'not nit noi'."
Nit Noi' meaning *very small, or little bit,* or just in case you're
leaning back too far...therefor 'Not Nit Noi' means BIG.

A few flashes and up came a page, yesterdays date and a list
of contents. Then the first few pages were general stuff about what
we had been discussing with Jerry for almost a week.

Focksy scrolled down and then came a page that was, eye
wateringly, bum clenching, earth shatteringly heart stoppingly 'oh
shit. Bloody hell.'...and that was an understatement, for us two
anyway.

Travel Risk Assessment: Orig. JS...CMTH...07/10/18.

Threat level.XXX: Assassination Potus.

Threat level.XXXX: Anti Regime / Potus Demo' s.

KEY INFORMANTS and SUSPECTS.

Suspect 1. ID F.S. Ferdinand 'Focks' S*******.**

Suspect 2. ID H.B. Harry B***

POTUS International Itinerary. Summer 2018.

01/26. Switzerland. Davos.Keynote & Piers Morgan. FIS:

01/10. Quebec. G7.   RCMP:

06/12. Singapore. Peace meet Pres. Kim J. NRK   SID:

07/11. Belgium Brussels. NATO Summit   GISS/VSSE:

07/12. UK. Accom. Ambassador Residence Regent Pk. London. Proximity of Mosque, safety of Marine One flight path a concern. Streets unsecurable all functions moved ex London to isolated country estates - Blenheim & Chequers.

07/13. Windsor.UK. HM Queen of England.   UK MI6 / SB: PM May. Piers Morgan. AF1.In/out Evac Stanstead.STN

07/14-15.Trump Turnberry Golf. Ayrshire.Scot.   MI6/SSB: AF1. In/out/Evac. Prestwick.PIK.

07/16 Helsinki Finland. Pres.V.Putin.   FSIS: AF1. In/out/Evac.Helsinki .HLS

Unconfirmed.

Ireland. Doonbeg Golf. AF1 In/out/Evac Shannon.SNN.G-2/GS

Informants / Suspects: Referred to above: FS & HB.

Currently in Chiang Mai Thailand.

Where FS has a house & accomplice HB regularly stays.

Armed/Unarmed: It is not believed likely they regularly armed.

I.D.Documents : Both in possesion of multiple passports.

HB.ID UK/EI. Primary residence : Cornwall UK.

FS.ID US/EI/GER Primary residence :NY USA /Dublin Ireland.

Criminal Records Check.

CRC-FS. US. Zero. IRE.(60's) student protest arrests.

CRC-HB.US. Immigration overstay.(85) UK CND demo (60's)

****

"Well, stone me." I said, "That's really not good. He's named us both as informants and as bloody key suspects!"

Focksy and I sat back and considered our future dressed in Guantanamo dayglo orange if arrested.

Focksy looked decidedly pensive, "If all this *'informants and suspects'* stuff is because Jerry's filled in some kind of standard issue reporting form it's a piece of sh*t. We know he really liked it here in Thailand, maybe he really had overstayed or simply not done enough work, that he had to make up stuff for a report to his office and bosses. "

"If it's supposed to be a joke that we were meant to find in his laundry, or that he was going to email to us later, saying *'hey chaps, this is the sort of thing we do,'* It's also sh*t."

" If it is a joke, and we spent two weeks of pretty intense work, wasting our time, setting it all up, it's clever, but double sh*t."

"But if it's a joke, then that makes Jerry also a joke, in as much as he's not really US security at all, but just another bloody 'connected' dreamer' of the kind we often do meet out here."

"Mind you, most days he did disappear into the consulate for a good few hours, and he did have some kind of pass that always worked the entry gate, so I guess he's a Government employee of some kind. "

"If he's the real deal, why are we named in there as key suspects. I mean just a bit of basic research would soon show his boss it's a farce, so I can't understand, unless he's trying to set up some kind of false trail or a delaying action for someone. We do know that in these days of fake news, that one of the best ways to hide something is to bury it in fake news or conspiracy crap."

"If he needs to set up a serious smokescreen, is it because he, with his shooting skills and all that, is himself planning an attack on the President back in the USA. If so, that's very serious to say the least. "

" On the other hand, maybe he hid the stick in that laundry because he was trying to get it out of the country without those 'angry men' getting it. Unless they were just angry because Jerry had overslept, he did have a lot of beer last night."

I held up my hand, "Hang on, this is all getting a bit wild and James Bondish. Given he told us he was with 'A' US Gov't. security service, which has now, from his laundry address at least, become a CI -A security service, surely he would have e mailed it."

"If you are right about him needing to keep it from those guys and get it to his office, we should either ship it with his clothes- which will take quite a while- or go and bang on the door of the Consulate, explain, and hand it in. "

Focksy-practical and informed as ever said, "Regardless if he's the real deal, or not, even if he's already e mailed it, with our names all over it, I don't think we should just hand it in. *If the consulate people here get to look at it, their first reaction will be to suspect us...and I'm starting* to suspect*, that there's a story here,"* he continued, " With reference to your 'Stone Me' comment earlier, actually, with *this* not from the first look of it, being a Middle Eastern problem, requiring a Middle Eastern solution, I fear waterboarding US style more than stoning, whilst they try to get you and I to admit something. "

" I read that the new lady head of The CIA has much experience of same...waterboarding that is. In fact, when I was in Washington I watched her at various formal hearings about her appointment to the job. She was dressed in nice momsy homely clothes - charming and smiling at the committee- although, should we get apprehended and interrogated , I suspect she won't be bringing us nice soft fluffy towels afterwards."

" Based on the accusations on the first few pages. *If Jerry has already put them into the US system, for whatever reasons are in his bloody head, we're in the shit."*

" We know we're innocent, but it could take quite a while for us to explain our way out of his accusations and worse, whilst we try to do that, we could both find ourselves arrested and given a free flight to somewhere we really don't want to go to. "

" According to wiki something, plane spotters suggests that those US secret rendition flights were most likely to be on planes with old historical links back to Air America, about whom your mate wrote the book that inspired the movie. As it happens, in 1968, I was rescued from Laos in a small plane operated by them so I have good reason to like them- but I fear my Air America frequent flyer miles have expired by now."

"If there's a chance of us getting arrested, we do need to quickly get some copies of that stick to a places of safety, like my office, who can then fight our case. You know it's ridiculous, I know it's ridiculous, but the ridiculous seems right now to be bloody reality which may take some explaining. But first of all we need to copy the contents on another few sticks to hide somewhere and send to friends, as well as e mailing them."

That seemed easier said than done as my old lap top appeared to lack any more sockets in which to insert a second memory stick. Bim observed me lifting the lap top to inspect it all over for extra orifices, sighed, and said, "Mr. Harry you want to make copy use Blue Tooth. Just copy it to your new computer or Focksy's by Blue Tooth, for anyone else send it e mail."

Given that Focksy and I had by now totally forgotten our concerns about any possible evil CIA Fishnet killer software being installed on the stick we gave that a go, although Focksy reminded me that the CIA and Israeli killer software was called Stuxnet not Fishnet. The two computers blinked and whirred- not that I could hear the whirring as the girls in the bar were by now watching and loudly encouraging 'Thailand's Got Talent' on TV.

The actual contestant looking about ten years old...juggling blindfolded with three fully operating chainsaws...*and I'll prove it by cutting this watermelon thats balanced on my sisters head in half*...until I saw that, I had been thinking that helping to avoid US Presidential asassination and other forms of demonstration or regime change was exciting enough for one day.

The blue teeth having finished chattering , at Focksy's suggestion I set my new lap top to do a full security scan- not that I really expected it to tell me much compared to the technical might of the NSA / FBI / CIA wizards...but on the other my '*free with your new laptop,*' security system was courtesy Russian hero and millionaire Mr. Kaspersky, so maybe I had better chance of sniffing out anything dodge than most.

As I helped Bim remove a flood of condensation off the glasses from our table and gave her a 'yes' thumbs up when she offered to get some '*crunchy and extra ped fried moo*' to aid our concentration and our thirst, Focksy was speed reading Jerry's files...making the odd 'oooh' and 'oh' and once a '*Feck me*' as he scrolled through the pages.

As he closed the lap top and adopted beer time lean back mode, "My first question," I said, "Is what was it that made you say Feck?" His response would have produced a Feck from Moi, but my Irish roots are a tad more submerged than his, unless there's a flood of Guinness or Murphy's which brings them to the surface.

"Well I've skimmed through most of it *and I can't decide if it's a research document to aid those protecting The President...or a bloody instruction manual for those out to get him.... He could well have called it 'Regime Change for Dummies'.*"

"Interesting. And so?" I responded, taking a sip from my beer..."*Feck - your fecking 'interesting'. Feck your- 'and so'* " said Focksy in his usual calm professional and relaxed style.

"It's got our fecking names all over it not only as researchers, contributors, advisors, editors and experts and the front bloody page lists us as expert in disruption and assassinations. Then it F**ing suggests that *'investigating and tracking Focks Sch******* and Harry B**** prior to arrest needs to be a priority.*"

Which produced a bloody big gulp, not a sip, from my now refilled glass...I spluttered "Like you said Focksy, Feck and indeed F**k...So you are right we urgently need to lodge copies somewhere safe."

Silence fell as we sipped our beer and started to nibble on the fried moo snacks that Bim had delivered. This resulted in some stereo and rather high pitched 'Fecks' from the two of us as the Pikky Noo chilies that Bim scattered all over the crispy moo turned out to be very ped and more than Scovilley lethal.

(*Hi There. It's the Ed again. I could add here that 'Ped' in this case means 'Spicy.' In case you are not keen on chili - 'Mai Ped' means not spicy. Those little tiny red or green extra spicy chilies are called 'Pikky Noo'...which means mouse shit.*

*Feck : By the way, that popular daily much used and very Irish 'Oh Feck' was not invented by the writers of the wonderful 'Father Ted' or 'Mrs Brown's Boys,' to get 'Oh F*ck' around the TV censors. It was in popular use before TV was invented as an everyday much used general term of bing pissed off or annoyed. Even angry Irish Grannies have been known to use it. So now you feckin' know.*)

As we recovered our voices, and resumed normal breathing Bim came over and reminded Focksy it was well past time for him to go for his booked haircut. At the usual hackneyed jibes, 'well it'll take them longer to find the hair than cut it,' he started to say that he'd not bother as he was too busy.

But then just as he was just about to e mail the file copies to various chums, he stopped suddenly, "I just realised, all our lecturing Jerry about the free WI-FI here being part of the US Consulate system and them reading all our stuff going in and out. I'll email the copies from the barber shop as it's quite a way across town, it might help. Whilst I'm away you check the original files."

Which is exactly what I started to do : Despite it seeming more than bit bizarre reading what basically suggested, *'And the Most Wanted are'*, it seemed to be a 'rolling document' with pages and pages of generic info about protecting POTUS & FLOTUS.

Responsibilities, circumstances, eventualities, contact details, facilities, equipment supplies and maintenance. Some was quite revealing- but it really went on a bit, but the key points were vary scary and on the surface appeared quite incriminating for Focksy and myself. Under arrival/departure there were pages of guff about motorcade specifics, with endless quick reference sections on: *Delays, responsibilities, traffic accidents.*

Medical Emergency: Potus. Other and Media.

I noted that the medics travelling at the ready for Potus were not available under any circumstances to aid or assist others. Pages on timetable breaks-seemed not about 'time to have a cuppa and dunk a biscuit or two' but detailed stuff on suspicious reasons for delays.

Just pages and pages...on and on...I really could hardly contain my apathy and then, I turned the page and there it was or there we were: and bloody hell, or as Focksy said, "Feck and Feck again." *Focksy and I were listed as having revealed detailed plans for the disruption of or potential assassination attempts on Potus on his trips to: England, Scotland and Doonbeg in Ireland. Our background knowledge of the places, and informed views making us urgently requiring further investigation and tracking.*

Now I don't know about you dear reader but so far I haven't noticed any specific suggestions that Focksy or I were in Carlos the Jackal or Lee Harvey Oswald mode, or even practicing pushing the big plunger on a silent movie style box labelled 'dynamite.'

We had it is true, using our fevered imaginations to keep the free beers flowing, at Jerry's request and suggestion, come up with a range of potential sabotage and other demos likely to catch the attention of the world media...and which thus needed preventing.

Assassination had only been mentioned as *'wow that Secret Service job is bloody risky for all concerned'* I sipped my beer and pondered: May be it was Focksy's intransigent views that *the CIA under Allen Dulles had a lot to answer for both at home and internationally* that had upset Jerry.

I turned the page and there was a list of many of our wildest points and crazy inventions. On checking my notebook...that's as in paper and pencil book comparing the listing, it seemed Jerry had either a remarkable memory or he had recorded our words and suggestions and now they were neatly laid out virtually verbatim. The titles seemed to back up Jerry's claim as to his day job.

Advance risk assessment. POTUS /FLOTUS Euro Trip.
Threats: Snipers, IED's, RPG's, Gas, Bio. To follow.
Disruptions Demonstrations. See below.
Arrival / Departure. Here there was all sorts of detail about the potential use by protestors of gas filled weather balloons and kites with long tails to disrupt Presidential helicopters.

There seemed to be a real concern about smoke emitting fireworks, we had shown Jerry their partisan use by European football crowds. So he now seemed concerned for their potential use by anti POTUS partisans : Smoke flares. Weather related. Note onshore sea breezes at most Golf venues.

Pages on the the need for direct and diversionary routes and avoiding blockages with attention drawn to current trends for terrorists to use driven vehicals as weapons. *Note drones and other powered light aircraft used by demonstrators, that all seemed quite generic.*

Crowd control was dismissed as being the responsibility of local security and police. Then I noticed something saying *'Advance agreement always required 'LHO Tentage. NB. Brits very sensitive about use LHO's. Will not allow in formal Diplo/Royalty situations. I wondered about the meaning of LHO?*

(*Ed here. LHO Tentage-is the portable tent set up providing a covered protected walkway between the Presidential Limo or other transport and an entrance into a building for use in high risk situations. LHO regretfully stands for Lee Harvey Oswald. Obviously 'Tentage providing cover from likely snipers.)*

It was all a mix of hard to follow or swallow- military jargon, Focksy's and my fevered imaginations and the bloody obvious. Hardly grounds for a global manhunt and arrest of two drinking chums from a bar.

Sabotage and disruptions to buildings was next, listed as: PRP had me baffled until I found reference to Presidential Related Properties. They apparently referred to The President's businesses, hotels, condo's golf resorts and suchlike. He apparently firmly retains control of at least his Golf Businesses and spends much time promoting them, although his spokesperson says : *'The President uses his time on the Golf Course to think about important matters.'*

For other attacks on the PRPs many of the concerns came back to Focksy and my upgraded 'practical joke' kids comics stuff.'

Or as set out in Jerry's position paper: *'Social Media have created an uplift in protestor awareness of modern protest items available. Old style 'dead fish' behind a heat source or 'stink bombs' replaced by: Timed release maloderant / skatole capsules secreted in public areas of PRPs .*

But then the report then came back to Jerry's constant ' Potential nerve or bio hazards with Haz. Chem.' That's quite fair I guess, reflecting recent Novichok events in the UK.:

Current nerve agent status UK -High Alert.

But back in the world of 'Joke Shops' and High School Japes' came more: *Pressure broken flat sachets. See Maloderants above: dead fish / tom cat / smoke. Live Skunk not found in Europe.* I loved that 'Live Skunk' not found in Europe! That, despite the seriousness of our position could make Focksy smile.

But then Definitely near hysterics from me as I arrived at Jerry's header of: *New Swell Balls:*

Even in his dry as a bone, serious, situation report, Jerry had realised the reader would be amused so he continued: *Before you smile, these can instantly paralyze an entire PRP building. Originally developed for 'instant repairs' to water tanks, roofing, sports boat hulls...on contact with water they swell up and set rock hard. One or two part Hydrophobic Foam.*

<u>Simple stage one</u> SB: Golf ball size H Foam reactant. In waterproof plastic outer. A few pencil sized holes made in the casing and then when dropped in a toilet and flushed...instant swelling and setting reaction and the U bend drain is blocked and that toilet is out of service. If blockages occur deep into the building plumbing system, they can take months of work to clear.

(Ed. I must say I'm really keen to buy some and test it in a bucket of water. Now we move on to creepy crawlies.)

Vermin / Rodents. Infestations in Public or PRPs are serious and require specialists.

Focksy had remarked that it seemed a bit extreme to have the secret service employed as Rodent Specialists, a point on which Jerry had concurred saying," *Defence and prevention is Us. Disposal and destruction is Them."*

Which had set Focksy and I off again thinking of cartoon fave's Tom and the other Jerry. But then I turned the page and found I'd arrived at:

Threats: See Snipers, IED's, Grenades & RPG's, Gas, Bio. Well this was the serious stuff. The Real deal. Nasty too. Gas and Bio hazard stuff. Sniper positions. Range of various rocket propelled grenades, and I started to have second thoughts about mocking the Presidential Armoured Limo.

Then some detailed concerns and serious warnings about IED's, Improvised Explosive Devices.

My immediate thought being that these days IEDs kill so many, that to be honest they don't fit in these pages...so even before we were asked Focksy and I got out the censors blue pencil.

(Ed here. 'We were advised by those that know this stuff- That any and all, life threatening threats and or suggestions, incitements to

and or encouragements for, even when clearly made as part of a fiction for action against The President, his family, staff or others, is an offence under various criminal, civil and security statutes, laws and various emergency regulations in The United States of America'.)

So it seems for the lawyers, that *'Assassination, doing him in, or making him 'Late'* as the wonderful Botswanan phrase puts it, as reported by Alexander McCall Smith, is all a bit OTT...

I'd had enough....Jerry seemed to have intermixed Focksy and my imaginative views into a fairly standard -for them- PARA report, but quite why, I have no idea....

(Ed's note: Whilst Harry sinks into a slough of despair, I can report that the legendary book about Air America...later made into the movie...is 'The Ravens by Christopher Robbins- a mate of Harry's from school days. Telling the story of 'the war that never was', where the US- whilst denying any involvement- dropped millions of tons of bombs and landmines on Cambodia and Laos.

To maintain their deniability- in the UN and elsewhere- the US used a secret CIA operated air force owned by a 'private company generally known as Air America. The (incredibly skilled and brave) pilots flew planes 'legally owned' by that company and they, the engineers, navigators, ordnance operatives, medics were all employed by 'the company' and thus not by the US Airforce.

Harry recommends the book- not because author Chris was a mate and fellow music nut, but because -along with Josef Heller's Catch 22...it's an amazing read.)

Chapter 6. *Summer 2018.*
Most Wanted: The Desperate Duo.

OK, Harry's had enough, sitting there, head in hands, his peaceful hols in smiley Thailand disrupted by disruptors. But I smell a story developing so I'll take over the narrative for while. Focksy's Tales: Most wanted: The Desperate Duo.' Actually 'Most Wanted' as the reality of the situation sunk in, was a double shot of something seriously alcoholic to steady the nerves, as we planned how to avoid 'Saying Hi to the FBI.'

As *both* the glass of restorative but medicinal tasting Danish Gammeldansk Bitters *and* the situation sunk in, Harry suddenly moved seats to sit along side me facing the inner bar - away from the street and behind a jungle wall of pot plants...my enquiring look produced a surprising answer.

"If that ' *Key Suspects'* accusation of Jerry's is already in their system as you suggested then people could already be looking for us." He continued, "Obviously we are not, have not ,will not, have never had, any serious intentions of carrying out or even organising the assassination of the current or any US President...or anyone else in fact. "

"Although, thinking about it, that bloody kid who spent eleven hours kicking the back of my seat on the flight here from London came very very near. My serious point is, when it comes to such things, the Yanks tend to shoot first and ask questions afterwards. That's as in, *'guilty until proven innocent'* and it might take a while any of our pleas of *'innocent till proven guilty'* to be heard...I am also starting to think we need to take evasive action."

"I am also more than a little allergic to having lights shone where they should not probe about my person - although that does also make me recall a strong desire to murder that specialist doctor with the pointy finger who who wanted to check my prostate situation. If I recall your comment at the time was that 'It was probably worse for him', was most unhelpful, correct but most unhelpful. So that's two on my assassination hit list, or three if I include you with your smart arse comments."

I started to suggest that with 'smart arse' Harry seemed to be developing a bit of a fixation but luckily Bim arrived with a tray of wonderful looking and smelling Khao Soy chicken curry for two. To her great surprise we refused offers of more beer or wine. Our 'we need to think about work right now-not make any mistakes,' produced a disbelieving, *That's a new one on me from you two'* shrug.

As I started to enjoy the always fragrantly tasty Khao Soy, very much a Burmese or Chiang Mai speciality with all it's little fresh veggie and spicy accompaniments, Harry's "Enjoy it, the next few meals may be bread and water," failed to put me off.

But then his follow up, "Or if we're held here in Thailand I guess it'll be rice and water," started to make me think my chum was seriously worried, especially as he was only picking at what was usually his feast of the week.

It also sent a shiver down my spine, which prompted me to say, "It's weird, I hadn't thought about it for years, but I have just had a flash back to my week in a Laos army lock up in the sixties. After I returned to Europe back then I did have a few nightmares for a while-but they are long gone. It's my fault for making bad jokes, but I do seriously think we need to make a proper review of where we're at."

"Oh yes, and here's a thing, when I was at the barber shop, Duncan came in, Cathay Pilot Duncan. He'd flown in to Chiang Mai early this morning from Hong Kong as usual, and guess what? As he was walking inbound along that glass walkway from his plane, he saw Jerry on the other departures walkway, boarding a flight to Moscow. He recognised Jerry as he had on that same Hawaii shirt on that he'd been wearing when they met on my birthday. "

"So that means Jerry was never in Bangkok." Harry nodded vigorously, as he was at last unable to resist the aromas and was rather focused on his Kao Soy... after a few moments, Harry munching, me cogitating, I started in my best TV reporting style:

"OK . Here in Chiang Mai right now we have a tricky situation. What the hell can we do, but first how did it all happen?"

" One: You and I both did a simple and not unusual polite *'Hail new friend in a foreign land'* and over the next ten days we had casual and then deeper conversations with the new friend who was previously a total stranger, now known as Jerry."

"Two: Total Stranger Jerry turns out to be some kind of protective cop or security connected to the President of the United States. Or, possibly we now think ,is just *'claiming to be connected.'* Something we have heard a zillion times before out here. "

"Three. Total Stranger Jerry tells us that POTUS, *who is less popular than many, but with his people more popular than most*, is as ever, always at risk of assassination. That being a fairly regular American habit or at least threat, hence his -Total Stranger Jerry's preventative planning work. Loose lips or careless talk? Not really. Just a general, but now and again, fairly detailed, series of conversations."

"Four. But then our problem starts: Total Stranger Jerry, our new best friend in the bar, on discovering that you and I were and are *'well travelled, well informed and well good blokeys'* starts to pick our brains on the subject of 'potential threats liable to embarrass his boss' -that's POTUS- on any upcoming foreign trips, the next one being to Europe."

"Jerry insists on getting the drinks in as he says he needs help as he's, *'Running late and light'* on useful information about Ireland and Scotland that he needs to report back to his office. Like any good blokeys chatting in a pub situation we are happy to casually help, just as of course we'd provide a friend with an alibi if he or she were late going home."

"We were happy to accept Total Stranger Jerrys light hearted suggestion of consultancy fees 'paid in beer', as it was way more interesting than the footie, rugby or the current FI season. Also, although we are both semi retired journos we can increasingly sniff a good story in there somewhere. And anyway a free beer is a free beer and not to be sneezed at, especially not when poured the German way with an inch or so of foam on the top."

"Five. The casual conversations develop over a few days, into quite serious discussions about the real threats and dangers that unpopular politicians may encounter. For what it's worth we put our own knowledge of such matters into the mix. Our knowledge coming from no more than a lifetimes reporting from around the globe, our ancient but fertile and fevered imaginations and reading too many spy books."

"Six. Then today it gets stupid. A series of 'coincidences' or possibly 'contrived setups' involving the sudden departure of Total Stranger Jerry. Some forgotten laundry. A perhaps conveniently lost memory stick is found: And we now bloody find, that our ' informed but mostly innocently invented' advice has been carefully noted by Total Stranger Jerry in real detail, and is probably now flashing its way by fibre optics to those most concerned with keeping POTUS breathing."

" It should be noted that we have learned, mainly when Jerry had too many beers, that, due his deep concerns about global warning being ignored by the President and his people, that he- Total Stranger Jerry- is not too *personally* concerned if POTUS bloody breathes or not. But he is still, with the day job, or claims to be still, *professionally* responsible for keeping him -POTUS- off the Abraham Lincoln, James A Garfield, William McKinley, John F Kennedy listing. You can add to that listing Theodore Roosevelt and Ronald Reagan who were both punctured but survived."

"Total Stranger Jerry now known to be Jerry Smith, has for reasons best known to himself suggested-possibly to his bosses-that he has uncovered a real plot...where two Euro blokeys in their sixties are planning to lengthen the aforesaid listing of Presidents suffering early deletion or at least deflation."

"When I was waiting for my haircut, before Duncan came in, it occurred to me that there are other things that don't ring true with Jerry. For instance, first he said his dad was a draft dodger, but then he said he'd been here in the sixties. And of course we now know from Duncan that Jerry was lying about being in or going to Bangkok. "

" *I am starting to wonder if Total Stranger Jerry is the one actually planning some kind of attack on The President.* But if so, why refer to us in a memory stick that would, should or could soon be at CIA HQ with his laundry, and which, if they took it seriously could alert them more than somewhat? So could he be trying to set up a red herring or a smoke screen."

Harry, interrupted, "After all the miscommunications between various US security agencies meant they missed the early warnings on loads of important events from Pearl Harbour to 9/11, surely that means that now, they must pay lip service at least, to any and all stuff that lands on their desks. Even if it's obviously bonkers, someone has to check it, even a little, although bag of clean laundry and a memory stick is pretty bonkers."

I raised a hand and said," Now don't jump on my words and say your usual -'No more conspiracy theories Focksy.' What if the CIA have reverted to form, and are so increasingly concerned that the current President, due to his extremely simplistic views and knee jerk reactions, or even due to him suffering some kind of mental health issue, or with his unprofessional Tweets is causing their very wonderful country to become a global laughing stock."

" Or as in the past they, the CIA, are again being influenced by big business, who are pressuring them that Trump's erratic trade policies, whilst at first sounding good, are really setting the country up for some serious long term damage to trade and industry. And it must be stopped."

" So the CIA, with serious concern for 'The State Of Their Nation' have decided or might at some time decide. enough is enough, there's only one thing we can do: Make POTUS an EXPOTUS, in fact with all other legal, and almost legal methods having failed, could they be prepared to make him a DEADPOTUS, or more accurately a DEADEXPOTUS."

"And Jerry is the man who has chosen the long straw...Or... is being set up-to carry out the task. But in the real world, for them to get involved in 'Regime Change-Do try this at Home' (again) and not get caught, being creatures of habit, they need to refer to the instruction manual. This advises, going down, the old, once successful, Lee Harvey Oswald route of setting up a gazillion red herrings, smokescreens, dead ends, cut outs, blame some foreigners, cover stories. Set up a patsy to do the deed. Pretty much all in fact just as Dulles most likely did in Dallas, and you and I, Harry, have become part of the new plot."

I sat back, and somewhat automatically reached out for my beer-until I remembered we were on the wagon.

Harry nodded, and saying, "I rather agree with you...firstly, that there's enough that's correct in there for your suggestion to be realistic more than conspiracy stuff, and secondly we need a beer."

As if she could read our minds a few minutes later Bim arrived with two glasses of Guinness, "I know you not ask, but I think you two not work so good if you not have Guinness, and what you want to do with Jerry's laundry clothes. Mooey say they not heavy and cost nearly same same to send by FedEx as EMS post and the FedEx man come here collecting more boxes soon?" And she departed with an armful of dirty dishes.

The Guinness with it's peaceful and always descending bubbles in the dark glass was obviously aiding our thought processes as indeed a thought occurred to me, and I asked Harry. " You read through the stuff on the stick in more detail than I did . In all pages of detailed threat suggestions, did it mention Hawks or Eagles? I didn't see any."

He responded that neither had he, but he'd quickly skim through all the pages again to check, which produced a Bim style sigh from me and... "For Christ's sake Harry just put Eagles in the bloody word search in the Jerry file-and you'll know instantly."

This he did and drew a blank each time, and double checked with and without caps, alternative spellings and all that malarkey. Absolutely-nothing. Which we agreed is very odd because the day we had my birthday dinner-- just four days ago in fact- when we came back to the bar here, Jerry, who was a bit merry to say the least, was going on and on about sodding Eagles and what great killing machines they were.

Telling us in great detail, how, way back in the history of many nations, how they were used as as weapons to eliminate amore than a few Kings, princes, tribal leaders and warlords of the Genghis Khan variety. At least the squeamish Harry wasn't eating by then.

Jerry had explained, that somewhere, a *Falconry expert could be training some fast eagles to dive down from a great height and attack a thatch of blonde hair, wearing a baseball cap.*

An aggressive falcon or more likely a Golden Eagle, with cruel curved beak and fearsome talons at the ready, could be plummeting down- in inch perfect perfect control at 150 miles per hour...yes seriously, around 150 MPH... its hawk eyes having spotted the President's own blonde thatch of hair from five or ten thousand feet above.

*In the Raptors mind...*one targeted thing. *Every time for the past year when I have really attacked the yellow hair in the red hat, on top of the scarecrow people dummy, with and without the golf club, concealed under the hat and hair I have always found a tasty snack of freshly chopped rabbit and chicken.*

He agreed with us when we pointed out that by the time a Secret Service sniper or an operative with a handgun had drawn their weapon the aforesaid Raptor would either be feasting on Trumps brains or be a mile away more than a little pissed off...and anyway rifle or handgun bullets would be lucky to hit the bird and not the boss.

But then, back on my birthday, Harry and I demonstrated our combined knowledge of both Aeronautics and the History of British Falconry- the *'Other Sport of Kings'* which reduced Jerry to a heavy sigh and a long drawn out,"Jeeeez."

Our contribution being: Back through history in the British Isles the liking of Kings for the sport of Falconry is well documented...in particular Kings, William, Alfred and various George's- especially George the Third...but then it seems King James the First preferred *'Training Fish!'*

Training Fish?...

Don't ask...I don't know.

But back to today: Harry looked at me and did his usual: "And so what now?"

I sipped my Guinness and said." Given that an eagle attacking a Presidential bonce at near 150 MPH was in Jerry's- all be it, a drunk-opinion, one of the worst case scenarios both for the security team charged with keeping POTUS safe, and probably for POTUS who could easily suffer life threatening injuries.

" *If that's so sodding bad- why isn't it- the one thing that we discussed in most detail- why does Jerry not put it in the report?"*

Silence fell - or as silent as busying bar ever gets and Harry added, " As I said, we do know that on the only occasions when Jerry confided in us about climate warming tended to be after he'd had a few drinks. When he talked about the eagles and stuff, and how much he loved them as a kid, what did he say, *'the ones we reared were like family,'* he was completely drunk. That was also when he described an attack on POTUS. So that either means he deliberately didn't want to include them in the threats listing, or all his stuff about them that night was just the alcohol talking."

We sat there for a while considering our options and the implications of the situation, Harry looking quite morose actually, and saying. "Well we can't just sit here and do nothing."

I replied, "OK . I agree. Actually it occurs to me that training a flight of eagles to attack specific targets would presumably take a goodly number of months -if not years. So if-repeat if Stranger and Stranger Jerry is panning something it's more likely to be with a rifle, he's already told us he's an ace shot. So here's what I think we need to do: "

"First: Based on the fact that we can both smell a potential big story here, we hot foot it to the President's next few international meeting and golfing destinations, that's Scotland, possibly Ireland, Helsinki and then, if he hasn't been Punctured or Peregrined we go back to the US, where I'm due at TNoTN soon anyway."

" It'll be good to go to those places, and *'How We Saved the President or Maybe Not'* could be a good story anyway. Serious if he becomes EXPOTUS or lighthearted if nothing happens. It'll be more than enough to get both our expenses paid by my office."

"Secondly: We need to sort something to protect ourselves-regardless of if Jerry's the real deal or not. Either way, banging on the door of the consulate and saying, *'Look at this'* could be very dodgy for us. Or at least very time consuming whilst they think about it, and we could lose out on what may be a great story. So we tell Bim to ship Jerry's clothes...but without with the memory stick. "

"Thirdly: "We do letters to the head of security here at the US Consulate and someone at the Brit Embassy in Bangkok, which we leave with Bim and tell her to post them in say, seven days time. By then we'll be well clear of Thailand and hopefully well ahead on the story. In the letter we set out most of what happened. *'We met a youngish American blokey. Now we realise he obviously a bit unhinged, who wanted to talk about assassinating POTUS all the time. He claimed to be with US security, and even gave us an address of the CIA, which obviously he could have found on line."*

"As ancient but experienced journalists we're well used to loonies and conspiracy theorists. But then, after the blokey had gone, we found a bizarre memory stick which seemed to suggest Total Stranger Jerry, had been well unhinged, as he listed all sort of ways to embarrass or even assault POTUS."

" Our view is that obviously he nuttier than a fruitcake as he even proposed we were potential asassains. As a couple of unfit sixty plus blokes who like hanging around in bars this was obviously quite ridiculous, but we thought we'd better pass it on to you- just in case there's a problem developing. The problem being that your citizen Jerry, also claimed to be a crack shot and have numerous other skills that could be threatening to POTUS."

" We'd only gone along with spending time with the bloke as although we on holiday, as ex newsmen we thought there could be a good story in there, and quite frankly he kept buying the beers "

"If they want to see the stuff on the memory stick they should send us an e mail and of course we'll email it back ASAP. Oh yes, we tell em in the letter, we'll be in the USA in two weeks, we give 'em my TNoTN New York office address. Shows willing."

As if by magic Bim arrived with two more carefully carried glasses, and we asked her to send off Jerrys clothes and we'd think a bit more about the memory stick.

Whilst Harry started his favourite pastime of seeking 'least journey time' air tickets I sat back and started to figure out how soon I'd be able to further investigate the mystery of why the bubbles always settle downwards in my Guinness or Murphy's in my favourite pub in Dublin- when suddenly Harry sat back and closed his lap top.

"We're stupid. Again. Second time today. Assuming that this consulate WI-FI system is bugged, and although it's a bit bizarre- currently they -who ever they are- are the last ones we want to know where we're going- so let's just go, pack up the house, go to the airport and buy a ticket to somewhere-anywhere in fact- and then go on from there."

Chapter 7. *On the road. Or in the air. Summer 2018.*
Turn left and welcome.

Focksy Writes: One of the main advantages of having a TNoTN company expense account is not the odd free dinner. Not even these days, in this itemized receipts age, a few bonus booze offerings in the airport duty free shop. The real perk- as I constantly tells my boss, is if we are to keep fresh and working across the time zones of the world' is Business Class travel'.

Of course, as is the way with these things, a week had passed by the time that Harry and I had packed up the house, or actually his wife mostly packed up the house whilst he and I fretted about being *the most wanted.*

Then, as she drove over the mountains to Sukhothai to spend time with her family, and sort out her street food business that she's opened there, Focksy and I casually -oh so casually checked in at Chiang Mai's excellent little airport.

Our hearts survived the *'Are we wanted men'* flight down to Bangkok with business class just being just an empty seat between us They were pounding again at final passport and documents check prior to departing at 20.55 from the busy but spotless Bangkok Suvarnabhumi to Doha, on a mighty Qatar Airways Airbus 380. Actually this time we didn't turn left on boarding as is usual with most first and business class, this being an A380, we were ushered upstairs.

There, it's the wider seat and the extra leg room that counts. Not even the 'free' champagne, the allegedly 'gourmet food' or the 'specially chosen rejuvenating well being enhancing vitamin enriched organic face and hand creams' in the little zippy bag they give you. The description of the organic cream with its vegetable and flowers photo packaging making me wonder for a second if it was actually for use on my soon to be served *'garden enhanced'* salad. 'Garden enhanced' has me worried by the way.

Harry- as a self employed freelance, is of course usually responsible for his own travel costs, so sitting 'up front here' as my guest is a welcome rarity for him, and he's on the second glass of champers before I can remind him that with seven hours to Qatar- and then about the same on direct to Edinburgh- there's work to be done and plans to be made. He's on my expenses claim form as an 'expert consultant.' *(Ed: No comment about that.)*)

He was though, most appreciative of the 80 inch-count 'em-leg room...this removing most of the likelihood of another seatback kicking kid being added to his 'due for elimination' listing.

As I, immediately we were allowed, had started to peruse the exact details of *Jerry's Regime Change for Dummies* manual on my apple with the big screen (not the model with the crappy keyboard) I thought Harry was being a tad ungrateful considering his spacious accommodation when he hissed at me, "Turn that bloody thing off for gods sake."

His explanation being that, very visibly reading a detailed instruction manual on assassinations, sabotage, projectiles, bombs and such whilst sitting aloft at 30,000 feet was perhaps a bit uncool. He was right and I sat corrected.

Having apologised, I leafed through one of the selection of magazines in the rack by my seat. Usual stuff, mostly stuffed with property investment adverts, not having several million of anything immediately to hand to invest in a 70th floor triple level condo with Gulf and Desert views- I turned the page and was confronted with a large Nat Geo style detailed picture of a bloody falcon or eagle staring me in the eye.

I reached over, quite a longish reach required in these big seats, to nudge Harry and show him my find, only to have him show me a whole range of similar photos from a complete library of different magazines he had opened. Seems the sport of Kings is also still that of Emirs, Rulers, Sultans and the many Princes.

He leaned over and said: "This all widens our search, I think we had agreed that once we got to the Highlands and Islands of Scotland we were on the lookout for a couple of Haggis hurling kilted McNasty's carrying huge birds around -or if in rural Ireland - some Mick with birdshit on his shoulders holding his Guinness or Murphy's in big leather gloves."

I agreed, "I'd forgotten that Falconry is still a seriously big deal in most of the Gulf States. I also note from today's paper that Trump's meeting in Helsinki with Vladimir Putin is confirmed. I don't know too much about Helsinki except that they gets lots of snow there and so they play golf with orange balls...so that gives him a built in advantage."

The next few hours passed agreeably as we tucked into our gourmet choices, elegantly selected and served from a traffic jam of of trolleys and really rather good. We came to the conclusion that 'Garden Enhanced' salad must mean that the veggies were all grown under glass in a hydroponic or similar system. Then, despite our choice to go easy on the alcohol, we both became a little hysterical imagining the lettuces and tomatoes being allowed out now and again to be 'garden enhanced' in the great outdoors of a shaded kitchen garden somewhere.

But to play fair with the boss, our dedication to working in our *spacious work enhancing area*' would easily pass inspection on this seven hour sector of our journey to Scotland. The parts we could read of the mainly Arabic print magazines suggested that there was a quite a trade in falcons from Scotland to the Gulf States, with much licensing required. Just as with race horses, certain breeding bloodlines and pedigree's having considerable extra value.

With a seven hour leg stretching and snoozing wait at Doha to get the ongoing flight to Edinburgh- we had plenty of time to use the free Wi-fi to continue our researches. Then, more by chance than with any advance planning it turned out that on the next flight we had on board wi-fi so we were able carry on working.

We discovered that in the world of falconry, there were quite a few nefarious goings on-going on-outside the obviously well regulated 'officially recognised' breeders and dealers. Seems that less scrupulous types, illegally traded and exported eggs and fledglings, and had even tried to entice pedigree birds out for a quick fly by, with pheromones and such, to come and bonk receptive lady falcons hiding in the nearby bushes.

With seriously big money at stake- Harry found details of an old court case in which the defendant claimed that 'the birds had already flown to the Gulf,' *albeit exported on a plane not on their own wings'.*

Various Scots newspaper reports also expressed concern from local farmers about the possibility of falcons and eagles escaping from breeding or training establishments and endangering their chickens. Given what we had learned about the their ability to see a target from ten thousand feet, and drop down at more than 200 mph, talons and beak at the ready - it would appear those famers might have a legitimate concern. Then again, with some birds apparently valued at thousands of pounds one would imagine that their overnight accommodation was well protected from both incoming robbers and outgoing birds.

One of the magazines also had a feature on, as they put it 'What to wear when enjoying traditional grouse shooting and deer stalking in The Highlands of Scotland. Which reminded both of us of the recent news story about Scotland being home to more rifles than any other part of the UK.

Harry remarking, "There's two points about that. There's really only been two gun massacres of innocent people in the reasonably gun free British Isles, one of them was in Scotland at Dunblane. Makes me think that, of all the places in the UK the Scots police and others must have a well strong hand on gun licensing and how they are stored. Although I guess someone with evil intent, would not choose to use a licensed weapon. Mind you with deer stalking and shooting such a big- and lucrative business up there that a lot of sporting rifles must be temporarily imported."

Despite the detail and serious nature of Harry's reports-all rather removed from his usual cheery demeanor we both then got almost five hours decent sleep, and only awoke as the lights came on and landing announcements started.

Harry then shattered my reverie with his, "Well , just about an hour and we'll be at our hotel - unless Edinburgh immigration has been alerted to our wanted status, in which case we're about an hour away from Edinburgh nick."

Thanks for nothing old mate, and it was interesting how -even though we knew the accusations were a ridiculous fabrication-how the heart pounded a little as we approached the immigration barrier and desks. As we did so a uniformed women stepped out in front of us, hand raised...

Which Harry told me afterwards- nearly gave him a heart attack- but she was just pointing us to the automatic passport recognition channels-which eventually allowed him entry with his UK passport, although I had to show my Irish one to a human.

With first and business class travel allowing us two pieces of hand baggage each, so no need for checked in bags and thus no waiting 'for downloading' as Harry's wife calls it, we were actually checking in to our hotel just off Edinburgh's Royal mile well within Harry's suggested hour.

Experienced travelers that we are - despite having had a good sleep on the flight, we were both very 'groggy'. My view is that even on short flights the change in air pressure on the plane is what really makes you tired. So we agreed-subject to snooze attacks- to 'hit the phones' in our rooms to see what leads we could gain from any local press and other media contacts. The problem being that - not wishing to give away too much about our potential 'exclusive news story' there wasn't too much we could tell people.

As I said to Harry, "In fact all that's sent us half way round the world are Jerry's drunken claims to have 'sniper skills' and his pretty wild stories about falcons. In reality we don't even know if a falcon or an eagle can really be trained to attack humans, or if that's just a wild goose chase."

Which prompted an interruption of "Don't forget all the assassination details on the bloody memory stick, that was, forgive my words- the trigger...and anyway...it's falcons, not wild geese."

He continued, " I'll follow up on those stories about people caught smuggling eggs and chicks out of the country. Despite them being quite old- the stories that is, not the chicks- they could still give us an opening to start a conversation with various wild life and bird protection groups. If I'm lucky I might get a few leads to a dodgy dealer or a flaky falconer and can learn something real."

We agreed to meet - in the bar of course- at around seven.

Chapter 8. *Scotland. Summer 2018.*
Bars smell.

Focksy writes: Having been used to the mostly open air drinking in Thailand for a month or so, now in Scotland, even with the well observed' 'No Smoking' ban removing the fug of tobacco, the bar smelled.

The stale, slightly airless, split beer smell of the Edinburgh hotel bar depressed me a little when I walked in. As did the slightly tacky feel to the tartan carpet, which for a moment make me recall the alleged Trump ban on Irn Bru. Despite the still bright evening outside, the heavy drapes on all the windows, made the bar late night gloomy. Eventually I spotted Harry, who, showing supreme advance planning skills was watching two Guinness settle, almost ready for much needed consumption.

Turned out that he was mightily depressed. Not about the bar atmosphere, nor as I suggested, "Could it be the jet lag, it's a known side effect?" ..."Err No."

"Could it be that, to impress the tourists, the bar was totally tartan from top to toe...so much it was hard to tell if we were inside a pair of Billy Connolly or Jackie Stewart's tartan trews, or at a Bay City Rollers re-union with Rod Stewart as 'special guest'. So an overdose of tartan?" Err No.

It turned out that this was his first trip in twenty years back to Scotland, and he had come to the conclusion that his linguistic skills and / or hearing had suffered a systems failure.

"I worked in Scotland for a good few years in the sixties-as a trainee journalist and then pop columnist. I went everywhere, I mean everywhere, Highlands, Islands, even the dodgy back streets of Glasgow reporting on knife wielding gangs in Easterhouses."

"In later years with my music company I made more than few recordings of all kinds of Scots music. We even had a Christmas Hit record when we re-released-Andy Stewart's traditional old Scots folk song version of 'Donald Where's Your Trousers.' Which now on You Tube has now been taken up as a 'Stormy says Liar Liar Pants on Fire' anthem about the President."

I sipped my Guinness and asked: " So what's upset you quite so much?'"

Lifting his head from his hands he said, " I can't understand a word they're bloody saying. Not the receptionist when we signed in. Not the lad who showed me to my room--and now not him," he gestured at the barman, busy as good barmen should be when they're not busy- polishing glasses. "

"Not a word of any of their Scots accents, it's not Highland, not Islands, not Glasgow...none of it's working for me."

"I can't tune in."

Being the kind considerate chap that I am, I really didn't like to see my chum in such depths of hopeless despondency, but before I could speak to him the receptionist came in saying:" Ah. Mr. Schnauzer, I found you. The car hire man is here, and he needs you to come and sign for the car."

As I stood up to leave with her, and noting her name badge 'Magda Urbaniak', I asked, " And where are you from Magda?"

Her response of-"Krakow, Poland", was quickly followed by, "and so's Petre"as she nodded at the barman and continued, "He's my brother- there's lots of us here, although Oleg the bellboy, he is from Ukraine."

As I left I patted Harry on the shoulder and said, " You see, sometimes being one third German helps the old human auto translate systems you know... and I'll have another Guinness."

On my return, having signed away my life savings , or actually those of TNoTN for whom I work, on the cheapo car rental 'optional' extra's, optional in this case meaning bloody expensive, I could see Harry having a very animated conversation with the barman. Harry holding an orange and two lemons and circulating them around his head.

I approached warily, as first sight suggested that Harry's depression had advanced into some kind dementia-of which there are actually hundreds of variations...although fruit waving was so far not known to me. He acknowledged my approach with a nod and said ,"I'm just explaining to Polish Pete here the reasons why it stays light so very late here in Scotland during the summer months, but it gets dark very quickly all year around six to seven in the tropics nearer the equator in Thailand where we were last night."

I think he noted my slightly puzzled frown as he continued, " This lemon being the earth, that one being the moon and the orange being the circulating sun...and that's your Guinness, which does also play an important part in the sunset hours of most of the world." He raised his glass, as did I, and took a welcome sip.

Harry also had important information to impart, "Pete says that, despite the Chef being Hungarian, that the Hotel Restaurant is actually way better than many. Especially for the fish and seafood, all particularly fresh- as since the Chef appeared on one of these TV tourism-cookery type shows-on your very TV channel Focksy-the place has been full to busy every night."

Despite us both usually deeply distrusting and avoiding Hotel Restaurants -our view being, most hotel guests are new to that locality, and so they prefer to go out and eat. Our theory continues, hotels only have restaurants for rainy days, and because they have to have enough space to serve breakfasts to almost all guests at about the same time each morning.

But in this case-not only did the Anglo-Irish- German-Polish gastronomic intelligence service prove to be remarkably well informed, but with it's soft mossy and highland heather colours, grey slate and lots of muted Harris Tweed and Fair Isle - the restaurant was remarkably restful on the eye.

Being both slightly travel jaded, we opted for The Light Supper...(*The Ed..Oh sure!...With optional extra's.*)

Starters, Salmon selection : Hot smoked over whisky barrel oak, marinated Swedish style and pate with little oaty biscuits. Brilliant. Then an immense dish to share of meaty delicate pink langoustines - not long out of the cold local waters, which has made their export along with Salmon such a success for the Scots fishing industry.

All with side salads so garden fresh they must have wept many a dewy morning tear for their glasshouse chums imprisoned and needing 'garden enhancement.'(*Ed..Oh for Gods sake!*)

We then, at Polish Pete's recommendation, had negotiated with the waitress (Lena Walenca- so Polish again) and followed up with main courses of double servings of one of the local speciality 'starters'- Cullen Skink. Despite its slightly alarming name, this, almost chowder like thick slightly creamy soup of smoked haddock with onions and potatoes really hit the spot. So much so that 'the restful on the eye' muted colours around us soon became positively soporific as we struggled to stay awake.

Of course it might have been the effect of two pints of Guinness each, and then a bottle of New Zealand Marlborough White Sauvignon, or more likely the jet lag. *(The Ed. Jet lag! The expenses claim clearly shows three bottles of wine.)*

But, regardless of all that, having checked our watches at 9 pm local, we realised it was 3 am Thai time.

Well past our respective bed times.

Such was the relaxed evening, that our rather needed 'Desperado Detective Duo's planning discussion' had come to nothing. So we scheduled a breakfast meeting...is that professional or what!

Mind you ,with our double dishes of the Cullen Skink neither of us thought we would ever need to eat again.

Goodnight.

Chapter 9. Scotland Summer *2018*.
Full Scots Breakfast.

Focksy writes: Breakfast TV in the UK tends to start around 6.00. Unfortunately I awoke at 3 am. That being my usual Thai wake up time of around nine-ish in the morning.

The only advantage being that when eventually the 8 am breakfast meeting time came around, despite the skinful of Cullen skink the previous evening, I was bloody starving. That's despite having eaten several packets of tartan packaged shortcake biscuits whilst using up all the little sachets of tea and coffee making stuff that the bedroom offered.

Seemed pretty much the same for Harry, whom I found in the now brightly sunlit-but still restfully decorated restaurant-obviously enjoying a *'Full Scots Breakfast.'* I gave him a wave and attacked the breakfast buffet, loading my plate with some enthusiasm, and having ordered English Breakfast Tea from a passing Polish waitress I joined him.

To my astonishment he said, " Stop. Don't touch your food I have to take a photograph of it." Given that he and I both are of a generation for whom food is for eating, and all the better for not having many fingers arranging it on ones plate like a piece of TV friendly modern art.

Even more astonishing was the fact that he then started to re-arrange my bacon, sausages, mushrooms, eggs and the little arty farmy chef ramekin full of baked beans, so that it would apparently look better in the photo. Having checked the photo on his phone he said, "Tuck in old bean, what kept you."

As I was sitting there mouth agape in astonishment at his change of media mind, it seemed a wasted opportunity not to put something in it so a forkful of sausage did the trick.

Harry, who had moved on to toast and marmalade, which looked reasonably bitter and chunky unlike the mystery sachets of clear orange goo we were used to in Asia, then made a suggestion.

"I think that we should alert the authorities here to the situation. Waiting for them to react to the letter we gave Bim to post in a few days, could backfire on us or even the President if Total stranger Jerry, is one of the bad guys. Or if he's a 'a good guy' gone bad., or even trickier if he's a good guy, now tasked with being a bad guy." I raised a finger to pause him whilst I let that one sink in, but he continued...

"Whichever way, there's a chance that with Jerry's much boasted about huntin' and shootin' skills, with rifles, longbows and even crossbows, that the President could be in real danger. Also, although this is a bit extreme, he could be at at risk from a falcon or eagle. Although how the hell we could get someone to take that eagle business seriously I don't know. I came to those conclusions after I bloody woke up at at about 3.30 am,"

I pointed at my self and said, "Me too,"

Harry nodded and continued, "Not only that, but if Jerry has shared his ridiculous accusations with someone- and something actually happens , and we have done nothing to alert the authorities, that can seriously backfire badly on us. At best it makes us look stupid."

" Despite this President's polarizing effects on the world, let alone the USA , we'd rather see the due processes of either law or the ballot box are followed, than a lucky shot, from a golf links grassy knoll. Or, even, apparently in a long gone echo of Central European-Asian history, felled by a falcon or eviscerated by an eagle."

" Even if the local cops have already got us on a 'watch for' list, we get brownie points for walking in to them. Not only that, but I suspect that even the worst of prisons here in Scotland are likely better than some blindfolded air travel and compulsory face washing whilst the Guantanamo guards lounge about smoking cigars just rolled on the Cuban thighs of local ladies. "

"But moving on, what also went through my mind is that we both look pretty bloody stupid if we can tell the story to the cops, but cannot provide who ever we tell, with a single useful photo of Jerry, with whom we just spent two weeks...In selfie mad Thailand. "

Both his points were correct, although the waterboarding thought did slightly put me off my final forkful. *Mushroom, bacon and the final piece of saute'd spud, mopping up the last of the egg, if you were wondering.*

But Harry had news, "So I called Bim and asked if she or the others, had any photos of Jerry. At first she she seemed surprised to find that neither she nor any of the girls in the bar had a single picture of him. But then she said, 'I think about it now, he always move or not want picture taken, but we are all quite used to that, we know many Farangs (foreigners) not want photo's, because they got wife or girlfriend at home who can get big surprise they not want next time they check their Face Book, Line or Instagram'."

I nodded, as my primary task was by then, checking out the marmalade that turned out to be as bitter sweetly good as it looked, especially with the Scots Breakfast Tea, as the lady from Poland had called it when she delivered and poured same.

But Harry had an update - breaking news even- "Then Bim called me back half an hour later and said, 'You remember when that truck bang away the satellite dish off the wall of the bar, and so we got no tv for a week, then we turned off the electric for the TV box, I see now, as well, we turn off security camera we got at the back of the bar, and forget to turn on again. So it still got pictures in it from when you and Jerry in here. I download some now and send to you'."

As I sat back in my chair well breakfasted I said, "Lucky break. Bim saves the day again. Have you got the pictures?"

Harry nodded and said, " Good HD stills and some video that's a little bit jerky but still clear."

"When I talked to Bim and told her it was breakfast time here, she asked for pictures of the good breakfasts, 'So that,' she said, 'they could make sure when we went back to Thailand we would get *same same.'* Seemed a good enough reason to break the habits of a life time and send photographs of our food."

Having agreed, and whilst I was considering if there was a discrete way of loosening my belt a few notches, Harry volunteered the fact that whilst he had not found out much about dodgy falcon traders, a Mr. MacGregor from one of the wild life preservation organisations had called him back just after seven this morning and given him a useful lead.

" No apologies for the early call, I guess those guys work farmers hours so he was probably on his mid morning break by seven. After some general chat he suggested we contact, or better still, visit, a guy named Matt McButton."

" Seemed McButton is one of those good folks who whilst making a living- in his case a mix of 'teacher -and paddle surfing guide' was totally devoted to taking care of injured wildlife- mainly birds. Apparently he was one of those who originally found and exposed the stories of the illegal export trade and egg smuggling and such. He's also been very involved in the re-establishment of some of the endangered species."

" Mr. MacGregor then said to me, ' McButton. The poor man's inundated. Everyone who finds anything from a chick that's fallen out of the nest to a wounded grouse, or any injured animal knows that he's the man to help. He simply 'Canna say Noo'."

I told Harry that we could get by quite well up here north of the border, without him lapsing into sad versions of the *'moose aboot this hoose'* vernacular' and enquired where we might find the apparently excellent McButton.

Turned out that Mr. MacGregor had told Harry in some typically Scots way, that McButton *'stayed' in Barra, during the summer.* This part of the story, fortunately required no more of Harry's ham English idea of a typical Scots accent. As it happens in most of the country the accent is more akin to a Swedish or Scandinavian lilt than the usual 'Och Aye's' of comedians and TV.

But back to Barra- or we would be if we knew where it bloody well was, helpfully Mr. MacGregor had said "'It's only an hour's flight from Glasgow, but only at low tide'."

We stood to leave, even though it was only just after nine there was some quite pointed and noisy 'laying up of lunch tables' going on and a Polish lady hovering with a hoover waiting to start work. We agreed to meet in the lobby in an hour and a half. I'd try my luck with the local police and Harry would try and contact McButton.

Chapter 10. *Scottish Summer 2018..*
'Hello, I'm calling to report'.

Focksy reports: Mid morning in most hotel lobbies is generally a bit of a lull. Those checking out have out checked. Those checking in are still in transit. The business men and tourists have departed for the day. There were huge-I mean really huge-giant size, tartan wing backed chairs in groups, around coffee tables, scattered all around the lobby and in some alcoves. At least the size of the chairs, and the gloom, concealed some of the distinctly tired tartan carpet. I started to wonder if it was the tatty state of the carpet that made the managers keep the curtains mostly drawn.

Finding Harry required walking round the giants nests peering into the depths of several chairs until I found him, and when I did he was more than little taken aback by my tale of apathy.

" I had expected that finding a real person, interested in Presidential security or even vaguely responsible for same in the Scots constabulary not to be easy. But so far I have failed. Totally, and as you know, as a TV newshund I'm not known for failing. "

"Not only that but when I found signs of even the slightest interest their only concern was, 'and who's going to foot the security bill for The President's round of golf, may I ask'? "

" I quite expected, of course, and got the usual run around from patient 'but beleaguered by nut jobs' telephonist's, *'Certainly sir. That is very kind of you to call. Would you care, to write in, visit your local Police Help Desk, or send us an email'.*"

" Which you can interpret as 'would you please piss off'. All of which I got several times. I deliberately didn't want to say I was from any TV news network as that would have transferred me to some slick and spinning PR operator. "

" Then the final bloody call, after lot more holding, fecking crap music, and if I hear another *'don't drink and drive'*, *'mind your purse and pockets'*, and *'do think first and avoid being cheated when banking on line'*-I'll shoot someone myself. Anyway, after an age, a wee young lass, as you would say, from the sound of her voice-came on and said,' Hello Mr. Sneezer. Sorry to keep you waiting. I believe you've lost your dog'."

Now Harry is a long time friend of mine, and he knows how sensitive I am about my name. Obviously that goes back to much teasing during my school days, since when it's always been the source of much merriment and many problems. Outside the USA that is, inside the US odd names seem an every day event, not an affliction, and are on occasion a proud affection.

So I was more than *eagle eyed* to observe any signs of mirth from Harry. But he seemed free of any smiling smirking or shoulder shaking. Perhaps just a tad of the latter. I suggested, "Given my so far, total failure to assist in *'making Scotland a safer place'* - let alone *'making the world a safer place'* and taking into account the day is passing. How have you got on?"

Better than I had it seemed. First of all he had not only contacted Bird Man McButton, but he'd had a useful conversation with him, although whilst on the phone, Bird Man was balanced on a paddle surf board some miles off shore, presumably with his phone in a special plastic bag.

Harry "It was interrupted now and again, with the odd whoosh and slurp sounds of wind and water, but generally he was chatting away quite happily. Bit Scots now and again, but as soon as I mentioned potential falconry felons and a need to save the world he was very happy."

" So much so that he seemed to fall off the surf board, but was soon back on line, and saying that, *'He was around all the rest of the summer. Just give him a call when we'd be coming to see him'*. Mind you, thinking back about it now, he might have been thinking global warming actions, when I said we were apparently tasked with 'making the world a safer place. "

" It was only when, I told him what I needed to discuss was quite urgent and asked him for recommendations on the best way to get to him that I suddenly remembered Barra was an Island, so I guess all that global warming stuff might be a bit crucial for him. "

"Anyway he said, 'There's a couple of flights most days from Glasgow with the times subject to the tide. Or a car ferry from Oban'. And now we know why. Because the planes land on the bloody beach. But when I tried to book a flight. No Go. Completely full all this week. I guess it's holidays. So whilst I look into ferries from Oban- lets see what can be done about getting you back on track to tell the authorities something that might be useful."

" Given that they 'the authorities,' in their wisdom have decided that any one who calls in to them with warning is a nutter- or as the Thais would say a bit Ting Tong and not 100%. They hardly deserve our help." There then followed a brief discussion about the likely non PC nature of the word 'nutter' these days, quite acceptable in our young day, but we suspect no more.

Harry, despite his apparent memory fail about some of the 136 permanently inhabited islands of the British Isles, as he does sometimes, came up with the winning ticket. And this time he really did, in this case a business card which he eventually recovered from the dusty depths of his computer bag saying," You remember that book I did about terrorists and modern drone dangers to our normal peaceful lifestyle ?"

I nodded. (*The Ed. We've done that already -but Just in Case you forgot, It's pretty good actually, quite a thrilling story.*)

Harry, "One of the people we mentioned in the book, who was concerned about the threat from drones to our cities, was the then English Foreign Secretary Sir William O'Rafferty. You also met him a few years later in China, and interviewed him about some trade delegation. I just recalled I still had Sir William's business card, so try calling him. As a member of Parliament he'll have the direct contacts to get something done."

Which I did, fortunately Sir William's still an MP even if no longer Foreign Secretary, and even more fortuitously he was in London when I called. I gave him a very abbreviated run down- and Bob's your uncle- ten minutes later, we hardly had time to order a coffee and a sandwich from a passing Pole in a tartan uniform, when I get a call from senior copper here in Edinburgh.

Brief word- which seemed to do the trick- although I then had to endure yet more complaints about, '*and who's paying all those costs so The President can play golf*'. I explained all to Harry, also saying, "They're sending a car to collect me shortly so I told them I'd be in the lobby."

He and I agreed, I'd do what ever I could to help the authorities here and he'd take the hire car to Oban, and the ferry from there, we agreed we'd meet up- probably back here in Edinburgh - in a couple of days.

As we waited for delivery of our sandwich order, we started discussing the chances of there soon being original Polish tartans. After all tartans have been created for almost every name and nationality in the US phone book. Even New York Lawyer Michael Cohen has tartan jacket. Him being a famous lawyer and all, we assumed he'd have an impressive certificate of Tartan Authenticity. So why not Urbaniak or Walenca Tartans for those from Poland.

With a slight interruption for some boringly predictable 'oldie but goody' Harry humour when a police car or ambulance passed by outside, sirens blaring, " They'll never sell any ice creams driving that fast." We started to enjoy the sandwiches (*The Ed. More Scots Salmon, with Swedish style sweet mustard and dill sauce on brown whole meal since you ask.*) But then with just about one mouthful taken, three Policemen- in ultra smart uniforms- came through the swing doors, removed their caps, and started the 'find the body' search through the maze of tartan chairs.

Which gave bloody Harry time for, "I told you so, can I have the rest of your sandwiches, if they take you away?"

Which I ignored as - after much waving in the gloom- the coppers spotted me and advanced, hands out to be shaken, as I nodded to their, 'Mr. Schnauzer'?

So the first words were good. They got the name right, their second words were comforting, "Many apologies for descending on you in full uniform, we usually try to be a little more discrete, but we're extra busy right now, and we were at a meeting just across the road. The office mentioned a little of what this is about, so here we are."

After some polite introductions, and 'Yes please, two coffees and one tea would be more than welcome-we've been on the go since the early hours.' I briefly explained the backstory, which seemed to interest them, although they did exchange raised eyebrow glances when I mentioned the potential attack by falcon or eagle plot, so I decided to wait a while before I introduced the concept that the CIA might be behind the plot.

But when we then explained that Harry was en route to Oban and then Barra to see some bird expert name of McButton they relaxed totally, one of them saying, "Bird Man McButton, fine fine man. We work with him a lot. On paddle boarding lessons, and quite often on injured birds that get delivered to us for various reasons. 'Canna say Noo' when there's any injured animal. He's inundated you noo."

I just had time to confirm that indeed I did noo, when as the teas and coffees arrived-good to see that copper's still can't resist the biscuits- when officer 765 -I hadn't caught all the names properly yet- continued. "Aye we work with McButton to teach some of our lads paddle surfing, not so much for fitness or fun, but it gives them a feel for the water and gives them confidence which they may need one day. But more to the point- why are you going to Oban and the ferry, why not take the plane from Glasgow?"

Harry explained it was full all the week, and both 765 and 941, after a brief nod of heads- obviously agreeing something, said "We'll get you on the plane, if it's a police matter we have some priority seats we can get. When's the next flight?'"

Harry's, "It'll have to be tomorrow, today's is at 2.45 and it's getting on for 1.00 now." produced three grins-and a- "How quick can you leave here-laddie?"

Harry held up his hand baggage saying, "Right now." Actually I could swear he said 'right noo.'

The third copper said, "I'll get you to the plane - it's just over sixty miles- with a spot of traffic here in the city. The guys here will get the booking and the check-in sorted, but you'll still have to do airport security. We'll get them to hold the plane -but they can probably only do that for ten or fifteen minutes, because of the tides. It lands on the beach you know."

With a swig of his tea, he grabbed Harry's bag and they set off, him calling back to his police colleague, 'Jimmy, I'll get Harry a place for the night at Mrs McNeil's.'

I sat back and said, "This has all gone as Harry's dad used to say, 'From the sublime to the gor blimey.' First of all no interest and then all this."

765 who seemed to be the senior officer, said," Well first of all, none of us- especially the chief constable want to be remembered for losing an American President. Even Mr Trump. Although you didn't hear that last bit," he continued, "and to be honest we're a wee bit fed up."

I interrupted "Not the cost of the golf, I've heard all that."

The now -two policemen both grinned and said, "No, finance is not our department, but we're a bit pissed off with the 150 page very detailed US Presidential Visit security manual we're supposed to work to."

" I mean, for instance, every manhole and drain on his route, and one alternative route, from the Prestwick Airport to Turnberry Golf Club has to be inspected and sealed. That's a legitimate security concern, and all well and good in a city street, but, with the the alternatives that's fifty or so miles of country roads. But then there's pages about exploding golf balls, sabotaging plumbers, stink bombs and Christ knows what. "

I pondered a response, but decided a concerned shake of the head would be best. Constable 941, who had been both listening and speaking with someone at Glasgow Airport laughed and said, "Aye and then after we've welded up all the bloody drains, he'll likely take his helicopter."

We agreed to move back to their offices, "A tad more private so we'd best get a taxi." said 765. I suggested that we could take my car as, if and when, they decided they could let me go I wanted to see a friend in Dundee later.

Twenty minutes later, settled in a meeting room at the Police station, I recounted the whole story again- and agreed to them recording it. 'Not as any kind of evidential statement but in case we need to check things.' The more details I revealed the longer their faces became, and the more folks they called and said, 'Pop into my office, there's some stuff I want you to hear.'

A good few hours later I had ended up with with seven or eight men and women all firing questions at me. Including one who said he came from the Army at Hereford-so a polite way of saying he was SAS Brit special forces, and one of the women, from MI5 or 6, who seemed very dismissive of my 'It's the CIA going rogue again.'

I suppose it's 'all spooks must stick together,' but I went through the story yet again, and also downloaded the images that Bim had sent, identifying Jerry in them.

It turned out that of the seven cops, one soldier and one lady from the security services, six had been to Thailand. Mostly beach holidays in Samui or Phuket. two had been up to Chiang Mai...so with a quick glimpse of the map- and google earth, they figured out exactly what we were talking about. Their google earth seemed way more detailed than ours, but I suppose that's to be expected.

After a good few hours, 765, who seemed to be the senior officer there, said , "I think that we will have to let you go soon, it would be good though, if you kept us informed of your movements. I suspect we may need you and Harry to come in and scan some CCTV images, on the off chance - you see your Total Stranger Jerry. Just wait here a wee minute, the boss would like a word."

I sat there for a while pondering his *I think we'll let you go,* 'deciding that he wasn't joking, but pretty quick 765 returned and we were ushered through to a big corner office with some spectacular views of the castle.

There, with lots of silver braid, chains even on the shoulder I met the Chief Constable. "Excuse the formal dress uniform, I'm on parade tonight for various functions. Probably means you won't recognise me in November this year when I'm on the beach again in Kho Samui."

Turned out that he had also been to Chiang Mai, " Came up by road from Bangkok, to Sukhothai with their wonderful old City, then over the mountains to to Chiang Mai, Chiang Rai and then a really nice luxury rice barge for a few days down the Mekong."

"My wife and I loved the food, the markets, the people- but the driving, Jings! I'm already in trouble at home as my daughter and her friend are off on some gap year travels around that area- and it's the driving that's got us worried the most. Both of the girls are black belts at judo so I think they can take care of themselves... but the taxis and the mini bus driving. God."

He turned to 765, " So I understand we might be able to score a few brownie points off the Yanks when we tell them they may have a rogue agent on their hands. That would be good. But I also hope we find the bugger, I don't want anything untoward to happen on my patch."

Having run through the story basics - yet again, I was just leaving the Chief's office when I said, "Hang on, before I go, let me write down a few of your names and numbers in my notepad, with my jet lag they'll be gone from my head in the morning."

As I got the pen and trusty spiral bound paper pad out, a folded bit of paper dropped out, and floated away under the desk, I reached down to get it saying, "That's handy, I wondered where that was. It's the paper where Jerry wrote down some notes for me. "

Well, as Harry's Cornish farmer friend Mandy always says, 'Suddenly there was hell up' with the Chief and 765 pushing me aside almost rugby style, "Don't touch that, it could have Jerry's finger prints on it."

The Chief Constable saying with a broad smile, "You wait till Jimmy asks the other lads if they thought about fingerprints. That'll be a worth a few drinks in the bar later I reckon."

It was only late afternoon, but now the day two jet lag did cut in, so I scrapped my visit Dundee plan and went back to the hotel, and having decided to put my feet up for a brief rest, fell straight into a deep sleep.

Chapter 11. *Scottish Highlands & Islands. 2018.*

Harry In The Hebrides. *I'm writing: I've had a lot of thrills in my life, but the ride in Constable Rory's police car from our Edinburgh hotel to the front door of Glasgow Airport, ranks as one of the best.* Mainly thanks to some skilled driving and a little use of the blue lights and once, a remarkably effective siren. Even with quite a lot of traffic as we left the city we made the 65 miles in about 45 minutes.

Once out of Edinburgh and on to the M8 motorway I gave him more of the background to the story. Several phone calls, or I guess police communications calls, hands free of course, confirming flights, airport security, and one that I totally failed to follow with a lady on Barra getting me a room for the night on an apparently totally booked up island.

Rory reporting," You're lucky there, Mrs McNeil, will get you the finest breakfast of your life in the morning...mind you there's no alcohol allowed in her wee hoose (he did say hoose I promise) and on Sundays not a lot of breathing even. Oh yes she's the Chief Constable's aunty."

As we swung into Glasgow Airport straight off the motorway, Rory bade me goodbye saying, "I have a feeling I'll be seeing you again- and I don't mean on the beach in Chiang Mai."

We pulled on a bus space right by some heavy duty bollards and just steps from the doors, where two burly looking armed police in the usual flak jackets, and a couple of other people waited.

I muttered my thanks, and "See you again I hope," neither having the time nor inclination to correct his geography, Chiang Mai being 500 miles or so from the nearest beach.

Having grabbed my bag from the back seat, I was swiftly escorted by the policemen, and it turned out, the head of airport security to a crew check in desk, where I got a boarding card, and although they hadn't asked, they were happy to scan my passport.

"As ID only, although Barra folks like to think of themselves as of another country, so far you *'noo need'* a passport to visit.' Then embarrassingly escorted to the front of the security queue and through-the usual body scanner and luggage inspection.

At the gate, the airport guy scanned a key code, opened the door, and we descended a few steps into the sunshine on the tarmac, just meters away from one of my favourite planes, a de Havilland Canada Twin Otter.

Boarding card exchanged with a smiley cabin crew lady at the bottom of the steps, her saying," You're the last, I kept the front seat, we'll put your bag back here. You'll get it back on the beach."

I just had time to mouth the word 'thanks' to the copper, against the noise of a nearby airplane and climbed the four steps. Having squeezed my way to front, I endured the usual fifteen seconds of 'about bloody time, he's the last one,' embarrassment as I as I turned to sort out the seat belt and faced the faces facing me.

By which time the cabin crew lady had the back door shut, and followed me to the front, and turned out not to be the cabin crew lady but the First Officer, and she was flying the plane.

Someone made the usual pre flight safety announcements, quickly followed by the really very nice reassuring sounds of the engines running up with slight 'chocka chocka' sounds as the propellers gathered speed. People worry about small planes, but in so many ways they are safer than jets.

I'd like to give a graphic description of the delights of the islands as we flew, fairly low I think, for the just over an hour flight to Barra, but I was jet lagged asleep before we'd even taken off. I guess it was then the changing engine note or the PA announcement that woke me as we commenced our decent into Barra airport, in this case onto the beach.

Quite a lot of salty spray from the wet beach, brief taxi, usual wait whilst the props revolved for a minute or two to cool the engines. Then the prop plane thing of putting out a little chain so no one walked in to propeller area- and with just 18 passengers I was soon standing on the damp sand in a considerable salty breeze.

Retrieved my bag from a glo coat man, and walked up the sand towards a smart and real old 'aerodrome' style building with a little glassed control tower on the roof. Really was just like the retro classic 'airport ' on the front of the box of Lego I'd given a friend's daughter for Christmas.

I kind of figured that Matt Mc Button was the bearded guy standing by an old long wheelbase Landrover, with two surfboards on the roof...and indeed he was.

With a broad grin, he corrected my *'surfboards'* to *'paddle boards,'* "Usually a tad more buoyant and a wee bit wider, more stable , particularly for the beginners," and continued, "Paddle boarding has taken off like crazy over the past few years, maybe you'd like a try tomorrow. Looks like it's set to be a braw day?"

Before I could reply, he said, "Hang on here for a moment, I've just to got wait till the plane's left again and do one wee thing. So while we wait let's go inside, collect a cuppa, and you can tell me what all this is about. After you called me from Edinburgh, about ten minutes later I got a call from the Chief Constable's office, telling me three things."

" Firstly that you'd be staying at his Aunties, secondly, my meeting you was vitally important for the good name of Scotland, and the safety of the world. Which sounds a very dramatic, and thirdly that I should 'stop chasing seals and mermaids' and if I bring you back here tomorrow for your flight he'd pay for me to have breakfast at Mrs McNeil's. Which sounds very good to me."

Matt then continued saying, "Sling your bag on the back seat, it's never locked on the island here, and it'll be safe enough with Percy in there, we'll go and have that tea."

So I opened the door and was faced with a very big and very live eagle or falcon, similar to those that had stared at me, just a few days back from the pages of the in flight magazine. Which made me step back more than a little...Mc Button laughed, and taking my bag, slung it on the seat and said, "Take care o'that Percy, we'll be back soon and you can have a fly."

In the Airport building which housed the single check in desk- incongruously 'normal airport' looking- and a cafe with some good looking cakes on display...each labeled, I noticed with the names of various local home bakers. Even as the passengers went out for the final departure of the day very few of the cafe tables were emptying out, Matt explaining that the cafe was popular with locals as well as tourists and passengers.

He then added, " Thinking about it, grab a seat on one of those benches outside there, I forgot they'll be closing for an hour soon to get cleaned up and ready for the evening rush for their fish suppers. I'll fetch you out a tea or coffee and a cake if you want some." As I went outside again he called after me..."And mind your face and hat now, the propellers blow up a bit of a sandstorm as they turn to leave."

I sat watching the passengers boarding the plane, the glo coats packing away the bags and then the chain barrier and thinking how very different this was to the mega airport terminal at Doha... although I guessed there was a lot of sand around there too. Seemed a long time since my first Eagle encounter in that in flight magazine.

Then, having watched the plane taxi and take off from the sand, more trails of spray, my second thoughts were that it was an incongruous location to be discussing global security. Or at least the security of one remarkably divisive person whose demise could have a considerable effect on that security.

Despite not having any update from Focksy, I figured that, given the message from the top cop, that I should fully brief Bird man McButton, which I started to do. Also very attentive were the two airport cafe dogs, although as soon as the cake, biscuits and the airport spectators had gone, for them, the attractions of the incoming tide soon became more interesting.

McButton, on the other hand, sat back, listened attentively, nodding now and again until I had completely given him the whole picture. Then and only then, he spoke:" Right. I get it. Despite many of us disliking President Trump for so many reasons...people with any kind of realistic view would prefer he faced legal or electoral sanctions than had his brains blown apart by a bullet or scattered by a seriously heavy blow inflicted by the beak and talons of one of the fastest animals on the planet."

He stopped, and I was just about to speak when I realised that he hadn't finished. I was starting warm to Bird Man McButton, obviously his often solitary hours patiently dealing with wildlife or on the water had instilled a real sense of 'think first - then speak', and when he did follow up on his initial words my view was rather confirmed.

He continued, "You know if Trump was out on the golf links, the first thing he would know about an attack by an eagle-that's way more likely than a peregrine or any kind of falcon, by the way, would be the sound. Really quite loud, as it descended wings back in the perfect aero foil pattern - they call that 'The Stoop' at, yes, around 150 MPH to 200 MPH."

" For peregrines their preferred prey- is other birds that they like to attack when they are also on the wing. They are also much smaller and lighter than eagles, so if we're looking at a real threat, a Golden Eagle, which prefers to hit its quarry on the ground, is the most likely. Could be any one of a number of other big ones like Percy here , he's a White Tailed Sea Eagle, but I'd focus on the Golden Eagle as they go for more inland quarry. They've been known to take lambs and baby deer, and there's a thousand years of legends about them attacking humans."

"Let me think about this for half an hour or so, I just need to get Percy out for a flight and then we'll go and have a proper talk...and may be a wee dram. I think you'll be fine there, it's fairly sheltered and you'll get a good view of Percy, as he hopefully goes for a fish. Back in a minute"

And indeed he returned in less, with the huge bird perched on his gloved wrist. He grinned, McButton not the bird, saying, "Before you say, 'he's huge,' actually he's only a youngster yet, but when he's full grown they're the biggest eagles in the UK, and fourth biggest breed in the world. Well more than six foot wingspan."

" I've had him for about six months now, some bastard had snared him at a fish farm. Those fish farms can lose a lot of stock to these beauties- and although there's many protective regulations- some- only some, of the fish farmers, and gamekeepers- that's Ghillie's up this way, on the big estates, charged with running salmon rivers, and breeding game birds as a business, adopt some nasty ways to cut down on the eagles and other wild birds."

" Normally, if you want to rehabilitate them- re-introduce them into the wild- you'd avoid handling them like this. But in his case he was so badly injured we almost had to teach him how to fly. Unlike other types of eagle there's not a history of Sea Eagles being used to hunt, as with falcons and golden eagles...mainly as his preferred diet is fish or sometimes carrion. I'm pretty much having to teach Percy to fish to survive. Now that they're washing the runway," he nodded at the beach which was rapidly disappearing under the incoming tide, "I've got some fish in my bag - and the idea's to encourage him to grab them when he sees them in the waters."

" The airfield folk like me to fly regularly here to establish it as 'falcon and eagle territory' as there's always a concern about bird strike on the aircraft here. So just as with many airports around the world, birds of prey, Falcons usually, are used to scare other species off, I can tell you Percy in flight is impressively scary."

With that he handed me a slightly fishy smelling booklet called 'Raptors of Scotland. Highlands and Islands, 'and walked down the sandy path to the beach.

I was torn between reading and watching Percy flying and on occasions diving down towards McButton who seemed to have walked out half way to Glasgow, oblivious to the waters lapping around his trousers.

The booklet, told how the mighty white tailed eagles of Scotland had been totally wiped out by humans before the first world war, but some reintroductions (from Norway) back in the seventies, and more recently, is bringing back breeding.

These days it seems, that in addition to modern hazards such as electric pylons, cables or wind farm blades, there are, still such strong rumours, about them taking game birds, fish both wild and farmed, and even young lambs, that they are at constant risk of being illegally killed. The booklet notes: 'Much vigilance is required.'

Nothing in the admirable booklet though about vigilance required by golfing Presidents. Although in my first few minutes with McButton he'd confirmed that there was potentially a serious threat to both the President's hair and his life.

Which he then confirmed even in more graphic terms when he walked up the exit path from the beach runway-carrying not in his case, a travelers case- but a presumably now well fed, Percy.

Before I could enquire about the development of Percy's fishing abilities, McButton, as promised had indeed been pondering the problem whilst out wading, as his first word were," Aye, the incredible sound of the wind whistling over eagles wings would likely be the last thing the President would hear. If he was 'na killed - it would take quite a while for him to be able to think and function again. That is if he actually thinks even now."

"With a big eagle weighing in at fifteen pounds, the females are heavier by the way, with their beaks, and awesome talons, they'd be well able to deliver a cutting blow with bad lacerations and possibly even smash or at least seriously damage a mans skull."

As we walked back to the Landrover, where he installed Percy on a padded perch in the very back, and before I could ask the question forming in my mind he answered it, continuing, "As I assume you're not too up on raptors generally I do think this could be a real threat. In the USA their sacred Bald Eagle or much more realistically a Golden Eagles could do it, although there's way stronger regulation there about keeping most kinds of birds."

"I think a bird trained from birth could easily learn that a certain hat and or specific face and hair always provides a tasty snack. It would likely take eight months or so. What you have to know is that- raptors, like most birds don't have any inbuilt instinctive knowledge when they're born. Not even flying really. They learn from observing the parents. So it's important that if you want them to become an attack weapon, they have to be taught that from birth. That's why if they have learned their feeding and survival from man- eagles and other hawks that choose to run off to the wild generally don't do very well."

"You just saw me conditioning Percy with those fish. If you have a falcon or an eagle to train depending on the hunting you want to do- you use lures on long bits of cord, which you chuck and then pull back in to imitate the quarry you want them to hunt. Your lures can be rabbit fur covered or with feathers from different breeds of bird- crow, pheasants, woodcock etc. *In this case using a Tattie Bogle would be the way forward.*"

I held up my hand...saying, "Tattie Bogle, what the hell is that?" McButton laughed..."It's a scarecrow, straw dummy of a human, up here on the islands they call them Tattie Bogles."

" So using a scarecrow dummy, Tattie Bogle, with tasty food under a hat is only another form of conditioning. They say these birds are not too bright-but I'm not sure. Falconry and zoo displays teach the birds to do all sorts of things, taking hats and such, mind you that circus stuff is not encouraged these days thank God , but past experience shows it can be done."

"Given an eagle can spot a mouse from a mile or so, and they definitely recognise their handlers- the ones who feed them- I would think they could even be trained with some good Tattie Bogles to distinguish between a Trump look-a-like and any other golfers."

"There's a few thousand years of history behind that 'weaponising' -as they would say these days- eagles. Right across central Asia from the Mongolians-who still fly a lot-all the Stan's, the Far East...and in all cases they taught their war birds to recognise individuals or at least specific uniforms. One thing is for sure-for pure attacking power if would be a Golden Eagle, and they exist in all those countries. Fewer in North America but generally almost world wide."

After brief discussion we agreed that he'd drop me off at Mrs McNeil's, for a restorative snooze- whilst he went and sorted out the rest of his aviary- or menagerie really-and he'd come back to collect me around six thirty so we could have further conversations over a "dinner and a wee dram."

Chapter 12. Scots Summer 2018
Tattie Bogles and Whisky Galore.

Harry writes: Waking up at six in the evening after an hours sleep was terrible, as of course it was midnight Thai time. When Matt Mc B arrived, I noticed that he'd taken the fairly 'well used' covers off the two front seats of the Landrover.

"If I don't, Chloe, my girlfriend won't get in the landy of an evening, especially as we're in and out of the sea most days in the summer when we're here on Barra - or soaked from walking around with the birds on the high moors inland, in the winter."

Matt continued, "I hope it's OK with you, but given it's such a great evening, and with a nice breeze to keep the midges away, Chloe had the idea we should go and have dinner outside by the beach. A fisherman friend of ours, Sandy Fredricksen, has a few tables in his garden and on three evenings a week in the summer cooks up whatever he caught earlier, Chloe's got the cool box with beer and wine in it."

I nodded saying, " Sounds really good to me, I've spent too much of my life in restaurants. It's terrible to own up too, but I've become what I call, 'menu blind' when nothing looks interesting or appetizing. So your Chloe's plan sounds better than you'll ever know, she must be a mind reader."

Matt continued " Well the really good news about all that is that the chef, some of the locals, especially the full time fishermen, call him 'Fairweather Freddie,' as he only fishes in the summer. But thats because in winter he's a chef at a famous ski lodge in the USA somewhere, so a good reason to let him cook our dinner."

Good was not the word, great, seriously wonderful fresh fish, simply cooked, locally garden grown and foraged vegetables- and lovely people. Not only that but by some quirk of fate- New Zealand white wine, seemed to be overstocks from a wedding that Chef Sandy and Chloe had catered for. Chloe, on my arrival, said," If you're not a fishy person, then Sandy's brother makes fantastic sausages. "

To my shame I then proposed that," As I've flown six thousand miles or so for this, may be we could have a few sausages afterwards to 'help finish the wine." Which we did. Matt and Chloe-who were, I guess in their late twenties, early thirties, kindly feigned interest in the tales of my 1960s working days as a trainee journalist in Scotland- rather alarmingly- almost thirty years before they were born.

Matt saying, " That explains it, I'd wondered how it was that you just nodded when I said about the midges. It's the first question for most summer visitors, mind you most of them assume they bite like mosquitoes. Most of us on the islands think that the tourist boards should boast more of the fact that with the usual sea breezes the Islands are way less affected than the mainland."

An hour or so later, as we sat back full of fish- and in my case still 'testing sausages,' Matt said, "If you'll just excuse me a moment, I'll just check my emails on Sandy's wi-fi, which also prompted me to log on, a little sadly, to 'the real world.' For me, luckily, nothing urgent, and nothing from Focksy or anything of interest from anyone else. Quick connection though.

As Chloe and I chatted about their island and winter lifestyles, Matt meantime had wandered away and seemed to have a more then focused conversation and then made a few more calls.

When he rejoined us he said, "Well. Hard to know where to start, several messages from Jimmy Brydon, one of the policeman you met in Edinburgh this morning. "

"Seems your friend Mr Focks, downloaded some photos of your suspect Jerry for them. Now, through some face recognition software they've got on trial up here, they 'think' he stressed they 'think' your Jerry visited Scotland in February a couple of years back, last year and again in February this year."

"Jimmy said, when you get back to Edinburgh tomorrow afternoon, they're hoping you and Mr Schnauzer can drop into the Police House to take a look at some of those photo's. Oh yes, Jimmy said your friend Mr Schnauzer has turned his phone off, so he assumes he's sleeping." Which left me some fine ammunition to tell Focksy how I'd been working so hard whilst he snoozed.

Having discovered that the island had brilliant internet connections- even Mrs McNeil's, Matt saying, "She has 'na even got a mobile phone, let alone a computer, but The Chief Constable needs it when he's here. We have a feeling that's why the telecoms folks made sure we have very good connections to the global fibre optics networks. Mind you Scotland's Loch Fyne, was the first place in the world where they tested the subsea fibre optic cables that now connect the world for 95% of all international communications. So I guess that helps."

The evening then took a turn for the worse, as Chef Sandy and few others joined us, whisky bottles in hand and before long it became-appropriately it turned out, Whisky Galore. That's 'Whisky Galore' as in, 'Oh not again,' sighs of the locals who'd heard that phrase and the story way too many times all their lives.

But Chloe was more than sweetly polite, confirming or really reminding me that, 'Yes, Barra was indeed where the Compton Mackenzie book of the same name had been set.' Great story- and wonderful 1949- black and white-of course- movie telling the story of a shipwreck off the local coast. Nothing, too remarkable about that, except that on board there were 50,000 cases of fine Scots Whisky. So, much excitement, as crafty and thirsty locals set about salvaging and concealing the spoils, whilst the local customs and excise officers did their damndest to stop them. I happen to have seen the newer remake on a recent flight- and that's one of the delightful exceptions where the update is as good as the original.

So stupidly it became Whisky Galore for me, and when a few local musicians arrived, it went further down hill and my jet lag seemed to have gone. Although I managed to maintain my lifetime record of never dancing, had I known what the morning would bring, I would have been a little more careful...probably...but as it was..." Aye, well, since you insist-just a wee one."

Chapter 13. *Summer 2018. Harry in The Hebrides.*
Mrs McNeil's Miracle.

Harry Writes: I'm not a believer in boring the reader, or friends with tales of morning misery, such events are usually self inflicted. So I won't. The presumably Presbyterian, apparently abstemious, 'church once, if not twice' every Sunday, Mrs McNeil, nevertheless had a twinkle in her eyes as she handed me a steaming mug of tea at the little table in the sunlit alcove just outside her kitchen door.

"I'm hoping that young Mathew and his Chloe did'na lead you astray last night, it's often hard to tell what's in a glass in the evening light." she smiled and continued, "Based on your '*deep sleeping*'- and young Mathew not being here yet, I've delayed busying the breakfast for a few minutes- to let you wake up properly."

Whilst I sat-and enjoyed both the air and the welcome cup of real tea-I was considering the awful truth of her, '*based on your deep sleeping,*' and wishing that the old adage '*snoring is one thing you can't catch your self doing,*' wasn't quite so precise, when she popped her head around the door and said, "Oh yes, one of the Police called on the telephone in the hall and said, "Would you give him a call."

She handed me a bit of paper with the names and numbers written, oh so neatly, in, I am sure, real ink not an old biro or scrawly pencil. Not actually needing her nicely described 'telephone in the hall' as I used my mobile, and having been put through to 765, whom I now knew to be James Brydon, the real world arrived with a bang.

" Morning, Jimmy here. Change of plans for this morning. We're sending a chopper to pick you up in about an hour, and I'm just off collecting your friend Mr Focks and we'll be on our way to meet you in Oban. Hope that's OK? We were going to go through a few photos to see if they ring any bells but automation and events have overtaken us. I assume Bird man Matt filled you in last night, that we think we may well have found an ID for your man Jerry?"

Hardly waiting for my muttered, "Yes." he continued, "Well we've had a few developments since then, I'll give you the full SP now, if that's OK ?" Without waiting for a reply from me he carried on, " Last night I was reading the report of a traffic accident that yon man Jerry apparently had near Fort William a year or so back. Although Jerry had the accident, a woman, who we now know to be American, had the rental contract for the vehical which was a Land Rover, and gave her address as a cottage near there. I noticed in the police report that the woman driver, her name is Theresa Smith by the way, so a relative we assume. On her passport she's listed as an ornithologist."

" When I mentioned this to Matt late last night, I think you'd taken to your bed by then, he said that he knew the area as there used to be ospreys or something regularly nesting there for some years. Apparently it's a well known site for all kinds of wild birds - so ornithologist sounds likely. Seems many of the birds are tagged, some even with satellite tracking and microchips and stuff, so the whereabouts of almost all breeding pairs are known, at least to McButton types."

"Then even later last evening, having noted that the huge estate that cottage is on, is probably owned by a Russian, I say probably, as the real ownership will be buried behind various offshore companies, I really knew the name rang a bell with me. Then Rory - your driver from yesterday- who's better on the computer than me came up with the answer."

" Back in March 2016 that estate had a break in and four sporting rifles were stolen, as far as I can see not when yon Jerry was in the country. Any ways the guns were recovered a few months ago, dumped in a ditch, as being too hot to handle I would think, so we took them off our current list of worries. It turned out that the rifles weren't properly registered or licensed for temporary import here, which is a very serious matter. So when the matter came to court the estate manager claimed a couple of guests had left them behind- 'but were soon to return.' "

"The local magistrate took a dim view of all that and set a massive fine and banned the estate and the estate manager from holding any weapons for a few years. That's why I mentioned the ownership can be international but the gun licensing has to be local, so what's why the estate manager took the blame."

" I called up the local constable up that way, got him out of bed I think. He'd been the one dealing with both the traffic accident and also the affair of the stolen rifles and he said two interesting things. One that the woman who had rented the cottage had stayed using it for quite a few years, as she was making a film about eagles. He said she was quite well known in the village and had even given some talks about the birds to the local schools. She also had an alibi for the night of the theft, as she was abroad somewhere."

" Then Constable Foster really spoiled my evening, and this is the bit that makes the helicopter urgent, he's heard there's long been a rumour around the villages and cattle markets that actually it was six rifles - not four - that went missing. So that's put them straight back on the bloody list again. Oh yes -and he knows the woman was still here in January this year, as she had been in to the police office to sort out the final papers on the driving offence."

"So a lot for you to take onboard and all before Mrs McNeil's Miracle, as the chief constable calls her restorative breakfast. If Matt's been able to re-organise his day's teaching then he'll come with us and take a quick look at that cottage. It will be good to have him with us in case there's any eagle stuff we need to look at. "

"It's also not very popular with farmers and Ghillie's to have a bloody great black and yellow police chopper landing amongst their grouse or deer- so the more good reasons we have to be there the better. "

I was just about to ask some questions when Jimmy continued... "With Russian estate owners, stolen and found again rifles, and a possible sighting of your man Jerry, and ornithologists it was all enough for even the Chief to agree it makes the cost of the chopper worthwhile. Also it seems lives may be at stake." Before I could ask my questions he concluded, " See you later." and rang off.

With fine timing, I heard and then saw Matt's old Landrover arrive, and after a few minutes Matt emerged from the kitchen carrying two mugs of tea. As I ventured 'Thanks for last night," he just raised a hand to his head, saying, "Have you spoken to Jimmy ?"

My nod brought a smile of relief, "I dinna think that man ever sleeps. He was on my phone at nearly midnight last night and again at 6.15 this morning. Which, after last night's fun, didn't help negotiations when I had to persuade Chloe to guide my paddle board bookings for today and tomorrow, and to take care of Percy and the other animals so I could come with you. "

"Mind you the clincher was, when I suggested she came with you in the helicopter instead...nothing personal. She just hates helicopters."

As he said 'helicopters' Mrs McNeil came out with two very full looking plates, and catching what he said. "Mathew, you'll call my nephew and remind him he promised no more helicopters in my field ever again. After the last time -Mrs Fairman still claims all her daytime unmentionables and other washing were blown across the sea to Glasgow."

Between hysterics, hangover and handing round the toast, and me noting there were real saute'd spuds, not the evil of hash browns, Matt assured Mrs McNeil, the chopper would be on the beach and not in her garden at about 10.00. Apparently satisfied, our fearsome but really very twinkly breakfast chef left us to it, with Matt whispering to me, "Did she do her usual, 'I heard you deep sleeping' thing?"

Which at least made me feel a tad better, about snoring the house down. It was the absolutely best breakfast ever...but sadly from now on, fewer lifestyle details in this tale.(*Ed Goodbye from me then...probably!*)... Just a focus on the facts, as 765- sorry- Chief Inspector Jimmy Brydon- had just said, "*Lives may be at stake.*"

Chapter 14. Scottish Summer 2018.
'Aye. It's a braw day for flyin'.

Focksy's tales: It wasn't till I was tucking in to my solo hotel breakfast, at about seven thirty in the morning that I realised that I hadn't turned my phone on. Very unusual, for me, but so, these days at least, is sleeping for almost twelve hours on top of my bedclothes - fully dressed. Sober.

The jet lag, and I guess the more than stressful conversations of the last few days had caught up with me. Messages and missed calls there were many. The main ones being from Jimmy the policeman saying: *'Change of plans, if it was OK with me, he'd come by the hotel and pick me up soon after eight as 'he wanted to check up on some information that had come in over night.'*

That closely followed by another from Jimmy saying, *'Oh yes, we'd be going by helicopter, so bring an overnight bag in case the weather closes in.'* Given that I hadn't even gotten as far as the toast and marmalade yet and it was already 7.30 I sent him an SMS saying. *'Will be ready and in reception from eight'* and bolted down the rest of my breakfast as quick as I could.

I also noted one from Harry saying. *'Me working not sleeping. Police now saying lives possibly at risk, so we taken seriously I guess. See you later.'*

I noted that was timed just a few minutes before I reconnected to the world, so obviously he's awake and probably knows more about what's going on than I do. I suspect it also means there will be more smug 'I was working not sleeping' from him.

Exiting a hotel with an overnight bag, but keeping one's room, fully intending to return (thank you TNoTN expenses) is never easy, as usual the nice people at the desk -politely concerned- needed some reassurance that I wasn't doing a runner without paying. Sadly I didn't get a chance to look back and see their faces, when a full on white police Range Rover turned up, blue yellow and red marking all over, blue lights on the top. Rather assuming it was for me I wandered outside.

Handshakes, several. "Sleep?"..."Yes fine- thanks-obviously needed it...Sorry about turning off the phone. " and with the door hardly shut and me still finding my seat belt, we were away, with Jimmy saying, "Aye. It'll be a braw day for flying."

Well that's as may be, but still tasting my moments before breakfast, let alone digesting it, the thought of a harum scarum ride to Glasgow Airport was not very high on my current bucket list. Although if the flight then turned out to be bumpy- a bucket would be the best answer.

I'm not sure if it was the effect of 'The Big Sleep' or I am just a bit thick, but Jimmy's then saying , "Not Glasgow this morning, we'll drive up and meet the others at the little airport in Oban, that's about three hours along the road," just induced a nod and shrug from me.

Jimmy continuing, "Sorry about the rush, but there's a lot occurring. I've already shared what we have with Mr Buckle, so I'll give you a quick update. Overnight, with some facial recognition stuff we have on test at the airports and docks, planning for Brexit I imagine, we think we have found a good image match for your Jerry Smith. With the name matching also. We found a few more details, such as him staying with a Theresa Smith as he had a traffic accident when he was here."

" Back in February 2016, he came in to Shannon Ireland from Colorado Springs via New York. A few days later he flew Dublin to Edinburgh on Ryan Air and two weeks later in the first week of March on the 5th he made a quick return trip to Bordeaux returning here on the 8th. Those dates he was away are important as that's when we had a theft of some rifles up near where he was staying. I'll tell you about that in a moment, but for now it seems from the gun theft investigation papers the Smith woman-his sister or wife- flew out to Bordeaux with him and returned with him, although I don't have access to the paperwork yet."

I interrupted, saying ,"Sounds like the right person, and I do recall him saying he had a sister."

Jimmy continued..."But then we have no departure details for him from the UK, which, with our systems here is not that unusual, but is embarrassing as we also have him noted as arriving back in again in late Feb. The next year. This time Boise Idaho to

Denver and then a few days later on Norwegian Air, Denver to Gatwick. Again a few days in Ireland, and on to Edinburgh."

" I canna recall if I told you or Mr Buckle any detail of that accident in 2016. It was quite serious, up near Fort William, and the reason it's on our files is that a cyclist was injured. The Landrover was rented by the woman and actually, you're right, the alibi notes from the gun robbery and the accident notes show her to be his sister."

" On her passport she's listed as an ornithologist. By the time it was decided, almost a year later, as that cyclist had been injured in the accident, that there might be a prosecution, the court papers were sent to Jerry Smith, as the driver, at the cottage the woman had rented, but he had gone by then. But then last night I spoke to a local officer in Fort William, dragged him out of bed I think, and he added a few interesting things. "

"Firstly the Smith woman is still here, or at least was here a couple of months back, as she had called in at the police station to sort out the driving offence. Someone's scribbled 'insurance' in the margins of the file, so nothing unusual there."

" Secondly, he confirmed that the cottage- which is way out of my area- is one of several on an estate where there had been a break in at the big house, and those four sporting rifles stolen. "

"The guns were recovered, quite quickly, dumped in a ditch a while back so that took them off the worry list. Or they were off the list until last night when Constable Foster told me there were growing rumours in the village that it was six rifles stolen- not just the four that were recovered. No hard evidence just 'village gossip."

" By the way, we did get some finger prints from that paper that fell out of your note book, so there may be some prints to compare with at the cottage. It's about five miles from any public road, but does have a long rough but drivable track to it- if you've got a Landrover I guess. As part of the bird protection mafia, McButton knows the Estate Ghillie and the area, so he's coming in with your colleague on the chopper from Barra."

With much talk of Ghillie's, stolen guns, and even when we passed near Dunblane, of the appalling school massacre. Inspector

Jimmy, telling me that top tennis player Andy Murray and his brother James were pupils in the school on that fateful day.

The three hours to Oban passed -if not very pleasantly- but fast enough. We pulled into the airport car park- just as they were refueling the yellow and black helicopter that had collected Matt and Harry from Barra.

As we waited , Jimmy got a call from the MI5 or 6 lady, telling him that her US contacts had responded to her notifying them about Jerry, with a simple.' Your concerns noted, we will respond soonest.' Which, Jimmy, found a little lacking in urgency, "But then again they probably had a lot of people to check, America's a big place."

I did remark that, "Based on the Chief Constable's words yesterday, he'd quite like it if the local force here could put one over on the Yanks." Jimmy smiled, and said, "At the end of today, depending on what we learn, we'll need to circulate an update to all agencies, on the threat position. Most likely including yon man Jerry and now including attack by birds- given that Matt has confirmed it could be a reality. Just as you explained when you came in to us, I'm feeling a bit of trepidation about likely reactions to the eagles bit of the report. Also, quite frankly between us, I suspect the Chief's not going to be too pleased about the possibility of more rifles still being unaccounted for."

With Matt installed sitting next to the lady pilot, "Another one," said Harry, which he explained to me later, Jimmy suggested Harry and I took window seats in the back saying, "There's some of the finest sights in all of Scotland to be seen out there."

We took off over the sea, but then turned inland. Around twenty minutes later, having seen acres of plantation pinewoods, a lot of wind farms, and indeed some spectacular, and very empty looking highland moors the Pilot brought the helicopter down about 100 meters from a collection of buildings. The situation then became a tad more 'real' as Jimmy insisted we exit from the chopper by the door furthest away from the cottage and out buildings, and stay where we were, keeping the helicopter between us and them. "We're not sure what kind of welcome we'll receive."

He scanned the buildings with a pair of binoculars, and then, as a quad bike with two people on it came round from the rear of a barn, relaxed. "OK, that's Constable Foster from Oban. He wasn'a too happy at six this morning when I told him to meet us here, this place being bloody miles from the proper road, so I guess he's got the Ghillie to bring him on the quad bike. The Ghillie being here actually helps a bit on the legality of entering the cottage."

Introductions for us, with Matt already knowing the Ghillie, and it turned out that the local copper, Richard Foster, was actually Matt's partner Chloe's brother. So small world, made smaller by helicopter. Jimmy introduced Focksy and I to the Ghillie, as being 'concerned with the car accident insurance and a few other matters from a few years back,' which perhaps would have been better had he told us in advance, but as he spoke, he had given us a broad wink of apology.

As we wandered across the scrubby heather to the cottage, to be quite frank, I wondered if I had inherited Harry's regional accent deafness. Between Matt, Constable Foster, Jimmy and the Ghillie- the accents and local wordage- seemed to have entered a whole new linguistic field, although Harry did then kindly whisper to me the meaning of 'Tattie Bogle.'

As Matt and the Ghillie, took the quad bike across to a fairly tumbledown looking building in the shadows of a small stand of trees a few hundred yards away, Harry and I took a quick look around the cottage. Nice enough, very spartan and very damp- but I guess it had been empty for some time.

Leaving space for the two policemen to check around in detail, we found a seat in the sun at an outside table. Now, despite having been hatched in rural Ireland, I spent my schooldays in New York and Shanghai China so I am very much a city guy, and Harry very much a beach and country dweller. But as the sound of the quad bike faded, apart from the odd word we we could not quite overhear from inside the cottage, it became very silent. A few birds, not much sound from not much wind.

I ventured, "I have to say, Harry, I've always wondered about your liking for farm life- but I must say this is very nice. Big sky's, good sun, seems like a fine place to unwind or write a book."

Harry's response surprised me. "Right now Focksy, it's idyllic, but, being neither an eagle nor a Highland red deer, between the midges, the rain and snow, long dark windy winter nights -this place is not at all on my wish list. Take me back to your place in Thailand anytime," he paused, "or by the Atlantic rollers on a beach in Cornwall."

Whilst it seemed much ornithological and detective work went on around us we continued chatting for a good hour as he updated me on his Barra findings and what sounded like an excellent evening. We were then joined by the pilot, carrying a wicker hamper. "Lunch," she grinned," We share a hanger and offices at Glasgow Heliport with a Heli tours and shooting company, so organising a picnic lunch was matter of moments, and a little bit of trading with some extra footie tickets that we had."

"Couldn't quite run to their usual champagne though."

"But there's flasks of boiling water in there, for a brew. These chopper's have a couple of special power outlets for spotlights or medical kit, so the Heli tours team have their kettles wired up to the same plug sizes. Actually seems that hot drinks, are as much in demand amongst grouse shooters or deer stalkers when they get picked up, as the champagne or the drams."

Having done a 'told you so' nod to me about the need for hot drinks, Harry then ventured on to what seemed to me these days very dangerous ground, in suggesting that a male pilot might not have had the foresight to organise a picnic lunch.

A comment that I feared could go very wrong, but then he explained that his pilot the previous day had also been a lady, the conversation moved on to how these days it was very much an equal opportunity job. Seemed our pilot had been a nurse with an Air Ambulance service and had loved flying so much she had then spent four years-'and a lot of money borrowed and risked' qualifying as pilot. "We're not actually employed by the Police, we work for a helicopter company that provides the services to them."

Whether it was the sight of the sandwiches or our slightly steaming mugs of tea that attracted them, but we soon joined by the other four. The Ghillie only briefly, as he had to go and feed some animals, and we were apparently dropping Constable Foster back near his car when we left.

Our Pilot, had discretely wandered back to the chopper, leaving our conversations private- telling us- 'Don't forget the picnic stuff, and all the rubbish when you're done.'

To our slight surprise, much had been discovered. First of all, Jerry's original fingerprints on my notebook page, did match some found in the house. The cottage was completely clean of possessions- so despite having paid the rental through until the start of this years grouse shooting season in mid August, it looked like they were gone for good.

Having asked how the hell they managed to check the various fingerprints so quickly, we learned that, there was a good mobile phone signal, even way out here in the wilds, with repeater aerials probably paid for by the estate to keep their wealthy shooting clients happy. So Jimmy and Richard had dusted for prints, photographed and then emailed details back to the experts at HQ and received the ID results back almost by return.

Matt's revelations were also interesting, although, we agreed they could have put us off the sandwiches if we hadn't been famished. "There's evidence in that wee bothy over there, that someone was doing some hawking or falconry. In fact from the bird droppings left around- I'd say they were eagles, as there's not so many feathers in the droppings."

"There's stands there, and traces of them all being used, possibly for five or more birds. Although I canna' believe anyone could fly five birds up here without anyone noticing, but it would or could explain why the ospreys that used to nest just over that range of hills for years, got moved on, as eagles are quite territorial. "

" Then again, Angus the Ghillie also told me that although he or his people are supposed to check all areas of the estate weekly, that after they had the break in and those guns stolen, two of his three assistants, had been spooked by all the attention and had left. The one guy that remained, who is Angus's brother by the way, stays up this way - well ten miles away- but he had smashed his quad bike and his leg, pissed one night."

I could see Constable Foster nodding in agreement at all this, as Matt continued, "So in reality it could have been at least six months that no one was up here regularly, except for the rental lady and a few hikers passing through. The couple who have followed the ospreys and the eagles around these hills for years, have gone to the Himalayas trekking, I'll send them an e mail, but goodness when or if I'll get a response."

Jimmy started to raise a warning hand, but Matt said, "I'll check the mail first with Richard so I don't put my foot in it." Jimmy's raised hand was transformed to a thumbs up... and Matt continued, " They've also had little or no deer stalking or grouse shooting for two seasons, because of all the licensing troubles."

He turned to Harry and I, " Bothys and cottages are only usually available outside the main shooting seasons, so the Smiths were either lucky to keep this one, or the Russian owners are working with them."

Jimmy said," The office called whilst Richard and I were doing the fingerprinting. I checked the dates again, and both the Smith woman and Jerry returned here a few days after the robbery when the investigation was in full swing."

Jimmy, took a sip of his tea, and said," Inverness Police, this side of the Caledonia Canal is all their area, would have been delighted with any alibis quickly removing two suspects. Quite correctly so back then , but now we need to look and consider if their 'trip away ' was a contrived convenience. There's a note on the file that says the rental for this place was always paid with travelers cheques. So finding clues from the banking and travelers cheques will be possible, but will take a time. Richard's going to visit the estate office this afternoon and recheck the rental files."

Matt then said, "There's two more things, in both cases I'm not sure if this is good news or bad, but I suspect they are both quite interesting. Angus and I dug these out of an old plank of wood up there" and he revealed half a dozen rather mangled bullets. Jimmy and Richard instantly did the, 'Don't touch them any more, there could be fingerprints.'

As Matt started to apologise, "Sorry guys' I should have thought of fingerprints," Focksy interrupted saying, "In all my life of reporting on gun crime, I don't think I've ever known good prints to be found on the actual slugs, only on the cartridge cases."

Jimmy added, "Actually you're right Focksy, but we canna' be too careful, but I will drop them in a wee bag here and get them checked. So sorry Matt for interrupting, what was your second point?" Matt, stabbed at his phone and held it up so we could see the screen..." Seems to be the remains of four quite life like Tattie Bogles stored up there." There was a stunned silence around the table...just those few birds and the breeze to be heard...

Jimmy seemed slightly underwhelmed with Matts scarecrow revelation- saying, " God. Thanks Matt. I can just picture the scene, security folk from the around the world, CIA, NSA, MI 5 and 6, Special Branch, the SAS and only God knows who else...all with their latest crypto reports, spycams, satellite images, sniper trajectories, bomb sniffing robots and hi tech hardware of all kinds: and then it comes to me...and from Scotland... Officer Jimmy bloody Brydon, and I have to report our main concern is all about scarecrows... Tattie Bogles and eagles...Thank you for nothing."

I thought I might be pushing it a bit when I said, "And don't forget Jimmy, you might have mislaid a couple of sniper rifles somewhere..."

As we packed up the lunch rubbish, Jimmy's response of, "Mr Schnauzer, remember you are my invited guest on that big black and yellow helicopter, and if you keep recalling difficult facts, I am minded to leave you here...and it's a more than a wee walk home," was fortunately accompanied by a broad grin, as he continued, "Time to move on I think, we don't want the pilot running out of hours, so I'll just take a one final look around the cottage and we'd best be away." '

Matt having been away on the quad bike, took a quick look around the cottage and turned up something else interesting. In a log store at the back he found a wooden box frame with some oldish looking cables coiled over it. Jimmy saying, " When I saw that earlier I wondered if they were growing a bit of marijuana up here to pass the time, but I decided we had enough more important things to worry about."

Matts response that, "I think it's an old egg incubator."

This time produced a rather more positive reaction than his previous revelations, Jimmy saying, "Well at least that's a bit more factual than piles of bird shit."

He and Richard having photographed the incubator and decided they'd get it collected later, partly due to it not being very very easy to lug on to the helicopter, and partly because they 'd need the Ghillie's or someones permission to remove it.

Having dropped, Constable Foster back at his car, with Matt, their plan being to have chat with a few villagers and the lady in the local shop, Matt saying, "I'll visit my mum in Oban and get the ferry back to Barra tomorrow."

We three, Jimmy, Harry and I had 'the luxury,' of a flight direct back to Edinburgh. Jimmy explaining, "A luxury, because with the flying cost per hour, there's all sorts of budgets, requisitions and permissions to go through in order to use the chopper."

" But with these," he waved the bag of bullets, "needing urgent checking before Mr Trump arrives, I'm giving myself that permission, " adding with a broad grin, "and that also means we'll be home for tea, or a drop of something stronger."

So it was, that just over an hour later, just a few minutes drive from the Edinburgh Airport helipad we were a dropped off by another brightly marked police car back at the hotel.

We agreed to return to the bar, and probably the restaurant, after all, Cullen Skink is designed for those who've spent a healthy day out striding across the highlands.

Helicopters optional I guess.

Chapter 15. *Scotland & NY..NY. 2018.*

The people are revolting...*or in the UK, they were demonstrating. Harry reports: The Summer of 2018 visit to the UK by US President Trump brought huge numbers of protestors out on to the streets.* Big enough crowds for him to have boasted about had they been at his inauguration...and big enough for the Brits to be forced into arranging a schedule that, in the main, kept him well out of the way.

Jimmy came round to our hotel for a beer on the evening that the President arrived in London, telling us that the US security liaison people had denied all knowledge of Jerry and had merely thanked the Scots police politely for the fingerprints.

He had run the various prints and photos' through the Interpol system-and again drawn a blank. Apparently Interpol hold the worlds largest database for lost and stolen travel documents and 'no alarm bells rang over Jerry's details'.

With the President being kept well away from protestors in and around London, few demonstrators likely even caught a glimpse of their target. "Here in Scotland", as Jimmy explained, "As the Turnberry golf course is the only place that the Scots could actually catch a glimpse of the President, I expect a huge turnout there over the weekend."

Despite no alarms being raised on Jerry by the Yanks or elsewhere, and also despite, we suspected, our Eagle's warning being ignored, Jimmy and presumably his various Chiefs were concerned enough to get Harry and I to spend a good few hours looking for Jerry's face, on recordings and the live TV broadcasts around the President's two golfing mornings.

So a remarkably repetitive and boring 24 hours really, that actually makes you wonder how effective security cameras are. Only as good as those looking at them I suppose, which brings us back to the urgency for those developing auto recognition systems.

The only real excitement of the President's visit being when a Greenpeace protester, ignoring the declared 'no fly zone' buzzed low over the Golf club terrace in a para glider-carrying a protest banner, forcing the President to smartly move indoors.

The word around Police HQ was that, "The Chief's hopping mad about that, saying,' it makes us look stupid'," Jimmy said as we took our leave of him, " The boss is right, that could have been a lot worse, the pilot could have dropped a bloody grenade or something and taken out all the people on the terrace, including the President. Does confirm the need to be ready for anything though. It also means that-if they try that again when the President visit's, forget him being shot- that flyer- Greenpeace Flag or no Greenpeace flag will get a bullet up the backside."

He thanked us, for sharing what we had with them, saying, "I have a feeling in my bones you're on to something."

When Harry pointed out that media reports suggested it was dodgy Russian money behind the Trump golf projects so we may well return with a different story to follow up, Jimmy did one of his trademark sighs and shrugs...saying, "I've had enough of you two...away with you now, back to New York, before you spoil more of my week, or I'm tempted to retire to Thailand."

Despite me informing my office about the basics of the potential story I was getting under increasing pressure to get back to the US and explain things. So Harry and I decided that rather than follow the President to his meeting with Vladimir Putin in Helsinki, where there'd be a TNoTN news crew anyway, that we'd get the first available Monday flight to New York.

As it happens that TNoTN crew were kept well busy reporting on Trump's secret one on one conversations with Putin which later grabbed weeks of headlines cross the US, as did the word from London- that John Bolton had mentioned- Trump had thought Finland was part of Russia.

With Edinburgh, being a smallish city, despite being the capital of Scotland and home to the Scots Parliament, we were surprised to find four choices of direct flight to New York. Harry and I chose United, as they flew in to EWR Newark, which for my apartment is way more convenient than JFK.

Before we left we had a long phone conversation with Matt McButton, explaining we were leaving but wanted to keep up to date with local events and relevant news. So I offered him £150 a month retainer for some part time freelance work as a researcher-making it clear that anything he found out, must be exclusive for TNoTN. He seemed more than happy to accept.

The reality - as Harry and I discussed, is that whilst the current core of the story seemed to be here in Scotland, it would soon switch to the USA, and whilst Matt might come up with some local stuff, the main advantage for us was that it should discourage him from contact with any rival news teams.

With an early morning departure, a flight time of only just over seven hours and of course the time change, by lunchtime New York time Harry and I were having a reviving cup of tea on my terrace overlooking the Hudson River and the skyline of Manhattan island. Thirty years ago I had stretched myself financially and bought my apartment in an old riverside warehouse conversion, in Weehawken, New Jersey.

Ten years back, depending on who tells the story, I became good friends, but not romantically linked with my neighbour Maisie Todd. Harry's wife desperately wants it to be like the classic TV adverts where love blossoms between neighbours over shared cups of coffee.(Yes they have those commercials on Thai TV also.) As it happens she's probably more correct than she'll ever know, but Masie is younger and wiser than me, and instead has become one of my closest friends.

She's in the TV business as well, as a freelance stylist and now director. She's mainly connected to a different network than I am, and of course as she's more into lifestyle features and I'm mostly news and politics, there are very few occasions when we're rivals. So when trouble flares up it usually only requires intervention with a peacemaking glass or two of wine to sort it.

When I moved 'over the river' many of my chums thought I was mad, leaving the fashionable parts of the city, but from the Weehawken pier, just short stroll away, I had and still have a choice of ferries, running from early till late to several Manhattan destinations. The most frequent being to the Mid Town Ferry terminal where there are always cabs waiting...and I have the river views, which are sunset spectacular at night and I get the sunrise reflected on the buildings across the river in the mornings.

So never a moment's regret, although with a useful branch of Harry's favourite steak house chain, Ruth's Chris, right by the pier, and some great old style New York- or rather 'New Jersey' style Italian restaurants just around the corner in Hoboken, I sometimes fear we'll never get rid of him.

Despite our best intentions of getting straight back to work, I talked to Maisie, who was in Europe, researching a thriller to be made about fake olive oil smuggling. Seemed located in rural Greece, Tuscany and Provence -such a hard life those features folks have. I then leafed through a pile of Sunday papers that had accumulated in my month away- whilst Harry had crashed out and was 'Singha song' in, albeit beerless, Thai fashion on the sofa.'

When I woke him, apart from him claiming that my air-conditioning had given him a sore throat and stiff neck, he said,' I'll go have a snooze on the bed...right now I might be in New York, but no one's told my sleep systems where the hell I am yet."

Chapter 16. *NY..NY..Summer 2018*
So good you see them twice:

Focksy writes: Even though the view of the city, and then the repeat with the lights reflecting on the river was oh so familiar to me it was still good to take a moment and let it all sink in.

As it happens, depending on the time of year, with daylight saving and all that stuff, six in the evening Thai time, is around midday 'Scot's' time, and all that is around six in the morning New York eastern time. So after what then turned out to be almost twelve hours dead to world for both of us, I found Harry, with both evening wine glass and breakfast coffee mug at the ready, on the terrace, watching the late night lights of the city across the river.

The first issue was: Harry couldn't make the Wi-Fi work, and it took us both a good few minutes to bloody figure it out. Again.

Just before I'd departed to Thailand a month earlier, TNoTN in their wisdom had decided that with scanners and new technology all our communications were at risk. Some boffin, let's spell and pronounce that, buffoon, probably more highly paid than most of us, but, 'obviously not of the real world' had decided that all our passwords would in future change at midnight daily.

The new log on required the addition or subtraction of a number involving the date and the second letter of the day of the week, except for Sundays where the second letter was x.

Quite how this buffoon had expected this to operate where TNoTN folks were reporting hot news 24/7 , from a zillion time zones around the world, and they all needed to log on to the home system I do not know. Complaints there were many, reactions from 'the bosses upstairs' there were none. The suggestion around the office was that they also weren't getting the messages...

When he was staying with me in Chiang Mai, Harry, had noted my problems with the system saying, "Seems to me that the Hilary Clinton method of using your personal e mail for most business when out of the office is a fine way to work."

Eventually, we were into the system , and thirty seconds later Harry let out a long breath and said... "Focksy, we've got a long mail here from Matt Mc Button, looks like he's taking his researchers expenses deal very seriously."

From : Matt Mc B. To: Harry / Mr Schnauzer.

I'm on the Oban to Barra Ferry, and will send this when I get home. Was good to meet you both. Trust flights were good. I tried to call you yesterday morning but you had checked out. Some catchups for you. Turned out that my Ma needed help with something so I stayed in Oban for an extra day.

Richard and I went back to the village near the cottage, and got a lot of facts and gossip. I guess he's reported direct to Jimmy, and I'm not sure of their policy on sharing info, so I'll update you myself...see No 5.

1. Theresa Smith, was making a documentary about eagles, to be called 'Up Where We Belong.' She and her mother had been staying around the area for almost three years.

In their years there they both got quite involved with the village primary school during that time, even taking a youngish eagle in there once. I asked if it was in a cage and it seemed she had it on her gloved arm, so I guess that proves some degree of Eagle training going on.

She told the teachers that Eagles, particularly the Bald Eagle of course and The Golden Eagle are sacred in the USA, with it being illegal even to keep found feathers, let alone the actual birds without a hard to get permit. She came to Scotland as she wanted to focus on Golden Eagles as part of a world wide look at hunting with birds.

**Back in Barra now, and Chloe has just showed me the links to the old Joe Cocker and Jennifer Warnes recording of 'Up Where We Belong' which I suppose is old style music you both probably know.'

2. The mum, who's name was Pamoon- call me Pam - apparently described herself at first to the kids in the school, as being ' Native American '. According to the head teacher, 'having got the kids attention- they were quite young as it's a junior school- she then went on to explain the various preferred ways to express that these days 'First American, Native American / indigenous people / persons' and suchlike. It's had for us to keep up with being correct...although, actually as she came from Canada, I suppose it could be Native North First American Indian, but, as a Scot, I'm not sure of all the exact correct details. Mind you as we Scots hate being called English, I can fully subscribe to the importance of getting it right. The shop lady said Jerry was Theresa's twin..

Harry interrupted my reading and said, "Here we go again- Jerry and Terri, still sounds quite cartoonish, but twin rings a bell although as the Scots cops have both their passport details we all should have figured that out...or maybe they did. So good stuff so far, despite his suggestion about our taste in golden oldies music."

Matt's mail continued: I mention that in the first year- that's 2016, the two women took a lot of time participating in activities at the village school who obviously absolutely loved them. The head teacher saying they had brought music, art, story telling and nature studies (as she, the head teacher called it) to life. I suppose that casts doubt on the idea that they were all up to no good, or they would have surely kept a low profile.

Then it seems clear that the mum- Pamoon-was more than a little confused. The headmistress said Theresa had confirmed that her mother - Pamoon- had seen some specialist doctors whilst in the USA and she had Alzheimer's or some similar dementia developing quite rapidly.

3. The village shop and post office lady, was a real old style gossip. When I mentioned Pamoon developing Alzheimer's , she said it became quite pronounced, fairly quickly but she always had a carer with her when she came down to the village. Partly as the carer, who she said was Spanish, or Terri drove the car. She also said that Terri Smith had loads of incoming post, mostly nature and scientific magazines. I guess she could see that from the packaging.

She was still getting stuff and wanted to know if we had a forwarding address. When Richard was looking through the uncollected mail, he found one from a travel company marked, ' Your next trip,' which he 'accidently' opened.. and bingo. He discovered it was offering discounts on Transatlantic crossings by ship for 2019. Nothing surprising there, but Rich spotted that the letter opened with 'As regular travelers with us.'

When he mentioned this in the shop, the woman just said, that Pamoon the mother hated flying, something to do with her dementia she thought. She also said, the Smiths must have more family at home in America, grandchildren she thought, as every time one of them went back to the States they'd cleared out her stock of Easter Egg chocolates.

Richard passed this on urgently to Jimmy last night, and he then told me this morning when he took me to the ferry. 'That it had answered a lot of questions.' It had showed up Jerry's missing departure dates, as several times he had also travelled back to the USA by sea on the Queen Mary 2, from Southampton to New York. Each time departing at the beginning of May.

4. Richard and I both went up to 'The Big House' where Hamish the Estate manager said both women had called in a few times to pay their electric bills, and also when they had problems with some slates blowing off the roof, and a water pump that had packed up. He described them as ideal tenants, wished he had more like them. He also said he was still holding their damage and security deposit, and didn't know where to send it

back to. Richard arranged for him to call in if the Smiths contacted the manager at any time to get it back. We figured that meant the ladies had left in a rush.

5.. Finally, the best bit, *and I understand Jimmy is under strict orders not to share this with the media, but as I tipped him off I thought I'd pass it on...Yesterday evening,* when Richard and I were in the pub, watching the repeated and repeated TV coverage of Trump departing to Finland from Prestwick Airport, I remembered that a few years back when I had got involved in advising on the use of Falcons (Peregrines and hybrid Gyr Falcons, actually- now that you are both Raptor experts), to scare away flocks of birds at Prestwick, that on the side of the main runway at the airport there's a memorial to Falconry.

It's called the Shaw Tower or Shaw Monument and was built three hundred years back. Fifty foot high, stone tower, circular stairs inside (crumbling a bit back then when I used them) going up to a viewing platform where the 'Laird of Shaw', who was getting on a bit and not able to follow the hunt any more, could view all his precious birds from the tower. You can see the tower quite well on google earth.

I mentioned this to Richard, saying that although the tower is in bad condition, I'd been up to the top, about five years ago and it was a great vantage point.

Given that Richard and I had had a pint or two by then I jokingly said, 'good vantage point for an eagle or a sniper.' Richard freaked out- and rushed outside to phone Jimmy immediately. When he took me to the ferry this morning, he only said that 'Thanks to me he'd made another useful call to Jimmy,' and it was so important he couldn't share the results even with me.'

So either it was just a good tip off, or they found something. If I hear anything I'll let you know, I can't ask Richard, as it puts him in an awkward place. All the best, Matt McB...Chloe sends her love to Harry.

Harry, looked up and said, or rather announced:

"Well quite a few answers and as many questions in that. But now, two urgent things for you Focksy. If Matt is suggesting that rifles have been found in, or are about to be found in, or even just that the Scots failed to check that old falconry tower, then surely you need to be alerting TNoTN, before some other operator in the TV news game gets a sniff of the story. Also at your birthday dinner Jerry remarked on what a brilliant shot he was with a hunting rifle."

His words, correct as they were, instantly removed any lingering desires for more sleep-but also required thought before action, so I played for time, asking, "You said there were two urgent things?"

Harry, who, is still rather more 'News is for tomorrow morning's printed papers,' than the ever breaking second by second, often speculative approach, needed by more modern 24/7 rolling news folk such as I, replied, " And I'm hungry."

Silence fell, only the distant sound of a siren of some kind in the 'City that never Sleeps,' across the water, and the deeper 'chugging thump' engine sounds coming from the shadowed outline of a largish boat as it passed along the river seven stories below us.

So the problem was , if I called Dan Groom, today's editor, at the TNoTN news desk and alerted them to the possibility there was a breaking news story about guns or even just 'items' found or even not looked for by the Scots, Brits or US security. This involving a stone tower at Prestwick airport, that would blow our chances of a major exposé of 'Jerry, mystery security man or assassin?'

We, couldn't even do a face saving 'Sources, as yet unconfirmed suggest that President Trump had a lucky escape when... ' as this would simply wake up our rivals.

I said to Harry, " I think that this time all I can do is risk telling Dan nothing till I see him tomorrow."

So hunger became the main story. Given the bizarre hours and travel schedules for both of us, Maisie and I have the luxury- of sharing a daily house keeper, name of Ermalinda. She's from Angola, and before you ask she does have a proper visa and all that stuff. Thanks to her efforts, inspection of the fridge revealed it well stocked with plenty of fresh basics, and with my oft quoted mantra being: provided you have pasta, water, a few cans of tomatoes and some cheese you can survive the end of the world. '

But here is not only 'The city that never sleeps', it is also 'Where temptation never rests,' and also the city that 'Never stops eating'. So the kitchen notice board was covered in menus offering multiple solutions to all those points. With the Lincoln Tunnel likely fairly traffic free at this time of the night we could have ordered national specialties from a hundred different cuisines located all over Manhattan Island and still had quick delivery.

But having agreed on the first principle, this was a late dinner - not an early breakfast- I knew just the Italian takeout in Hoboken to deliver, even after midnight.

Hardly time for Harry to set the terrace table, candles, and for me to open the wine and the door open system chimed.

As Harry unpacked the packages, Maisie called, an early start for her, setting out to drive from Tuscany across to Nice. Having wished her a safe journey and assured her there would be no romantic 'Lady and the Tramp' sharing one strand of spaghetti moment for Harry and I.

As he and I addressed both the food and the story, Harry spoke- or mumbled with a mouthful, "It seems to me that with events inevitably rolling on, and with your office and news desk likely to start pressuring you for more confirmation of facts or fiction- that we need to firm up what we've got and where we're going."

I nodded, as I was somewhat lasagned at the time, and he continued." Firstly: Except for Matt's rumour of 'something nasty in the old stone tower', which you and I have chosen to interpret as possibly finding more of those missing rifles, I think we should delete rifles and guns completely from our future research. Here in the USA they really are a non story."

Still lasagned, I realise now that apart from an airline breakfast which was obviously, by Harry's report of Mrs McNeil's Miracle not even qualified to be called breakfast-let alone a miracle, that I had eaten nothing for ages. So just another nod to Harry, with a thumbs up to show further participation and interest at least.

He continued, " I say that as there are probably more shotguns, rifles, pistols and military hardware with the potential for Presidential puncturing going missing every hour here in the US as go missing in a few years in Scotland, so much and so many that it really is a non story."

Fortunately, his pause, coincided with a slight moment of indecision on my part, having to choose between a lush slice of crusty garlic bread, or a slice or two of mozzarella and heirloom tomato. 'Heirloom' being the compulsory description of any random tomato these days in the USA *(Ed. Careful, focus on the bloody story, I'm still around)* so this time I was able to speak."I agree, so that means we need to focus on the Eagles."

Noting that Harry, who has been a bearded blokey for all of the forty years I've known him, was now wrestling, and losing ,the battle with those long stretchy strings of cheese that inhabit the best of pizza's, lasagnas and other Italian joys, I continued,

" I also agree I need to deliver something to TNoTN soon, so we need to try and overtake the events train, and focus as the old news paper editors used to say, on the WD40...Who, Why, Where , When and 'For God's sake How!"

Who?: Jerry. A US Government employee, ex employee, would be employee, or slightly deranged and possibly disgruntled opportunist. Harry, by now, in the main free of cheese string, just the odd snack lurking in his beard, then made the Jerry listing longer by adding, " Or he could now be a mercenary engaged by one of the insulted shithole nations. "

Why?: Political rivalry here at home, although physical assault is a bit OTT for most of them despite concerns by many over potential damage to the name and business of USA Inc.

Where: That wonderful Brit newspaper, ' The Guardian' referred to *'Homebody Trump, packing his ketchup'* to travel internationally. So with the President pissing off most of the rest of the world, nation by shithole *(Ed. You've done that shithole bit already)* nation, it appears increasingly likely that the Donald would remain in the USA. At least for a while.

So for Where? We currently just list. Golf courses.

When: TBC. We are trying to report not influence, so 'sooner rather than later' is an inappropriate answer to this one.

How: This really becomes a multiple choice question, and you really don't need all the options repeated here.

Harry, has many skills and one of them, which he actually learned from his kids, is operating a real deal espresso coffee machine. Not the little home ones 'squish squash a sachet' into steam, but the full on, two three or even four station Gaggia, as used by the best baristas from Rome to Rio. I had been given such a gleaming gem for my fiftieth birthday...and it turned out that whilst he was raiding my fridge earlier for wine, Harry had already refilled my machine with fresh water and turned it on.

So I rewrote the abbreviated listing , whilst he cleared the dirty dishes, and then delivered some of the best coffee I had had in the past month... bit even that couldn't lift my sense of,' what if?

The reality is, the mega news organisations of the world, in conjunction with tens of thousands of security experts are daily, hourly, minute by minute concerned with finding, stopping or reporting any and all legal and illegal realities that can make POTUS into EXPOTUS, a DEADPOTUS, or even as previously mentioned : a DEADEXPOTUS. So it's very unlikely that the combined resources of just us two, are going to break *that* story first.

Harry has now started thinking Jerry's clues, no matter if deliberate or accidental slips under the influence of alcohol, are pointers to a mercenary hired by an indignant or enemy nation.

'Take Care America, no matter how hard you try with all your millions and your technology or military bully boy tactics, the old world ways and right will triumph over might in the end.'

I pointed out to Harry that his 'Take Care America' wording sounded both like the opening to a modern computer game, and the tabloid reporting of Al Qaeda- ISIS type rumours.

By now the Eastern skys were lighting up the horizon, although the city light pollution tends to blur the 'in-between' bits of day and night. Minute by minute the sound of traffic across the river and on the river was increasing as the commuters on the road and on their morning ferries arrived to kick start New York's business day.

Harry and I decided that whilst I went and showed my face in at TNoTN, he'd focus on trying to find out more about Jerry's sister and mom...and he'd also write up the Thailand to Scotland part of the story to see if it delivered any more useful memories or clues.

Chapter 17.   *Big Apple Tales Summer 2018*
Stop the World I want to Get On.

*Focksy Reports: Reading the morning papers, or at least
checking the front pages, as I sat on the ferry and then in my cab to
my TNoTN office, as usual one could imagine that the rest of the
world had disappeared.*

No mentions of deadly floods in India, earthquakes in
Lombok and Japan. A hobby drone attack narrowly missing
President Maduro of Venezuela, Elections in Germany. Not even
much on Chinas growing business influence investing all over Africa
and many other countries. Nary a scary headline about Brexit.

As usual the US media was us, us, us, or more accurately
U.S. U.S. U.S. To question that narrow focus was to invite an
onslaught of viewer/ listener/ reader accusations of being Anti-
Uncle Sam, even when there were positive lessons to be learned
from 'abroad' and even better business for America Inc to be had out
there in the big world.

It was in this very insular situation for most of mainland
USA, and with a focus on 'America First' that, confounding the
'know it all' pollsters, pundits and politicos of Washington and
beyond, that Donald Trump was elected.

Despite all the media tears, tantrums and claims of
'Collusion,' ' We was cheated' and 'He had help from The Russkies'
(even if he hadn't asked them for help) 'The Donald' - with his
simplistic and often incorrect claims and tweets was doing just fine.
His support base was legitimately increasing, so a victory of 'Power
to the People' in wresting control away from the Washington
Political Elite.

As for the US media ignoring the rest of the world, in reality
they had no space for anything that wasn't Trump, mostly either
violently Anti or enthusiastically Pro. Mind you name calling,
accusations of corruption, philandering, telling lies, vote buying and
blatant support for certain 'friendly or usefully located' businesses
was and is nothing new in US politics. I always loved the old, but
overused Adlai Stephenson quote- *'I will make a bargain with the
Republicans. If they stop telling lies about Democrats, we will stop
telling the truth about them'.*

Even President Kennedy, also somewhat dubiously elected was quoted as saying- *'The worse I do, the more popular I get.'*

The only difference now, and it's an important one, is that since the turn of this century, the stories and reports both fake and fact are globally available in seconds...and social media is now the main source of both news and opinion here. So it is rather easy for outrage to fan the flames of bigotry...especially when the President himself sets so many fires with his inflammatory Tweets.

As I fumbled for cash to pay the cab, I was pondering what would happen if indeed an assassin of any kind 'took out' the President. When Kennedy was shot, the world recoiled, wept and respectfully mourned.

If Trump becomes 'Late', I really can't resist that Botswanan way of putting things, I suspect that apart from an initial degree of sympathy for his young son Barron, and I suppose for any other 'offspring' yet to be revealed, the general reaction on the streets of the USA will be a mix of celebration and armed anger.

Obviously the media have contingency stories in place ready for the death of Kings and Queens, Presidents, sport heroes, real media stars and more transient celebrities. Should something happen, in Trump's case, the mainstream media will start out by being factual. That followed, I assume in unseemly haste, by two faced, insincere politicos of all sides saying, 'Well we disliked him and disagreed with his policies' but this is a step too far.' Whilst rubbing their hands with glee-carefully off camera.

Then of course they will blame, The Russians, The North Koreans, The Iranians, The Mafia, Al Qaeda or Isis, those Shithole Nations, various 'deranged persons' or as they used to be called, 'madmen'...and last of all, shock horror, as usual, The CIA.

Pausing at a cart on the street corner to pick up a breakfast hot dog, and then buying an expensive latte from a shopful of muffins and cronuts, I waited again, for the lights to change to enable me to cross the street to my office. With skilled juggling of phone, computer bag, coffee and an armful of newsprint I was able to grab a bite of my wonderful, but definitely mystery meat, hot dog even as I crossed the street. Wow it was good and it was good to be back in New York... no wonder they named it twice.

Meanwhile, on the seventh floor terrace overlooking the Hudson, matters are a tad more internationally flavoured. Harry is desperately trying to recall the Portuguese words for 'Accident and Sorry.' He actually speaks the language quite well having lived and worked in Lisbon for a while, but under the indignant rapid fire assault of Angolan Portuguese from Ermalinda our housekeeper his wits have failed.

The object of all the exasperation was Harry's cheese and tomato shirt with which he had shared some of his lasagna the previous night. And the basic translation was, 'How the hell do you really expect me to get this clean for you...I remember you. Last time you were here you expected me to remove an entire vineyard of vino tinto from your special evening shirt.'

Harry's overworked language recall system was saved, as with a exaggerated shrug and sigh, a slight stamp of a flip flopped foot, Ermalinda flounced out of the room...hardly had he managed sit down to recover when she was back...this time, big smiles and, " Eu faco-te uma Bifana voce faz-me um cafe.".

She was bearing a steaming Bifana, thin thin sliced hot pork in a sweetish bread roll, dripping with plenty of fried onions, garlic and her special chili chili Piri Piri sauce. A more than fair trade for delivering a real coffee 'just as Ermalinda had requested' from the complicated Gaggia machine.

Harry smiling as he remembered his son who had worked in an Algarve beach cafe for a while telling him that working the machine was bad enough -but then you had to understand and recall Portuguese for all the named variations of coffee made with, hot, cold, lots of water, or just a drop, hot or cold milk, foam no foam.'

Additionally of course the names and exact recipes varied between the Algarve, city folk from Lisboa and the blow in's from their old Portuguese colonies of Mozambique and Angola.

Having admired Ermalinda's many photos of her many grandchildren, back in the increasingly prosperous looking but very corrupt Angola, and survived a tidal assault as she washed the floors around his feet, Harry messaged his wife:

'New York now. Really great to be back in America'. He pondered also doing the 'New York, New York. So good twice thing, but figured that Mali, who was still in Thailand on family duties would struggle slightly with the English of that part.

Over the river at TNoTN, Daniel in full news editor mode was still trying to pull together confirmation of that John Bolton loose lips quote that Trump thought Finland was in Russia, and also a story out of London- also Bolton related tittle tattle that Trump had expressed surprise to Brit PM Theresa May that the UK was a Nuclear Power. So he-Dan- was also more than slightly dubious about the chances of my 'Eagles as a Weapon' story coming good. But then half an hour later, he urgently pursued me round the building with a slight change of mind.

Having found me, Dan had something very cool to impart. As a follow up to the news story of a drone bomb exploding near Venezuelan President Maduro, a report had come in of the French Army training Golden Eagles to attack drones in order to protect their President, Palaces and other establishments.

The fact that they had chosen to train Golden Eagles was a real bonus, for Harry and my story. Not only that but the birds were named , d'Artagnan, Athos, Porthos and Aramis- as a suitable homage to Alexandre Dumas's book 'The Three Musketeers, 'so that was another bonus for any TV report.

I studied the incoming press release, which came directly from the French military at the Eagle training base at Mont de Marsan in South Western France. Them keen, I guess, to show what ever is the French is for 'a little one-upmanship'. It also detailed that training birds to go for *specific targets* was taking about eight months, exactly as Birdman McButton had predicted.

I then realised that Maisie and her basic camera crew were still in Southern France and so was able to persuade our, normally very budget conscious editor, to commission her to go and shoot some background video footage.

When I called she was extremely pleased to get the extra work, although she blanked my suggestion that I deserved her bringing me some vintage wines or special Calvados (my favourite) on her return, saying she would instantly earmark the windfall cash for her crew and her to have dinner at La Tupina in Bordeaux, which she'd seen in a Rick Stein travels show.

I was so wrapped up in the confirmation of military use of eagles especially about the eagle training times, that it was only as she mentioned Bordeaux, as being just a few hours away from the military training base, that I woke up properly and recalled it had been on Jerry and Terri's travel listings.

Later, as I walked in the door of the apartment, Harry was beside himself as he had noted during my birthday celebrations back in Chiang Mai, that one of Jerry's favourite restaurants was actually in Mont St Marsan. So for now, more celebrations -modest ones at least were in order, having made some real progress at last.

But generally a good day...and starts to look like our bizarre and so far fairly relaxed Grand Tour is going to stand up as a story... one way or another...*all we have to do is find the right people...and the right birds...in the billion or so flocks of both.*

Chapter 18.   *Summer in the City 2018.*
First find the right question to ask:

Focksy writes: Then it should be fast forward. Another fabulous August day, Harry and I on my terrace. Brilliant place to work and using the combined files of google, bing, yahoo, baidu we're searching the entire globe and beyond in milliseconds as to the likely whereabouts of the Smiths.

Surely today we will find some answers, especially as for the past two days we have been helped by a focused flock of eager and informed interns over in the TNoTN News Room. They probably searching in ways and deep dark places online that Harry and I have never heard of.

Or they were.

Our mood of gloom and despondency soon returned when Dan Groom called to say that as his intern team had so far found nothing, he'd have to move them on to new tasks in an hour or so as they were getting behind with their Presidential fact checking.

It seemed that rumours of a big story were emerging from the White House, Trump's people , advisors and election consultants were deep into the machinations and intrigues of Ukraine. As ever Dan was trying to disentangle the fact from the fiction and the claims that everyone from Trump's man Rudolf Guilliani, Paul Manafort, and even Joe Biden's son Hunter seemed to be benefitting from what he called 'The Axis of Easy Dollars.'

Hence him needing to reassign our interns...explaining this to Harry, I pointed out that I'd worked with Dan for years and understood the pressures he's under to keep *'his news'* ahead of his rival's *'their news'*.

Harry's response was apposite," I do actually get the news cycle for you guys. Actually today I've been pondering another story, about Ermalinda's hotter than hell Piri Piri. I was wondering earlier if there's a new angle to the story on the addictive nature of spices and chili's. Scarcely a day goes by without you or I discussing same or craving some Thai food. "

"In fact right now, focusing on getting no where, it's midday why don't we take a break. I'll order up a Thai delivery and also rustle up some seriously Thai side dishes, you send a thank you to the intern team at TNoTN and as it's late afternoon in France see if Maisie managed to get any footage of the French Army and their Eagles." Turned out that the answer was both yes and no.

The French had suddenly gone all coy and according to Maisie, *'Regretfully Madame' our Headquarters in Paris will no more allow the TV in here. Reasons of Security.'*

So a bit of a shame, on the other hand she did at least get what in the trade we call 'establishing shots'. That's pictures of the Army base, distant shots of some soldiers through the fence and some 'high flying eagles.' *Mais sur l'autre main (Ed. Dodgy French there Focksy)* the French have established some very strong privacy legislation making our use of such snatched video quite tricky.

She was also miffed at the French Army person calling her 'Madame' and not the younger 'Mademoiselle'. But then she struck lucky, and chatting in a cafe, learned of a couple of locals who apparently kept a few eagles further into the Pyrenees. So she was intending to check them out tomorrow. But as she signed off, she did remark that, around Mont St Marsan town they seemed to be very proud of the Eagles growing fame, saying that *' Even the Americans, had sent the Army teams to learn from us.'*

I figured this was something positive but for Harry it produced the opposite reaction to the one I had expected. He explained, "Given that his existence was officially denied when we were in Scotland, we still don't know if Jerry is the real deal. If it turns out that he is, and they have plans to follow the French and set up a US team of trained eagles, that'll be an even bigger nightmare than the one we have now. "

"The US military own, operate on, or have closed off, millions of acres of land all over The States, if the US Military, CIA or a private contractor are setting up eagle research then they could be hidden away for years on those DoD lands. After all they've managed to keep the reality of UFO s in all those *'area somethings'* secret for almost fifty years. So hiding a few eagles compared to a fleet of spaceships filled with bloody aliens is nothing."

I nodded and sat back, quite depressed, even more so when , Harry added, "If the military want to start messing with Eagles here in the US it could also quite understandably upset the locals traditionalists more than bit. Although I suppose that could suggest, that the US might want to do their researches well away from the USA...like Scotland or France."

He was still hammering away at his computer. "I just checked out any 'US Military and Eagles' news, nothing more than pages and pages of history and ceremony on Eagles. Many references to Falcons trained and used as bird scarers at airports and military airfields. There's even a mention of falconers being contracted to the US Navy to scare seagulls- they just call them seabirds- off various Navy installations, even a couple right here in New York and New Jersey."

He continued, "I also notice that here in the US, when injured or rescued birds are able to be returned to the wild - hacking they call it-after they've been trained and conditioned to at least start to hunt for themselves -they are sometimes given the names of fallen military veterans. Which is very cool." He shut the computer and said, "I'm wondering if we've embarked on a project that we can't complete."

I just nodded, in agreement, 'win some' ...'lose some.' Or I guess, or in this case, 'So near yet so far'. Harry and I were discussing the constant demands of the world of news -*kind of skirting round the real question of 'Is it time to give up?'* when a message came up on his phone asking him to call Bird Man McButton.

Whilst he waited for Matt to answer, he suggested that the Isle of Barra might be a fine place to escape the pressure of the 24/7 news world. Apparently it still had fine stocks of smuggled Whisky when you knew whom to ask...although Matt had suggested that any old style bottles with labels half washed away offered for sale now, as apparently having been 'hidden in a cave all those years', were fakes. So there, even the bottles of booze needed checking.

Then, listening in to Harry's conversation, it seemed Matt Mc B was in good form, in fact he was positively merry-as he'd been to a wedding which was also pretty much a school re-union for both him and Chloe.

But facts he had, and apparently brilliant ones at that. He'd sent us a detailed email yesterday, but had just noticed, there had been some island internet connection problems, or possibly a glitch in his computer, so to be safe he was re sending his report right then. The other reason for his call, was that Chloe's brother, Policeman Richard, had confided three things, which he hadn't wanted to put in the mail in case it caused any problems for him.

Firstly, the Shaw Tower Monument Prestwick Airport. No rifles or similar found, but there were several Marks and Spencer water bottles and sandwich wrappers up at the top. They had 'best before' dates on them ' suggesting that someone had been up there during Trumps arrival or departure, they were now being checked for fingerprints.

Secondly. The bullets he had found in the old shed up at the cottage had no fingerprints on them, but their markings did match one of the stolen guns that was eventually recovered, but they could have been fired many years before they were even stolen.

It seems that although Jimmy and Scots Police had now very much re opened the file on the gun robbery, they had confirmed again that both Terri and Jerry had alibi's. Back then they had no reasons to keep any files open on them as even the minor matter of the car accident had been dealt with, now however they had asked Richard to keep sniffing around. Matt then asked us to check his mail arrived OK, and said he'd be awake for a few more hours if we had any questions. Sure enough the mail had arrived, so Harry thanked him and we opened a treasure trove of facts.

From: Matt Mc Button. Barra. Friday/re-sent Saturday.

To : Harry and Mr Schnauzer.

About half of Oban seems to have arrived here on Barra for the long weekend, and amongst them a whole bunch of our school friends for a wedding. Call me to fill in any details.

1. The older lady at the cottage, Pamoon.(Mrs Smith.)

A Spanish couple had arrived with Pamoon and lived up in the cottage, the woman as carer for Pamoon, the man seemed to do odd jobs and stuff. They spoke English quite well, and as they did most of the shopping they met a lot of people in the area. Every one remembers the woman's name which was Bitxi - she always said- 'Bitxi with an X'- but no one can recall the guy's name.

2. Yes it is very likely they were rearing birds up at the cottage for at least two years. No actual confirmed numbers or breeds, as this information came from a couple of 'non birders' who had been out several times exploring off road --trespassing on the Estate really- on their motor bikes. But they hadn't noticed any Tattie Bogles.

3. This may be useful. Sarah, one of Chloe's friends, is over for the wedding. Her dad is a taxi driver around the area. Apparently he had driven the old lady and the two carers a few times to Southampton to get the Queen Mary 2 ship to New York.

It came up in conversation as obviously this long job was seriously unusual as it was more than five hundred miles, each way. A hundred mile trip to Glasgow or Aberdeen is considered a long way up here, so the Southampton's were a big deal. I'll see if there's anything else from him tomorrow as soon Sarah wakes up and can call her Dad. (Might not be too early given this is a big party.)

4. Going back to my last mail about Terri and her Ma, talking to the kids in the village school. One of the teachers, Miss Melbourne, who used to be my teacher, is here for the wedding. It still seems a bit strange sitting having a bevvy with her, but she had a lot to say about eagles.

She said that what really stuck in her memory of the Smiths talking Eagles was the fact that in The States, any and all found feathers or even dead birds must be sent to the US Fish and Wildlife Service. I just checked this out on their web site at the National Eagle Repository and it explains a lot, basically saying:

For hundreds of years Native Americans have used eagle feathers for religious and cultural purposes. In recognition of the significance of these feathers to Native Americans, the U.S. Fish and Wildlife Service established the National Eagle Repository in the early 1970's, at the Rocky Mountain Arsenal National Wildlife Refuge northeast of Denver, Colorado.

Its purpose is to provide a central location for the receipt, storage and distribution of bald and golden eagles found dead and their parts, throughout the United States. The eagles, and their parts, are then shipped to Native Americans and Alaskan Natives from federally recognized tribes for use in Indian religious ceremonies.

As it is illegal for any unlicensed person or organisation to possess a bald or golden eagle, including its parts (feathers, feet, talons etc.) the repository service provides a legal way for Native Americans to acquire eagle feathers for religious purposes. This reduces the pressure for birds to be taken from the wild and thereby protects eagle populations. Only licenced conservation agencies, zoological parks, rehabilitators, and certain others may legally possess bald and golden eagles.

Not sure if this background helps your search, but it confirms that the birds remain sacred to this day, and also that to possess any you need to have some kind of registration and licencing, but I guess you found and checked all that already.

I'll get you anything more from Sarah's dad tomorrow, and in the mean time I leave you with an old quote from Miss Melbourne,

She said,' The Persians, had a legend that said. 'Eagles are the heavy weapons of War, and Falcons their faster killing sisters.' Best Matt.

Chapter 19. *Mid Summer 2018.*
There's a lot of haystacks online.

Focksy's tale:And when you're searching for needles thats a little unhelpful. Sunday: Wandering out on to my morning terrace, after a good long sleep, free of annoying jet lag wake ups, I find Harry, he also reported having had 'a good night.'

Then, as our resident Gaggia driving barista, having offered me a 'coffee' he chucked me over some pages of notes saying, "As I started work earlier than you this morning, again, I've sketched out your opener for the program, if there ever is a program."

Intro Focksy. Sincere to camera: *"Having spotted its prey from airplane height, say ten thousand feet, the Golden Eagle then, wings and tail feathers streamlined back, plummets down, in what's called 'The Stoop' at around 150 MPH. But in inch perfect control, massive talons and cruel razor sharp beak at the ready"*

Silence and pause for effect. *"The first The President, he being the Eagle's chosen target, would know, seconds before the mighty bird crashed into him, lacerating his flesh and splitting his skull, is the fearsome- unholy almost, banshee like scream of the wind over the birds mighty six or eight foot wings. That likely closely followed by a similar scream from The President."*

Long pause and then you continue in reporter speak mode:
"Experienced falconers and experts who have seen these birds 'taking' deer, goats and other large prey agree, one saying 'If he, The President survived, I wouldn't think he would be fit to work or think for months..."

"Any of the President's Golf courses in the US, Scotland or Ireland would provide fine open hunting ground for several species of Eagle. Training the Aquiline aggressors from birth would take about eight months. "

" Security experts charged with protecting the President say it would take quite some skill to target a bird coming down in the stoop-at such a speed, by the time they had focused, targeted and fired they'd be just as likely to hit the boss.."

Focks Schnauzer brings you this extraordinary and exclusive story on The Newsiest of Television News...TNoTN.

By the time I had read and re read that, and it's really rather good, Harry arrived with our coffees. Complete with little almondy-biscotti biscuits in the saucer. Such is his growing barista style that I dared not tell him that when I was alone in the house I had become an Oreo man...but then again I know Harry at heart is a McVities Digestive fan.

"Brilliant old mate. Seriously good intro, well told ,punchy and grabs the attention, real TV style. Good coffee as well."

He smiled contentedly and then of course I then added part two, " But the reality is, we haven't got the faintest idea where the birds or the bloody Smiths are. We don't even know if they're here in the USA, for all we know, they may be lurking behind the Kremlin aiming to attack President Putin although his golfing habits are unknown to me."

As newsmen we are pretty well connected, but it was hard to see, apart from inspired, but random online searches, how or from whom we could get help in finding our elusive Smith family. For sure, they'd stand out from the crowd with a bloody great Eagle perched on their arm, but one could assume that for any training purposes they'd be way out in the middle of nowhere in the US, just as in Scotland.

This is not the place to get into the right's or wrong's of carrying weapons in the USA, but there are millions of genuine hunters, mostly responsible. Millions more fishing fans, not to mention birdwatchers and serious enthusiasts for the outdoor life. Plus millions more casually enjoying the remaining wilderness areas and the national parks on a day by day basis.

Given the sharing effects of the internet, particularly for wild life photography, Harry and I figured that the sudden arrival of any licensed or unlicensed European Golden Eagles - anywhere - would be noticed by someone pretty darn quickly, even if they didn't note the exact species. Even in Colorado where there's more than few they'd still stand out to anyone with good eyes or a pair of binoculars, and America seemed to be overly well populated with amateur ornithologists.

Having said that, with several species of eagle migrating to and from the even bigger wilderness areas of Canada, Harry and I noticed many comments about *Tourist Eagles*.

We assumed at first this referred to the migrant birds -but this turned out to be the slightly disparaging name used by more expert ornithologists to describe the many sightings of 'buzzards'. Apparently when wheeling high in the sky, they-buzzards- are often and easily mistaken for Eagles, so there does seem to be some room for confusion, or concealment by the Smiths.

Given that a little tissue paper wrapped biscotti is less of a breakfast than breakfast- our thoughts turned to brunch, and as great minds think alike, and we both craved Thai food again.

So the kitchen notice board temptations listings came to the rescue, with Harry suggesting that he'd get the lunch fixed whilst I could gather our scanty facts and suppositions into factoids that could possibly provide a better focus than sticking google pins blindly into the map of continental North America.

So working backwards, I noted.

Target: A Presidential Golf course or where ever he liked to play. Having waded through pages and pages of *'book a room, a game, restaurant, travel with us'* pages, I then focused on the maps and decided to un-prioritize urban courses. That's those close right in the edge of any big cities.

All the while I was working on this I could hear aggressive chopping sounds from the kitchen and, soon I too was getting angry with the confusing links of most hotel or resort internet searches, so it was to my relief when Chef Harry arrived with a tray of freshly delivered 'Thai takeout cartons.'

He had also made some good looking crunchy salad - together with a bowl of 'Harry's Special Thai Seafood Sauce.' This being finely chopped fresh chilies, cilantro and shallots in vinegar and lime, with a good shot of Nam Pla-Thai fish sauce, and softened just a tad with palm sugar and a splash of dark soy.

"Good." He said, indicating his sauce, "For *'waking up'* the already tasty looking Thai delivery, the salad and us."

If *'waking up'* was the same as blowing off the top of your head, then we may have found another threat to The President. But

Harry's considered view on that was, "Given that there's tens of thousands of Thai restaurants across the fifty two states, I hope we can ignore that. And anyway, he only eats hamburgers."

He agreed with the golf course targets I had selected but then suggested we add the The White House lawn to the list, as any attack there would be making powerful political statement.

We were just finishing a really rather good and very *'woken up'* lunch when a 'ding dong on the door bell' announced the return of Ermalinda. Good timing, as she bustled in and cleared up the dishes for us...sticking her finger in the nearly finished seafood sauce bowl and tasting it, then with a shrug suggested it was not hot enough, saying *"Need real Ermalinda chili chili Piri Piri."*

Harry and I having concluded that her Angolan origins were stronger than her Portuguese genes we got back to work.

Without making these ornithological reports drag on for much longer, I should add that whilst Harry was checking out more eagle background he found an encouraging story. It seems that at one stage, ddt poisoning had reduced the numbers of America's national bird and emblem -The Bald Eagle- so seriously, extinction was a real possibility. Now though, decades of dedicated work from wildlife guardians, rescuers and refuges have brought the numbers back up to reasonable levels.

Turns out that much wonderful work has been done by 'The American Eagle' foundation which is based on some steep hills close by Dolly Parton's 'Dollywood' Theme Park outside Nashville. There, people get a chance to see and show their kids the majesty of many kinds of raptor...falcons, eagles, hawks...but the organisation has also gone on to breed and release more than 150 birds into the wild.

Harry I both agreeing that inspiring kids is a vital part of the survival puzzle, and the release of the birds is seriously good news... although not quite so helpful for us when we were looking to identify just one or two specially trained aerial asassains.

He then informed me that 'He also now more clearly understood the full implications that, just as Birdman McButten had explained, and now also, Gerald Machoukow the French military falconer training their eagles had confirmed, that the birds need to be focused on *'this is a food target'* from the moment they hatch'.

Having heard Harry's rather detailed lecture, I just nodded again, and thinking this was all going on a bit I did an exasperated, "And so. " But he set off again, "Don't you see Focksy, this means that the Smith gang couldn't just catch a few fledglings or young Eagles already flying around. *They needed to have them from the moment they hatch out of their eggs. Does that mean, given where eagles usually nest, that Jerry still had his climbing skills he had boasted about, enabling him to collect fertile eggs from eagles nests high on rocky crags. ?"*

I nodded, and rather pointedly didn't quite stifle a yawn, but Harry, who was getting rather agitated just continued, "In Scotland the eggs are mostly laid around mid March to mid April and hatch 45 days after they are laid. Depending on the nest location, altitude and usual weather patterns in the Central and Western states of the USA, the dates are about the same."

I nodded again, and I am sorry to say, I did another exasperated, "And so what? "

Harry was getting more and more worked up. "If you had eggs that were laid soon after Easter, say mid April, that means they'd mostly hatch towards the end of May."

I held up my hand. Now I was interested.

"Harry did you say Easter? "

He nodded and said "Exactly. Matt Mc Button reported that the village shop lady said the Smiths cleared her shop of all its Easter Egg Chocolates each time before they set off back to the USA by ship...and those voyages were all in the first ten days of May."

I sat back, as did Harry, who said, "There was even an egg incubator at the cottage - so they knew what do do- if you're also thinking what I'm thinking..."

Before he could answer, the Tsunami that is Ermalinda arrived back on the terrace. Bearing gifts. For Harry she delivered his cheese and tomato shirt, cleaned and ironed...and Bifanas for both, saying, " Eu faco-te fazer uma Bifana con chili chili Piri Piri Angolana, agora voce vai fazer um cafe saboroso."

As Harry stood obediently to go and rustle up a coffee for Ermalinda he took a big bite of his Bifana, *whilst giving me a thumbs up for the possibility of Eagle Eggs actually, having been kept warm at the cottage, on the journey to Southampton, then being smuggled into the US as Easter Eggs...having presumably been kept in the correct warm incubating conditions on the ship.*

As he disappeared towards the kitchen I heard him gasp and and start to hyperventilate as her chili chili Piri Piri got to him.

Forewarned I just took a nibble from the edge of my juicy, wonderful smelling roll. Some minutes later when my eyes cleared, and my heart had slowed, I just sat munching and tried to figure out if the enjoyment was macho, sado, masochistic madness or simply just mind-blowing...a mix of all four was my conclusion...and more to the point we had what could be a real clue about Eagle egg smuggling across the Atlantic.

As Harry and I then sat, sipping our coffees-feet up- as Ermalinda enthusiastically unleashed a perfect storm of terrace washing around us - we agreed that- whilst we still had to resolve the minor matter of where in the entire continent the eagles were, the last two days had at last, brought about real progress.

Chapter 20. Summer 2018 simmers on until:
'Assumption is both the food of fault-and the catalyst of discovery' *Focksy writes: Harry has often quoted these words, which his father, a teacher, used to write on student work he was marking. The sentence usually continued, 'Sadly in this case it is the former, but perseverance usually triumphs in the end'.*

This afternoon, after the euphoria of the morning, Harry was somewhat philosophical," I think that logically, in the real world, trying to figure out 'who dunnit?' or more realistically here and now 'who might do it? requires so many assumptions that the list will be long and wrong."

I nodded in agreement, and he continued, "Without going into real detail lets at least start to make a list of likely miscreant nations, those with an interest in Regime Change in America. We need it on file-in case something does happen-a bit like the 24/7 'just in case'- 'death duty' news pool at the White House"

We started with the obvious:

Russia. Putin Govt. *Officially Unlikely.* Given collusion confusion Trump is causing here and internationally, probably quite keen to keep him...whilst he behaves. U*nofficially quite likely.* The Oligarch Initiative. Need to free up frozen funds, travel restrictions, grow business. Oligarchery apparently directed by Putin. Eagles a bit 'old style' for Russians, in their case the 'fickle finger of fate', now 'the sticky fingers of fate', they favour more modern methods of assassination.

Ukraine. In the minds of the US public until details of recent events started to emerge, Ukraine was usually included in with Russia. Although the reality is, they're seeking to 'get away from, or stop any further Russian encroachment so they're investing big time with the US. So again plenty of Oligarchial backstory.

North Korea. *Unlikely.* They, currently at least have some kind of door open to the world. Quite what we will find behind that door is not yet clear, sticky door handle notwithstanding.

South Korea. *Unlikely*, but they do have old traditions of hunting with Eagles, and have plenty of agents in place in the USA.

China. *Likely.* It would suit them if the next US President could calm the Trumpled world of international trade. China, as well as Mongolia and other enforced friends along the Silk Road have a thousand years of skills working with Eagles...and where traditions are revered.

Iran. *Reasonably likely*. Majority of Iranians are keen on keeping moderate government at home, as it slowly re-opening their world to travel, trade, and liberal lifestyle. Along with most of the world, they had great-hopes for the Joint Comprehensive Plan of Action, or the Iran Nuclear deal as it is known. That working treaty then bombastically broken by Bolton & Trump thus playing into the hands of Iranian extremists.

The old Persia, now Iran, region, for a thousand years, the home of Falconry and hunting with Eagles. Any demonstration of ' The Old Ways' would 'prove a point' for Iran, who have created their own drones, fighter aircraft, missiles & other 'home made weapons.'

Israel. Govt. Activity and interests of Israeli Criminal Gangs, closely linked with globally powerful Russian Mafiosi, pushes them to equal top of the list of *very likely*. This has absolutely nothing to do with any anti or pro Jewish sentiment it's purely criminal. We assume the formidable skills of their legendary security agencies have matters under control.

Then there's Turkey. Bounded on all sides by interesting and interested players, still keen to be in the EU, home to various US military facilities and weekly wooed by and wooing Russia. Rumours afoot of wheeling and dealing going around various Trump people and the affairs of the Turkish 'Halkbank.'

Al Qaeda/Isis/other terrorists. *Very Likely*. They have the skills, the grievances, have shown themselves as long term planners. Searching for scary Muslims still an understandable mania for US Security.

Mexico/South America. *Unlikely*, although Eagles already fly happily over any border walls.

Balkan States. *Unlikely*. Very much part of the Mc Mafia, so more criminal than political, but not really their thing. Unless of course Melania still has any green eyed ex admirers there.

Arabia. *Unlikely*. Despite their extraordinary love affair and history with Falcons and Falconry. The CIA once traced Osama Bin Laden to a Falconry hunting party but didn't act on the information.

There's an up to date backstory, in the world of Falcons. One of the reasons behind the boycott of Qatar by several other nations in the region- is that just a couple of years back, 24 Qataris and 2 Saudis were kidnapped whilst on a Royal Falconry hunt.

Despite $500 million-- yes that's five hundred million dollars- of the ransom being seized on 16 April 2107, at Baghdad Airport-in cash. Eventually a huge ransom was paid, billions more dollars they say, and the money used by various terrorist groups.

Whilst Harry and I we're pondering the huge sums of money involved, his phone sprung into life: 'Matt McButton' he mouthed at me as he both answered and grabbed paper and pen. Brief call, Harry jotting down a phone number and he rang off, and reported.

" After a seriously good night at the wedding party. Matt's a bit groggy but had to get up to sort out his menagerie, so he called the Taxi guy. Told him we are neither Police nor Revenue Men, and he's expecting our call. The the guy's name is Angus, same name as the Ghillie, it's all very Scots. Mind you, Matt using the old style term 'Revenue Men' for 'tax officials' is really quite Whisky Galore, he said to call now, as Angus is an early starter'."

Harry's conversation with Angus the Taxi man went on for quite a while, and completed with effusive thanks, Harry, saying he'd check the message and call back if there were any questions.

Harry to me," Well, we have some good stuff coming, Angus keeps good records as he doesn't want *any more troubles* with the revenue over cash receipts. He's sending names, dates, destinations and times. Seems he even picked up Pamoon, and her carers when they first arrived in the UK, and did all their trips from then on. "

Hardly had H. stopped speaking when his phone did its annoying Whats App cuckoo noise with an incoming message.

Angus to Harry.

Psngr Dtails Years 16-18.

7. May 2016. To: Cunard Terminal Southampton Docks. Drop Mr Gerry Smith. For Queen Mary 2. Dest. NYC.

7. May 2016. From: Cunard Terminal Southampton Docks. Collect Mrs P Smith, Mr Anaut Olaberria, and Mrs Bitxi Olaberria. Ex Queen Mary 2.in from NY Via Seville.

29 March 2017. From: EDI.(Edinburgh Int Airport) Collect Mr G Smith 14.45. Ryanair Ex Dublin.

8 May 2017 To: Cunard Terminal Southampton Docks. Drop Mr G Smith, Mrs P Smith. Mr and Mrs Olaberria for QM2. Dest NYC.

22 June 2017 From: Cunard Terminal Southampton Docks. Collect Mrs P Smith ,Mr & Mrs Olaberria. Ex QM2 in from NYC.

4 May 2018. From: EDI (Edinburgh Int Airport) Collect Mr G Smith. 18.30 Air Lingus ex Dublin.

10 May 2018. To: Cunard Terminal Southampton Docks. Drop Mrs P Smith, Mr and Mrs Olaberria. For QM2 Dest NYC and Boise Idaho.

14 May. 2018. To : Rental. Mercedes Sprinter Van. Ms T Olaberria. Oban- CAL Campbeltown Airport. Call me...Angus.

Apart from us both immediately adopting the old as the hills 'Call me Angus' Harry did exactly that, and then listened again very intently, made a few notes, asked a few questions and then with even more effusive thanks, rang off, and said, "F*ck me"...and continued, "I don't know where to start except to say that we have some real clues here. Going through in order of the list from Angus:"

"About the Spaniards, Anaut and Bitxi Olaberria, at last we have their proper names- Angus said he got to know them quite well, partly from the four very long-ten hour drives he did with them to and from Southampton- and around the village. "

" He says that although everyone said they were Spanish-they were actually Basques. I guess that explains the X in Bitxi's name, I've travelled around there and there's lots of 'xs in the Basque language."

" Angus also said that whilst the two women always sat in the back of his car, Anaut sat in the front with him and they chatted quite a lot. Because all the time they were in Scotland there was so much publicity about Scots Independence, Anaut told him a lot about ETA, the Basque independence group. He even suggesting the Scots should take a few lessons from the ETA bombing and kidnapping campaigns, 'And then they'd get a bit of action going.' Angus, did stress that was more light-hearted chat on a long drive than a serious threat."

Harry continued, saying, "Hang on there's more. Let me make some coffee, whilst I do that, you look up Boise Idaho, Angus said that's where Pamoon and the Olaberria's were headed."

Harry was back in no time bearing biscuits, bananas and coffees...saying somewhat excitedly "No time for a real lunch today." My response stopped him at first sip of his coffee," Two things: Without even much of a search, just putting 'Boise' into google maps and there in big red letters on the map, about twenty or thirty miles outside the city are the words, 'Birds of Prey Reserve.' I haven't checked that out yet."'

"Then in the first few the first lines of the city story is a reference to a large population of Basques. On top of that, I notice that there's a even a small town or suburb north of the city thats bloody called Eagle! It must be the right place."

As Harry eventually manged to negotiate his coffee cup to the broad grin that was now lighting up his face I continued, "Seems to me, as you said, taxi man Angus may well be unlocking the mystery for us. Let's hear what else you got from him, before we get digging. Oh yes, did you notice he spells Jerry as Gerry, not sure if Jimmy's researchers looked into that but I guess they did."

Harry replied, " We'll come back to that spelling thing, he then said, that Terri, Miss Smith to him, flew back to the USA. On 14th of May this year, that's the van rental on the listing. He said he had to rent a van because of all her boxes. I asked him if he knew where she went and he said he wasn't sure, except she said she was intending to meet up with her Ma and the Olaberria's, so he assumes it was Boise also."

"But then he added that he had found one of her box labels on the floor of the van when he cleaned it out before he returned it, and he thinks he's still got the paper on his garage desk as he jotted a phone number down on it one day when he was driving."

" He *thinks* it says CAL - to COS or MO PU or MUO, something like that. He'll let me know asap, he's obviously very proud of his professionalism. "

Whilst Harry was speaking I put MOPU, as an airport identifier into my computer and got nothing. I did get Mount Pleasant Michigan for MOP, and Colorado Springs for COS, but then trying MUO the result shocked- or kind of surprised me-or not, if I thought about the conversation of the past few minutes. I turned my mac round to show Harry: MUO. Mountain Home Air Force Base. Boise. Idaho. Western United States. Speechless, we both just sat back and gazed at the river and the skyline beyond, until Harry then said, "Where's that Campbeltown Airport then?

I inserted the letters and again simply turned the machine round to show Harry: CAL -Campbeltown Airport/Ex USAF/ RAF Macrihanish. Kintyre Scotland.

As we toasted our success with a banana each, Harry was furiously punching his computer computer keys and then said, "I'm going to call Angus again. The map shows Campbeltown just over a hundred mile drive south from the cottage, way down on the Kintyre peninsular... but there's only two flights a day from there...both small planes...Barra island types...and they only go to Glasgow."

" It's crazy, if you didn't take that road south but took another one soon after you left the village or Oban you'd be driving straight to Glasgow anyway and also about 100 miles. I'm also wondering if he knows where Gerry went this year. I assume on the Queen Mary 2 like the year before with his mum."

Harry called up Angus, this time the conversation was fairly brief- Harry mouthing at me-'He's got passengers in the car.'

A few minutes later he was doing a major, "Thank you, thank you so much. You have really been very helpful. That's a good bottle of something we owe you."

...and then adding, and laughing, " Yes, when you're not driving the next day. Thank you again."

Harry, leaned across the table, saying, "Shake on this now Focksy...we're bloody nearly there...I think we almost have a story."

" Terri's freight boxes included nine or ten live birds. Angus thinks they chose to fly from Campbeltown, which closed as a US Navy and RAF base ten years back, but is still open for commercial flights, because all this year, loads of questions have been asked in the Scots Parliament and the local press, everyone getting very uptight, about too many US Airforce planes using Prestwick."

" According to Angus, the plane that was at Campbeltown was 'not like the big ones that flew in all Trump's cars and stuff to

Prestwick a few weeks ago, this one was smaller, same military colour but it had a green white and orange striped flag on the tail, not US markings on it'."

I really couldn't contain myself- after all these weeks of wondering, and was just about to suggest we deserved champagne when Harry said..."And for finishers. Jerry!"

" On the same day, Angus took Miss Smith to CAL, Jerry, was taking a Toyota SUV, *that he had bought from Angus-'my old taxi' but well looked after* ...to Ireland on the Stranraer to Larne ferry...with more birds in boxes."

We both sat there, quite frankly exhausted. After a good half an hour, I suggested to Harry,"Why don't we call it a day for now. It's coming up to six. We could walk along to Ruth's Criss, have a much deserved celebratory steak and a really good bottle of wine."

Harry's response ,was simple: " I think we deserve several really good bottles of wine...and tomorrow I have a feeling we'll put this story to bed. ?"

Chapter 21. *Idaho bound. Summer 2018.*
Two Hundred bottles of wine.

*Focksy writes with considerable effort: I stress that two
hundred is the number proclaimed on the front of the wine list
from the almost always excellent Ruth's Criss Steakhouse, and not
the quantity consumed by Harry and I in party mode last night.*

Although from the way I feel right now I fear we, and some
friends and neighbours who we met there, may have made a valiant
attempt to drink them dry. It was only the sound of Harry operating
the coffee machine that encouraged me out of bed, although to my
ears this morning, the hissing and whooshing sounded more express
train than espresso.

 Harry, to my horror was fine. Annoyingly so, really
annoyingly so. "Morning Focksy. Big coffee here for you, plus some
extra hot water and even some milk in case you need it. Lots to
report." I grunted, and studied his evil smiling bearded face...as he
continued. "Good night last night, nice folks your neighbours, pity
Maisie wasn't here as well."

 I grunted again, and raised-with considerable effort, one
finger...asking, "Did I give the game away about our story to them,
one of those chaps works for CNN. I used to work with him at Irish
TV years ago, so he's a good mate, but it's 'finders keepers' in the
news business."

Harry's response of "Nope. You spent quite some time, really
quite some time, discussing the legality of Donald Trump's lawyer's
or ex lawyer's Tartan Jacket. I think Mr Cohen has more than
enough on his plate for now than to be worrying about the origins
and validity of the tartan."

I relaxed, and decided that the day could only get better,
until Harry continued, " Although I suspect that come Christmas or
your next birthday, your CNN neighbour chum has some fine
phonecam video to share with you and your chums. You sitting
there, slurring words, wittering on about highland history, clans,
kilts and all that stuff. I didn't stop you as it was keeping you off the
dangerous path of revealing what we were really working on."

I just nodded. Harry, then said, "Anyway, was a good night.
For some reason I'm in good shape this morning and started a while

back, but now something's really bugging me. First of all. Obviously Boise Idaho is a big bloody place to search around, regardless of focusing on the Basques. So when we get there we'll need help from the police or others, and we know what credibility problems we've had with them already."

I nodded and said, "So what's changed for better or worse then?" His response. " CAL. Campbeltown Airport. You may recall yesterday me saying the US military or department of defence had long managed to conceal the rumoured secrets- such as they are- of aliens and god knows what in the the various 'Area's'...Vast no go bases in New Mexico, Nevada, Arizona and such. That all of course creating even more interest and conspiracy gubbins...well it seems that CAL is the UKs own 'Area McMystery.' "

"Anything Area 41, 51 or whatever the bloody number is, can do, CAL can to better, it's built on just about the most remote place in the British Isles, with one of the longest runways in Europe. It's been used for spy planes (U2's) and as a potential space shuttle landing site. The US stored tactical nuclear weapons there in specially built bunkers, protected by their own guards. There are pages of rumours of sighting at CAL of everything from UFOs to US war planes that did or didn't exist."

"None of that really affects us, *except we already know that us suggesting there's a plot or plan to 'Decapitate the Donald' using trained Eagles is already more than little lacking in credibility.* So when we introduce Campbeltown, with it's very flaky reputation for rumour not fact, it will look even worse for us."

I sat back, somewhat fact attacked...but Harry had more, this a mix of positive and negative. "I just can't see," he went on, "how a plane with foreign or even Irish markings can come swanning into the UK. Land at an airfield with no customs or immigration facilities, and then go away again without anyone noticing."

I held up my hand...and said, "Unless you have done more searching than you have mentioned, we don't know if anyone has noticed. We're not there, and we haven't asked around locally. Yet"

Harry, paused and nodded saying. "OK. Point taken, maybe I'm a bit het up over the credibility factor...so near and yet so far and all that, but at the other end of the journey- look at this. Angus has now sent us a photo of the found freight label which he had used to jot down a phone number. "

"Does say 'CAL- COS-MUO / *PUW* and there's a black smudge or fold where it got dirty I guess on the floor of the van so nothing more is readable...no address or anything. So again we're back to 'so near and yet so far'. COS is Colorado Springs which is shared with Petersen Airforce base, and yesterday you pointed out that MUO was Mountain View USAF base in Idaho, so both having a military connection. But MOU that's near Boise so hopefully that could help."

I spoke. "If I say, well done Harry, good stuff, brilliant detective work and thank you, will you rustle me up another coffee and I will then be capable of booking you and me tickets to Boise."

Harry said, "I will indeed. Oh yes, I also sent a message to Matt McButton, I suggested that Constable Richard might get some brownie points with Jimmy if he quietly found out from Angus the number of his old car- the one he sold to - Jerry. Richard can tell Jimmy, Jerry had apparently taken it, and a few eagles, from Stranraer to Larne in Northern Ireland on the ferry."

" I didn't say anything about the missing rifles though."

I nodded and said "Brilliant, really brilliant. Now, please please Coffee. It's almost brunch time.

The coffee took a long time, booking a flight to Boise did not. But when Harry returned it was with the ultimate in revivers (non alcoholic) for us Irish and the Brits.

Bacon sandwiches. Harry saying, "I used the the last of the Scot's bacon I smuggled back with us, it seems we both need it," then continuing, "I was thinking about CAL, the airport, Matt McB said that mates of his handled bird scaring services for a few airfields in Scotland, so maybe he knows someone who knows something about it."

I responded, mouth full of almost miracle breakfast, "He's on the payroll, send him an e mail and ask him, give him the date Terri and Angus were there just in case it helps." Which he did.

Restorative having restored- the conversation turned to the reality that even in Boise, we had no clues how to find any of the Smiths, and it's a fairly big city. Harry had already suggested that expats often tended to stick together so searching around in the Basque community there for anyone who knew-or knows the Olaberria's could be a slightly more focussed way to proceed.

We started to make list of, or at least look for Basque societies and organisations in the area and found a lot, but then Harry's phone did it's cuckoo sound again, and after he listened for a while, he grabbed a pen and scribbled furiously. All followed by yet more exuberant thanks.

I realised than that he'd been talking to or at least listening to Matt McButton. He...Harry...not Matt, as far as I know, started to behave bizarrely...for him...punching the air and shouting..." Yes Yes Yes."

Eventually, he calmed and spoke. "OK. Mr Schnauzer I accept that employing Mr McButton as a freelance assistant was of course entirely your idea...but I suspect you are lucky he's not working here or he could nick your job...and probably mine."

" He has come up Trump's to use the original, not the current meaning of the phrase: I present to you, the address of a Mr J Smith near Boise Idaho, here on my Whats App messages."

" Richard knew Angus's old car number- small town I guess. As a copper he immediately got the address and full details online from the DVLC -the UK's national vehical licensing computer. They included the full change of owner ship details as inserted by the ever efficient and professional Angus McCabbie. "

"Cops in the U.K can get in big trouble these days, for sharing DVLC details with non cops and especially the press, but as Richard pointed out to McButton, all we needed to have done was to call, 'call me Angus' and ask. When you sell a car in the UK, it's your responsibility to notify the change of owner with the new owner's address, to the DVLC, because otherwise you are still liable for any speeding, parking or other fines the new owner might incur. Matt did say, don't forget that info didn't come from Richard, as we don't want it getting back to his bosses."

"Secondly. He does know someone who does some thing at Campbeltown Airport, not a bird scarer, he thinks the guy cuts the grass. Anyhows, who ever it is was at the wedding, Matt, hasn't got a number for him, but will try and find him before he leaves Barra."

Having booked us on a 7.30 morning departure to Boise, even with nearby Newark being just twenty minutes away, it still meant a 4.30 wake up to allow for Monday morning traffic-and all the usual security lines that characterise air travel these days.

So the kitchen temptations board board came into play again for an early supper, and a planned alcohol free evening.

We discussed booking a local camera crew in Boise. Back in Scotland we'd regularly talked through the obvious need for video footage to build the story, but back then we didn't know if we even 'had a story', and as far as getting a TV news production budget from Dan Groom we simply did not have enough facts.

The conclusion in Scotland had been that if the rumours and our 'imagination' stood up' we could easily get a local Scots crew in later to pick up some shots of the The Cottage and any other relevant material. Harry and I now also agreed that as Birdman Matt McButton had become such an integral part of the discovery process we might need to return to Scotland, and even Barra to get him on camera.

Harry saying, "I think he'll be unwilling at first, but provided we can promise him some decent screen time to also put his case about the need to take care of the natural world and it's inhabitants I think he'd agree. There's also a secondary story story to be had reminding people about Barra and the Whiskey Galore story. Even Mr Groom would be happy to get two stories for the cost of one.

But here in the US, TNoTN had access to retained crews nationwide so we made a call to my office and booked a two person crew -camera and sound- to meet us at Boise Airport tomorrow lunchtime. Just in case.

No real surprise there from the logistics team at the office, but Dan Groom, did call, to enquire if we did 'at last 'now have a story after all these weeks of costly research work.

Home made lemonade and cookies.

Harry writes: I've taken over the writing duties, as Focksy is in TNoTN newsman mode today. Or rather he hoped to be. Currently, we're sitting at a ramshackle barbecue table under the shade of a big old tree with a delightful lady, 'of a certain age' enjoying her home made lemonade and cookies.

Exiting Boise airport, late of course, or if you prefer, late as usual, we spotted- or were 'spotted by' our local TV crew. They, on recognising Focksy turned on a blinding light and their camera. 'In case you needed an establishment shot of your arrival'. This attracting both much attention from fellow passengers in the arrivals hall and a distinctly pissed off growl from Focksy that, *'We're trying to be discrete round here.'*

Once in the TV crew minibus, Focksy, having vented once more, *'I suppose it's just lucky that we're not using your outside broadcast truck with stickers, slogans, badges and a bloody great dish antennae on the top. I assume it was already booked today, and that's why we got the 'B team'.*

He sat back and pointedly started to check his messages, but couldn't resist his demeanour improving somewhat, with Susie the camera woman and Kenny the sound guy telling me that on their last job with Focksy, it had been in mid winter, way up in some nearby mountains following up on a 'Big Foot was here' abominable snowman story. Then a mega overnight snowfall meant that the story of course never happened, but they were all trapped in a remote ski resort for a couple of days.

Focksy brightening up recalling, "By the third day, they eventually got the roads passable again thank god. I say thank god as by then 'these two'," he indicated Susie and Kenny, "These two, had drunk the entire resort dry of any alcohol."

Susie, who was sitting at the wheel, said. "So where to Focksy? Assuming it's not another wild goose chase through the woods on another natural world mystery about big birds that is."

Her comment shut my exuberant chum up for a moment, until he got it, "You've been talking to Dan Groom haven't you."

Susie turned in her seat and smiling said, "You got it Focksy. They wanted Kenny and I to sign a 'non share no disclosure to others' form about your *'might be eagles story'* before we set off."

" We did that, of course, and here's our signed copies for your file. You might notice Kenny has noted that, 'We will not share the story, but we reserve the right to share any and all available supplies of alcohol'."

Kenny, said, " Dan, or I guess you, sent us a first location address, so I suggest we aim up that way, it's about forty minutes or so into the mountains. There's a decent coffee shop soon after the highway exit, we can stop there and make a plan."

Which we did. It was interesting watching and listening to them make a professional plan, first drive discretely by the location, and hopefully on the return find a parking place across the roadway a good few yards further along from 'the target.'

Susie explaining to me, "Never right outside, because when you pull up right outside, even with a discrete TV crew, people are instantly nervous and nosy neighbours get in the way."

With Kenny having taken over at the wheel after our coffee stop, and having found the address we had received from Scots Cop Richard *(Ed. You mean from Angus McTaxi!)* we did the drive by- the only shooting being Susie, with her camera through an open window.

Nice old house, one of a several set back from the road, in this case with what turned out to be a 'Nice Old Lady' operating a leaf blower, tidying up the front lawn. Also on the front lawn a real estate sign that had obviously said 'For Sale' but now had a 'Sold' sticker over the top.

Focksy said, "I think we'll start gently, just Harry and I, you two stay here in the van for now." We slid open the van door and slowly approached the old lady, both of us with big smiles. Once she noticed us, she shut off the noisy machine, removed her ear plugs and enquired, "Can I help you gentlemen?"

Focksy said, " We're looking to find Pamoon Smith, or Terri. We've come all the way from Scotland where they were living for the past few years, we're working on a story about the work some folks are doing helping endangered wildlife."

Well to be fair to Focksy, all true, and seemingly inspired as the old lady relaxed visibly, saying, "OK. We've had some funny people coming round once the for sale sign went up, and my son, who'll be back in a couple of minutes, always said to take care with any folks who come knocking."

She continued, "Pamoon's not here any more, her family have booked her into a care home as she was becoming too much even for her home carers to handle. They sold the house to pay for that."

Focksy nodded and said, " We heard about the dementia, but we understand the carer couple, the Olaberria's, were very kind to her, but we hadn't realised she had deteriorated so much. That's never easy for families and terrible to deal with."

Now knowing the Focks the way I do I thought he was over doing it a bit now, especially as the old lady was very smart, getting in the early mention of her son's imminent return, but again he was well received. The Old Lady, held out her hand and said, "I'm, Jenny Baxter, my husband Matt and I've lived here since 1980, Pamoon and the children moved here around Christmas in 1988."

"I know the date as it was the same year her husband Andy had been killed, so with her two children being the the same age as mine, I think we helped to make that terrible first Christmas a little bit easier for her and especially Terri and Jerry. Mind you, Matt, my husband- he's away fishing -again-Matt always said that with all her secrecy there was something funny going on. But she was a good friend to me over the years."

" When she came back from Scotland this time I was completely devastated at her rapid deterioration, she was on occasions quite violent with the Olaberria's. She'd been back here most years for a few weeks or so I knew she had dementia, but it's a terrible sickness as it develops."

She paused and looked away for a while, obviously upset. Then she said, "It's a terrible way for nice things to happen, but my son Joshua and his wife, having seen what has happened to Pamoon, have now bought this house. They say they just want to move back with their children, my grandchildren, to the area they grew up in, but I know they really want to be here in case the dementia gets me also. I'm exactly the same age as Pamoon, but so far for me the old grey cells seem to still be working." She smiled.

I decided that needed some input from me and said," Well Mrs Baxter, we've only just met, but I have a feeling your grey cells are in better shape than mine and my friend Mr Schnauzer's. We came here as we wanted to ask Pamoon and Terri a few questions about Eagles and other wild life, as Mr Schnauzer said, for a story about the work that people are doing trying to bring back threatened species of birds all around the world."

Mrs Baxter said, "My son can tell you more about what they've been doing, he does that internet thing, and so he was always able to stay in touch with the Smiths when they went to Europe. If you can wait, " she indicated a table in the shade under a tree, "As I said, he'll be back in a moment or two. If you can, I'll just pop into my house and get some lemonade, I made it fresh just this morning when I thought it might be warm day."

Having accepted, we watched as she walked across to the rear of the house next door, Focksy walked swiftly over to the van and after a brief conversation returned to the table.

"They're going to drive off after she comes back with the lemonade and return when I give them a call. Susie says she's got quite good footage of the house and us. What Kenny wants us to do is put our phones on record and on either end of the table, so between us we should be able to record most conversations."

Just a few minutes later Focksy leapt to his feet, and rushed to assist 'Mrs Baxter ' as she was carrying a heavy tray loaded with glasses, a clinking ice filled jug of lemonade and what looked like a tupperware box of biscuits. Four glasses either meant she was bluffing well, or she had called her son and established he was on his way, she was so nice and trusting , I rather hoped it was the latter. Which, happily it was, as minutes later a battered pick up truck pulled into the driveway and we met Joshua.' "Call me Josh."

Josh recognised Focksy from his TV work so I figured it was lucky we had at least mentioned to Mrs Baxter that we were 'working on a story' about wildlife rehabilitation .

What we discovered, and were able to double check later from our phone recordings was firstly Joshua repeating that that

Pamoon had moved to the house near Christmas in 1988, "There was snow on the ground I recall that. They'd come here soon after Mrs Smith's husband, *who was something in the military,* had been killed abroad somewhere. Over time we learned he'd been killed in Persia."

He continued, "Dad always says that back then for years there had been all sorts of problems between the US and Persia, I guess it continues now with Iran. They'd had that revolution a couple of decades earlier, then they'd invaded the US Embassy and taken loads of US hostages and President Carter screwed up a rescue attempt-losing helicopters, transport planes and personnel. I think that eventually the hostages were released on the day Reagan was inaugurated. Although all that was way before Pamoon's husband was killed."

"Dad always suspected and still suspects that Andy, had some kind of special forces connections from various things Pamoon said over the years." Josh going on to say, "I'm the same age as both J and T, so we really did a lot of stuff together, we went to college together. Actually for both of us, more trade school than college, so it was very good to see Jerry last month-even if only for a few days. He arrived a few days after the others and was here to help settle his mum into the care home. "

"I made them an offer to buy the house and they were both real happy about that. Got a bit complicated with the lawyers as it's in Mrs Smith's name, and she can't figure things out any more, but it's all sorted now. I hope when I'm finished renovating it we'll be in for Christmas."

His mother cut in, "Terri told me several times her mother had refused to sell the house when she was living abroad. She said it was because, her mom had brought up the kids in a very nomadic farming style, with just a very basic house. So this was her first real home, and in her mind it was also very special to the kids."

I asked, "Did they show much interest in wild life, falcons eagles or even keep any of those things when they were kids.?"

Josh replied saying, " They sure knew a lot, from where they'd lived before, out in the wilds, but they never kept any, there's very strict rules about all that you know."

Focksy interrupted saying," We're aware of the regulations, they are a bit rigid when well meaning folks want to get involved and help, but generally I suppose it's for the best."

He continued, "Back in the day, given Terri's ornithological studies, or when she came to visit did she have anything to do with any of the Eagle reserves or other falconry or wildlife places and organisations around here, there seems to be a lot of them."

Josh laughed, "I can answer that one, I'm a builder and my boss - who I've really worked with right back from our college vacations is a big wild life guy. Mind you he does go shooting, but anyway- we've always done a lot of work- some paid- some volunteering, to build specialist stuff like displays and breeding cages, even offices for many reserves, zoos and other places all over the North West, so I've always had heaps of free entry tickets for most of those places."

"So as long as they lived here, or at least from my college days I always offered the Smith's free tickets, and whilst they were polite in thanking me- basically Mrs Smith said, 'Over my dead body, birds should fly free and never be caged long-term. ' Terri and Jerry simply said, 'We're with Mom on that' and I never saw any weakening of those views even in recent years. "

" She was very strong minded, looking back I guess they were all angry and bitter about some things, for instance the three of them always went away for two weeks around July fourth 'back to the wilderness' they said. It was to escape all the celebrations and stuff around the Fourth because their dad had died on the Third."

Mrs Baxter said, " Josh is right, all three of them were very bitter about his death, as apparently he was accidently killed by The US Navy. Mind you losing your dad at such a young age can't have been easy, and I don't think Pamoon ever recovered, maybe that's what contributed to bringing on her outbursts of aggression in her dementia so quickly."

She paused and looked sad again, as Josh stood up, and rested his hand on his mom's shoulder, saying, "If you'll all excuse me I've got to collect the kids from school, but I'll be back here before the hour to carry on the work in there." He nodded at Pamoon's house.

Focksy, standing as well, saying "We must get along too, especially as my friend Harry here has eaten more than his share of the cookies. And thank you for the lemonade, as I live in New York, it's a long time since I had homemade, sitting peacefully under tree, although I hope our questions didn't upset your day."

He continued. "Just one last question, about the Olaberria's what's happened to them now?" Mrs Baxter replied. "Anaut and Bitxi, they were very nice by the way, just like you said, they arrived first with Pamoon. Terri and Jerry were only here for week, but the Olaberria's stayed for almost four weeks to settle Pamoon in the care home, and helped clear the house. In fact they've shipped a lot of the family furniture back to Spain for when they go home."

" When they went, Bitxi was so sad about Pamoon, but she also knew it was for the best, she and Anaut really had been on the receiving end of some of her violent rages."

Focksy stood up, and retrieved his phone as we shook hands and thanked Josh again, saying ,"May I get your phone number in case we think of any more annoying questions for you?"

Josh laughed and giving Focksy a business card, said, "No problem's, I'll keep an eye out for more of your TV programs in future. Which reminds me, I need to get a satellite dish or cable sorted here before we move in." He kissed his mother and with a 'see you later' backed his truck out of the drive as Focksy walked down to the street, phoning for our van.

Mrs Baxter gathered up the glasses and other items from the table and I remarked, " Those chocolate chip cookies were lovely. Seems to me that this city is full of chocolate lovers, we were told that when Pamoon was in Scotland, she cleared the local shops out of Easter chocolates every time she came home here."

Mrs B laughed and said, "We'll we do like our chocolate, but that was always the Olaberria's. They had so many relatives in the community around town they had to bring something for all their nieces and nephews. I remember them saying European chocolate was the real thing, and much better than American style."

She paused, "I'll miss them and the Smiths, but at least Terri said she'd be back from Moscow regularly to see her Mom, and she'd come to see me and collect any mail that comes in."

Noticing that Focksy seemed to be talking to an open van window and gesturing towards the house now and again I assumed he was 'recording a piece to camera,' so I said to Mrs B, " Sorry, did you say Moscow?"

Her response surprised me and I feared it would open a whole new avenue to our investigation...she said. " Yes she's moved to Moscow, she must be crazy, it's very cold there in the winters. I'm glad you enjoyed the cookies, I hope we helped with your program."

Chapter 23. *Harry writes, eats salmon and leaves.*
From Sockeye to Red Eye.

We just managed to catch a 'Redeye' flight out of Boise to Newark. First class and no bags helped us get through the terminal in time, and Focksy and I were soon sitting eating some seriously good Sockeye salmon during our two hour layover in Seattle's Tacoma Airport.

Outside the Baxter's, before I got in the minivan, I quietly told Focksy that I had probably resolved the mystery of all the chocolate taken by the Smiths on their trips. More to the point, I told him that Terri Smith now seemed to have moved to live in Moscow.

As we boarded the van Focksy muttered to me, "And Andy Smith, was we now learned, rumoured to be a military spook, and killed in Persia or Iran if you prefer," and then continuing to Susie and Kenny, "I fear Harry and I will have to escape the perils of an evening with you two, could you aim for the airport whilst I see if there's a red eye flight back back east to the office we can get on."

We were in the Airport by five, and aloft just before six in a prop driven Dash 8 , aiming completely in the wrong direction. West to Seattle, there, following two hours on the ground we'd be on an Alaska Airways flight direct to Newark. The five hour flight, getting in , because of all the usual time zone gubbins at 4.30 am, but as Focksy said, "Just time to get home before the rush hour traffic really starts and either have a snooze or get to work, which ever way, it's better than wasting tomorrow."

We agreed that by chance, the transparently open and honest Baxter's had answered many of our questions. It was sadly apparent that even if we gained access and permission to speak with Pamoon that we would achieve little of credible value.

There seemed no point in staying to further investigate any of the Eagle sanctuaries, as they appeared likely to be devoid of Smiths, and probably any of their Eagles. I did ask Focksy about dropping by MUO - Mountain View Airforce base, but realistically we figured any questions about 'mystery flights' from 'mystery locations' in Scotland or elsewhere were unlikely to get past guards of slick PRs and would be referred to Airforce HQ.

As we enjoyed our salmon-*'sustainably caught'*, said the menu, but then again don't they all say that these days, for the n'th time on this story we started to make a list, this time of the new facts, and both outstanding and new questions.

Andy Smith: Many questions, killed in Iran 1988. But killed by the USA. So blue on blue killing one of their own if he was on 'Team USA. Or 'an enemy' killed in action by US if he wasn't.'

Apparently a military man, allegedly- according to Matt Baxter as reported by son Joshua, 'a spook or special forces.' Focksy saying" That'll be Oliver North and all those Iran Contra secrets then, but I thought that was all over by '82. In the office we have at least five hundred hours of files on all that, God help us, but we'll have to take a look."

The killing, whatever the reason, had quite understandably set off a strong blame and hatred of US military or more accurately- as Mrs Baxter had said, 'The US Navy', in Pamoon and apparently the kids. Which made Jerry's claimed current employment by US Presidential security even more than a little suspect. Depending on his underlying attitude now, if he really was employed in that role, it could seriously compromise the POTUS protection squad.

Food for thought, which made Focksy again raise the question that we had discussed on our first morning in Edinburgh : "At what stage of a journalist's investigation does it become a duty to share information regarding a discovered threat to a person, nation, place or organisation?"

Given the acres and hours devoted to the constant alleged threats to both the President and national security, we swiftly decided that, whilst we were unravelling a good story, we didn't have hard enough evidence to make anyone take much notice.

Focksy adding, with some optimism, "Yet."

As we flew east on the Air Alaska flight, we agreed:

'Productive and worthwhile trip, but as many questions as answers, although I did add, "Sadly I think we can close down all the 'Eagles Eggs smuggled as Easter Eggs."

I suggested to Focksy that," Terri having moved to Moscow, moves the Russkies way up on our likely miscreants listing, and that's going to be way more criminal conspiracy than collusion."

This causing Focksy to recline his seat, pull a blanket over his head and say, "Just shut up Harry. Get some sleep. I fear we're in for a busy tomorrow."

Bleary, but to be fair, having had four hours good sleep, in First Class space, it was only 5.00 am EST as we settled back into the town car Focksy had booked to meet us at Newark. Focksy turned on his phone, whilst I just sat back, gazing out of the window pondering that 'Liberty' was a very inappropriate name for the airport considering all the armed guards, defensive bollards, warning signs and security queues. "Shit," Focksy exclaimed, handing me his phone. "Message from Matt Mc Button."

CAL. Grass cutter also in local fire crew auxiliaries so worked night May 14/15. Plane. Dassault Exec Jet. Seats out freight mode. Not Irish tail flag, that Green /White/ Orange this Orange/White/ Green. Ivory Coast, Cote d'Ivoire. Ukrainian company and crew.

In from ABJ / via France XMJ 8PM on 14. Then out at around 4am on 15 to COS (Refuel) Dest: Moscow PUW. Loaded boxes and 1 PAX . Refueled by truck from Aberdeen Airport. If you need more I have Grassman phone. Matt McB.

By the time I had taken all this on board we were at Focksy's place, so we agreed, shower, coffee and catch up with a siesta later if needed.

The first and simplest point from Matt's message was that it confirmed Mrs Baxter's final words to me about Terri Smith having gone to Moscow. But the Ivory Coast, connection was odd, but then Focksy turned up a story about the French DGSE security service assisting the US/ CIA in the construction of a massive drone base in the Sahara between Niger and Mali. As did another story about Moldavian and Ukrainian Airfreight companies in the region being much used by the French and US military and security services with the planes badged with with local African registrations.

Modern day Air America style, using unattributable airplanes I guess, "About par for the course out there," said Focksy, "Good clandestine stuff. As they always say in Africa, 'If the airfreight docket says machine tools or engine parts,' the first question's always, 'Is that with or without ammunition'? "

Focksy said, "I guess that with that flight coming in from Abidjan Via XMJ Mont St Marsan where the French are training their eagles, makes me wonder if the plane taking those boxes out of Campbeltown was 'officially but un-officially' US authorised - if you see what I mean. Or even if if was delivering as well as collecting. "

"If so that opens up the entire Scots Eagle training business to a whole new level. In as much as -is it, or was it, being done in France or Scotland as keeping Eagles -even officially- is so restricted and well policed here in the US."

The morning news was overloaded with Trump positives or negatives depending on your choice of channel, and we were in the main too busy to pay much attention. But we did notice that The President was planning a trip to Ireland after he had been to France in November around it being the 100 year anniversary of the ending of the First World War.

I was typing up my notes of the afternoon in Boise, when Dan Groom called. Focksy wandered to the end of the terrace and had quite a long conversation, on his return he said, "Well sorry to say, old mate, but Dan's pulled the plug on this story. Too many other things they need me for backing up. "

"I tried the Moscow angle, which I had emailed him last night, and he said that was pretty much what made him decide to pull the plug, as he is convinced we'd find out b**** all there. I also tried him on the Irish visit angle, as we can assume the Pres. would want to play golf at his Doonbeg course after France, and he said he was ahead of me. He'd got that travelling info yesterday from a White House press briefing, and it wasn't clear if Ireland was on or off.'"

"So we're, or should I say, I'm off the story from next Monday, which is almost a week away. Then I've got to turn up in Florida as the hurricane season approaches the research team are checking to see if the President's Mar El Largo Hotel and golf course developments get any preferential treatment when hurricanes actually threaten. Dan seems a bit pissed off this morning as he growled at me when I suggested he could do on screen graphics of The Donald's hair blowing around to demonstrate the various levels of those hurricane winds that regularly hit them down there."

I suggested to Focksy that I'd wander down to the nearby deli and pick up some rolls or fresh croissants whilst he made some 'Will the Eagles strike back?' notes, which I could either use, or just file for future use. He replying, "If you want to keep sniffing around this story, as ever you're welcome to stay here as long as you want... or as long as you can survive the daily assaults from Ermalinda's Piri Piri."

With fresh coffee made, rolls and stuff all sorted, I found Focksy still on the terrace deeply engrossed in his lap top and remarkably cheered up. "Sorry Harry old bean, I haven't sorted out my notes yet, I've been a bit busy looking at placing a few bets on the chances of The Donald being attacked or even deposed by an Eagle. Quite a few online bookmakers in the world are taking bets on many matters Trumpian. So I 'm just trying to see what odds they'll give me on possible Presidential Puncturing by an Eagle. I figured out I might at least try and re-coup my time and effort with some dollars from a bet if something does happen."

I decided to leave Focksy to organise his betting coup, and have a siesta, as I've said before, even shortish flights just wipe me out. By the time I re-joined Focksy on the terrace it was lunchtime, and my chum was looking smug...as I sensed a gloat building up...so I simply said, "Yes?"

He continued. "With you now needing so much sleep in business hours, I thought for a moment I was going to have to fly without you." I just nodded again, so he continued: " We're booked on the 18.10 British Airways flight tonight, Newark to Bilbao Spain. Gets in at 11.15 lunchtime tomorrow, Wednesday. Rental car booked and several nights hotel in the Spanish Basque Mountains near I think- The Olaberria's. Or at least near the destination for the freight they shipped from Boise."

"I am booked to return ex Madrid on Sunday lunchtime, direct to Miami, getting in Sunday night. Positioning me to return to TNoTN duties at Mar El Lago first thing Monday as ordered. Gives us almost four days in the Basque country to have a sniff around. Given that the whole area is a gastronautic wonderland- even if we find no eagles or evidence- it could be the end of a remarkably fine - but possibly pointless adventure."

I enquired, "So where, when and how did we get the address for the Olaberria's freight shipment?"

Focksy responded reasonably gloat less. "Joshua Baxter called. He'd taken his mum in to visit Pamoon this morning-using his car- not his usual work pick up truck-and realised he had some copies of the shipping details in the car. He'd helped the Olaberria's with the shipment by using his office printer and stuff. "

" He emailed me a copy of the freight pages, and I got the address from there. Postcode and all. Oh yes, Pamoon seemed fine, although they suspect she's on some quite strong calming drugs but I guess that's good under the circumstances."

" Maisie also called. She says that she has got some wonderful evocative shots of mountains, eagles, villages and stuff... she also said that it is very clear the locals all stick together as none of them would give even one word about other local Basques, French or Spanish, keeping Eagles. But she is convinced they all knew a lot."

I had to admit defeat..."Great stuff Focksy. Really great."

He somewhat smugly continued," Oh yes, when Joshua Baxter phoned to tell me the freight address for the Olaberria's, he also told me how Andy Smith- Jerry's dad had died. Shot down in an Iranian passenger plane in July 1988...shot down by the US Navy ship USS Vincennes. Explains a lot I think, but also raises yet more questions."

I could only nod.

Chapter 24. *In the Pyrenees. Late July 2018.*

Focksy writes: **X marks Everywhere** *when you study the map of the Spanish-French Basque region. The map these days- usually digital and rarely those huge sheets of tyre or gas company sponsored, crackly strong paper, requiring careful re- folding to restore it to anything of manageable size.*

The practicality of GPS related, location locatable, and instantly located- digital maps are a brilliant resource. Sitting in the spacious business- not first- class of the British Airways flight to London and then on to Bilbao, and poring over a huge sheet of the Michelin map of the Basque region of Spain, I agreed with Harry that on occasions the printed sheet still had its uses.

Trying to get 'a broad overview' of a whole region using a map on a phone or pad and the detail is tiny, and the names, from which you are seeking 'interesting routes' more than 'destinations' are too small to read. Of course it's instantly expandable, but then the sense of distance or scale is lost, together with the general feel for the practicality of driving from A to B, or in the case of the Basque region from X to Z, or even EKZ .

Our need for an over view being that, although we had an address for the Olaberria's furniture shipment from Boise, closer online examination of the detail- not actually undertaken by Harry and I until we were waiting to board our flight, revealed the delivery address to be a warehouse type building in an industrial estate on the outskirts of a town called Extarri-Arranatz. In that case the digital map street view showed us right to the loading door.

As I mentioned, X Z and K more than ABC usually mark the spots in the wonderfully hilly to mountainous, geographically and gastronautically privileged Basque region of North Eastern Spain. It then continues - via valleys, peaks and passes over the Pyrenees mountains into equally Basqueish parts of France.

Our freight depot target destination was about 100 miles from Bilbao, located-according to both digital and folded paper - soon after the turning to Santxolopeztegi and after Ideazabal town. Although to be fair the signposts for Durango looked a more familiar, and sparked off several miles of discussion with Harry and myself about the origins of names across the USA..

The sleepover flight had been on time, although quite why British Airways, have chosen to make the seats face each other in Dreamliner business class I really don't know. Waking up, facing Harry- even six feet away is more nightmare than dream. The changeover in London easy, and by some quirk of fate the rental car line was speedy, even if the car-despite being a chunky looking SUV- seemed to be less so -as it struggled slightly to cope with the early gradients of the Pyrenees.

Despite our professionalism, many years of experience, a committed urge to deliver the story, and tight deadlines- to be honest, Harry had slept for the entire first flight and I'd dozed and studied some well connected recommendations for restaurants around the region.

So plan B- assuming getting to where we are had been plan A- was a bit lacking in detail. In fact soon after noon, as we passed Ideazabal we agreed that truthfully we had no Idea.

At the freight depot, no signs of life-total siesta mode and all operatives gone home to avoid the heat of the mid day sun, and not even any dogs-mad or otherwise to- apprehend or even comprehend an Irish Englishman or a German-American-Irishman. We parked in the shade of the building, Harry saying, "I'm more fed up than hungry, but I suspect that's the early onset jet lag cutting in."

He did however engage brain with a suggestion, "Given that the freight company have depots in a number of towns in the region, we could also assume that, ignoring the chance that the freight blokey here is a relative or great friend of the OB's, that the final destination for the goods -is, was or will be- within a shortish distance of where we are parked."

I agreed, saying. " Yep, agreed, right now although it's late wake up time in New York, we know from experience that we'll both soon have serious brain- if not- body fade. Air pressure on planes and all that crap. I suggest we make for the hotel, check in and adopt the excellent Spanish siesta habit and engage brain again later." Which we did...and what a hotel.

These brief words fail to describe the lovely old building, with huge beams, tumbledown flowers hanging all over, and when we walked through the arch to the rear, away from the road, there was a shade dappled courtyard, awesome mountain views...and even, I promise, a fast running ,clear, splish splashing river twenty or so feet down from the terrace.

Harry, wheelie bag following obediently along beside him, simply said. "Wow and wow again Focksy. I bow to your research skills...if you have not cocked up the booking process as you did once in Macau, leaving us to sleep in a hotel that rented rooms out by the hour, then you are forgiven for many sins. In fact if the rooms and food are as good as it seems, then you are absolved from any and all sins you have sinned on your entire long life."

And they were.

Or our two rooms were wonderful, old farm furniture, small framed windows, and a bathroom with a shower that could strip paint and a bath big enough for a battle ship.

As the sun lowered and reddened the sky, we met in the bar, much refreshed, and in the case of Focksy absolved from a lifetime's sin. Not only that but he had again triumphed when I was sleeping...although this time he had the good grace not to gloat simply saying, " I was checking my emails and stuff, trying to think of a good one to send to Dan Groom, who is obviously feeling guilty about taking me off the Eagles Revenge story, and messaged me suggesting dinner tonight at 'Ayada Thai' in Queens."

"Any way, I was looking at the emailed paperwork sent from Josh's office, and realised that in with all the tracking numbers and delivery stuff there's a Spanish phone number...you know starting with 34. It's not one of the freight company numbers, or at least not one of the ones on the front of their building. So I am wondering if it's the Olaberria's, it would be quite usual to require a delivery recipient number on the paperwork. I haven't used it or tried it yet, as I thought we'd engage brain first-oh yes, I sent Dan a text and said sorry we already had a plans for this evening at a Basque restaurant...but thanked him for his invitation."

As ever with our professional deliberations, they seemed to coincide with the need to first order a drink-- it was by now seven o'clock. Basque aperitibos were off the menu for Focksy and I as experience had taught us- albeit in some of New York's Basque restaurants- that most were very good, but way too sweet for us. So we plumped for locally produced dry cider.

The waitress hovered, waiting for more on the order and we suddenly woke up enough to realise we were in the world of Pinxtos, or Tapas to most of the world. That part was easy, "Just bring what you recommend, and keep bringing them until we say 'please stop'!"

(Ed here...this book having evolved into a rambling travelogue but with a slightly unusual reason for the voyage, has had more than enough about food and beverages...although I do realise that, here in the Basque country we're in foodie heaven.

So despite lives - or at least the life of The President of The United States being at stake, I will allow Focksy to point out, that just one of the many stand out dishes of any dinner here--is their aged beef. As it happens, this evening rather sensibly for once -but taking into account it's been a five thousand mile day- the boys are eating lightly with some local trout. (That's trout the fish not moi)

Tomorrow though with the aromas of this evenings grilling over the open fire already wafting over the terrace it will be 'Txuleta.' A rib eye, bone in, to be shared.

In the US, 'USDA' accredited beef must be no older than 30 months...it may then be aged 'hung 'for a good while after butchery. In the UK most beef sold is around two years old. Here in the Basque country, good beef for grilling or other preparations are usually slaughtered at about twelve or more years old, they often having been milk cows...So more flavour and texture, and not always quite US style 'you can eat my beef with no teef,' but seriously wonderful.)

After some discussion, some cider and some deliciously tasty red peppers and then *(Ed NO! We've done the food stuff.)* we sent the message to what we hoped was a number for an Olaberria.

>Hola. Josh Baxter tells me they visited Pamoon yesterday and she is settling in well and seemed calm. Jenny will visit again next week. We also just returned from Scotland where we missed you- and Jerry who we know well from Thailand. My colleague Harry Buckle and I are keen to meet you to learn more about The Eagles. We are here in the Basque country until Sunday. Rgds Focks Schnauzer.<

"It's gone through, in as much as it's a real number...I don't know if the system here will tell me it's been opened or even delivered. Maisie is still in France- along in Bordeaux now, but if anything came up she can be here on the AutoRoute in a few hours.

All in all a perfect relaxing evening, neither of us are 'phones on the table when eating or drinking types' but a faint 'ping' from Focksy's buried in his laptop bag had us excited for a moment- hoping it was the reply we were waiting for...sadly it was some kind of automated signal from the Focksy door entry system to his apartment causing him to say, "That'll be Ermalinda screwing up the entry codes again."

" Luckily Winston the doorman knows her well enough to expect it. He also knows how to re-set the system, in time, before all hell breaks out. Even regularly giving him mega cash tips, it's still way cheaper than the call out fees from the security company."

We agreed that with the sun well down now, candles and lights flickering, the river sounding louder for some reason- Focksy saying 'maybe the breeze had dropped at sunset, so we're hearing the water over stones clearer, that nothing could be much further away from the hustle and bustle of New York, New York.

Unusually for us pink wine was the choice, it seemed refreshingly right, and coming from Irrulegey -was better in today's food miles rules...'source, cook and eat and drink local,' which is more than can be said for us two consumers.

Despite the fact we'd eaten sensibly, even been quite light on the booze, and it only being late afternoon in New York, by ten, when people were still arriving for dinner, we were both yawning and struggling to stay awake...and still no message back.

Jet lag and an old style sink into a deep feather bed, sent me off for a good long sleep, in fact right through until early sun coming in the windows woke me. Having then -eventually- managed to adjust the shower to avoid being 'jet washed and depilatoried' too violently I was very awake when I wandered out onto the terrace soon after seven. With, a slight touch of early morning chill in the air, a big - and steaming cup of coffee, with hot and foamy milk on the side, with a couple of mini churro style sweet pastries provided a fine start as Focksy came bustling out of the hotel, rubbing his hands, and asking, "Sleep good?" and without waiting for an answer continued, "Did you get my message?"

My, "Actually I left the phone off over night as most people think I'm still on New York time." produced a sniff...but some good news. Focksy, "I got a message this morning about six, presumably from an Olaberria- asking if we could meet in the Plaza del Castillo, in central Pamplona at around ten thirty. I of course said yes, and got a response that they'd be there, and we should note that it's a walking street, so park somewhere and take a cab is best in this tourist season."

He continued, "I just hope that it's not the bull running festival in Pamplona, as I'm not Earnest Hemmingway, and neither am I a fast runner these days. But then again I guess all I need to be is faster than you, so I'll probably be ok. "

Having informed Focksy that I thought the, 'I'm OK, as long as I can run faster than you.' was a very old line more applicable to Safaris and face to face confrontation with lions, and recommended the coffee-we agreed that this morning's riverside terrace- was in many way's superior to our riverside home in New York.

Half an hour later we were on the road and by ten we were looking for a parking place in Pamplona...eventually we succeeded. As we had circled and circled the town we were totally disorientated but back in the world of digital maps, we both marked the parking place on our phones, and then discovered that by chance we were just a few hundred meters away from the Plaza del Castillo.

Coffees ordered, and eventually delivered, Focksy's phone then rang, and he explained we were sitting at the top of the square, at the Cafe Iruna, or at least the big writing on the awning shading us suggested that.

After a few more words he said, "OK. No problem," and then to me, "He'll be here in fifteen minutes, and suggested we moved to the Windsor Cafe which is almost next door."

We paid for our coffees and as we approached the outdoor tables at the Windsor a man sitting at one of them stood, and said "Hi I'm Anaut. Pleased to meet you."

Hand shakes, and he said, "Let's sit inside if it's OK with you. I am sorry to move from the other Cafe but we are concerned why you should want to meet with us, and we don't really want to be in any TV show with secret filming. After we talk with Mrs Baxter and Joshua last night, we are all surprised you should come all this way. But it will be good to know what you want. It is Joshua that tells me that you are from the TV people."

I guess we were both feeling over caffeined, so water for us and a coffee for Anaut. Focksy said, " First of all it's good to meet you- we heard a lot about you from Scotland and then in Boise- which to my surprise I now realise we only left the day before yesterday."

"Could I start by explaining that both Harry and I are indeed journalists...but right now I can assure you, we are alone. Neither are we filming anything with secret cameras, and to show willing that we are not recording anything I'd take the battery out of my phone, but it being an apple that's pretty impossible. I doubt Harry knows how to get the battery out of his Huawei either-but if you want to take them and put them in your bag, or behind the bar for a while that's fine. "

Anaut raised his hand and said -"No, no I trust you...but why have you come here?"

Focksy said, "Well it's a long story that started back in Thailand with Pamoon Smith's son Jerry. He got us thinking that someone was planning to assassinate the US President...which I think you could imagine could be quite of interest to a US TV company and most news outlets worldwide." Anaut nodded, and Focksy continued. "Then as we sniffed around the story it appeared that trained falcons or eagles, could be the weapon of choice."

" To be honest, it's such a crazy idea that it would make an incredible story that would go all around the world- if it was true- or even, as they say these days, 'If it was Fake News. So regardless of truth or not my boss at TNoTN is dreaming of headlines like 'The Revenge of the Eagles'...or The Eagle Strikes Back."

"In a nutshell, that's why we're here. Seems like a story if it's a fact, and also still quite a good 'light-hearted tale 'if not."

Anaut smiled and said, "I have spent some time in America and we have some crazy news outlets here in Spain also, so I can see what you say. I do know a bit of a lot about Eagles and although it would be quite difficult to teach a bird to do what you say, it is not impossible. Difficult to be sure, with guaranteed success to make an attack on one special person in a group of people, but with careful training it certainly can be done accurately. And that's actually what warriors across Asia and elsewhere around the world managed to do for thousands of years."

He continued, " I can see a lot of people are upset today about the President the American people chose, but killing him is not the way. I am fifty eight years old, and so I was born in 1960, I came here in 1978, an important year for Spain, not because I was here but that is the year of the first democratic elections here elections since 1936, and that only became possible since the dictator Franco had died- of natural reasons -in 1975."

" Of course here in this region we also had many troubles to receive some kind of independence, and right now, even in these weeks, not far from here The Catalans, are on the street in their millions, as they want to escape a bit from Madrid."

"So I think we know a lot about voting for Presidents and also about changing things with actions direct. Mind you, your Mr. Trump does seem quite loco!" And he made the universal finger drilling into the side of his head to make sure we got the meaning of loco. Anaut adding, "Please excuse my English it's no so good on everything."

Having reassured him about his English, Focksy said, "Well Harry and I rather agree with you, firstly about the President being what Harry's wife calls, 'Not one hundred percent' although I think 'loco' is more expressive."

" Secondly. Yes, he was elected in an election, probably as straight as any other in the USA, and removing him is better done by legal means at the next election. Or if he's acted illegally, by the correct court proceedings. So we agree with you on that."

" Thirdly. Just for your information, actually he is not 'our President.' Harry is Irish English and I am mostly Irish German, so he is *their* President not *ours*...although his impulsive tweets affect and endanger our world as much as theirs."

Anaut said, " It is good to hear that, but I am not sure what I can do for you, although we agree about your - sorry - *The President.*

Right now I can assure you, hand on my heart that, that as of right now I don't know anymore where to find any Eagles who may attack the president. None is now under my control. So I hope you have not come all this way for nothing."

Focksy said, "Well first of all, it's worth coming just because it's one of the most wonderful places in all Europe. In fact tonight Harry and I are planning on having Txulata," Anaut interrupted, "Ah well, that's good, and where are you staying?"

Focksy answered and continued, "Just to go back to why we are here. There is one other aspect to the story that we are following up. When we spent a week helping Jerry with research in Thailand *it started to look like he might be the one actually planning some kind of drastic action against the President."*

" When he was in Scotland, or at least nearby, there was a robbery of some sporting rifles, some of which may well still be missing. But regardless of all that, we'd like to see him again- partly because we had some good times with him, and also so we can kill those parts of the story- before someone tries to kill the President."

Anaut frowned , saying "Well, he's our family, but I am not sure about if he actually wants to shoot the President for real, or if he's only like so many of those people, like we see on TV, who shout angry things like that all the time. I saw Jerry for two or three days, when they clear the house in Boise, but I have no idea where he went next. Last night when we get your message, you say about knowing Jerry in the message and so I try to call him on the only number I have but his phone says -not a true number. Look, I'll try again, I have it on redial."

He sat, back and after showing us the response to his redial, said," I am sorry but now I have to go, my phone also tells me my wife is waiting for me. I am sorry I cannot help much, but you now have my phone number. If you think some more questions-you can phone me anytime. Remember here in the mountains sometimes the signals come and go a bit, but I will always call back to you. Now please excuse me I just have to speak to the barman and to pay for these few drinks. "

As Focksy and I were offering to pay, he stood and went over to the bar, and some minutes later, returned bearing a bottle of wine, saying." Please take this from me, and enjoy it with your Txuleta tonight. Open it and stand it still for while when you get back to your hotel, it needs to get some life in it, it's been waiting in the bottle for you for many years."

As we thanked him, handshakes and all that stuff, he said, "Here, we have some words that really make some sense for your story...they are, '*Naturak zaintzen gaitu bainan batzuetan natura zaintzeko borrokatu behar gara,*' and with that he walked to the back of the bar and out into an alleyway where we could see him get on the back of a motorbike, and he was gone.

Focksy and I sat back. He was the first to speak, "I hope it was ok with you to have told him so much about Jerry, the guns and stuff, but I was just reacting to his reactions."

I replied, "Hundred percent mate, good job and I think the honest way you did it probably got a little more from him than we might have otherwise. "

"It seems to me, there's a lot to discuss after all that, it also seems to me that as it's only just after twelve, whilst we could to whole spectacular lunch thingy here in Pamplona, I quite fancy getting back to the hotel terrace. A real Spanish, or I suppose Basque omelette or a salad, by the river there, putting us in a good place for a siesta and a pleasant evening. After all we did tell Anaut that was reason enough to come here."

As he stood Focksy responded with, "I agree- and we know we work best by rivers."

Chapter 25. Txulata the same day. July 2018.

Harry writes: Dinner was, what the travel shows and paragraphs like this tend to call: Spectacular. Wonderful food and wines, beautifully presented and served in an idyllic timeless setting. The soundtrack provided by the gentle rippling and splashing of the river below tumbling over the rocks. As the sun's last glow faded, soft lights and flickering candles were reflected in the glassware on the tables.

If those audio, visual and taste sensations were not enough, the aroma of cooking over the open fire - Sometimes meaty sizzle, sometimes herbs or a waft of wood smoke- all added a further magical dimension to a perfect evening.

Except of course my dining companion- although a long‧ time good mate, was far from perfect, and certainly not a romantic one. Also our conversation, whilst relaxed- as we enjoyed actually one of the best dinners of our lives- was centred, yet again, around assassination, assignations, accusations even aspirations.

Although on the latter Focksy said, "*Aspirations? Just knowing the bloody answers would be enough. I have no desire to amaze the world with a mega TV scoop ....unless CNN or Fox look like they're on the trail as well.*"

As we paused for thought, with perfect timing our much anticipated beef arrived. Sliced and enticing, on a remarkably hot plate...and looking enough, as Focksy said said, "To feed a rugby team."

I got the the rugby connection immediately as we had both once eaten brilliant meats cooked over an open fire in Buenos Aires, where our dining companions were some of the Argentine Rugby team, 'The Puma's.' The Pumas we spoke to, were very appreciative of our support for our home team-'Ireland,' nodding their approval, and when we added that internationally, we were also big New Zealand All Blacks fans, their nods became shrugs of 'well of course' followed by *'But just you wait-the Pumas will show them.'*

The main thrust of our conversation *this* evening was trying to figure out if we were making any progress. Focksy was quite depressed, thinking we were only making progress through luck. Catching up with with Anaut was well done - although getting his phone number was *a bit of luck*. Luck again he stressed, in a story where *'luck'* has played a major part...starting with meeting and talking with Jerry...and then Duncan spotting Jerry boarding a plane to Moscow. Although I maintain, by then, we were already deeply suspicious and had been alerted by being named as suspects on the memory stick.

'Luck' in being put in contact with Birdman McButton, thanks to contacts from a wildlife specialist I had called at random. Although my view is, once we had contacted the Edinburgh Police, they would likely have sent us to see Birdman to get his expert advice anyway.

I did suggest there was a degree of luck with Birdman McB, finding the taxi driver contact who gave us so much useful information. Focksy differs, Constable Foster was on the case there anyway, and would have eventually found the details...although when, or even if, the Scots police would have shared them with us is another matter. Focksy suggested Mrs Baxter being out blasting leaves off her lawn when we arrived, I didn't see that as luck, we would have banged on the neighbours doors either side of Pamoon's empty house.

Eventually we wondered if we were clutching at straws by analysing everything again and again, although Anaut's careful choice of words when he denied any current eagle activity needed thought. We both recalled them exactly, him saying *'Right now I can assure you, hand on my heart that, that as of right now I don't know exactly where or how to find any of Jerry or Terri's Eagles who may attack the president. None is now under my control. So I hope you have not come all this way for nothing.'*

It seemed churlish to doubt him, especially as we were just finishing the last of the red wine he had kindly given us, but really the question and his answer were and are the nub of the whole affair, and his words seemed very carefully chosen. As we sat back and pondered, the hotel receptionist arrived, bearing an envelope. Addressed to me. We were both intrigued, Focksy suggesting it was the hotel bill as maybe TNoTN had sacked him and his credit card wasn't working...but no, it was a handwritten note.

"Gentlemen. Excuse the impersonal note, but I suspected having spoken at length with Anaut that you were the English Irish kind who thankfully turn off their infernal phones when in restaurants. I wanted to get this message to you before you turn in for the night, as a fine dinner in this part of the world can render most of us comatose.

This is to invite you both to lunch tomorrow. As I say I have spoken at length with Anaut and I am interested to learn more from you. Please send him one of those txt/sms things if you are available.

Someone would pick you up from your hotel (bring your passports) at about 10.00. Early I know but there's a bit of a drive.

I would suggest that you allow most of the day- until the early evening for this. I am not sure I can sparkle in conversation but I can guarantee a fine lunch.

May I request you leave your mobile phones and any tracking or recording devices at your hotel to save any embarrassment later. Sadly in this day and age such precautions are more necessity, than just being the quirks of an old man. PS. I enjoyed Harry's book 'Just In Time'. Interesting and easy read set in one of the biggest potential problems most of the world will face. As usual reality sleeps whilst politics play...

The signature was just a dash of the pen and unreadable.

I couldn't resist observing, "Obviously, whoever they may be, he or she are a fine judge of the written word, so we must of course go to lunch." Focksy then bringing me down to earth saying. "Firstly it's a he. *'He'* refers to quirks of an old man in the letter."

" Secondly, when I was having my siesta I was thinking about our situation. Say we are right about almost any of the who might 'puncture the president' scenarios, including God help us-the US, other nations, criminals, pissed off or deranged individuals, it could appear to them that bit by bit, day by day, you and I are getting closer to exposing them."

He lowered his voice and leaned in," Given that round here used to be the bad lands of Europe with various iterations of ETA, their independence party, killing hundreds- many of them innocent passersby in the street-until the tortuous and very slow peace processes eventually came into effect in more recent years."

" So just wandering off to lunch- we know not where -with a total stranger-might be not so clever. I agree, that's a bit dramatic- but you're the one who told me about your travels around the mountains here in the seventies, with all the signposts shot to pieces. I agree it seems calm and settled on the surface, but we don't know what's festering beneath the surface."

Silence....Broken only by the murmuring of conversations, the snap and crackle of the fire, and of course the river.

Then Focksy, continued, "Actually, as I said, I considered some of this this afternoon, although I didn't know about the invitation to lunch then, so I kind of have a backup plan, so yes of course we go to the lunch. But first - just as we did when we were leaving Thailand and concerned if we were likely to be arrested, we lodge with Dan Groom the basics of where we are, with an update of what we've found, including details of Anaut. "

"We tell Dan we're off tomorrow-Saturday in the morning on some deep research...without phones or similar communications- and should he not hear from us by Monday morning New York time, -then he'd better quietly and discretely start looking for us. We stress this is for his eyes only."

I nodded and said. "Good plan. You go and get your phone from your room to accept the invite, I'll organise whatever is Basque for a Calvados."

Chapter 26. Part One. Basque high country.

Harry writes: ' **Naturak zaintzen gaitu bainan batzuetan natura zaintzeko borrokatu behar gara.'**
So now you know. Actually if you do, you're one up on Focksy and I, as neither of us have yet got a translation sorted.

Breakfast was a little subdued, partly as we'd over done it the evening before , but there was also a little trepidation about today's planned adventure. Focksy saying, "I've sent the 'where are are, what we're doing,' email to Dan this morning, with an extra copy to Maisie just in case."

At ten we were in reception where we were greeted by our driver. Good, if heavily accented English, him saying, " I've just told the reception lady we're going to St Jean Pied de Port to meet friends for lunch, and that you should be back middle of the evening. I hope that's all OK."

Outside, fairly usual basic Mercedes taxi, although the driver then removed the taxi sign which seemed to be stuck on the roof with suction pads. He left the electric connection in place, sticking it down with a scrap of duct tape which seemed left there for the purpose. As we settled ourselves in the back he said, " Taxi sign really makes a big wind noise on the road. Now we go to meet Anaut, actually we meet him at the famous Ham Shop just before Francia. If the traffic is nicely then we get there in just more than one hour. "

The journey was fairly silent, I suspected the driver had run out of easy access English- and then as Focksy said, after miles of major highway, then a largish road, but with endless twists and turns as it climbed through tree lined valleys, "I give up. No chance of remembering the route or the names, all I know is we're on the N135 and there's signs to 'Francia' every now and again"

On arrival outside The Ham Shop, which seemed to be in quite a narrow village street, we suddenly turned right, and then a few yards down a lane stopping outside what looked like 'The Village Hall', next to a large barbecue grill, stood Anaut.

Hand shakes, " Do you have everything from your taxi ?" and he showed us into a fairly battered dusty old Toyota 4X4. Wisps of straw on the floor, and a distinct smell of dogs. "Excuse the car, we live on a farm, and in the winter here the roads get snowy and icy, and we're not even at the peaks."

" For reasons I will explain later, I have to take some precautions, not to be followed so we go now." We pulled out onto the road, the taxi following us, and continued in the 'direction Francia', for a few miles, when suddenly just after a few sharp bends, we pulled into small farmyard gateway and stopped behind some buildings.

Anaut saying, "If you don't mind gentlemen we change cars again- the last time-I promise, but be quick as we can, and just stand behind this wall a little."

We exited the Toyota, and somewhat to our surprise three men jumped in it and immediately drove out of the yard, continuing along the the way we had been travelling. Arnaut pointing and laughing as a minute later, the taxi passed the open gateway, it followed by a line of traffic, " Good to see Alain got his taxi started again, it's so unreliable." He went on, "Of course, him blocking the road is an age old game and not really very effective, but anyone eventually getting past him, and then following my car can still see three people in it. But better than nothing, and better than asking you to tramp some hills and wade across a river or two."

He opened a gate and behind it we got into a four door Hi Lux pickup truck, (made by Toyota Thailand I happen to know) the mystery of the dogs being solved by the two large shaggy occupants in the open back of the pick up. Anaut saying, "Of course if there's two or more watchers, one will have stayed back near the ham shop, expecting something simple or stupid. Their problem is, there's only five small roads , lanes I think you call them- out of the village."

" If they have done their research or know the area- which actually I don't think they will if they are following you- from the map or sat nav, they could expect for us to take the lane we're on right now. It will show in their Sat Nav, as the Barrio Bixkar. What it will not show, is that in about ten minutes- we cross a grill in the road, there to stop sheep and cattle from passing, and after we do cross over it, actually into France, the grill will be pulled up, and they cannot pass. For them to find another way round will take more than a few hours."

The country side was almost very English, Cornish even, high moorland, stone walls ,some heather and gorse, close cropped grass- hungry sheep I assumed. Ten minutes later, having passed a few cars parked off the road, "Walkers or bird watchers I would think." said Anaut, we drove over the grill across the track. Me telling Anaut, "In England we call these cattle grids, but they don't usually have pulleys and weights to bring them up in the air and block the road."

Focksy adding, "Like old castles really."

Anaut, getting back into the car having pulled up and locked 'the drawbridge up,' saying, "The gateway is supposed to be 'up' all the time, with just four or five farmers having the key, because their land and so their animals go both sides of the border. I have a key. I have a feeling that some of those people, who crossed it when they found it down, will be angry and have a long drive back to where they came from."

Twenty more minutes of twists, turns, trees, valleys then up again where in the high shadows there was a dusting of snow- and suddenly we crossed another grid- Anaut saying, "Cattle grid , I must remember that".

He brandished a remote control and said, "This one has 'electric parts Chinois'," as a farm style gate swung shut behind us, him commenting "The electric gates are easier for my uncle."

We pulled into a farm yard, old stone buildings on two sides, and we parked in the shade of a barn filled to the rafters with big round bales of hay on the third. A man appeared driving an electric wheelchair, which made Anaut's 'Easier for my uncle, electric gates' comment clear. The driver greeting us warmly, "Hi. I'm Paul, or Paulo if you wish. Good to meet you, sorry about all the bloody car changes ,on the journey, but needs must. I'll explain later."

Anaut had released the two dogs from the back of the pickup, huge and shaggy, so Pyrenean I assumed, as we introduced our selves, to both Paul and the dogs...firm handshake from Paul, disinterest from the dogs...Paul saying, "Follow me, there's a chill in the air up here now despite the summer sun, but the terrace stones will keep us warm."

Well. If the hotel terrace took my breath away, this was even more spectacular. The house was built into the side of a steep hillside, looked out across several miles of valley, with hills rising to what looked like the highest Pyrenean mountain tops in the distance. Round the terrace, waist high double stone wall, the center beds filled with geraniums and other flowers. Big old slate and granite slabs on the floor and a stone columned, pergola with massive beams and a vine or something growing over it. Under which was a table set for lunch, and some easy chairs round a fire piled high with burning logs.

Paul saying, "Not trying to warm the world, but we must cook to eat. Now having noted your nationalities, I can offer you some chilled Guinness- only bottled I'm afraid-or local anything and everything."

As he spoke a women came out of one of the doors from the house, dusting flour off her hands, she saying, "Hello. I'm Bitxi, Anaut's wife. Excuse my hands, I was in the kitchen, and as we have the last of the cherries and first of this years apples, I'm trying to make an Apple and Cherry Crumble. I spent two years at school in England in the seventies - and I can't remember anything I learned, except some of the cooking ."

Again more handshakes, Focksy saying, "Well Guinness and crumble would be worth walking here from Pamplona, although having said that, I haven't a clue where we are. And actually, I'll just have a glass of wine or I fear the Guinness will bring on the jet lag."

I nodded, and added, " Wine of any colour that you advise will be good. Given that I have often observed my friend Focksy here sleeping in chairs on terraces in Thailand, after lunchtime Guinness, I am happy he has spared us that sight and sound."

As we took our seats, around the fire, Paul saying, "It's fascinating the attraction of log fires. It's a sunny day, not even much past noon, and yet we are drawn to the fire. Primitive man and all that I guess." He continued, " You mention Thailand, I think you live or at least spend a lot of time there." I nodded again saying, "I'm the lucky one, Focksy has a holiday home in Chiang Mai, and I get to use it rather regularly."

Paul, slapping the arm rest of his wheelchair said, "Before I needed wheels, I went to Chiang Mai once or twice in the mid to late sixties. I'd been up to Ubon and Udon Thani a few times, and had a few weekends off with some flyers. The wild ones made for Bangkok, and those who wanted a bit of peace and quiet went to Chiang Mai."

" Loved the food and the people. It's funny, they use a surprising amount of spicy peppers in Spanish and the local food around here, but it's not 'spicy and lime fresh' in the Thai way, although 'lime fresh' sounds a bit like a deodorant spray."

Bitxi delivered a tray with glasses of wine- ice cold reds, and a selection of sausages and crispy looking vegetables and roasted peppers. Focksy saying, "I guess a lot of the locally grown peppers here are used in chorizo like this." He continued, " Please *do not* let me overdo this wine , ice cold red wine, still catches me out every time. It just slips down too easily."

He asked Paul," I assume that, visit was when the US had a whole bunch of airbases in North Eastern Thailand, used as forward supply bases for Vietnam, and all the bits we don't mention, Laos and Cambodia."

Paul nodded and said, "I agree Mr Schnauzer, I'm eighty eight and I can tell you, even at my great age, the ice cold reds, can make driving this more than interesting."

Focksy said," I appreciate you getting my name right-but the world knows me as 'Focksy' so I would be honored if you would call me that. Harry, has a very English habit of saying, 'Oi You,' to which I also answer."

Paul said, " Thank you, " paused and took a sip from his glass, " I think that we all know why you are here. As Anaut said to you yesterday, we're not sure if we can answer your questions, but I will try. If I fail, we will, knowing Bitxi's skills, have a fine lunch anyway- which would seem to be a good enough reason to meet. Also I have enjoyed Harry's books, the ones I have read so far, and some of your TV work. "

"I only say 'some', as the constant invective and rhetoric of most TV channels- on occasions including your TNoTN, is more than I can be bothered with these days. If I could figure out how to work the bloody record machine for the satellite system I would probably see less rubbish and more of you, but it tends to be 'view what's on."

"The younger members of my family cannot believe how the service I joined in 1956 operated with no mobile phones, computers and suchlike." He reached out and stirred the logs with a poker, "Although I am not asking for this discussion to be 'off the record' I suspect, that as we've asked you not to make notes or record stuff, the least I could do - as what I have to tell you covers a good few years - is to start at the beginning."

He moved his chair nearer Focksy and I and continued. " My parents were farmers and had emigrated from around here just before the first world war. I was born in 1930, and my brother Andy in 1937 on a farm a few hundred miles south of Boise, Idaho."

" *I assume you already know I was with the CIA.*"

Focksy and I glanced at each other and nodded, casually, despite Paul's first few words being a bombshell. Both of us, as we recalled later, thinking, actually all we knew was some claims from Jerry about himself and the security world, and some rumours about Jerry's dad, Andy, from the Baxter's. In fact we hadn't even really given much thought to Paul's existence. Until now.

Paul continued, " Actually I joined, or was signed up as a trainee in 56, so I was 26, it was only about the tenth anniversary of the company -in name anyway, less than a thousand people, most of them left over from the war."

" I had a very basic college education, I was considering joining the military, but based on reading about the horrors of the second world war through my teenage years, and then about Korea I was not too keen to get sent there. Or anywhere actually. Andy and I liked life on our small farm. Very isolated but it was what we knew. We didn't even have TV. "

" Mom and Pop had taken on some very basic land- presumably very cheap- down in Northern Nevada, their farming style was very much the same as here- raising sheep and cattle in th high pastures- provided there's a source of water- and over wintering in the valleys.

"Some of the family had remained around Boise, I stayed with them when I went to college. Most of their contemporaries, those that didn't try to find their fortune in America, remained as farmers here. Some still are. How I ended up at the agency, and not in some muddy trench on a battle field, or still out tending sheep, is weird."

" Apparently my relatives did garden work and other maintenance for some branch of the Angleton family who still lived in Boise. The Angleton's son James, of course went on to run counterintelligence for the agency from 54 to 75, was born in Boise in 1917. His family had then moved to Italy, where James, after university in the US, had a considerable role in security after the war, he eventually ended up working for Allen Dulles, as did I."

"James still came back regularly to visit family and friends in Boise around the time when I went to college there. Somewhere along the line, when the military called, folks at the college pushed me towards the very new world of intelligence and the Angleton connection. I was one of the few, if not the only Basque speaker in the agency."

" Our paths crossed now and again, of course I was years younger and so an agency junior, he was both a legend- and an oddball- from the start, but for some reason, every time we met, even years later, he'd say, 'Us Boise folks must stick together."

"Of course in later years when he became convinced there was a Russian mole high up in the CIA he eventually became somewhat discredited and quite rightly I was questioned several times about my connections. The fact that I'm still on the payroll is not necessarily an automatic indication that I was completely absolved of any suspicion-as usually we keep the suspects close at hand as it's easier to keep an eye on them that way. But then over the next God knows how many years I've been trusted with so many 'interesting projects' that I guess I passed the tests."

"In later years, I concluded, that originally someone in the agency, knowing they needed more people in Persia, hired me, as at the time many people were under the misapprehension, actually many still are, that the Basque and Persian language were one and the same.... Some words are similar, but that's it."

"Anyhows. In 1958 I ended up in Teheran"

Anaut came out from the house saying, "Let me refill those glasses, food is on it's way. I'll be back in a minute, but one of the dogs has been rolling in something terrible, and I need to go and hose it down before we have more farmyard inside the house than outside."

Paul laughed and said, "A daily occurrence. Really big dogs like that are kind of better outside- but I like having them around. But anyway back to the narrative, it's 1958 and I arrive in Persia. Tehran to be exact, with the big US embassy , later to become very famous- or notorious if you like. In 1953 the agency had helped strengthen the position of the Shah by getting rid of their elected Prime Minister who had increasingly revealed socialist leanings. We can assume 'Big Oil' was pulling the strings, and of course Allen Dulles and his powerful and well connected brother James Foster Dulles -actually almost the entire US business community had anti communist mania. "

" So I arrived, as the office new boy, trying to learn Farsi as quick as I could. One thing we were doing there , was using Persian-forward air bases and all sorts of planes, to snoop around the fringes of the USSR. All along the border with Azerbaijan, Turkmenistan, up towards Ukraine and Crimea. The operation was called Dark Gene, one of the key objectives was to test the Soviets and see how fast their air force and defence reaction times were."

"So I was busy liaising with the Persians all over the country, where most people there were very pro US at the time. We had a good life style there, remember the US was still recovering from the war whilst all across Europe with it's bomb damaged towns and cities, there was food and fuel rationing. But we had great accommodation, wonderful exotic food-from fantastic markets, servants, cooks, drivers, tennis courts, swimming pools. The lot...and a real eye opener for a lad from a farm in Nevada."

"So much so, that at Christmas 1960, I arranged for Andy, my kid brother to come out and stay. He was 22 or 23, and as life on the farm was quite basic I thought I'd show him the world. I figured the oil business there in Persia was growing and knowing a few folks might have helped him. I couldn't share too much of my work with him, as we were doing those secret overflights, remember this all before satellites, so we were using U2 aircraft. They flew very very high, but with incredible camera's we focused to get information about Soviet ground positions, rocket sites and strategic bases. "

"You don't need me to tell you all about that U2 stuff, but I do remind you, the President -that was Eisenhower back then- was trying to get some disarmament talks rolling, and forbade any more U2. flights. The planes were based at Interlik in Turkey, but were all a bit visible there, so they launched from Peshawar in Pakistan."

" For some reason, still argued about today, politics or agency ambition, in April '60 a brilliant pilot called Bob Ericson took some risks in his U-2c and came back with incredible pictures of various Soviet rocket and bomber bases. One of them was the Tarutam Missile range- that's the now the Baikonur Cosmodrome, that we see on TV so much, now even working with NASA."

"Bob's plane landed back in Persia, on the Zahedan air strip, over near the Pakistan border, so that kept me busy. Then just a few days later, disaster struck when the Soviets shot down Gary Powers in his U2, causing huge embarrassment to the US, and they say the collapse of the disarmament talks. Of course these days they suggest that was a Dulles plot... but what ever."

" Noting that we're alone out here right now I'll finish this story quickly, whilst I was busy, running all over Iran-Persia-chasing planes and secrets- my young kid brother was busy in Teheran...a bit too busy in fact. As he managed to make a young Persian girl pregnant."

"Pregnancy was bad enough, but she was only just sixteen, and from a very high up and influential family. Her parents were geared up to kill Andy, and possibly her, so a major diplomatic incident looked like it was brewing and it would also kill my career."

" Fortunately my local boss, was both understanding and keen to avoid an incident, so he arranged for them to flee the country using Canadian passports. That of course strangely fore telling what happened in the Embassy hostage crisis twenty years later. Of course as you will have figured out the girl was - and is Pamoon, and of course, the baby was and is- although he's no baby now- Anaut."

"For me. Probably no harm to my career. Dulles, Angleton and most of the US were so fixated about the growth of socialism around the world, this included the fast growing anti Franco separatist movements in Spain...Catalonian and Basque mainly, so I was posted here- under deep cover. Back to the family farm, but with a little money to make some discrete improvements and a day job with the agency as well. So once again the Basque language gave me a career...Having said I didn't suffer any career harm, I'm still employed, albeit out here in the wilds...so who knows."

Fortunately for Focksy and I, as we were near collapsing at all the revelations we were hearing, Paul, paused as Bitxi came out carrying a small notepad, she saying. "You told me not to forget to give you these papers to remind you of things. I know this is the first time you have told this story, despite Anaut and me telling you for years to write it all down, and we all know you not like to be interrupted. But these guests have got to eat. I suggest I start bringing out some food, and cook the lamb on the fire- and I promise not to interrupt any more."

She turned to Focksy and said, "Interruptions and help are not allowed. We get growled at sometimes if he's on the computer with the office door shut...only the dogs allowed to scratch the door and go in. Mind you when he gets his wheels stuck out in the fields if it's wet or snowing, if he's lucky, then we help him, otherwise he can have a cold night." With that she gave the fire a vigorous stir, releasing a cloud of sparks, and went inside.

Paul laughed," Domestic bliss eh guys. There is no one in the whole world I would rather have interrupt me or help me than Bitxi. Have you noticed - no one ever says wheelchair. It's always wheels. When I got injured in summer of 1980, I was very screwed up, blaming the world, and taking out my problems on everybody."

"My poor late wife had to put up with a lot, but the habit of never referring to the *"F*ing wheel chair'* seems to have stayed with all of us. When Anaut met and married Bitxi, in 1982 it was, things changed. There was this slip of a girl, new to the family, I was fifty and she was just coming up to twenty. I upset her one day-in my misery and self pity-and she came and sat next to me then, and quietly said: *'There's people worse off than you. You can move* around a bit, speak, eat, drink. You have good money from your old bosses, more than most people round here.'

' You got a whole world outside your room here' she meant this terrace- they'd built it in when I was first home on the wheels- 'You can see the hills, the animals, the sky, feel the rain'.

I remember the exact words, she then went on to say, '"So your world has changed- but you still have a chance to change the world. As they say here, ' Naturak zaintzen gaitu bainan batzuetan natura zaintzeko borrokatu behar gara."

"So that's what I've done and what I'm doing... and Bitxi is the one who woke me up to the opportunity."

Focksy raised a hand, and waited, until Paul who seemed a bit overcome with his long and emotional speech, smiled and said, "I see an interruption, yes Focksy. "

Focksy asking," Simple really, but what's the meaning of those Basque words that mean so much to you?."

Paul really smiled and said, "Of course,"

" Naturak zaintzen gaitu bainan batzuetan natura zaintzeko borrokatu behar gara... Nature takes care of us- sometimes we must fight to take care of nature."

"...and that's what I'm doing."

Chapter 26. Part Two.
Somewhere in the Basque high country.

Harry writes: Focksy and I were still rather overwhelmed with Paul's revelations- despite that sounding like a Biblical title- so it was with some relief we found lunch to be great fun...mainly due to the irrepressible Bitxi.

We ate- no, we feasted-and she kept up a constant supply of cooking, *"go on Mr Focksy, one more lamb chop. I know you can."* and as she served up endless side dishes -Pinxtos' really- with much information about *'who grew what and who made what in the various villages.* So lunch was much enjoyed by all- with much eyebrow raising, shrugs and smiles, from Paul as Bitxi bossed him into only eating what was allowed and then forbidding him more wine.

Eventually Anaut, waved the white flag and said, "I am not a big food expert, but I think a wait of some time now would be good. Maybe in an hour or so we have more coffee and some of the apple and cherry pie crumble."

Some discussion followed on the differences between pies, cobblers, flans and crumbles...with Focksy adding in a few Irish names to confuse matter even more, ' barm brack, yellow man, carrageen pudding, and lots of soda breads and Guinness cakes.'

So it was quite a while later that Bitxi said, "Anaut and I will clear all this up, you all carry on with your storytelling."

Which is what we did, Paul saying, "Before I tell you what we've been doing recently, I'll just finish the old days first, which, you'll be pleased to know I can run through a lot quicker than this morning's history lecture. Pamoon and Andy went back to the farm in Nevada, our parents were getting on a bit and needed help, with Pamoon hiding from being 'Persian' by telling that she was 'part Indian from Canada'. "

"They stayed there, partly because they both loved it- but also as they needed to keep a low profile- it was almost a Fatwa- that was called out on both of them from her family in Persia. I say 'almost' as it was more family than religiously endorsed- but was still serious. Jerry and Terri were born there in the early seventies, Anaut stayed there on the farm till about 1975 or 6, and then came back here to Europe as I was getting very busy with agency work and also needed to keep this place going. Luckily he knew pretty much how to run this place when I was wounded in '80. "

"Here, it was interesting times through the sixties, with Franco as dictator. The various Basque separatist movements were partly political and sometimes radical, ETA is just one of the factions, perhaps the best known around the world. "

"The Vietnam war was underway, and I worked on various agency projects, including before you ask again, various activities Laos and Cambodia. As well as the obvious concerns about The East Bloc, the agency was very active in much of Africa. I spent over a year in Angola, as the agency again got languages confused and assumed that as I spoke Spanish I also spoke Portuguese. "

"South America was of great interest and there were always fears that another Caribbean Island would go the way of Cuba. So I worked right through the whole string of Presidents- Kennedy, LBJ, Nixon, Ford, Carter, right through to Reagan, Clinton, a pair of Bushes and on to today. "

"My bosses changed over the years, including Helms, Colby, G W Bush -briefly, Casey, Stansfield -Turner. I always assume they left me here because either they forgot me-or I was still the only Basque speaker they knew. I've been here for over 65 years, all as an agency employee. In fact I've lived through so many world changing events that on occasions I feel like Jonas Jonasson's wonderful '100 Year Old Man', Allan Karlsson."

" My original mentor, James Angleton was both honoured but as I mentioned, in the end regarded as a liability due to his narrow focus, mania almost, on potential traitors in the system. His credo was that we had to assume that every security agency in the world had been penetrated by an enemy, that made him play his cards very close to his chest- and towards the end, too close really."

" It was sad and in some ways left too many questions unanswered when they forced him out- but it was probably time to move on, although of course-he was re-hired, but just kept off the books. Of course these days, with hindsight, behind every event or error lurks a conspiracy, many of which are the results of the need to balance immediate political ambition at home with events developing elsewhere in the real world."

"The first really big conspiracy story- other than the JFK affair, was for me here in 73, when someone set off a huge bomb killing Admiral Correro Blanco, who was shaping up to be Franco's chosen successor. Of course the CIA, got the blame, which I think really kick started a lot of the rumors swirling around about our regime interfering activities in Italy, Libya, Egypt, Turkey, The Congo, South America, Cuba, The Caribbean."

" I was involved in, or aware of many of those actions and deceptions, so I can understand the kneejerk 'blame the CIA' for everything. With reference to suggestions we had set the bomb that killed Admiral Blanco, nothing could be further from the truth. He was very anti communist, and although we wanted the process of democracy to *move forward faster here* in Spain- replacing the dictatorship of Franco it was,' better the devil you know than what may come next'. "

"There's lessons there that the US should have learned, with their mania for *'democracy-the American way'* they insisted on changing or trying to change the tribal, ethnic and religious status quo in some of the sandier and oil rich regions of the world. That was never going to bring about lasting situations."

"Here, decade by decade the lot of the average Spaniard improved, tourism grew as did many freedoms, of course slower than the extremists wished but better for the majority. We cannot ignore the crimes Franco's regime committed in the early days, and during the war, but it mellowed over time, he long planned to restore the monarchy, which he did actually, just before he died."

" For the US, we'd had air bases and naval establishments here for decades, they still use Moron down near Seville. I used to have to go there secretly every month to meet with various folks as we thought communications at the US Embassy in Madrid were compromised."

" I say secretly, as things were quite hairy round here, even after Franco died in '75. Soon after in 78, they had the first democratic elections here since 1939, but things were not moving fast enough for some of the factions. ETA and others with bombs and ambushes killed many, the peace processes were many and varied, and my work was cut out trying to 'help but not blame,' neither was I policing things. Here in the mountains, memories run deep. In the villages they say, *'The hills have ears and eyes, the villages have memories'.* "

" I always had to watch for my security and not many people around here even know I speak English, but I go to the markets most week buying or selling produce or animals. Generally there's a kind of neutrality in the region thanks to the peace progress and with the hope for the new generations."

" These days the main the reason for all the games of hide and seek bringing you here is not so much that we don't want people to know where I am-- most here know- but they will never tell. But what they don't want, we don't want, is a media circus following you dragging up the facts, the fictions, and local skeletons of the still too recent past."

"However, now at 88 years old, I have developed some concerns that in future years- political expediency will turn the fake news, conspiracy theories and all that- into a travesty of the real story. So *I have now become determined to set out the facts and the reality before I become carrion for the wild eagles to pick at.* "

"Jerry told me quite a lot about both of you-back to when he was in Thailand actually, which may surprise you, and then, I think fortuitously, following some dogged story chasing, you've ended up right on my doorstep. "

" I want to set the record straight as applied to actions I was involved in directly and indirectly, very much including those now seen as errors. That's from 1958 through to today, so a good few years- a lifetime indeed. *The question now is, would you be interested to help me tell my story."*

He paused, but before Focksy and I could gather our thoughts to make a suitable response Paul continued. "It is not clear to me- and possibly even to you both, if your pursuit of your current story is a for a quick big headline and move on...or if you have interest in the bigger picture. My suggestion is, that I show you a few things relevant to your current story..and then tell you a little more of my history. After that we adjourn for a few weeks and consider our various positions."

"I must make it clear, I am not trying to place you in the awkward position of feeling you are auditioning , any reluctance to 'let go' and get started is entirely mine. But there are also serious responsibilities and liabilities, not to mention dangers to knowing old and current secrets, hence me suggesting you two will want some time to think- in the event that you are vaguely interested,"

Focksy said," I know I speak for Harry, when I say we would be very keen to look into this. In fact if I recall correctly, I even said to Jerry, that- we, Harry and I, these days, generally took the long view, more than the splash headline. Mind you Harry and I tended to lecture Jerry a bit- when he seemed a little-shall we say-'hot headed.'"

Paul smiled and said, " I can imagine. Once I had decided to set out my tale, I decided a while back that I wanted non Americans to report it, not because there's any lack of writing and reporting skills in the US - they nurture many of the best reporters and writers in the world. But because Europeans - such as you both- have a deep seated independent understanding of much of the history."

Focksy said, "Just to lay a marker down, not in haste, but for real, I would happily take a year's sabbatical from the day job at TNoTN to have the privilege of working on your story."

I shifted around to be facing Paul, " Count me in- but in fact I'm also lucky to be here, especially after your failed attempt to do me in here in Spain some years back."

Paul looked quizzical, "Go on, give me a clue."

I replied, smiling, " 1966 Monday January the 17."

Paul hesitated and said, "Well I was here for most of that year I think. The notes that Bitxi gave me probably have the details but the date doesn't mean much to me."

I continued, "Mid morning, I'd been in Cartagena over the weekend, as a journalist, doing a story on a Spanish pop group, called Los Brincos. I'm driving along the coast road toward Gibraltar Airport...just near Palomares, actually near a village called Aloe Vera, and the car is suddenly enveloped in a cloud of dust..."

Paul said, "Christ. I know. There'd been an aircraft refueling accident and a B52 dropped four Atomic Bombs on the coast road. One drifted off into the sea, one fell into a pond, and two exploded, not thermo- nuclearly-but still scattered pounds of deadly radio active plutonium everywhere. Some flyers died. Terrible day."

Paul, "Hell of a mess. We denied it at first- but in weeks it was all over the worlds press. I do remember going down there, as a Spanish speaker, the Navy had brought in ten or more ships with all the latest hi tech equipment to find the bomb that had landed in the sea. They failed for weeks- if not months- and refused to listen to the local fishermen, who kept saying, 'It's right there amigo's, in the fishing grounds. Right there.' "

" He laughed and said, "I can even remember the name of the guy-Francisco Simo- who in the end showed them exactly where it was. " He continued, "You know some of the land is still fenced off as there's radiation in the soil. Plutonium is very nasty stuff with a half life of 20,000 years or something like that. And it was only a couple of years back, 2016 I think - fifty years after the accident- that US Secretary of State, John Kerry agreed that the US would at last clean up the area properly. That exactly kind of adds a poignant reality to those words,' *Naturak zaintzen gaitu bainan batzuetan natura zaintzeko borrokatu behar gara.*' I'm glad you survived though."

"Before it gets too late I want to show you something. "He turned to Anaut and said, "Could you get the things laid out on the other terrace, and and we'll be around there in a minute or two."

He wheeled his chair- or I guess, 'wheeled the wheels' nearer the fire and chucked on some logs, "They'll burn up well, as soon as the sun goes in the temperature will really drop. Whilst we wait for Anaut, let me quickly skim through the rest of my story-- 'back story' seems to be the phrase of the day. "

"I mentioned that I was injured in 1980. The US Embassy hostage crisis in Teheran, which had started in November '79 ,when more than fifty US citizens were held after the Embassy had been invaded and taken over, was in full swing. Any and all Farsi speakers were called in including me. In early January I went into Iran, using a Spanish passport as they were not so hated as the US. There was a real need to find out where all the hostages were, as some were being hidden by the Canadians. They were eventually sneaked out, nothing to do with me, at the end of January."

"President Carter still had misguided ideas that he could negotiate, although with 'official talking shops 'closed, the US was relying on some fairly flakey characters to help us."

"Whilst I was there, I went to see Pamoon's family, it was almost thirty years since Andy had made her pregnant, and over time- her father had died, and her mother really wanted to see Pamoon- and her grand children. The meeting went well, and basically, she agreed she wanted to come to Canada, we hadn't told her of the real destination back then. Obviously, right then was not the time to start, but she seemed very keen."

" Anyway, It's not clear if my cover was blown, or if it was an unfortunate meeting with some smugglers, but a few days later I was ambushed. That all happened way away from Teheran- over near Zahedan on the Pakistan border, where we'd kept some contacts since the U2 days mainly to keep an eye on the drug and arms smuggling. "

"I was shot in the lower back during the ambush, by chance I got rescued by a Pakistani Army unit- who had a great young doctor with them. Brit trained actually, although at the time I blamed him for me ending up on wheels," he smiled as he spoke, "But in the months that followed, the specialists back in the USA couldn't believe what a brilliant job the the guy had done- in not much more than a first aid room in a country hospital."

The final part of all this is the most difficult to tell, eight years later, with me stuck on my wheels, Andy my kid brother went back into Iran, to see if he could get Pamoon's mother out. All unofficially, in fact I only found out after he'd landed in the country. Anyway, I got a fax in very colloquial Basque, so reasonably coded I guess, from Andy at a Teheran hotel saying that the following day, July 3, 1988, he and Pamoon's mother were supposed to be on Iran Air flight 688 from Teheran to Dubai, via Bandar Abbas. "

"The plane was then shot down by the US Navy guided missile cruiser USS Vincennes. There were no survivors. The Vincennes was later shown to have been in Iranian waters, and the event was blamed fairly and squarely on a blustery old school and very gung ho, 'I listen to no one' US Naval captain name of Rogers. Neither my brother's name nor Pamoon's mother's name were on the passenger lists, but we have never heard from them since."

" He would of course have arranged to be travelling under an assumed name on a non US passport, but the agency, who tried all they could to help, never established what the name was. Although it could be said they may well have had alternative reasons for wanting to know if Andy was amongst the dead."

"Jerry- who, as mentioned is understandably very bitter about the event- believes his dad was able to buy a false passport in Thailand, which was reasonably easy back in the eighties. So modern day Iran is not much spoken of around here-although as you will learn in a minute I follow some other aspects of their long past history quite closely."

Chapter 26.   Part Three.

When the Eagle chooses, it seeks and touches the deepest blue of the sky'. *Focksy writes: These days I'm not so good at recalling quotations, and neither is Harry, and we both used to know quite a few. We have a theory that 'instant recall' technology is changing the operating systems of human memory. So I have no idea- unless I stop writing and google it- who came up with those emotive words about eagles and the sky.*

Following Paul along the terrace, around the side of the house, then down a longish slope, Paul saying "Coming back up this path ten times a day, I turn off the batteries on these wheels, which usefully keeps me fit."

Harry and I were surprised again, this time, to find a huge open sided low barn- or aviary really, with quite a selection of Eagles and other birds- presumably falcons, of various types.

Paul," We've been keeping, and breeding birds here almost 40 years since about 1983, soon after Bitxi's conversation about my condition changed my life. Given your current storyline you may find it hard to believe but the plan then, was just to provide a safe haven and perhaps some new breeding stock for various failing species."

"Then over time-with no internet or satellite TV to occupy my evenings, for obvious reasons, I spent a lot of time reading and we all became interested in the legends of Eagles being trained as Warbirds and targeting specific people. Once they were of age Jerry and then Terri also became very keen. Of course in recent years bloody windfarms are decimating birds of all kinds, so most of our focus is back on helping in a small way where the numbers are are getting depleted."

"Once the birds are adult they are free to come and go as they wish, we're not breeding falconry style, to have hungry birds that hunt to order, although today, as we want to show you something, we kept a couple of the ladies in overnight."

Bitxi, emerging from a doorway, turned to us saying, "If you look on the table here there's twenty paper -or card plates...as you can see they've got very similar patterns drawn on the back. You have to look very carefully to see the differences. Come with me and you can set them out on the terrace wall here, all the way along, amongst the flowers is no problem. In any order, I will hide some fresh food under one particular one, it looks just like the others - except-the eagle can see the difference from thousands of feet away."

After we'd set out the plates, and for sure I couldn't see which one had food under it, let alone see any real differences in the patterns, she gave a loud, fingers to the lips whistle, "I learned that at school in England as well."

Anaut came round the corner of the building with an eagle on his gloved arm...which he then released. With immense and noisy flapping it left him, and was soon gone from sight, Anaut saying- "She'll be stretching her wings as it's a little later than usual that's she's been able to go out."

He held up a small silver tube and said-" This what they sell as silent dog whistles...inaudible to humans...but we had a theory that eagles could hear them from long distances. Paul had found some stories in old Persian books of whistles used when hunting with falcons and eagles. I'll give it a blow- and 'Sarah ' will look down from a few thousand feet, and figure out from the pattern on the plates which is the one with the meat under it. "

Whilst we were opening our mouths to ask about 'Sarah', he blew, and in seconds, with a clatter more than flutter she crashed down on top of the correct plate and ripped it apart with her beak and talons.

Paul who had been retrieving another bird from one of the cages, saying, "The amazing thing is we taught her to do that, twelve years ago, not only that but she flew away from here six years back, and only returned ten days ago, we don't track our birds so we have no idea where she was. So the 'imprint' of exactly where she would find food was still there, twelve years after she learned, and six years after she had last done it. There's a clue in the name Sarah about how long ago that was, when we were checking out how much the birds can see and remember, Sarah Palin had just been chosen as a Vice Presidential candidate - with John McCain, and she also seemed quite feisty."

As the huge bird on his arm, looked beadily around, and, sat or rather stood with its immense beak alarmingly close to Paul's face he spoke again. " You know, thirty years of doing this has been a revelation, although I have been rather stuck here for obvious reasons, I found and learned more and more from the old Persian, Greek, Chinese and Japanese legends and books. "

"Terri -sometimes with Anaut and Bitxi spent a lot of time researching in the Gulf States, Mongolia, Kazakhstan, Kyrgyzstan, Turkmenistan... all 'The Stan's' really. Travel to some of those countries is a good deal easier these days, so maybe some good came of all our anti communist agitating."

"But let me get Melania here aloft...she's a bit heavy on my arm. You know, I may be reading too much into the situation- but over the years I have become convinced the birds understand, I am stuck on these wheels. So many times when one returns from a flight, rather than crash down on my arm, as they do with Anaut or Bitxi , they'll land near me, and then step up close- so they know something. Right now look over the wall, and you'll see whole group of people...or rather life size straw dummies."

As Harry looked over he called back, "Tattie Bogles."

I explained to Paul that, being a Scot's term for scarecrows, him replying, "Well, I have their names in about fifteen different languages, but thats a new one on me, Tattie Bogles...I like it."

He continued. "If you want you can, nip down the steps and mix up all the hats and jackets, but I can assure they are all on the dummies randomly. What you can't see from up here so well, is that they have faces. Here in Spain we have tradition of making paper mache models of politicians, personalities and characters from films and cartoons. Then at festival time - like Las Fallas in Valencia- we blow them up with fireworks, it's a mix of religious festival and strong political statements."

"A bad or greedy local mayor or politician, will be modelled with an accurate face, possibly with a fat and slobby body to make the show better. They get the message pretty damn quick that the local people are not happy, when their effigy starts to appear on a hundred bonfires- stuffed with explosives."

"When it became clear over the last few years that President Trump, was going to totally ignore the mood of the world and take down the plans to slow global climate warming--I noticed that at Las

Fallas, and other Spanish festivals, effigy's of Trump were starting to appear, in the usual 'cartoon' style, exaggerating his characteristics. Then, someone on this terrace, naming no names, named this one Melania, so she's only been learning her dedicated target for a couple of years." Bitxi interrupted saying, "I think the whole Stormy Daniels story was going on then so I figured Melania would be very angry."

Paul continuing, "Actually it's interesting how wide spread the use of 'warbirds' was. There's so many narratives suggesting that they were commonly used by Genghis Khan and other warlords right across Eurasia, by the Samurai in Japan and others in China. They made accurate effigies of their various enemies- and took squadrons of eagles out to war - trained to attack just one person."

"In Roman times, and then later throughout the Austro Hungarian empire, across Europe, and into the mountain passes of India , Kashmir, Pakistan, Afghanistan and so on, locals taught their birds to 'attack any person *with a certain kind of 'uniform hat'*, or 'coloured sash'. So less specific but still deadly."

"We have less evidence from South America, but my initial studies suggest it was the same there back to the Aztecas and Mayans. So in addition to the majesty of the Eagle in bearing and in flight- there seem to be practical reasons why they are the symbol of so many empires and armies. The legends also spoke of eagles returning tens of years later, with the memory imprint still in place. But in some cases attacking their old handlers who had by then changed sides and thus were now wearing 'enemy ' uniforms."

"You guys go down the steps there, it's quicker than me using the ramp and going round. Check out the faces on the straw men- I mean Tattie Bogles-until you find Trump, change any hats or clothes you want, or move the whole bodies around. "

Harry , Bitxi and I nipped down the steps and after some careful looking found Trump not because they were 'bad likenesses' - but because, as Bitxi explained, they were all so similar. "We made them very alike to try and make sure the birds really focused and only chose the exact correct one."

At her bidding Harry and I swapped a few hats and jackets around, and after a while she said, "Step back here and I'll tell Paul and Anaut to let the rest of the birds out. These are not trained to any whistle, they just go in and out as they wish, but obviously we closed the doors today when we set this up to show you."

"Actually whilst these ones are not trained to the whistle, luckily Paul and Anaut are." And she gave an almighty fingers to the lips whistle, and soon we heard and could then see about half a dozen eagles wheeling about- most of them going higher and higher ... one perching on the top of a building.

She said, "Now listen." For a while we heard only the wind, then then was a whooshing sound- it got louder and with a heart stopping crash- and flap of mighty wings, the talons hit the dummy's head which shattered and fell to the ground- with the bird pecking and scraping away the food then revealed.

Bitxi said quietly, "I'm not sure if another will come, after the first one sometimes puts them off for a while...but we'll wait a little longer."

Two three minutes on, and she heard the sound first, "Look look, see the bird on the ground has covered her food in case it's a robber coming down to steal it."

But it wasn't to be...the mighty eagle pulled out of it's dive at the last moment and soared away... the frantic and slightly ungainly first eagle still hopping around concealing its feast.

Bitxi saying, "You see, even though she's hungry there was no Trump for her to attack so she pulled out of the dive. They look so terrible when they walk- but so wonderful when they seek and touch the blue of the sky."

Harry and I were too overwhelmed to answer.

Chapter 26.   Part Four.
Apple & Cherry Crumble.

Focksy's tales: I could resist neither the crumble-(with crème fraiche) with the accompanying glass of what I thought was champagne, but turned out to be local dry cider.

As the talk turned to 'working together'- I told them that Harry sometimes had his uses and he had written a very strong intro for our proposed TV report, using information gleaned in Scotland and confirmed with other researches including a video of Golden Eagles used for hunting in Mongolia.

Although I then added, "Mind you the world getting to see that depends on TNoTN being convinced there's a real story and also now, after Paul's suggestion, I should say *'If Harry and I choose to make and submit one."*

 Bitxi- of course it was Bitxi who said," Mr Focksy, can you recall the words of that intro. I ask as it would interesting to hear how an outsider see's it all." She looked at Paul, who nodded saying, "I very much appreciate the subtle but vital difference in your words from *'when'* you make, to *'if'* you make,' I like the sound of that. But as Bitxi says hearing a professional intro for a possible TV story would be very interesting."

I fished around in my bag and found the notes whilst explaining, "Of course unlike printed media where apart from a few stills the story has to be conjured up in the readers mind, for TV we have to take care that the narration is in synch with the images on the screen - sometimes before, to alert viewers to note something- and sometimes after for added emphasis."

" We also have to consider the need for 'a headline' to grab the viewers attention...so the opening is usually followed by somewhat more paced content. Of course we also have the benefit of emotive speech...so Harry's production instructions were:

Intro Focksy. Sincere to camera:*" Having spotted its prey from airplane height, say ten thousand feet, the Golden Eagle then, wings and tail feathers streamlined back, plummets down, in what's called 'The Stoop' at around 150 MPH. But in inch perfect control, massive talons and cruel razor sharp beak at the ready"*

<u>Silence and pause for effect:</u> *"The first President Trump, he being the Eagle's chosen target, would know, seconds before the mighty bird crashed into him, lacerating his flesh and splitting his skull, is the fearsome- unholy almost, banshee like scream of the wind over the bird's mighty six or eight foot wings. That likely closely followed by a similar scream from The President."*

<u>Long pause and then I continue in reporter speak mode:</u>

"Experienced falconers and experts who have seen these birds 'taking' deer, goats and other large prey agree, one saying 'If he, The President survived, I wouldn't think he would be fit to work or think for months...'."

"Any of the President's Golf courses in the US, Scotland or Ireland would provide fine open hunting ground for several species of Eagle. Training the Aquiline aggressors from birth would take about eight months. "

" Security experts charged with protecting the President say it would take quite some skill to target a bird coming down in the stoop-truly at around 150 mph, by the time they had focused, targeted and fired they'd be just as likely to hit the boss.."

<u>"End of report...roll theme music, logos and end</u>. "

I sat back, and Paul took up his glass and said, "Powerful stuff...really powerful. I can see what made you two a good team."

Bitxi adding, "I can imagine that with the pictures...Wow."

Harry, "To bring us back to the real world, any TV show, all revolves around the slant put on it. It could be sensational and newsy ' Will the Eagles get The President?' or it could be that the sensational storyline is just used to capture the interest of a huge audience - to whom we then have the chance of really setting out the true meaning of your Basque phrase..."

Anaut nodding and adding, "' *Naturak zaintzen gaitu bainan batzuetan natura zaintzeko borrokatu behar gara.*'

Paul said, "Well, the door is open to getting my story told, and we'd better all think about it before I fall out of the nest. Right now I am happy to sit here by the fire until late, but I believe you now have very early flights tomorrow and I suspect you have a lot to discuss and consider. Just to confirm, having at last shared some of my story, I feel somewhat liberated and I would be keen to continue - with you two gentlemen. If you have the time and inclination. "

"Of course, working with me, let's be clear, and keeping some of it confidential-may be legally interesting for all of us. My loyalties were and still are to America, but with hindsight and experience I can see that these days some revelations and corrections are needed to put straight some of the scurrilous rumours before they become accepted history."

"Those stories, despite any reasoning and explanations, will of course get me branded in the popular media as everything from a traitor to a spy for another nation or regime. Those co-operating with me in reporting this accurately will be branded with the same uncomfortable irons."

"So, whilst I have had enough time- years even- to consider what is best for our great nation and its people...you've had the opportunity- or the poisoned chalice- presented to you just this afternoon, so some careful reflection would be advised."

"Regarding Jerry and Terri, I am genuinely not sure what will happen next. Anaut indeed spoke carefully yesterday, but truthfully. *We have rather lost control of the situation with both Jerry and Terri, and we genuinely do not know where they or any birds they trained in Scotland currently are. They both really operated on a need to know basis-and we were not included in that. Partly I suspect because they couldn't judge which way my loyalties would fall.*"

"The one thing I can say is that if-repeat if-they are either or both- pursuing this attack Trump thing further, then the birds would need several months of conditioning to get used to the location that they are to target. You couldn't just drive up and let them loose in a whole new place, neither for security reasons would you likely to be able to fly from your arm, falconry style, as we have done here."

" In total 'released back in to the wild' mode they would roam over many miles seeking their usual prey, then one day, one year even, just having the happy luck to see a familiar target- a face, perhaps hat and hair they associate with free food...and down they'd come. But I confirm again, no birds were trained here other than for research, and right now, none of us, have a location-or any real confirmation of their target-or indeed the the whereabouts of the potential miscreants."

Harry and I stood, as Paul continued, "You'll be pleased to know it's a direct drive back to your hotel- no car changes. I suggest we contact each other at the end of next week...Bitxi will give you my e mail details. Given that you both seem quite taken with our ladies here-you could keep and fly some Peregrines or similar from your riverside terrace in New York. That would keep the seagulls away."

With many thanks, handshakes, and in the case of Bitxi, hugs, with extra thanks for the wonderful food- we made our way down to the farmyard, where our original taxi man awaited.

Paul had come down to the yard, and beckoned us both over to him, "In case it escaped your notice...as with many countries, old names often refer to the profession of the person...Brewer, Farmer, Carpenter and such... in Basque, Olaberria means New Smith."

As we considered that, more nods and smiles, Bitxi suddenly said, "Hang on"...and rushed into the house, emerging carrying some shopping bags, " Some souvenirs from St. Jean Pied de Port and The Ham Shop...even though you didn't get to those places you can think of us when you eat them in America."

Chapter 27. US *bound. Late Summer 2018.*

'Think of us'. *Harry Writes: Bitxi's words are still ringing in my ears and it's now five days later...and quite frankly I have done little else but think of her, Paul and Anaut since we parted company on Saturday evening.*

When we arrived back at our hotel at about nine after an extraordinary day, on livening up our phones we, or rather Focksy, found, that ironically as he was going to Florida to work on a hurricane story- the impending arrival of a tropical storm, although not yet an actual hurricane, required him to advance his travel plans.

His new 07.10 departure Sunday, now to Lisbon and on to Miami got him in there at 14.30 - hopefully landing before any incoming hurricane. Thanks to the joy of instant online booking, and needing to share our rental car back to Bilbao, I also changed to a similarly timed departure-via Paris- getting in to JFK, at 12.30. I figured it being Sunday the traffic over to Focksy's apartment nearer Newark wouldn't be too bad.

Of course getting back to Bilbao airport and allowing for check in time required us to leave the hotel at a regretful 4.00 am...regretful in wake up terms and also in having to depart from the peace and quiet of the Pyrenean foothills. Peace and quite, yes. Gastronomically fascinating and requiring a re-visit- which could be another reason to accept the suggestion we could abandon our current story and work with Paul.

Back in the US, sitting- back, post siesta and now late evening Sunday, on Focksy's terrace, glass of his wine, and eating some French made pate and biscuits, from our Bitxi goodie bags was good. All this rushing about meant that Focksy and I had little or no time to discuss Paul's amazing sixty five years backstory, and his offer for us to report same, instead of the current, 'Be there predatory eagles out there?'

So questions and quandary. Good pate though, and in the fridge, packages of Serrano, Bayonne and Basque mountain ham, French and Spanish cheeses, saucisson, jams, tins and more vac packs of pate to share with Focksy on his return.

Apart from some discussions of how Paul knew about Focksy's riverside terrace or more concerningly about his changed flight schedule for that morning- what he and I had agreed during our dawn drive to Bilbao, was that Focksy would e mail me his entire file of notes and part written pieces. Over the next few days, I would then assemble them -with mine- into some kind of narrative - which we could later, *subject to our conclusion about going with Paul's incredible life story or staying with the original Eagle Threat to The President,* on Focksy's return, submit to TNoTN or file for future use.

I await the return of a remarkably pissed off Focksy for the final decision, he is mightily pissed off because on arrival in Miami he discovered that the weather threat had postponed the making of his 'Presidential Privilege? Does the President's resort of Mar el Lago' get preferential treatment in Hurricane Season?' Something to do with TNoTN's insurance and the heightened risk of lightning strikes only allowing filming of news not features.

With most US channels alternating between their usual Sunday Trump loving or bashing, and inch by inch live progress reports on the *'not yet..but might soon be a hurricane,'* I fell asleep in front of the TV. The week then passed off peacefully enough with long days sorting through our notes and re-writing stuff.

But Focksy it seemed, whilst still in Miami and well clear of hurricanes, had then stirred up a storm of his own. On TNoTN and then much repeated online-he had poured scorn on some old 'live' reports on other networks- him showing and re showing footage of a rival broadcaster ' leaning into the wind, apparently bracing themselves against gusts- on occasions staggering, 'blown to one side,' whilst just thirty feet behind them, passers by strolled along with their dogs and shopping bags without a care in the world.

He then stoked the flames further by alleging that during storm Katrina years before one of his network rivals was actually kneeling in shallow water- not bravely standing waist deep to make their report from *'The developing disaster.'*

Dan Groom called me to suggest Focksy would be back on Thursday- flights permitting- him also suggesting he'd better, 'Get Focksy to a place of safety-*long pause*- before the other networks did him serious damage'. Dan also asked, as I was working alone if I needed any fact checking as he had a couple of work experience junior interns available. So whilst keeping silent about our meeting with Paul, both to Dan and in my story resume, I emailed them a whole heap of notes, so they could check stuff like time zones, chronology, spelling, place names and such like.

Thursday evening and Focksy arrived. Still irate as Dan predicted, fuming at his wasted week, although he accepted - after one or two restorative glasses of wine that there was a funny side to losing a hurricane story because of a non hurricane.

He also had big news...he'd asked Dan if he could take a year out from TNoTN duties to write a book. Focksy saying, "I thought I'd ask when I had pissed them all off a bit. If Paul confirms he wants to work with us that'll be good, if he's not ready yet, I've got plenty to catch up on. Dan asked if I was writing about the Eagle's but I explained I was hoping to complete a spy story."

"Dan needs to run my planned year off by the powers that be, but it seems that I could not have asked at a better time as there's someone retiring in a years time, and another person needing to come back and be US based right now. So provided I'm back on duty by November next year to cover the final year run up to the 2020 US elections I think they'll agree. Not only that but after my 20 years with them they keep paying me half salary and reasonable expenses.' I do have to give them a first option to report anything new that I do or write, but that's cool."

By the time he'd then enjoyed a 'Basque' dinner, *assembled* from Bitxi's gifts, he was back on good form, excited enough about the possibility of capturing Paul's amazing 65 years journey to make up for the possibility that we'd wasted near enough half a year on a story we couldn't stand up. On the matter of 'standing up' the story I gave him a list of bullet points: This is what we know.

Pamoon Smith. Iranian/Canadian. Mother of Anaut, Jerry and Terri. Her husband Andy (and also her own mother) *believed* killed in shooting down by US Navy of Iranian Air 655 July 3 1988. Mrs Smith now severely affected with dementia. Resides in care home Boise. Idaho.

Jerry Smith. Is or was a security operative of some kind for the US Government or military. Possibly with responsibilities for Presidential protection. Current status, location unknown. Due to death his father has deep seated resentment about aspects of the US Navy, although we feel conceals that as being anger over big business harming the planet.

Terri Smith. Biologist and ornithologist Expert in Falcon/ Eagle breeding/cross breeding and artificial insemination. Known to have advised certain Falconry 'associations or owners ' in Gulf States. Recently lived Spain, France, Scotland currently resides Moscow. Address can be checked with her mothers care home.

The Olaberria's: Anaut and Bitxi. Also experts on raptors, apparently spent some time in Scotland as carers for Pamoon Smith. Currently farming in Spain.

The Eagles. Alleged 'Attack Ready. Numbers target trained unknown. Locations likely: France, Scotland , Ireland, USA or Russia. Status, captive or free to fly (attack) unknown. Ends.

Obviously and very carefully this omitted any mentions of Paul. Reading and discussing it over breakfast on Friday, despite (yet again) nice riverside and Manhattan skyline views, some good coffee, and even lush French (imported by moi) biscuits- was a depressing affair.

Focksy saying, "*I agree with all that, despite all we've found, right now we can't produce a single eagle-let alone Jerry or Terri, the Olaberria's and certainly not Paul without betraying him, which I am not minded to do, with or without the deal to write his story. Nor of course any other 'real proven evidence' of a threat to The President, we have some evidence it can be done, but no actual threat.*"

He continued," I agree we *simply just don't have enough proof that will stand up.* Even on a quiet news day, if Dan Groom - believing in you and I as he does, allowed us to run this, then you, I, Dan and TNoTN would be struck by a mega storm of fake news disbelief, and general scorn'."

Pause, for long silence...I responded, "Sadly but realistically, I agree Focksy with all you say, and the likely effects, especially the scornful vindictive that will be poured on you and yours truly by those rivals you insulted about their hurricane coverage fakery."

"But what if we're right, what is our position? What if one afternoon in years to come, on a golf course anywhere in the US, or even Ireland or Scotland- or if some folks get their way- in a penitentiary exercise yard- an Eagle comes crashing down and seriously or even mortally wounds the Ex President."

Focksy nodded saying "For me, I actually don't give a monkeys about the legal position, neither will I have the slightest tearful 'Oh I should have warned them' remorse. What I do worry about though, is you, Dan and TNoTN professionally- if we've been sitting on the scoop of a lifetime all the while.

He sat back as we both considered-or perhaps- confronted 'the reality,' until suddenly his phone beeped...causing him to add, " Hang on a minute, I've got email's from Dan."

From Dan: Following from my interns: One major error Eagle story. PUW airport code is for Pullman-Moscow Airport, this shared between US towns of Pullman Washington and Moscow Idaho-both located about 300 miles North of Boise. Ends.

Second mail: Dan Groom To Focksy. Now you free of birdwatching commitment this confirms management happy you take year's sabbatical. HR will send you terms and conditions. Back here on duty by Oct Nov next year 2019. Oh yes-based your plan to write a spy novel you might care to note that the spies are more likely to be found in Moscow Russkielands than on the campus of a US college in Moscow Idaho. Good luck. You owe me dinner. Dan."

Focksy shrugged saying, "Three things. Bang goes our, 'It's the Russkies' theory, and actually also I cannot believe, given the fame of their Universities and all their sports excellence, that you and I both missed that US Moscow reality. Shows how too close focus *on the desperate wish to get a story* sometimes makes you miss the bloody obvious."

" Secondly. Subject to you also needing to make a living, If we do get to work on Paul's amazing 65 years on the frontline with the CIA, as always you're welcome to stay here as long as you as you can survive Ermalinda's Piri Piri, and water the plants. "

"Thirdly. How about another of your excellent coffees and I'll break open the special Basque calvados to drown our sorrows.
It's all very Catch 22 : Eagles...we don't know if they are there...and if they are... where are they. And are they where they are for what we think they are there for.

Chapter 28.   November 2018- November 2019.
Focksy's Sabbatical Year.

Harry Writes: Sorting out Focksy's obligations to complete stories and tidy up matters at TNoTN in the end took him almost up to Christmas, during which time I collected, collated and edited all our work so far in 'The Eagle's Tale...Fact or Fable.' That's pretty much what you've read in the preceding pages.

It seemed that Paul was also busy and so it was not until the end of January *that found us being greeted at Bilbao airport by Anaut and Bitxi.* "I hope you packed some winter clothes as I suggested." were Bitxi's first words...I gestured to my two large suitcases-and explained that as I'd been in Ireland and then Cornwall for Christmas it was chilly there, and of course New York also tended to get plenty of snow, so I was well equipped and used to the cold.

Focksy butting in saying," That's all well and good but I've come direct from a month in Thailand and I'm already bloody freezing. I need to drop into the FedEx office here at the airport where I hope there's a box of my winter clothes- USBs optional. They were dispatched by Maisie my neighbour and kind of 'wish she was' girlfriend. When I called her she still seemed to be celebrating Christmas and was distinctly merry...so there's a chance the FedEx box is full of beach kit for Florida."

Half an hour later having used the car keys to cut through the no tamper tape round the FedEx box- much to Focksy's relief it was full of his skiing kit." Bitxi, shielding her eyes at the bright bright colours, said, with a broad grin, "Well so much for discretion, everyone in the village, or actually everyone on the entire mountain will be able to find you Focksy." He responding gruffly with jet lagged ill grace, "Well at least I'll be warm.'

As Anaut drove, "A nice and direct route this time, so about an hour and a half." the conversation turned to Paul's health- which seemed to be excellent-although with Bitxi setting out some firm rules regarding work times and stress. Anaut adding, " He's been working writing notes like crazy, all hours of the day and night. Your plan to work together seems to have really given him a mission, so he's very happy. The only downside is that the dogs are getting fat.

They were used going with him on a longish circuit of the farm every day, using the track we set out years ago for his wheels...and they of course loved that. He used to go in all weather's. "Bitxi cut in, "Now they've found a new favourite, just lying in the warm of his office whilst he works."

I suggested that with Focksy being a fitness freak, he could jog round the farm perimeter daily with the dogs before we started work. Which went down singularly badly. With Focksy. He being notorious amongst his New York crowd for loathing jogging and joggers, and for never knowingly having stepped inside a gym.

Surprisingly then, during the almost six weeks of long days making notes, and long evenings discussing many aspects of Paul's life, Focksy and I had taken up walking most afternoons, with the dogs, the entire five or six kilometer perimeter of the farm. Partly to clear our heads, but also as Bitxi had suggested we need to slow the pace a little for Paul.

After that six weeks we departed our hard work, but much enjoyed Pyrenean home during the first week of March, Focksy back to Thailand and me back to join my wife in Dublin and then, spending some months based in Cornwall. I had to meet Mick the Brief my lawyer in Dublin and then travel around the UK doing some promotion work for my new book 'Just One Day'.

During our time with Paul, we'd enjoyed wonderful views of the Pyrenees from the guest accommodations on the farm with the mountains getting a dusting of snow many nights, good for the ski runs, and shadowy valleys, but most burned off by the daytime sunshine. As well as the dogs getting fat -Focksy and I were also. Well fed-both at the farm by Bitxi and at weekends when she and Anaut took us to some simple village cafes mostly off the main ski tourist routes. Hence even Focksy agreeing our head clearing walks were also much needed by our waistlines.

One part of Paul's story seemed to be completely off limits. No mention was to be made of his late wife, Paul saying-"This is story of events not a biography."

Focksy and I tried to suggest that to ensure credibility for his recollections, readers needed to know 'the man behind the stories', but we got no where. We did learn that she was Irish, and that he had no children, which Focksy and I quietly wondered at first was due to him being 'on his wheel's' but then we realised that he was 50 when he was shot. He was though a huge fan of traditional-or at least traditionally influenced Irish music. So we enjoyed many long and lively evenings in the farmhouse kitchen enlivened by some of his favourites-Horslips, Spud, Dolores Keane, Christy Moore with our particular choice being a more modern download of a few tracks by The Hooligans.

On our walks Focksy wondered, as it was long rumoured that the IRA had connections with ETA if there'd been any political connections that involved his wife...but even on a relaxed and well lubricated musical evening around the fire that door was firmly closed and so somewhat reluctantly ...eventually Focksy and I decided to go along with Paul's "This is more about the events than about me.'

Of course we learned a lot more about eagles- really a lot. More about conservation than the likelihood or not of any threat posed. On our arrival Focksy and I had said we wanted to focus on Paul's story and would avoid asking about Jerry or Terri, which was well received, Paul saying it," Much appreciated very professional."

Although Focksy and I still tended to trawl the internet every few days, but we could find no trace of them nor even anything interesting about eagles. We're both starting to feel that if-repeat if - Terri is indeed in the US with a flock of free flying eagles, with the US so well covered with enthusiastic bird watchers, hunters, and those Americans for whom the sighting, let alone capturing or handling of any eagle is significant, surely someone would have seen them...

This total invisibility gave us to conclude that either they were 'officially hidden' way out at the back of beyond on one of the numbered 'Area's- or else, we had the right Moscow in mind as their destination-the Russki one - first time around.

As departure day neared, we spent some time with Paul arranging the most secure ways to create and store our combined files. He preferred that we not communicate with him by email saying, "You've got detailed notes on about twenty years to work on-so any questions and corrections we can clear up next time we get together. The main folks who could break into our secure systems are the NSA , CIA, probably the Chinese or Russkies and definitely the Israelis. My concerns are mainly to keep this book away from any official scrutiny, as I have to inform the agency of any plans I have to publish anything."

" I think gaining permission to write would likely take a year or so to obtain, and even with God willing, I fear their idea of a year, or so will deliberately be very different from mine."

So his plan was to eventually submit the book in final form for a safety and security review, but tell the agency that for reasons beyond his control, copies of the manuscript were already in the hands of various third parties, presumably Focksy and I, who would carry on and publish regardless.

"I don't think they'll prosecute me, they might try legal moves to injunct the publishers, or they could excommunicate me and cut off my pension but I really couldn't care less about that. I don't think they could bundle me off in a secret rendition flight to distant islands without a serious court case." Him adding, with a wan smile, "Not unless they bring you two along for the ride." Which raised equally wan smiles from Focksy and I.

It was fairly late one evening when we discussed all that, relaxing in the kitchen- hunting trophies, some with impressive horns or antlers, on the walls and a collection of hunting rifles with telescopic sites mounted over the huge stone fireplace with it's crackling logs and flickering flames.

After some wonderful Anaut caught, Bitxi cooked, first of the season's local trout, Paul, raised his wine glass, savoring what he called, 'The last drops of my Bitxi rations,' and said, "If the agency still play silly bugger's, a very appropriate Brit phrase I have learned from you two over these past weeks, then we or I guess you- can just threaten to sign up to a Russian or Chinese online publisher. That'll concentrate their minds wonderfully."

We raised our glasses in a toast-"To freedom of speech."

To which Paul said, "*I'll add the old agency prayer to that...CI..Amen.*"

Chapter 29.   A year on. November 2019-20.
Harry Writes: **Time for Focksy to re-join TNoTN.**

Our travel schedule of the past year, similar to the previous one, mine with Ireland and Cornwall, then where it all started with Focksy in Chiang Mai. On to Spain - as we quietly and ambiguously referred to our Basque country sojourns- and as Christmas nears again we're back on Focksy's terrace in New York, sounds like the perambulations of a couple of wealthy retiree's.

Whereas the reality is we'd been working all hours, getting details on Paul's life, that incorporating his direct or informed participation in some of the most momentous geopolitical and often contentious events of the past sixty years.

Our online research and other work done using our old computers, but the new book now only created on our special new laptops where alarmingly 'programme, contents and machine will will destruct unless on switch and keys are used in a specific timed order, or if the case is opened in any way.'

The 'bookwork' laptops were never to be connected to the internet. Some Israeli security boffin recommended by Paul had physically removed the wi-fi and blue tooth connections and done something to the single USB socket so only some specific coded and numbered USBs he supplied would work in them. Their only 'connection' was to the electrics and that had to go via some magic transformer boxes that broadcast jamming signals to avoid any and all kinds of - or as the guy said- 'all known'- snooping systems.

Our boffin, became a little irritated when Focksy asked, "As we understand it certain parties-alleged to be Israeli- managed to get across 'the air gap' and into various Iranian, US and Russian computer systems to sniff or fix certain ultra secret projects. So how can we be sure ours can't be jumped by those same certain parties-especially if they also Israeli."

The response was terse. "Firstly these cannot connect to the internet and you can only use the USBs we provide. Even I can't get into the system once you've set all three passwords, loaded your fingerprint, eye scans and meaningful dates. If you scar your finger, get an eye infection, or forget the three passwords you're screwed, as it needs all of them to work and there are *no* second chances."

"Our second question was more practical, how about the times we needed to leave the laptops unattended ?

Our boffin scored bonus points with his immediate response, " You mean The Guinness problem. Obviously an opportunist thief won't know they can't open or sell the machines, but I'm confident for you to leave them concealed in your usual way. Do though conceal them in very different places so you don't lose both -as that's a real pain in the arse, for work you may have to re do."

"If you pour coffee into the machines or lose the passwords, don't come crying to us to fix them and retrieve the data, because even we can't do it. Also when you hit delete, delete means delete, it's not just compressed and buried in the system, it's totally wiped. Really wiped- and the drives are completely filled with other stuff, overwriting and underwriting old data. So doing back ups in the exact way I've shown you on those special USBs is the only way."

Which of course caused Focksy to explain how we'd got started on this entire affair, with us getting hold of a certain security person's USB and then checking out the contents. The response was predictable... " I only have two words Amateur or Plant. Amateur is obvious, and Plant being deliberate to allow persons to easily find what ever is on it. "

"As Focksy and I looked at each other, with raised eyebrows but little surprise he continued, with a cheerful, "I'll see you when you lose or destroy a machine, not to fix anything, that's impossible -but to bring you a new one." And he left us to it...

Back sitting in New York, in very familiar circumstances Focksy continued, "It's well over a year now since we met Paul, and my 'so called year off in a deliberate use of a cliché- it's just flown by'. Working with Paul, keeping an eye open for eagles on line, was fine, and just observing The President, but not having to report on his year was a lucky break."

"To be fair Trump did score quite a few home runs, mostly unacknowledged by the Washington media bubble, but generally he behaved like an arrogant ignorant moron, completely destroying years of much needed diplomacy, upsetting shithole nations and allies alike. Around the world, at every appearance, Canada, Japan, France his ignorance astounded and then rebounded as foreign leaders mocked him in ill concealed concern. In the UK his boorish behaviour and the crass ridiculousness of his family upset British society on all levels, and he seriously insulted the British Queen, who is one the most hard working respected people on the planet."

" Talk about the Ugly American, Trump has made America and The Office of The President a world wide ugly joke...and now I've got to go out on the road to endure his ridicule and lies, and also try to make some sense out of the mumbling and bumbling of Mr Forgetful Biden."

"We need those fecking eagles...all of them. Now."

As I nodded, Focksy growled and continued, "Right now on a frosty November morning I need a warming cappuccino and after that we get back to work. Me off over the ferry to to see what's what at TNoTN for the first time in a year, and you trying to join up more pieces of Paul's CIA puzzle. Hopefully -with coffee stimulants provided by you, and me having now to do the day job also, we'll still meet our deadline for the next meeting with Paul."

Chapter 30... 22 December 2020.

As the Election roller coaster slowed and stopped the Post Election ride is waiting to get started, Trump is insisting he's remaining on board.

By choice Focksy and I are partly in lockdown mode at home. Harry Writes: Home in this case still being Focksy's apartment in New York, the journey to work just a few steps, either through the door to our office, or for a bracing breath of air out on to the Hudson River view terrace.

What a difference yet another year has made: If Focksy's sabbatical year - flew by-then the last- twelve months have been a roller coaster for us, and after four tempestuous years, a pandemic and a close run election, they've been an even wilder ride for The USA.

Despite the extraordinary refusal of Trump to admit defeat and his rabble rousing claims of 'We was Cheated,' ' occasionally varied with 'It was Stolen', Focksy and I are mainly focused on completing Paul's life story.

Back in November last year, at the end of his sabbatical, Focksy wandered down to TnoTN to log on again to the news team...and almost before he'd even got into their offices, despite being their oldest working newsman- as their only Cantonese and Mandarin speaker- he was dispatched to Hong Kong to cover the fast developing Student Riots.

His month there then turned into a four month nightmare, as soon after a Chinese Christmas, he followed up on rumours of an animal related disease allegedly affecting a humans in a Chinese mainland city called Wuhan. For me, worrying about the house plants soon faded into insignificance as the disease-infection-bacteria-microbes-now virus - what ever, had spread throughout Wuhan before Focksy even managed to get there. It now had a name-Covid 19, which very soon became known as Killer Covid- and changed our world-probably for ever.

My wife had spent several months here including Christmas and New Year, but then in February when the talks of travel restrictions were breaking, with scary rumours of the disease likely to spread throughout Asia she'd returned to her family in Thailand.

We've been together for fifteen years and her close family-Thai style-are always an equal priority with me and my travels for work. Although she maintains I miss her Thai cooking more than her.

Obviously all visits to Paul, were cancelled for good reason, but I had plenty of his backstory to get on with, and then via FedEx came a couple of the special USB sticks. Apart from the fear of cocking up the 'coded opening process' luckily for me it was great-really useful. Hours of stuff, some written notes, but mostly recorded stories, more than enough, as he said, to almost complete the book.

Focksy had returned in March from Hong Kong, wheezing somewhat but with no fever. So more affected -we hoped- by a lungful of tear gas inhaled as he reported on the riots than by the disease. TNoTN had then, in both their wisdom, and in accordance with their wish for a good story -spent a goodly amount of dollars and doctors time in attempting to get Focksy tested for Covid. Finding a test was not easy even with the well informed and well funded TNoTN so that all turned into another, 'Chaos in the Covid System,' story for Focksy.

Focksy is working mostly delivering background news pieces to camera from his home office-but the lockdown and his Hong Kong injury has enabled him, to put in plenty of hours on Paul's story. Which is largely complete except for one significant event...The Kennedy Assassination.

As Focksy points out, "Paul's covered the Bay of Pigs, The Cuban Missile crisis, some of the stories regarding Kennedy's alleged marital indiscretions and the rumours of connections-of some of those women- with organised crime."

" He's gone into Kennedy's fractious relationship with the CIA , particularly Allen Dulles over operations in Italy and Africa. But on the actual assassination: Nothing. Lee Harvey Oswald: Zero. Jack Ruby: Zilch, and nary a mention of the Warren Commission investigation or any later ones, We need to get that assassination story sorted and then we're on the home straight."

Midmorning and as usual I set off to make the coffee, as I did so, we heard the familiar 'ding dong' of the front door opener from downstairs in the building lobby, Focksy remarking, "And now

I fear we have to survive the typhoon or cyclone that is Ermalinda."
Whilst the coffee machine hissed- I of course made one for her
before she demanded it- and so it was, we were able to greet her
with smiles and a coffee as eventually she arrived up on the seventh
floor. She in turn had something for us.

"Is good you here Mr Focksy, Winston the doorman down
the stair, he speaking to a man when I come in, and he have a
special letter *only for you*. The man - he really want to be sure is for
you- and he speak me. Big surprise he speak Angola Portuguese-
same like me...like I say big surprise, not many American speak that.
Anyway here's the letter he say only for you. *Him a very nice man--
sad for him he cannot walk and have the special chair to move him
around."* And with that she took her coffee and went off towards the
kitchen.

'Stunned, shocked, amazed'... dear reader you don't need all
that...but we were. Focksy opened the envelope and a memory stick
fell out...which we both looked at in...I don't know what...more
shock, horror...amazement... groundhog day instant recall...

Focksy saying " Hold on, lets read the letter"

Att: Focksy - Harry. NYC. Saturday 20 December 2020.

*First of all an update. I received this information only in the
last two days in a brief call from Terri. Of the Eagles shipped to US
one died soon after arrival. But the others- were transported by Terri
under contract to the US Military via Petersen Air Force Base to
some remote area within the Weminuche Wilderness in Colorado-
between Durango and Colorado Springs.*

*She confirms the initial work work was done outside the US
to avoid dramas with those who sincerely and traditionally regard
anything and everything to do with Eagles- including their spirits to
be sacred.*

*Terri mentioned on the phone, that she had spent a lot of
time in Mont St Marsan, so one assumes she also investigating use
of eagles as offensive / defensive protection for the US Military or
Security Services as the French are doing. But for most of the past
two years she's been way up in the high wilderness in Colorado as
she said, 'Just her and an ever increasing number of eagles'.*

It seems in the past six months she became even more disillusioned with US politics and extremism, she said she didn't watch much TV but enjoyed some remarkable journalism in the Colorado press. Anyhows she has resigned as a military consultant.

She told me how sad it was that just before she left, twelve of her best trained and imprinted birds had flown away, she knew not where. Aware as I am of your year's work-prior to meeting with me-I guess you can read into that what you will. I do recall her original plan was to release at least one on the West Coast, some here in rural Washington and some she hoped in Florida, despite that not being a natural home to Golden Eagles.

Actually as she said she had an ever increasing number of eagles I'm wondering if she's been working with other breeds here, certainly 12 birds released would seem to be more than she brought over from Scotland.

So if she has or is proceeding with her original plan, with their fifty year target imprint memories, I assume much ongoing vigilance needed by the alleged target for many years...especially, as the security services keep telling us, becoming an Ex President, does not also make you an Ex Target.

I am here in the US as I had a meeting in Washington yesterday. With reference our discussions on my terrace many miles from yours here- I'm looking forward to completing that project with you. I'll be out of touch for few days as I'm still sorting out a few matters very important for our nation. I am though concerned that something may happen to prevent me from implementing that plan to meet, so here's a detailed explanation in case we can't get together by early New Year and remember your Basque phrases. Best Paul...

And alongside that the memory stick had been taped.

Having shown the message to my speechless chum we studied the memory stick and decided it was not one of the special 'one chance only' type we were using for our bookwork, so I opened my usual laptop to try it and got...

------------**Password Please** ********

Apart from us having a serious heart failure -and another ground hog day moment harking back to the discovery of Jerry's original USB in Bim's Bar...the question was what's the password?

Focksy said," Seems to me that if what ever Paul is doing, is as he says, 'Very important for our nation,' he'll have used a decent password." I gazed at Focksy-somewhat bleakly, "Point taken, but knowing the world he moved or still moves in he'll be smart enough to know most services can unlock any password in milliseconds."

Focksy said, "I agree, although I was reading the other day that the more characters used the longer it takes. Some complicated ones can take even the largest machines months to decode. Or so they would have us believe. " He continued, "So how about..."

I held up my finger..."Great minds think alike,"

I'll type it in." *Naturak zaintzen gaitu bainan batzuetan natura zaintzeko borrokatu behar gara.*

Having done it- and checked the spelling-I looked at Focksy and as he nodded, I held my breath and pushed the enter tab. After what seemed to be the longest ever milli microsecond the screen flashed and up came the very welcome words:

Welcome both: Firstly there may-if there have been any leaks following a meeting I have just attended in Washington -there may be those who would wish for me not to remain at liberty to complete our project. If you do not receive confirmation of us meeting by second week January for final editing of the book, then I would suggest that you endeavor to get the book completed to your own satisfaction, and then set before the American people.

There's a video on here of the meeting in Washington.

The nine folks there all known to each other and either have had, or will have, some confidential responsibilities for the health and safety of our nation during transition and beyond. Three were well known to me, but six were quite surprised to meet me, an obviously old guy on wheels- sitting at the head of the table.

The fact that I managed to make this video recording, with out even any help from Huawei, despite the experts from three security agencies sweeping and checking the venue, I guess shows 'you can teach an old dog new tricks.' P.

Chapter 31. The Kennedy Ultimatum
Transition & Redemption.

Focksy writes. The video shows the setting for Paul's presentation: A standard looking meeting room. Somewhere. Apparently not so clean, as in electronically and physically swept, checked and rechecked, as had likely been expected by most of Paul's invited participants. Given this a matter for Washington DC, fairly predictably 'somewhere' is probably not so far from...
... Washington DC.

No name cards or initials-on the table -although a couple of the participants look familiar from various news reports. As the last of the nine took their places - with a nod to the others and a slight frown at the head of the table, Paul rolled his wheels right up to the table and spoke;

"Ladies and gentlemen, thank you for attending here, despite the election and electioneering apparently -in the eyes of some folks-not yet being concluded. In an attempt to immediately set your minds at rest as to why it was suggested by various mutual acquaintances we should meet, let me explain who I am and who I am not."

" I am not the representative of any political party in the US or elsewhere in the world. To clarify that, I am not particularly for nor against Team Trump Pence or Team Biden Harris, although given the personalities involved, the closeness of the result and with the current covid circumstances I have serious concerns regarding transition and the next four years."

"Neither am I in any way connected with or retained by any business or NGO here or elsewhere in the world, nor do I represent or work for any foreign regime nation or state...not even- Russia nor Ukraine. But of course I would say wouldn't I. "

"But most importantly, let me very clear, neither am I proposing to try and alter or interfere with the result of the vote by the American people."

"I am American, very much so, although I have not lived here in the US for more than sixty years. Surprisingly I am employed- despite my great age- by the CIA - and have been so since 1957, although I allow that might come as a surprise to many in Langley.

Particularly those who set the parameters for compulsory retirement."

"You will note that Mrs Haskell representing the CIA is not here-mainly as I don't want anything I might say to compromise her. Circumstances required me make my pitch to you before she receives my impending resignation...after which... she could at least say of me, 'apparently an ex CIA man'. Not that I am planning anything to particularly bring the agency into disrepute, although as ever folks are deeply suspicious if we get involved in even discussing national affairs."

"With every respect to those of you around this table, even after my many decades with the company, I still find my self amazed at how well these things usually work, I still like the concept of... ...'The FBI's job is to catch people breaking the law, and the CIA's is to break the laws of other countries by stealing their secrets'."

" Given miscreants especially in the worlds of terrorism and espionage are mostly multinational, the two organisations have usually meshed together...not always smoothly, but despite popular misconceptions in the media, with their dedicated and brilliant staff- they get the job done. For America."

" The fact that 'you' are here does not infer I am careless of any compromise that could involve yourselves, whichever office you come from but we all obviously value your presence."

" I was born in 1930 in Boise Idaho, of Basque immigrant parents. I joined the CIA in 1956. I was stationed initially in Teheran Persia, now of course Iran. I was wounded in an action in Persia hence the wheels, but have remained in active service since then."

" During my time of service, we the US and the agency, for better, sometimes for worse, weathered the storms and occasionally stoked or put out multiple fires around the world...mostly in the name of combatting-communism and of course defending our nation. In hindsight I realise that for many outsiders, the reasoning behind some of those actions was concealed, convoluted and confusing. For example, ignoring the overly analysed Cuban affairs there are those who know little of the hand we had in the failed French military uprising against General de Gaulle's plans for Algerian independence and the later attempts to assassinate him. As it happens I was very much up to speed on those situations, but on occasions even us insiders were equally confused. To this day on that one I am not convinced as to which side we were playing for."

" We -the agency- deserve a lot more credit than we get for work well done, but the overall picture is always more than clouded by the ever enduring conversations and conspiracy accusations regarding the agency, Allen Dulles and the Kennedy assassination."

"But I do not intend to waste your time by asking you here for an history lesson-*I asked you here on account of the damage done to the reputation of the United States by the President over the past four years, and the reality that regardless if he is restricted in his use of social media, that damage is likely to continue or even worsen despite or because of the narrow election result.*"

"As we all know it is less the policy, more the presentation, mainly in those late night tweets by him and increasingly by his family, that has reduced our standing in the world. The soon to be Ex President has demeaned diplomacy and reduced political discussion to below that of the schoolyard and the gutter."

"The Office of The President has been defiled."

" Taking into account the legal and historical objections that would be thrown up if attempts were made to ban or even censor his future output, let alone the impracticalities, we must therefor continue to fear the potential for the Ex President to go on making those damaging-deranged-rabble rousing statements, however they are broadcast. "

"As we all know they spark off a further onslaught of rhetoric from all parties concerned, all repeated and shared endlessly on social media. Without getting into which side of the fence they are on Facebook, Google Twitter and the rest are overwhelmed, by the millions -billions-participating 24/7."

" As are the TV networks, even fact checking, originally presented as an admirable control on truth, requires the re-stating of both Fact and Fakes...so the fires are fanned again. For so many-may be now including 'the majority'- those Tweets *are* the News."

I *stress again, it is not my position, to suggest interference with the -hopefully- fairly-but oh so narrowly made will of the people. That's assuming after four years, they 'The People' can still distinguish enough fact from fake, to have made considered choices for their votes."*

"Neither is it my suggestion-which conspiracy precedent suggests you would expect from an almost ex CIA man- that any physical methods are used to harm the President or as he will be the ex President. But I do think we need to find a way to restrain the extremes."

Several round the table nodded, one leaning in saying, "I suspect that the Biden Harris combination will likely be calmer and more professional."

Paul nodded and said, " That is the key point, even with a more professional team in the The White House, do we, just one of the many transition teams, need to take action. Surely we cannot risk four more years of the Ex President- when not golfing, finding ways to tweet or broadcast more of the same- tinged with bitterness- and all backed up with millions of voters saying -we were robbed, as the world will still be watching and listening."

A quietly but firmly dressed woman spoke, quietly and firmly, " I guess the CIA will get the blame what ever happens, they've weathered fifty years of conspiracy clouds so what's another fifty, although with Gina not being here I may be speaking out of turn."

Paul eased back from the table as the woman continued, " Our reputation can and indeed must recover. Over time the damage will be blamed on that rogue male, his family, and the more fanatical of their followers. Tea and insincere sympathy will be offered by most of the world. "

"In the case of President's Xi and Putin, with them both being more informed and astute than Trump has ever been, they are at least mindful of the need for global stability-despite them not exactly helping the cause here over the past few years."

The woman spoke again, " *Regardless of the reality, or not, of the old conspiracy theories, surely for the good of America, This America, Our America...ignoring any echoes of Dallas we need to take firm and direct action...Of some kind."*

Chapter 32. **The Kennedy Ultimatum.**
A Breath of Fresh Air. 18 January 2021.

Harry writes. And it is fresh - actually, clear and very bright but near as dammit freezing air- that is being well appreciated by four of us on Focksy's Hudson River view terrace. Myself, Focksy and guests Bitxi and Paul.

Bitxi and Paul relaxing with a coffee and whilst Focksy and I have been desperate to discuss learn more about Paul's Washington meetings, the first subject of discussion was of the continuing media and political fallout from the storming of the Capitol buildings.

But first: Paul and Bitxi's arrival to the apartment had required a little 'old style spy' subterfuge...involving Bitxi pushing me from their hotel, and then round parts of Central Park on some of Paul's 'wheels.' Me wearing one of Focksy's wildly lurid ski jackets- with my face well concealed in scarf and dark glasses.

She'd been doing that each morning with Paul wearing the same Hi Viz coat- for the past couple of days 'to get any watchers used to the routine.

Today, whilst I sat back and enjoyed the ride around the park, Focksy with 'The Real Paul' as we were calling him, on a spare set of his wheels, had gone down in a service elevator to the basement and into the back of a FedEx van, which then, drove across town, through the Lincoln Tunnel and using Focksy's key code- straight down into the basement parking of the apartment.

Later in the day, Bitxi and I, no wheelchair or Hi Viz colors, but faces still well wrapped up against the cold, and hopefully not recognised by any watchers, grabbed a cab to the Mid Town Ferry Terminal. There we took a ferry to Weehawken, jumping aboard at the last moment as the crew guy heaved up the gangway. We got growled at in classic New York style, but we lost any followers.

Paul, apologising for the old style spy routine, saying, "I'm fairly certain that no one's out to cause me any harm, but after the Washington meet that's not quite guaranteed, and there may well be folks keeping an eye on what I'm up to. Even more these days I'd like to keep a low profile about the book till we're ready to go."

With Maisie still trapped abroad by covid restrictions, Paul and Bitxi were staying with us, or rather staying in Maisie's next door apartment for a few days to hopefully enable us to complete the last few edits for the book. Paul, wheeling himself to look out over the river, "With us being used to the mountains and with the, albeit luxury, hotel becoming increasingly claustrophobic, this terrace-really is, 'a breath of fresh air.'"

I asked, "Given that Focksy and I, tease Maisie mercilessly when she decides to sunbathe out here, pointing out that there's at least 5000 windows-looking out this way from across the river, aren't you at all worried." Paul laughed and said, "Point taken and I appreciate all your efforts to at least keep my location reasonably low key, but if they figure things out, and that's a long shot from over the river, then they do. And we do need some air."

He continued, "Actually America needs some fresh air. At least Biden is now officially confirmed-and will be inaugurated imminently, and despite my need to focus on my book for these next couple of days, observing the disgraceful incursion at the Capitol incited by various Trumps, Giuliani and others-I would say that the various comments in the video you are so keen to also discuss now seem both restrained and prescient. I'd suggest we focus on the book for now and come back to considering more recent events- including that video when we run out of editing steam."

And so it was-fueled with my usual Barista skills and lunch made by Bitxi-sadly US style not any of her Basque specialties we delved back into the extraordinary worlds of the fifties and sixties. Although even today- Paul brushed past the Kennedy era with a "We'll get back to that one."

After some very productive-satisfying even- hours we were all startled when the doorbell rang and Focksy and I both said: "Ermalinda. We forget about Ermalinda. She'll be motor mouthed about seeing you again." Paul smiled and said, " I think I can fix that...leave it to me, and hopefully she's got the ingredients with her to make her famous Bifanas for an early supper, unless you have other plans."

Having agreed Bifanas sounded good to us, eventually we retrieved Paul from his deep and meaningful conversations with Ermalinda in the kitchen and got back to work. Back in the Basque country we'd learned to tread carefully around certain issues- as

Paul had a way of deflecting questions about sensitive matters by saying-"Too soon for that, or 'Too soon for this'." His words becoming acronymed into TSFT.

Late one evening in the flickering firelight of the farmhouse kitchen he'd said, "Regarding these TSFT situations, some of them we can clear up and include, others I think I'll deposit the facts somewhere to be revealed in ten or fifteen years time, so that'll fairly likely be after I've fallen off the branch. If you then do an 'All New and Updated 'edition it could be some useful new income for my family, and a pension bonus for you two."

So we were loath to push too hard about the Kennedy situation, as we'd noticed he sometimes relaxed the TSFT rules when things were getting set out in the way he was comfortable with.

After a good few hour's work the bulk of the work was done. As the lights started to reflect on the river, Ermalinda, produced Bifanas. Served I noticed on Focksy's best china.

As we tucked in appreciatively, Paul and she were chatting away-presumably in Portuguese Angolan. Pausing to take a bite he said, "Boy these are good and the taste really takes me back. I spent many months in Luanda." Between bites he continued, "Ermalinda tells me she gets actual Angolan made Piri Piri, or as she calls it Peri Peri, here in New York, that's 'Angolan Made ' as in made by Angolans using imported chilies. Given what I know about those home made sauces fermenting in the bottles and exploding, thank god she keeps it in the fridge and you guys use it up quickly."

With a brief break to scan the various News channels including the Focksy less TNoTN to catch up on the clear up and as Paul called it, "The blame game but not yet the whitewash," ongoing in Washington eventually we got back to business...and even more eventually-later that evening as we enjoyed a drink, the discussion moved on to author's differing styles in espionage books.

Focksy pointing out he and I had often discussed that some of Paul's East European exploits in the late fifties early sixties, would appear to sit well with the gritty grey postwar realism of John le Carre or Len Deighton...and then what a huge contrast that was, to the work in the sunnier parts of the Caribbean, South America and

West Africa. Not so much James Bond action, but sunnier climes often favoured by Ian Fleming.

Paul nodded, "Yes, very much of the mundane normal daily grind, was as portrayed so well by le Carre and Deighton. Although I didn't have much call to spend time in Berlin , as we've discussed I did have to be in and out of various other East Bloc nations."

"I was never much in Vienna-also much loved by authors of espionage...mainly as we viewed it also so impregnated-even after the Russkies moved out after the occupation. Actually I see nothing much changes , various so called 'Spy Exchanges' have taken place there- including the recent one where Sergei Skripal and others were exchanged for Anna Chapman- the Red Headed Soviet Temptress so much beloved of the tabloid media."

" Even just six months back a couple of Russians were arrested there after a Chechen dissident was shot dead. The long arm of Putin reaches out again...the killing took place on July 4th, so a not so subtle message to us and any and all persons viewed as traitors to the Russian state."

" In fact, I believe that most of the so called 'Collusion' and similar events such as the discovery of the various hacks targeting US elections, are nothing more than further very obvious messages from Vlad...'Don't mess with the Russian Bear'. No coincidence I feel that the hackers- or the ones they let us discover- I repeat-*they let us discover'* were named 'Fancy Bear' and stuff like that."

Paul then, took a sip of his drink and said, "For me more than Fleming and some others , the incredibly factual Frederick Forsyth was the reality. Obviously starting with 'Day of The Jackal'."

"In fact his storylines were so accurate and well informed that we had several files open on him and his books, as we were wondering where he was getting his information from. We came to the conclusion, as he'd done some work for some security agencies in Biafra, that he'd remained well connected with the British and French services."

We sat quietly for a while, watching the lights, and then with Ermalinda, having typhooned her way round both Focksy's and Maisie's apartments, leaving -with many sincere thanks from Paul for what he called 'A tasty run down memory lane,' Focksy opened another bottle of wine and breathing deep, asked about Washington.

Paul, leaned back in his chair- or rather-on 'his wheels' and said. "Well the first thing is, I am now officially an Ex CIA man, I'd handed in my resignation prior to the meeting for various strategic reasons. Turns out my pension is more than my salary-due to the number of years I've been paying in, which has surprised them and probably pissed them off- but not enough, I hope, to require a little subterfuge as to my whereabouts."

" Even without Trump's claims that 'The Election had been Stolen' the premise of the meeting in Washington was to quickly bring together an off the books, security based transition team. Transition between outgoing regimes had been so fraught on occasions that detailed legal requirements were instituted a while back. "

"We all know the over repeated story of the missing 'W's' on White House keyboards when George took over. I suspect, taking into account the passing of the years, and various clear-out's of personnel here at Langley, I have more experience than many of the matter. At least as it applies to international security, and this one's more scary than most."

" Most agree, to mix up the timeline a little, that the past few years have not been America's finest hour. So the question is simple, in addition to smoothing the handover of operations and power, are there ways to ensure the Ex President can be restrained from further harming America's good name."

Paul continued, "Despite my latest meeting being about the current transition *and controlling an ex President*, it was not unlike some discussions back in '62 or '63 with their, *'What to do about a problem called Jack'?* Although, I hope, despite rumours to the contrary, we will soon be more dedicated to keeping 'the nation safe and healthy' than some of those in the '60's, prioritizing keeping themselves and their friends 'safe and wealthy'."

"Back in those days, just as now, they were also concerned about the direction, as they, *The Washington Elite* saw it, that their brash new President and his Attorney General, who happened to be his brother Robert, were taking America."

"Although the Kennedy's were from a political family and JFK was part of a media favourite-celebrity-couple with Jackie, he was not really a Washington insider. Thus he lacked enough of the deep connections for the wheeling and dealing that even the most popular Presidents need to support their proposed policies. So right from the start he was up against some very entrenched views, *of those 'behind ' the military, the various offices of state, and the fiefdoms of the CIA and the FBI. "*

" So there really were parallels with Trump, although Kennedy was very smart, and in his case his intentions were more honourable. Actually, as is often the way, after the assassination the great and the good of Washington were the first in line to proclaim what a fine president JFK had been. Such was the mood of the people-the world even- that for quite a while no one dared question their original attitude-and eventually their probable complicity. These days, with social media, the rumours would have been out in minutes."

"But back to my meeting, the room was quite chill...and you could see and feel the palpable relief from some when I made it clear, that although I had been around- in an active way during the Kennedy asassination- I was not, repeat not, suggesting we remove today's -soon to be Ex - President- also by assassination."

"Having said that, several were starting to mutter that given Trump's narcissistic and erratic instability, any persuasive reprogramming to try and control him was likely to fail, but they restrained themselves. For a while at least. The conversation in Washington continued for several more hours until, one of the ladies, asked what she said was,' a rhetorical question,' that stunned the rest into silence.

She saying, ' *I guess what happened in Dallas, fixed the problem at the time, or at least, fixed it in the opinion of some powerful persons, a faction. Surely some kind of direct action must be an option for now. For the sake of the nation."*

Paul held out his glass to Bitxi, who, sensing the drama, refilled it immediately as she did mine and Focksy's.

Paul continued, "I can tell you if there was a chill in the room before she spoke-it was like a bloody freezer straight afterwards.

...and before you ask, I cannot tell you what conclusion the meeting eventually came too. Having confirmed earlier I would shortly not be employed by the agency, I was politely shown the door. But I can tell you what I told them, shortly before that lady's remark turned the room into a freezer."

"As the still locked away files will eventually one day confirm, the assassination of JFK was an accident. "

"Persuasion and politics having failed, in an attempt to get him to fall in line with the old guard in Washington, a plan had been hatched to, as they might have said at the time: 'To put the frighteners on him.' That is, scare him into co-operating."

"The idea behind 'The Double HH' project, as we called it was for a skilled sniper to put a hole in Jackie Kennedy's Hat and Handbag. Hence Double HH. Thus making it very clear to Kennedy that he or she would be next...unless he fell in line."

" Now of course, especially with hindsight, that sounds totally extreme. But back then you've got to remember, within the previous hundred years four Presidents-Jackson, Lincoln, Garfield and McKinley had been assassinated and more recently attempts had been made on both the Roosevelt's and Truman."

"For many, still in power or business, the gun running rum smuggling days of prohibition were a reasonably recent reality, with Al Capone only having died fifteen years before. The gritty story of Chicago gangbuster Elliot Ness, who only died five years earlier in 1957, was becoming a legend with *'The Untouchables.'*"

" On TV, the most popular show was Dragnet, with the nation captivated by the phrases, 'I carry a badge' and 'Just the facts ma'am, just give me the facts.' "

" Westerns were also wildly popular evoking an America that many still considered as being ' the real world.' So it was all a bit *Good Guy's against the mob* and *'Cowboys and Indians'* in a stylized America."

" Jeans, cigarettes, cars were all marketed using charred cattle ranch style brands, hence our use of the brand sounding *Double HH,* which was way more macho than *'Hat and Handbag'.*"

"Put all those together with the fact that organised crime was still -very powerfully organised-as both Kennedy's knew very

well, and so a 'mob style warning' was kind of in the realms of normal for those days.

The problem was, the organisers-whoever they were- then found a patsy to create a diversion, and unknown to him-take the blame. Oswald, had or was set up with, a back story of 'commie connections,' real Russian ones, and a mix of Cuban and Castro associations. Even an attempted asassination, when a shot he fired in April '62 at Texas politician Edwin 'Ted' Walker hit a window frame and missed."

"But on that fateful day in Dealey Plaza, Oswald, their crap shot- not crack shot- instead of firing in the air to create a planned diversion as instructed, somehow, with his slow and inaccurate rifle managed to kill the President."

"The actual crack shot sniper-there to deliver the Double HH, Hat and Handbag warning, only got off one round before the Oswald shots created mayhem. And we all know what happened next, the sniper got away and lived to work again another day-on another continent...Which is more than Oswald or Jack Ruby, or the President and later his brother Robert managed to do."

Chapter 33. The Kennedy Ultimatum.

19 January 2021. 'Now is the time to heal America.'
Joe Biden's much repeated words are still resounding
around the world, as are the pictures of demonstrators
inside the US Capitol buildings.

Harry writes: An early start for Focksy and I, both of us
bursting with questions after Paul's revelations of the previous
night, but to our disappointment he was departing early. Him
explaining, "I logged on a while back and it seems following very
recent events duty calls. Even for the recently retired."

He didn't volunteer any more information, other than asking
us to book them a taxi. As we had a coffee and waited, Focksy
showed us through his usual TNoTN morning roundup of the
world's front pages. Many were increasingly wondering if President
Elect Biden's *'heal the nation'* was the right way to go...with most
now suggesting no prosecutions, suggested carte blanche for future
Presidents to behave in illegal or dangerously undemocratic ways.
Their arguments backed up with photos and videos of Team Trump
inciting physical demonstrations if not quite insurrection.

Bitxi saying," Well from what I see and read, and I'm not
partisan in any way, this Joe Biden seems to be a very different type
of person. Regardless of any political maneuverings he appears to be
thoroughly decent. I see that as well as Kamala Harris he's adding a
lot of women to his team, which could be good provided they have
the skills and it's not done for show."

Paul, who was packing away his laptop, growled and said,
"Lets just hope he gets the chance to succeed, God knows the
country needs it, and it really doesn't need any more pointless shit
from Trump and family floating around whilst Biden does his best."

Paul went on, " Despite us losing a day here now, I'm happy
for you to complete the final edits. These transition months are
going to be chaotic for a good while longer, and I'm in two minds if I
should submit our work to sneak it through for approval now, or
wait." Focksy grinned and said, " I suspect it'll cause a severe case of
sense of humour failure regardless of when we submit it, and the
threat of Russki Harry and Chinese Focksy publishing regardless of
the rules, will have to be invoked. But we wait and see."

Having heard the downstairs entry door chimes, we started towards the elevator and then...with handshakes and hugs...they were gone. I've known Focksy for more than 25 years, and after the departure of Paul and Bitxi, the long-oh so long-silence as we sat on his terrace, diverted a little by the usual river traffic seven stories below us, was the longest I've ever known him to be silent.

"Well," he said, eventually, "Well, well, well and well, that's all interesting. We can and we will of course complete 'Paul's Revelations,' or what ever we're going to call it. I think we agree, with all due respect to the absolute master of the genre, Jonas Jonasson, that, *'The 90 year old spy who climbed out of his window and...'* although correct, is a not a very original title."

" Although of course, if Paul suddenly disappears over the next few weeks or months, we might be forced to re-consider that. Which actually make's me think, we'd best, before we do any thing else, think of a way to securely hide some safety USBs with copies of the book, Paul's meeting video, last night's corrections and I guess, our notes about spies and novelists."

I nodded and said, " On the subject of spies and novelists, I spent half the night thinking about Paul's words yesterday before we all turned in, referring to the real marksman in Dallas, *'He escaped and lived to work again -on another day-on another continent.'*

Focksy said, "*Yep, me too, and his mentioning Frederick Forsyth -Day of The Jackal* and all that. Put that together with him having told those people in Washington, that not only was he 'around' during the Kennedy assassination, but was also working in France during the De Gaulle assassination attempts."

I responded " If we start going down that route we have to consider brother Andy who was apparently a crack shot. Then there's those hunting rifles in his kitchen, Bitxi told me he kept one for sentimental reasons. But if-repeat if- what Paul told us is correct, and Oswald was, the lone killer of Kennedy, and in the case of De Gaulle, where again there were always rumours of a second gunman ...but again they missed...or never fired...so that rifle is innocent of any actual killing."

Focksy slowly shook his head and said, " Yesterday, did you notice he called the view over the river from all those windows to our terrace- 'a very long shot'. Was that factual concern or just him using a well worn phrase."

"You know if we were in Thailand or even better back in Dublin, we'd settle down to watch a glass of Guinness settle as an aid to our thought processes. But right now, as if all the political mayhem wasn't enough, I see photos of bloody Guinness tankers leaving the Dublin brewery with their 'All New Non Alcoholic Guinness 0:0'. Apart from it being sacrilege, I note they fecking advertise it as having fecking hints of coffee and chocolate 'just like real Guinness'...For what it's worth I haven't been aware of any coffee or chocolate highlights in any of the zillion or so pints of real Guinness I've consumed over the past 50 years."

"But back to today, or rather yesterday, taking Paul's story of the Kennedy assassination being 'an accident', does this mean, he, they or someone, is considering trying to control Trump's future social media output with a similar scary threat. God knows Ivanka's got a whole range of handbags they could shoot at, or one of Melania's, if she's not herself in markswoman mode that is."

"Then again Trump's so arrogant he's unlikely to be persuaded of anything, and even if he agreed to behave today -by tomorrow he'd have reneged on the deal -and be upsetting America and the world again. So that puts us firmly back in the realm of warning shots and...ooops...Sorry Donald."

" Although I can't see anyone agreeing to an assassination, surely too many people know about it already...including us, and for some reason we've got a bloody video. Of course a rogue loner could try something, but that's a standard everyday threat anyway."

"But we've just spent a couple of years and 242 pages trying to figure who might be planning to puncture POTUS so if anyone should have a clue who might make a move, it should be you and I and our readers.

So to answer the question, if this is '*officially*' being considered in Washington, collusion comes back in vogue as they will seek to blame someone else...or if there's no collusion but a foreign entity is to to blame, either way top of the list remains the one guy, '*Who gets the blame, but never seems to take the rap for multiple assassinations by modern methods* that's President Putin."

"He seems totally focused on those who betray, or fail in their tasks, or perhaps-scarily for Donald-*those who don't repay their debts to Mother Russia.* None of whom will likely escape the long sticky fingers of Russian secret service justice."

" Putin's probably quite pleased to have a bit of calm in Washington for a while, *on the other hand, he and the Russkies really quite like causing chaos around here-Because They Can.*"

I nodded as he rambled on unstoppably, "This whole journey started with Jerry, and as far as we know there's still a flock of '*Killer Eagles-Programmed to Attack Trump...Sometime'. Somewhere.*"

"Then, Paul tells us that the unreleased archives will reveal *'The Double HH Plan - JFK Assassination an Error'.* So is someone planning a re-run to scare The Donald into silence. "

Focksy sat back, and looked at me in a rather alarming and enthusiastic way, "You know Harry, I'm starting to think this can run and run. If we can do all this before breakfast just on Coffee, maybe we should give that no alcohol Guinness a try. Then there's: *Golfer Trump Get's A Hole For One: In the graveyard?*"

... cue music...

I just shook my head, recalling our quote in the opening pages about *Events dear boy, Events,* how over the long lifetime of any book, many events occur, don't occur, should have occurred or, should not, have occurred. In this case, the future reality of events Trumpian, is a clouded and confused unreality, and even that certainly didn't include the likelihood of the US seat of Government being overrun by demonstrators.

I'm not sure this journey can run and run, but *before you* go, read on...*Harry Buckle writes.* On the night of 22 November 1963 I was working as a trainee journalist for a Scots newspaper company in London's Fleet Street, home then to the UK's national press and the offices of most of the international press along with the world's news and photo agencies.

I was getting ready to leave the office at about 6.30 in the evening to make my way home, when suddenly I heard the alarm bells ringing on the teleprinters and wire machines in the news room. That only happened when the senders had something they really needed looking at urgently...a minute later the London News Editor rushed out of the room and yelled at me," Harry, run down to PA, Keystone, Reuters and the rest...get to the front of queue and get back here at the double with everything they'll give you."

About twenty minutes or so later I ran back clutching what turned out to be the first of many armfuls of still warm news agency photos(*I show one on our website) to be wired to our newsrooms in Scotland. Not yet trusted with writing stuff I spent the entire night belting round the various courtyards and alleyways of Fleet Street collecting agency news copy on punched tape, photo's, even some heavy printing plates- not to mention supplies of sandwiches, teas, coffees, cigarettes and more than a few bottles of whiskey.

It was around 6.00 am after a long long and dramatic night- so 23 November 1963- in one of the, very crowded, printers pubs near Bouverie Street that I first heard the story that the shooting of Kennedy had likely been 'an accident'.

The pub was packed with journalists from all the major agencies and papers- including several senior well connected US journalists then based in the UK. As a junior I nursed my pint 'not my usual breakfast,' and listened open mouthed as a couple of them agreed they had heard there had been a search for, *'a patsy to stage a Double H' job'* to try and deal with, what even back then, they referred to as, *'As a problem called Jack.*

One of them explained, *"The idea behind 'The Double HH' project, was for a skilled sniper to put a hole in Jackie Kennedy's Hat and Handbag. Hence Double HH. Thus making it very clear to Kennedy that he or she would be next...unless he fell in line."*

Now of course, especially with hindsight, that sounds totally extreme. But back then you've got to remember, within the previous hundred years four Presidents-Jackson, Lincoln, Garfield and McKinley had been assassinated and more recently attempts had been made on both the Roosevelt's and Truman."

"For many, still in power or business, the gun running rum smuggling days of prohibition were a reasonably recent reality, with Al Capone only having died fifteen years before. The gritty story of

Chicago gangbuster Elliot Ness, who only died five years earlier in 1957, was becoming a legend with '*The Untouchables.*'"

" On TV, the most popular show was Dragnet, with the nation captivated by the phrases, 'I carry a badge' and 'Just the facts ma'am, just give me the facts.' "

" Westerns were also wildly popular evoking an America that many still considered as being ' the real world.' So it was all a bit *Good Guy's against the mob* and *'Cowboys and Indians'* in a stylized America."

" Jeans, cigarettes, cars were then all marketed using charred cattle ranch style brands, hence the brand sounding *Double HH,* which was way more macho than *'Hat and Handbag'.*"

"*Put all those together with the fact that organised crime was still -very powerfully organised-as both Kennedy's knew very well, and so a 'mob style warning' was kind of in the realms of normal for those days.*

With the story still unfolding by the minute I wearily returned to my office to now do the day shift...

Only in later years as all kinds of rumours unfolded and were exploited by a sensation hungry global media did I realise I had been there at the very start-of the very first 'JFK Conspiracy Theories. Unless of course the still to be unsealed secret files reveal that the organisers-whoever they were- had indeed found a patsy to create a diversion, and unknown to him-take the blame.

Oswald, had or was set up with, a back story of 'commie connections,' real Russian ones, and a mix of Cuban and Castro associations. Even an attempted asassination, when a shot he fired in April '62 at Texas politician Edwin 'Ted' Walker hit a window frame and missed."

"*But on that fateful day in Dealey Plaza, Oswald, their crap shot- not crack shot- somehow, with his slow and inaccurate rifle managed to kill the President.*"

"*Was there indeed an actual crack shot sniper-there to deliver the Double HH, Hat and Handbag warning, who only got off one round before the Oswald shots created mayhem.*

And we all know what happened next, the sniper got away and lived to work again another day-on another continent...Which is more than Oswald or Jack Ruby, or the President and later his brother Robert managed to do."

Back in the pub...with Oswald still being questioned...and not yet targeted by Jack Ruby...the main more concern was 'Who done it? Rather than Why?

But back to today, today being 20 January 2021...

Having watched Trump's departure on TV, including his words both outside the White House and again at Andrews Air Force Base suggesting, 'Good bye but hopefully not for long' and then 'We will be back in some form,' I am increasingly wondering about 'The Problem called Donald.'

We can assume he'll have plenty of time on the golf course 'To consider his future,' and enjoy the sight of some majestic eagles wheeling and soaring in the sky above him.

Should he again start sending out messages denying democracy or-worse-demeaning and dividing America and 'The Eagles' don't recognise him- then I suspect he'd best watch out for a quiet man 'on wheels' who might introduce him to The Kennedy Ultimatum, and of course Melania & Ivanka have plenty of handbags.

In case Focksy is right and this story does run and run-or more to the point-if The Eagles Fly - we'll be updating things on our website where you'll also find backstories- updates- details of new books & more: www.harrybuckle.com

More books by Harry Buckle...

Some with his alter ego Focks Schnauzer...

Focks Schnauzer? Think Wolf Blitzer, but with ~~not so many~~ jokes !

All from amazon print & kindle- Bookshops can order from Ingram's.

Sometimes Music Is My Only Friend :The Accidental Spy.

Following career advice from James Bond author Ian Fleming, in 1962 Harry Buckle became a Fleet Street journalist. The book follows him from his years as the '60s most read pop guru, to starting his own music company, then to his surprise bringing you *a hundred or so* hit records. *Then he found himself reluctantly working with both the British and The Russian Secret Services.* ' A roller coaster tale with some fine, funny & true recollections of life as it developed.

Coming soon: *Just Not On* and *Just One More*.

On sale now: Just One Day. Just In Case. Just In Time.

More a collection of stand alone stories than a series.

The vineyards of South Western France, bordering the calm charms of the ancient tree lined Canal du Midi, with its sunbaked villages, much loved by viewers of Rick Stein's 'Odyssey' TV series and readers of Peter Mayle's timeless books about life in rural France often provide, at least the starting point, for Harry's Books.

The region is now home to Joel, an ex French Foreign Legion Brit. Aussie Mel and some other *'interesting' new locals.* When not relaxing with a glass or more of wine watching the canal boats go by they share their *'even more interesting skills'* with Brits Squeeze & Chris at Sven McMullen's Singapore based security company. (And yes he does know he's been living with that name all his life.)

Just In Time: As ever with Harry's books, an amiable thriller starting amid the Canal du Midi Villages basking in the sun of Southwest France. Sven, Joel, Melody & Squeeze race to find out more about a *'probable'* modern kidnapping & deal with the world's biggest bullion robbery. The search takes us from those canal side villages to Taiwan, via Germany, Portugal & France to The Badlands of Western Sahara. Will it end back in France with a celebratory Cassoulet or Catastrophe.

Just One Day: Again a relaxed thriller that gathers pace about a potentially catastrophic attack on the global network of 'internet' cables that feed, protect & connect us all. With *two remarkable 'guest appearances'* the storyline visits the gleam & glamour of the superyachts in Monte Carlo and continues to Sardinia and Corsica, where we find *The French Connections* still somewhat criminally inclined...Probably.

Just in Case: Despite the subtitle *'Suicide no longer required,'* In Harry's usual much referred to *'amiable style'* he reports as the British deploy their finest military and scientific minds to diverting death and destruction from above our city streets, by enlisting a helpful solution from 'Down on The Farm.'

If that wasn't enough, Sven, Joel, Squeeze & Chris are back dealing with the minor matter of an explosive shipwreck (true) in the shipping lanes of the Thames Estuary and a threat to close the few ports in the world able to handle the world largest ships.

As Joel always says, " *So what do you want us to do after lunch?*"

Backstories and more . Www.HarryBuckle.com
Published under licence from:
MarosaJokato Dublin & Foldgarth Press Australia. .

(c) Harry Buckle Marosajokato Dublin. 2021.

Bookstores TPB:ISBN 978-0-9935576-6-8
Amazon TPB: ISBN:978-1-9998849-9-4
Kindle eBook: ISBN:978-1-9998849-3-2

This story and characters are fictitious.
Certain long-standing institutions, agencies, services, public offices, persons, places: commercial, political and geographical are mentioned, but portrayed in this work as fiction and thus any and all actions, events or views they express are wholly imaginary.

No part of this publication may be copied, reproduced, stored in a retrieval system, or transmitted, in any form or by any means without the prior permission of the publisher. Neither may it be otherwise circulated in any form of binding or cover other than that in which it is published and without a similar condition being imposed on the subsequent purchaser.

The author and the publishers are not responsible for the content of or technical security of any web sites or other forms of contact, information or entertainment referred to herein which the reader may choose to visit.

Updated winter 2020/21 Parts of this book-were previously published as Regime Change By Harry Buckle & Focks Schnauzer

Dedications: As ever this book is dedicated to my families. My late wife Mandy: Sam. Joe & Vanina, now with my grand daughter-Mia.
Anne: Katy and Tom... and to my wife Mali.

And To: Philip Israel in Australia & Barry Purchase in Cornwall. Without their help...
Suzanne and Chris Todd, Diana Melbourne and
'Sir' William O'Rafferty for encouraging me through times both good and bad...and for saving me from the bad times - David 'Mick the Brief' Reilly with Anne, Dylan & Julianne.

It is also dedicated to you the readers.

I very much appreciate your time in reading my work-no matter if bought or borrowed-but I hope- not stolen. In 1962 I started out as a trainee journalist 'training' my typist fingers in the carbon paper age of typewriters in a smokey roomful of Fleet Street professionals. All of whom seemed to rattle out a million words a minute whilst smoking and sipping endless cups of tea-or quite often- something a tad stronger.

Embarrassed at my slow stutters & stumbles, no 'spell check' or other aids then, they encouraged me by saying, 'Just focus on the story-journalists write- printers spell and punctuate'.

Well, in these days with all the modern aids indeed one can focus on the story, but regardless of this digital dexterity, stutters and stumbles-particularly involving wayward apostrophes- still sneak through the system and my dimly recalled years of quite tough training.

So apologies and thanks dear reader- if you find an escaped apostrophe or other 'puncto or typo' running wild on these pages then let me know by e mail to harry@harrybuckle.com and I'll buy you a Guinness should we ever meet.

As you will see from the following pages I am quite fond of a drop of the black stuff, but so far I have no need to blame it for my terrible typing...although I can report a pint accidently poured into a laptop does not help either the laptop or my demeanour.

Printed in Great Britain
by Amazon

71257474R00140